Gifted & Talented

WENDY HOLDEN

headline
review

First published in Great Britain in 2013
by HEADLINE REVIEW
An imprint of HEADLINE PUBLISHING GROUP

1

Cataloguing in Publication Data is available from the British Library

ISBN 978 0 7553 8525 6 (Hardback)
ISBN 978 0 7553 8526 3 (Trade paperback)

Typeset in Abode Garamond by Avon DataSet Ltd,
Bidford-on-Avon, Warwickshire

Printed and bound in Great Britain by Clays Ltd, St Ives plc

Headline's policy is to use papers that are natural, renewable and recyclable
products and made from wood grown in sustainable forests. The logging and
manufacturing processes are expected to conform to the environmental
regulations of the country of origin.

HEADLINE PUBLISHING GROUP
An Hachette UK Company
338 Euston Road
London NW1 3BH

www.headline.co.uk
www.hachette.co.uk

B 000 000 010 2708

To Andrew and Isabella

Chapter 1

Isabel stared out of the train window. The English fields flashed by, sometimes with cows in, sometimes sheep, sometimes nothing but a couple of troughs or an oak tree with russet-leaved branches. It was autumn and the light was low and rich. Beneath the surface of the fields the ancient plough and furrow pattern rippled like a sea.

Isabel glanced at the man and woman opposite. Neither seemed to have noticed the view. The woman had boarded at Edinburgh, hours ago now. The scarf she was knitting, originally a woolly beige stub a few inches long, was now heading for two feet.

Isabel pulled the Branston College prospectus out of her bag and looked at the photograph on the front. It was of the college from behind a red brick wall and the central dome appeared like a rising sun of grey concrete.

'Every room's got central heating and there's a laundry and kitchen at the end of every corridor,' she had reminded her mother on the way to the station that morning.

'Laundry and kitchen, eh?' Mum had shot back, teasing. 'Didn't realise you knew what they were for.' It was a joke between them that Isabel's genuine intentions to help with chores always got sidetracked. Her mother would find her, ostensibly putting ironed clothes away upstairs, but actually crouching on a step, absorbed in poetry or a novel pulled from the upstairs bookcase.

Now, Isabel thought sadly, rather fewer clothes would be put away, and in record time. Books would stay in the bookcase and Mum would go back down afterwards to an empty house. No wonder, as they turned into the station, she had been staring through the windscreen, blinking hard. As had Isabel, come to that.

The train was drawing into a station. There were people on the platform, milling about, holding coffees, reading newspapers, picking up their bags, squinting at the carriage numbers.

A young woman on the platform was holding a baby. She was smiling at the child, talking to it. Isabel felt a sudden hot rush of tears.

She blinked hard, willing her normal composure to return. What had happened had been irrelevant for years. Although, of course, it had always been there, like a dark, mysterious cupboard at the back of a room. Ever since, that day at primary school, Moira MacDougall had said something about Isabel's mummy giving her away.

'Why did my real mummy give me away?' Isabel had asked her adoptive mother that night. Mum had hugged her tightly and explained that her real mummy hadn't wanted to but she wasn't able to look after her. But she had another mummy now who loved her very much. 'What about my daddy?' Isabel had asked, but alas no one seemed to know anything about him.

And then, after her adoptive father had died when Isabel was nine, being an only child with a single parent had become the normal way of life. A happy, settled way of life too. No parent could have been more loving than Mum, no place more idyllic and safe than Lochalan, that string of white cottages along the silver lochside with the green and purple mountains rising protectively behind.

But now life was changing, stirring, bringing all this buried business to the surface. It was on Isabel's mind as never before.

The train slid down the platform. The mother waggled the baby's fat little pink hand as it passed. Isabel, still blinking, lifted her long pale thin one in response and, then, as mother and baby disappeared, felt an almost overwhelming loneliness.

She wished with all her heart that she had allowed Mum to come with her today. She had wanted to save her a long, lonely return journey but perhaps, in retrospect, the trip back might have been a good thing. It would have given Mum time to adjust so, when she got back, finally, to the little white cottage by the still expanse of loch, she would have been prepared.

But now Mum would get back almost immediately and Isabel herself would have to face everything alone. The thought of all those new people made her heart thump.

'Just be your usual self,' Mum had urged her, but her usual self was shy, self-conscious and prone to blushing to the roots of her already-red hair. Only in books could she lose herself; only when working could she feel really confident and shine.

Would she know anyone? There had been, at interview, a girl called Kate. She had seemed very down to earth. But no one had been terrifyingly posh. In fact, apart from the beautiful buildings, the town had borne little resemblance to its popular image.

The train was slowing. The ticket inspector was yelling over the Tannoy: *This is Derby. This is Derby. Change here for Chestlock, Buxton . . .*

The train was about to depart before his very eyes. It was the last straw; well, the latest last straw. The hindmost straw up to this point had been when, this afternoon, the job at the *Chestlock Advertiser* had failed to materialise.

Olly had been delighted and hugely relieved when, after a whole summer's fruitless search for employment, he had landed an interview. The position was investigative journalist with the local paper of the small market town of Chestlock. Which was fine; Olly had never expected to kick-start his career on one of the national newspapers, as many of his well-connected fellow former students were doing. He would do it under his own steam. He would work his way up to London in the time-honoured journalistic tradition.

He had travelled to Chestlock, a journey of some three hours on the train from the university town. The file on his knee had been bulging with examples of his college journalism and his head positively swarming with ideas for features on the town he had researched exhaustively on the internet. For example, he had – admittedly after some searching – discovered Chestlock to be the birthplace of a minor poet called Ivor Tickle. Why not have a literary festival – a Tickle Festival, no less – sponsored by the paper?

He had only been off the train five minutes, five seconds probably, when he realised Chestlock was not a festival sort of place – of Tickles, tickles or anything else. The Victorian town hall that had been the main image on the council website turned out to be flanked by branches of Poundstretcher and Blockbuster. The town's northern border was a sprawling multiplex while massive rival supermarkets hemmed in the east and west. They were, Olly concluded, the reason for the tumbleweed blowing through the town centre.

It turned out, when he reached the *Advertiser* offices, that Chestlock was no longer a newspaper sort of place either. A porcine blonde receptionist called Hayley showed him into the battered office of the editor, a harassed-looking man called Don. He had wonky glasses, thinning grey hair and an air of defeat. He gave Olly the grim news, received that morning. The *Chestlock Advertiser*'s parent company was rationalising its platforms and diversifying its offer.

'What?' Olly had asked, uncomprehending.

'Or, to put it another way,' Don added heavily, 'closing down local papers left, right and centre.' The *Advertiser*, he explained, was one of many that would be going weekly and, with five days to gather the news, Don was expected to do it by himself with the assistance of Hayley.

Olly felt sorry for the editor, obviously a good man who had equally obviously not expected his own career in newspapers to peter out quite this way. Don had, he told Olly, his face lighting up for a moment, once worked on the *Manchester Guardian*. But, even more than sorry for Don, Olly felt angry. He knew Caspar De Borchy, whose father owned the *Echo*'s parent company. De Borchy had been at the same university college, although they had not moved in the same circles. Drunken, wobbly circles in Caspar's case. He had been one of the rich set; black tie permanently at his neck and bottle of champagne welded to his signet-ringed fingers, loudly guffawing in one of the quads. Whatever Caspar was doing now, Olly guessed, which was probably not much, his particular platforms would remain flagrantly unrationalised.

Skirting the puddles on the broken pavements as he hurried back to the station, Olly silently lamented wasting the last of his money on a suit. A horrid, slightly-too-tight, definitely-too-shiny suit, as well. And, actually, it would have made no difference if he'd turned up in a pink bikini.

Now he was broke. Very broke. His pace quickened. He could not afford to miss the train; after this one, the prices changed and he would have to upgrade his ticket at vast expense. Olly broke into a run.

As he hurled himself across the footbridge, the deafening yet indistinct announcements mingled with the desperate pounding in his heart.

'You can't go through there.' A man in a train company overcoat reared up forcibly before him.

'Oh, come *on*,' Olly pleaded at the flint face and the gloved hand sliding the barrier between him and the thrumming locomotive.

'Barriers go up one minute before the train leaves,' his opponent smirked. 'Says so on all the posters.'

As there was clearly no point in arguing, Olly simply twisted his body sideways and shot through the section the guard had not yet managed to close. He shouted after him, but Olly had reached the train and hurled himself on. He felt rather daring, like something from a film.

Ribcage heaving with the recent effort, he looked for a seat. There was one right next to him in the aisle, next to a youth plugged into an iPod and occupied by his guitar case. As an enormous navy-blue bottom was now reversing towards him down the aisle, dragging the buffet cart after it, Olly had no choice but to squeeze himself in between the guitar case and the back of the seat in front.

The youth removed his earplugs. 'Hey, man. Respect the Rickenbacker, yeah?'

'Bought that seat for it, have you?' Olly said dryly.

The youth scowled and shoved his earphones back in.

Olly ploughed on down the aisle. The mobile in his pocket buzzed. It was his mother.

'Just wondering how the interview went,' she said.

Olly regretted mentioning the *Advertiser* to his parents at all, but he had had to tell them something. If a whole summer without as much as a bite at a job had been a worry for him, it had been downright shocking for his mother and father.

Olly himself, on the spot, at least knew the way the economic wind was blowing – not too propitiously, even for students of his own prestigious alma mater. There were others besides himself looking for work, although not Caspar De Borchy, admittedly. But his parents retained the idea that a degree from the ancient university was a guaranteed passport to future greatness.

He sought now to downplay events.

'It was always going to be more of a chat than a formal interview,' he heard himself saying breezily. 'And it was very useful to go there. I mean, um . . . that particular paper's closing.'

'Closing!'

'But,' Olly added hastily, 'I've got other irons in the fire . . .'

'I suppose you mean your novel,' his mother sighed.

'Well, yes, actually,' Olly said defensively. 'It's going very well, actually,' he added, although in actual fact it wasn't. It was a rite-of-passage memoir, heavily influenced by *Brideshead Revisited.* Or at least this particular manifestation of it was. The work as a whole never seemed to get beyond the first chapter. He was wondering whether an experimental novel composed entirely of beginnings might have a future.

'I think,' his mother said, obviously trying to mask her impatience, 'that you need to get a proper job first. Get an income. Then write the novel.'

'I've got a few other possibilities,' Olly assured her. He hoped she would not force him to admit this was the cleaning agency he had, in desperation, registered with earlier that week. The owner, a no-nonsense Zambian, had told him she preferred to employ Eastern Europeans. 'Better than college students,' she told him. 'They want to work, not write novels.'

He had not mentioned his novel, but the Zambian lady had sharp eyes which could obviously see inside his head.

'Don't worry, Mum,' he said brightly before he rang off. 'Something will turn up.'

The train, he noticed, was drawing into another station. Hopefully someone would get off, make some room.

Isabel longed for a cup of tea but the buffet trolley had not passed for at least an hour. Probably ground to a halt in one of the crowded carriages. She wanted to go in search of it but was hemmed in by a large woman in the next seat. Isabel gathered her courage to tackle her.

The woman was reading a tabloid. As she occupied a considerable amount of space to start with, and required even more to read an open newspaper, Isabel could hardly help reading it too.

It was open at the diary page, full of gossipy items about prominent people and dominated by a large photograph of a very beautiful blonde girl in a very short leopardskin print dress. She was laughing with very white teeth at the camera. She was in the back of a limousine, surrounded by cream leather. Her long, slim brown legs spilled out and, alongside the diamonds at her ears and fingers, her confidence blazed from the page. Who was it? Isabel started to read the story that ran alongside:

> After a long hot summer on Mustique, heiress and socialite Amber Piggott is swapping Basil's Bar for books as the new university term begins. Pulchritudinous Amber, daughter of retail billionaire Lord Piggott, starts an English degree at—

The paper jerked suddenly and Isabel became aware that its owner was staring at her coldly. She smiled awkwardly, gathered up her bag and, muttering apologies, stumbled into the aisle.

The train had stopped and yet more people were getting on. In the foyer Isabel found her way blocked by a tiny, elderly Asian lady in a sari. Her enormous suitcase was almost the same size as she was. She was staring earnestly through a pair of very clean glasses at a young black man who was saying to her urgently and repeatedly, 'You get off now. Train about to leave.'

The elderly lady had evidently reached her destination and the young man, seeing the extent of her burden, wished to help her get off. Neither had yet acted on their urges, however, and the train was now shaking with the force of doors slamming prior to departure.

'Come on,' Isabel urged, moving towards the old lady's bag. 'You need to get off.'

The young man sprang forward. 'I do it. Is heavy. I do it.' He seized the case and pushed it forward. Panting, eyes bulging with the effort, he got unsteadily back down, out of the train, on to the platform. The old lady stood in the doorway watching anxiously. Just at that moment a short, bristling figure arrived. 'What's going on here?'

Isabel was relieved to see the ticket inspector. He would have the power to halt the train for the necessary time. She could hand over responsibility for the situation to him.

'This lady wants to get off,' she explained shyly.

The inspector ignored her. He looked the old Indian lady coldly up and down.

'Derby?' she chirped, hopefully.

'Too late to get off now, love,' came the inspector's snapped reply. 'This train's going now. Doors have been closed.' As if to make the point further, he reached to the door behind Isabel and slammed it viciously shut.

The roar of the engine could be felt through the floor. Isabel stared at the inspector in horror.

'You've got to let her off,' she said in a shaking voice. 'Her bag's out there,' she added, pointing down at the platform where the young man was looking anxious. 'And you've got to let *him* back on. He's not getting off here. He was just helping her.'

The inspector shrugged. 'Well, he's off now, isn't he? His choice. Train's going. End of.'

'It can't go,' Isabel protested.

'Persons not on the train one minute before it leaves are not permitted to travel,' chanted the inspector. 'Not my fault if these people can't understand the language, is it? Should learn English before they get here, shouldn't they?'

The revs under their feet had increased; the train was off.

'Derby!' wailed the old lady, her face a picture of distress. Through the window, Isabel could see, on the receding platform, the young man staring after the train in disbelief.

Olly could see him too. He had arrived in the foyer just after the inspector and had heard the conversation. And seen Isabel.

It was her eyes, Olly decided afterwards. Those beautiful, clear green eyes, filled with distress, between banks of red hair. Something had soared within him. He had not even paused to think. His arm had gone to the communication cord entirely of its own volition.

Chapter 2

The train had, fortunately, not quite cleared the station platform, so the old lady could be let off and the young man let back on. Nor was this the only piece of luck. Just as the ticket inspector erupted with fury at Olly, a smart young man standing by the loo came to his aid.

He was, it emerged, a barrister and he had an axe to grind, having been made by the inspector to surrender his seat at Crewe even though the double booking had been the fault of the train computer. Having to stand in the noisome foyer when he had paid for first class rankled and he was keen to avenge himself on the architect of his misery. Once the inspector learnt that Olly's actions were, in these particular eyes of the law at least, reasonable and defensible, he had backed down dramatically and hurried down the train, face ashen and ticket machine very much between his legs.

The barrister left at Birmingham, as did a great many other passengers. Olly and Isabel found seats at an empty table. The refreshment trolley heaved past and Isabel was finally able to get some tea.

They smiled shyly at each other.

'So,' Olly said, awkwardly breaking the silence. 'Where are you off to?'

'University,' Isabel said, shyly.

Discovering now that it was her first term, Olly was surprised.

No other student he knew, himself included, had made this significant initial journey alone by train. And all the way from Scotland.

'And you got in from a comp?' he added, warmly. 'God, you must be a genius. What college?'

'Branston,' she muttered, blushing at his praise.

'So you're a pickler,' Olly smiled.

'A what?'

'Branston College. People there are called "picklers". Because of Branston Pickle. You know.'

'I didn't know, actually.'

As the wide eyes turned upon him, Olly felt slightly disingenuous. She obviously had no idea that the nickname, while affectionate, also contained a hint of mockery. Built in the seventies – or was it the sixties? Olly wasn't sure – Branston embodied the best and worst architectural principles of its era: the abstract desire to make a bold gesture with its (literally) concrete realisation. The bold gesture that had resulted in Branston had provoked comparison over the years to everything from a nuclear processing plant to a multi-storey car park.

Not that he could talk, of course. His own former college, St Alwine's, was known throughout the university as St Wino's. About to tell her this, Olly stopped himself. She was bound to ask why and he would then have to admit the disrespectful diminutive sprang from St Alwine's being home to the university's most notorious drinking club, the Bullinger.

The thought of the evidently upright, thoroughly Scottish and dewily innocent Isabel linking him in any way with that despicable, dissipated and decadent institution – judging him, moreover, by its standards – sent a cold ripple through Olly's insides.

'It's quite a building,' he observed. 'Branston,' he added quickly.

'Oh, yes,' Isabel agreed with enthusiasm. 'It's the ideal of the modernist *Gesamtkunstwerk*, apparently.'

'The *what?*'

'*Gesamtkunstwerk* means "total work of art". It's a 1967 masterpiece in concrete.'

Olly stared at her. He had never met anyone who took Branston's architecture seriously. But were the old ones so much better, particularly his old one? St Alwine's was physically beautiful, being founded in the mid-fifteenth century. But its ethos and outlook were as antiquated as its buildings. St Alwine's was so stuck in the feudal past that the porters still ironed the students' newspapers.

'I didn't realise there was a connection with pickle,' Isabel was musing. 'I thought the Branstons who founded the college were in petrochemicals.'

'Mmm,' said Olly, determinedly not offering any further information.

'But I love Branston Pickle, anyway,' she said cheerfully. 'Frankly, I love Branston. They gave me a bursary. Paid all my tuition fees. I could never have afforded to go to university otherwise.'

'You must be seriously bright.'

'Seriously poor, that's all.' She smiled and Olly felt ashamed again. Had his own college ever paid anyone's full tuition fees? He'd had a scholarship himself, but the amount reflected the same 1446 values as everything else at St Alwine's. It amounted to less than a fiver a term and barely bought a pint of lager.

It was difficult, he was finding, not to stare at her. She had the kind of face that seemed ordinary enough at first, but the more you looked at it, the more compelling it seemed. It was an old-fashioned face, the sort you saw in engravings and Elizabethan portraits: wide eyes balanced by a long straight nose and small mouth. She had very beautiful skin, of a delicate, radiant paleness and almost unbelievably fine, smooth texture. Her lashes were thick and long, even without mascara. A sudden shaft of sunlight through the streaked window warmed up her auburn hair; set it on fire, in fact, to a fabulous, pre-Raphaelite red.

He found himself wondering if she had a boyfriend and how he could find out.

'What's your name, by the way? I'm Olly.'

'Isabel.'

Isabel. Isabel, Isabel, Isabel. The perfect name. Classic. Slightly serious. Scottish. Isabel, Isabel, Isabel, *Isabel.* It galloped through his body like his own heartbeat.

Can all passengers ensure they take all their belongings with them . . .

They were arriving.

On the platform, he saw Isabel was taller than he had expected, with long, straight legs in faded jeans. She was stamping long, slim feet in black ballet flats, presumably to restore circulation after the trip.

Olly had already decided to walk with her to Branston. If she would let him. It was a glorious afternoon for a walk, a golden curtain call by a summer not quite ready to quit the stage. And she was a glorious person to walk with, a red-headed fairy from the far north with eyes as clear as a mountain stream. Her shyness and her winning openness of manner intrigued him. He wanted to protect her. He wanted to do a lot of things.

But first he would help her with her bags. 'One rucksack? That all?'

'I've only got clothes.'

'Haven't you brought any books?'

'Just a couple of paperbacks,' Isabel smiled. 'I read the reading list this summer.'

'What? The whole lot?' Olly's memory of faculty reading lists was that they were very long and with very fat spines.

'Yes,' she said, sounding surprised that he was surprised. 'The whole lot.'

She was heaving on her rucksack. As she slipped slim arms into the padded straps, the movement made her small breasts shake beneath her white shirt.

'I'll help you with that,' Olly said hurriedly. 'It's a long walk.'

'No, it's fine, honestly. Anyway, it'll look funny with your posh suit.'

'It's not posh,' Olly muttered.

'Isn't it? It looks it. It's very – what's the word . . . ?'

'Shiny?'

She laughed, and he felt a burst of happiness. If it amused her, his suit was perfect. Who needed Armani?

They set off up the road. She had a fast, striding walk. He imagined her striking forth over Scottish moors, wrapped in tartan, her hair rippling in the wind like something out of a Walter Scott novel. Or his own novel, come to that. It rather lacked a feminine focal point at the moment.

The effort of keeping up with her made conversation a challenge, but Olly tried his best. Was she going to the freshers' fair, where all the university societies competed to attract members from the new intake?

'I don't know,' Isabel said. 'Sounds as if I should.'

He told her about his ill-fated audition for one of the famous university acting clubs. 'The character was called Lord Sebastian Holles but I thought it was pronounced "Holes".'

It was amazing how, after three years, he could remember the scene in its entirety. That barely suppressed air of mirth from the audition panel as he read the touching scene when Lord Sebastian tells his mother that, despite being an only son and despite the estate staff dying like flies in Flanders, he, too, is going to certain death on the Western Front. 'Mother, you must prepare yourself for a gap in the Holes family . . .'

She was laughing, he saw, gratified. He felt sufficiently emboldened to add his experiences as a second year with The Kynge's Menne, a short-lived group of student strolling players whose idealistic intention had been to bring Shakespeare to the people. The people, unfortunately, had had better things to do, at least in the small Norfolk villages whose empty church halls and schools they had graced. Then there had been the weather. There had been a couple of downpours so violent that *The*

15

Tempest had more or less performed itself. Half the cast had dysentery at one point, a rogue prawn curry in Cromer being fingered as the culprit. Finally, after a performance of *Othello* in Brancaster in which a pensioner and a dog had been the only spectators, The Kynge's Menne had wrathfully gone their separate ways.

Watching her laugh, eyes sparkling in the sunshine, it seemed to Olly for the first time that the humiliation of trying to act had been more than worth it.

They had reached the centre of town now. As many tourists as parents and students were walking up and down the sunny, pale pavements and sitting, eating ice creams, along the low walls. The teashops were thronging and the outsides of the college formal-wear suppliers were crowded with gawkers at silk- or fur-trimmed academic hoods, black gowns, mortar boards, college scarves and ties and cufflinks with college crests. The circular postcard stands outside the newsagents' were surrounded by people in baseball caps.

Isabel stared round at the fairy towers, the cupolas, the golden college buildings. 'It's all so beautiful.'

'It is,' Olly allowed. 'But you get used to it.'

Isabel felt she never would. It was all so new, so strange. So unexpectedly fast moving. People were whizzing past on bikes, ringing bells just before mowing you down. It made her jump. She felt grateful for Olly's help, most of all for his company. She shot him a couple of shy glances. He was tall, fair and broad; quite handsome really. He looked kind. She felt she could trust him.

'What do you do now you've left?' she asked. 'Have you got a job?'

Olly summoned a confidence he did not quite feel. 'I'm going to be an investigative journalist,' he said bullishly, then added, for good measure, 'I'm writing a book as well.'

She looked impressed, he saw. 'What about?'

'Sort of young man's rite of passage sort of thing.'

They were passing St Alwine's now and he could have kicked himself for saying it. But her smile was dazzling, and genuine. 'You mean about your time at university? I'd love to read it. I'm sure I'd learn a lot from it.'

She sure as hell would, Olly thought. Once again a wild urge to tell all overwhelmed him. He wanted to get it over with. Acquaint her with the fact that, in certain circles – specifically the liberal feminist circles in which he had sought to find love in the past – admitting you were at St Wino's was like confessing to some dreadful disease.

Isabel was staring at the carving above the gates, the painted shields, mythic beasts, portcullises and roses. 'What a wonderful place,' she murmured.

Olly shifted from foot to foot, hoping that if he said nothing she would lose interest and move on. Apart from anything else her backpack was dragging at his shoulders and it was hot.

But Isabel stood, it seemed, spellbound. He watched her wide, clear eyes take in the details of the façade.

Then the wide eyes narrowed and looked puzzled. 'What's he doing?' Isabel asked. She was pointing at the carved central lozenge of the college's eponymous saint.

Olly cleared his throat. 'Um, he's holding a palm in one hand. It's the traditional symbol of martyrdom.'

Isabel glanced at him in mild exasperation. 'Well of course I know *that*,' she said. 'It's the other hand I'm wondering about.'

Olly took a deep breath. The fact that St Alwine appeared to be holding a bottle had contributed in no small part to the college nickname. There were those who insisted the long-necked, bulbous object being held in the saint's carved fingers was a cosh by which the generally mysterious Alwine might have met his end. But they had always been a minority and a mocked one at that.

'It's some sort of club.' Olly raised his chin as he spoke, as if to deflect objection.

Isabel continued to look thoughtfully at the carving. 'It looks like a bottle,' she pronounced at last. She turned to him, eyes sparkling with amusement. 'What's this college called?'

'Saint, um, Alwine's.'

'How funny. St Alwine's, and he's holding a wine bottle.'

'A cosh,' Olly corrected, determinedly. He was now quite set on his course of non-disclosure. If she didn't know – yet – of his alma mater's reputation within the university, then why tell her? Did he really want her to associate him with a group of braying, champagne-swilling, window-smashing, cash-flashing toffs of the most objectionable kind?

Thankfully, Isabel had switched her attention to the statue outside the gate, of a man in a ruff, looking down at his open hand. Olly fell on the opportunity to transmit the relatively uncontroversial information concerning it; this, he told her, was the Elizabethan founder of the college, Sir Titus Alwyne, known as Texting Titus because his pose suggested someone sending a cell-phone message. Sometimes, he added, Titus would contemplate a pizza box or a can of Heineken, strategically placed there by an inebriate.

He had to stop himself adding that during Caspar De Borchy's reign at the Bullinger helm, Titus's dignity had been further compromised by bras and suspenders. Or adding that Caspar had made tearing up fifty-pound notes in front of homeless people one of the club's initiation rites.

But Caspar De Borchy was gone now. Although Olly had heard he had a younger brother coming up this term. It crossed Olly's mind that he should warn Isabel to give De Borchy minor a wide berth, but he dismissed it as unnecessary. Given the fact she was at Branston and terribly conscientious there was absolutely no chance of them ever meeting. Caspar was as snobbish as he was lazy and his brother was bound to be the same. If not worse.

They were crossing the river now.

'Is punting hard?' Isabel asked, glancing over at the flat-bottomed boats, propelled by long poles, which plied up and down the river.

'That depends,' Olly said evasively. Throughout his college career he had struggled to master the art of balancing on the boat's slippery rear and been consistently unable to remember which bits of the river were shallow and which deep, squidgy and likely to retain the pole – and him with it – if he pushed it in too hard. This was the reason why, however much Olly wanted a job, chauffeur punting had never been the option it was for several of his fellow former students.

Isabel was watching the boats. 'It looks so romantic.'

'It's very romantic. Especially when water from the pole runs down your arm into your armpit.'

As Isabel laughed, a voice Olly recognised, one with a distinctive Northern twang, floated up from below: '. . . known throughout the university as St Wino's . . .'

He looked down, horrified. A punt full of American tourists was being poled along by a chauffeur punter, a fellow ex-St Alwine's student called Kevin Strangways. Kevin had been, Olly recalled, even more of a fish out of water among the Bullinger hoorays. Apart from the times they had dumped him in the college fountain, of course.

Kevin was clearly eager to settle the score now: '. . . sexist, racist braying toffs from hell, basically.'

His voice, amplified by the stonework, boomed up from beneath the bridge into Olly's ears with what seemed to him unmissable volume.

'They have window-smashing parties with strippers and dwarves. They tear money up in front of homeless people.'

Olly felt panic rise. It was not difficult to work out what was being described.

'You're not serious?' gasped one of his passengers. 'You're making this up, right?'

Olly was almost running over the bridge, Isabel hurrying behind him. 'What's he saying?' she asked, straining back to hear.

'. . . bras and suspenders . . .' boomed Kevin from under the bridge. Olly plunged on through the crowds with Isabel's rucksack.

As they continued up the road the rich college architecture gradually gave way to new-build offices, apartments and hotels.

Eventually Branston's rounded concrete dome hove into view with the covered walkways that projected from it like wires from a skull undergoing some revolutionary and subsequently discredited therapy. The scrunchy silver of the exposed heating and water pipes glittered in the sun.

'Here we are,' Olly said.

They approached up a wide tarmac path flanked by yellowing rhododendron bushes. Age and weather, while it had mellowed the stone buildings of the town, had here done the concrete few favours. The front entrance had sliding doors, like an airport. Above it, a large rectangular clock with a red digital LED number display reinforced the effect. The doors meshed together by means of rubber edging which parted with a slight farting noise as people went in and out.

But Isabel, Olly saw, was gazing at it all with delight. She turned and smiled at Olly. 'Thanks so much for carrying my stuff.'

'S'OK,' he shrugged. 'Pleasure.'

Was that it then? Not so much as a cup of tea? But he could tell she was too distracted by arrival to consider niceties such as this. Her green eyes were swivelling everywhere, taking it all in.

As slowly as was possible, he peeled the rucksack off his sweating back. 'Perhaps,' he suggested, feeling rather desperate, 'I could take you for a drink later, once you've unpacked and everything.'

'Or I could take you,' Isabel suggested, remembering her manners. 'I owe you a drink. I'm not sure whether there's a bar here though.' She looked vague.

Olly hid a smile. Every college had a bar. They were the centre of student social life and some chose colleges entirely on the basis of them. But probably not at Branston, where the bar did not enjoy a good reputation.

'The Turd,' Olly said.

She blinked. 'I'm sorry?'

'The bar. The bar at Branston. That's what it's called.'

'Is it?' Her eyes were round with wonder. 'I don't remember that in the prospectus.'

He felt suddenly rather weak about the knees. There was something utterly adorable about her earnestness. 'It's not an official name.' But, as he explained, given that Branston's bar was concrete, subterranean, fatly tubular in shape and rounded at the ends, it was possibly an inevitable one.

He could see her absorbing this. The coarseness of student humour seemed as much a revelation as the Turd itself.

'Let's go into town,' Olly suggested. 'I can show you where the good pubs are.'

'I've got to unpack first.'

'Here then?' Olly pressed eagerly. 'About seven?'

She nodded, waved with her free hand and disappeared through the farting airport doors.

Chapter 3

All these excited teenagers, Diana thought. Arriving for the new term, full of hurry and excitement. They seemed to flow like a vital river in and out of the lacy buildings. Their youthful shouts and laughter wove like ribbons round the older sound of bells.

It should, she felt, have cheered her, but her spirits remained flat. If only she was starting this new job – this new life – at a time of year other than autumn. Spring, perhaps, with its new growth. Or among the glossy grass, daisied fields and blossom-weighted bushes of early summer. In the sparkling wastes of winter, maybe.

But the end of her marriage, the loss of her home: there seemed parallels to it all in the October bonfires in the college gardens. The sad, slow blue spirals of smoke, the rotting sweetness in the air.

Feeling the familiar pricking behind her eyeballs, Diana blinked hard. Tears were out of the question, at least until she was alone. She had to keep cheerful, for Rosie's sake.

And here was something cheerful. Diana stopped at a zebra crossing for a beautiful, smiling girl with red hair that rippled like a flag. Panting after her was a young man in a suit – an amusingly shiny suit. It was with some difficulty that he raised a creased sleeve to acknowledge Diana, staggering as he was under the weight of an enormous rucksack. He was carrying it for the girl, quite obviously.

Young love, Diana thought, half envious, half despairing.

'Mum?' Rosie piped up from the back. 'Your face looks all red. I can see it in the mirror.'

'I'm hot,' Diana muttered, although the mellow October sun was not as warm as all that and their ancient car had no heating. As Rosie was probably about to point out. She missed nothing. Diana could see, in the reflection, the vivid little face of her nine-year-old daughter in its frame of wavy brown hair.

On the grass outside a gilded college gate a thick carpet of brilliant yellow leaves lay in a circle below a naked maple. It was a quietly spectacular sight, the thick pool of gold surrounded by emerald grass. Every leaf seemed to have dropped at once, in a blaze of glory. 'Look at that!' Diana said.

'It looks as if its dress has fallen off,' remarked Rosie. 'It looks cold.'

Following its grand autumn gesture, the denuded tree looked thin and vulnerable. But it would survive, Diana knew. Even now, beneath the earth, things were stirring for next year. The cycle would start again: new buds would form on the cold brown branches; she and Rosie would drive down this road next spring and see the trees shimmering with vivid new green.

If they were still here, of course. But they had to be. She could not afford for anything else to go wrong.

'It'll be fine,' she said firmly, to her daughter, but really to herself.

Rosie nodded and returned her attention to *Matilda*. She could read anywhere. In a car, in a train, in – as had often been the case recently – the foyer of a solicitors' office.

The divorce had been horribly painful. Lots of people got divorced, of course, but she had never imagined it happening to her. Her disappointment and sense of failure were crushing.

The familiar questions pressed in. How could she not have known? Or even suspected? Not just the affair, which was bad enough, but the money? The split had exposed how much higher on the hog they had been living than Simon could afford. He had never talked money with her, and now she could see why. The villa in Provence, the first-class travel, the expensive cars. They had been able to afford none of them.

Rosie's nanny and expensive private school, it turned out, had been similarly beyond his pocket. Ditto her oboe lessons with the LSO and Saturday classes at the Globe. That last now seemed especially ironic; that Rosie had gone for acting classes, given the show her own father was putting on.

All on credit. Their entire lives had been an illusion so that Simon could keep up appearances. He had always been aspirational; lately, imperceptibly, it had gone up a gear. She had been too busy doing nothing to notice.

But doing nothing had been exhaustingly busy. The hair appointments, the lymphatic drainage facials, the lunches, the personal trainers, the clothes. Simon had wanted her to look a certain way: that glossy, yummy-mummy way. She had gone along with it; Simon was not the kind of person you said no to. He was vital, energetic, a showman. She had always been much more retiring.

Well, she had been well and truly punished for her passivity now. After years of sleepwalking, she had been rudely awakened. Simon was bankrupt, the London house sold and Rosie withdrawn with dizzying speed from her expensive private school. In what seemed no time at all, Diana was what she had never imagined being: a penniless single mother.

Simon had disappeared to Australia with his mistress, leaving Diana with Rosie. And thank God for Rosie. Thank Him, too, for the gardening course. Diana had started it initially as something to do that wasn't shopping. All her neighbours had employed contract gardeners to maintain the patch that sat behind each tall, stuccoed slice of town house and connected to the private garden square beyond.

The gardeners were a focus of intense competition, one neighbour losing no opportunity to remind everyone else that her particular horticulturalists also did Buckingham Palace.

And that the Queen's acres were inferior in various ways. Diana, despite all this and probably because of it, wanted to do her own planting and weeding. Simon had tried to talk her out of it but on this one point she had been adamant. And found, to her surprise, not only that she enjoyed it, but that she was good at it. She had passed her first few exams with flying colours.

Before events had got in the way, she had planned to take her studies even further, way out into the upper reaches of garden design, into water features, even building. She had had no definite ideas about actually working as a gardener then, but events had got in the way and it was while flicking through a gardening magazine in the dentist's – her last ever visit to the smart private one, but her teeth, if nothing else, would be ready to face whatever lay ahead – that Diana had seen the modest advertisement: GARDENER WANTED. BRANSTON COLLEGE.

The judder of excitement she felt cut through even the fear of the approaching filling. She had, in happier days, visited the ancient university town and remembered the glossy college gardens strung along the shining river like jewels on a necklace. Gardeners would be fighting to work there, but perhaps this was only a junior position and she might have a chance. An ability to garden was, anyway, her only saleable skill. She had to throw her cap – and gardening gloves – into the ring.

A university town had obvious benefits too. Renting a house there would be cheaper and safer than amid the unknown dangers of London's unloved fringes. There would also, presumably, be good schools. And, after what had happened, it would not be hard to say goodbye to the capital.

Diana went immediately to the local library and booked a slot on one of the computers. She was surprised to find that Branston College, which she had imagined all mellow stone and herbaceous borders, was one of the modern ones. It looked, in fact, like a multi-storey car park. And it was hard to get an idea of the garden, as pictures of it were so few.

Nothing daunted and, determined to land the job through

sheer enthusiasm if nothing else, Diana thought hard about which flowers could lift and soften concrete walls. The contrast could even be dramatic. She assembled an entire folder of drawings and sent them off. The day the letter arrived inviting her for interview had been her happiest in months.

Arriving for her interview, she had marvelled anew at the grand college entrances with their coats of arms and heraldic beasts, the stained-glass chapel windows, the towers with their gilded pennants.

At Branston, which looked nothing like that, she had marvelled at the fact that the garden itself was so much worse than she had imagined. It was a wilderness of scrubby, unloved, Action-Man landscaping, done originally, Diana guessed, by bulldozer. There were entire areas of arid aggregate or mouldy patios of cracked concrete slabs. The weeds were rampant, great glossy dandelions and ground elder as far as the eye could see.

There had been a gardener of many years' standing, apparently. Although perhaps 'sitting' was a better way of putting it. 'What did he actually do?' Diana asked, looking round in amazement.

'Sit on the bench, mostly,' sighed the fat official showing her round: the deputy head of the college, the Bursar. A new Master had been appointed but was yet to arrive, Diana learnt.

The money offered made Diana gasp – and not in a good way. 'Branston's not one of the rich colleges,' the Bursar said.

'Shit!' Diana now exclaimed, slamming on her brakes and twisting her wheel violently to the side. They were proceeding along the road at the back of Branston, to the staff entrance. Diana had been about to turn into it when something shot out and hurled itself at her.

'Mummy!' Rosie rebuked from behind. 'You swore!'

'Sorry, darling,' Diana said, heart hammering at the near miss. It had been someone on a bicycle. Why did these people never look where they were going?

A dark shape in a cycle helmet now loomed at her side

window. As the sun behind was too brilliant to see him properly and the window of her battered car had long since lost the ability to lower automatically, Diana had to open the door to squint up at him. She forced herself to smile, expecting an apology and determined, despite the shock, to be gracious about it.

'What the hell do you think you're doing?' he demanded in a grating American accent. He was looking at her piercingly; Diana was suddenly conscious of her hat, a charity shop affair in purple fleece which looked, if anything, even cheaper than the 50p it had cost.

'You were going too fast,' she objected.

'You could seriously injure people, driving like that,' he went on, angrily.

Diana felt Rosie's sharp little chin pressing into her hair as the child leant excitedly forward to listen. However unfair the circumstances, Diana knew she could not argue with another adult under the surveillance of those small, bright brown eyes. She had been fiercely protective of her daughter over the divorce, refusing to fight with Simon in front of her or – and this had been a struggle at times – say anything nasty about him within Rosie's hearing. She had no intention now of undoing all that good work by rowing with a stranger.

'*You* were the one going too fast,' she repeated, screwing her eyes up against the drilling rays of the sun. That he was tall was all she could see. The helmet obscured his hair and face.

'I think this jalopy speaks for itself, don't you?' the cyclist sneered at her car.

Diana knew that. Her current vehicle, an ancient estate, looked most disreputable. She had bought it second hand, its gear stick lacked a knob, there was no functioning lock and it had dents in both front wings. The boot would not shut properly and needed to be tied on for days like today when the rear was full of plants. It was a moot point as to whether the car looked better dirty or with the dirt cleaned off showing the scratched blue paintwork beneath. But while certainly not a car to impress people, it was perfectly serviceable for a gardener, and it was as a gardener – a poor one at that – that Diana had bought it.

Her aggressor was walking briskly away now. Diana, red faced and feeling, despite everything, unpleasantly bested, stared at the concrete college walls as he picked up his bicycle and cycled away.

'Who was that?' Rosie wondered with interest, watching as he disappeared down the tree-lined road.

'Just a silly man, darling.' Diana drove crossly into Branston's back yard.

'He was *American*,' Rosie remarked, evidently awed.

Diana smiled at her daughter. 'You get people from all over the world coming here to study.' She hoped, even so, that the aggressive cyclist wasn't typical of the town's international population. Still less that he was one of her new colleagues.

Diana got out of the car. Rosie, released into the wild, ran ahead into the garden. Her mother trudged after her, over the bald and soggy lawn, the sodden black soil scattered with worm casts, pine needles, straggly weeds, bits of rubbish that would have to be picked up.

Rosie was whirling round on one of the lawn's few lush patches, a few yards of intense sunlit green, which Diana had already identified as moss. Head flung back, soaked in light, Rosie seemed, not a child in an old pink sweatshirt and too-short tracksuit bottoms, but a mysterious, triumphant, celebrating spirit. Looking at her, Diana felt, despite her gloom, a sudden, piercing conviction that everything would be all right. After all, if Rosie was happy, what else could possibly matter? She crossed to the little spinning figure and gave her a hug.

Professor Richard Black cycled impatiently on, annoyed by the near collision with the woman in the car. Part of his agitation arose from the fact that, in his heart of hearts, he knew himself to be the guilty one. He was, as Amy had always laughingly pointed out, far crosser about things when he sensed himself partly to blame.

Stopping at a crossroads, he watched a family carrying what looked like most of the contents of a house – chairs, a TV, a bookcase – and Richard wondered briefly what it would be like to have a child starting university. That his and Amy's marriage had been childless had been her only source of unhappiness in an existence in which everything else seemed a delight. But of course, if they had had a child, he would be bringing it up himself now, alone. And what would that be like?

Difficult, Richard imagined. All the students he could see here seemed to have two parents. Adoring, concerned, proud parents into the bargain. The place was packed with happy couples and blissful families; what on earth, he wondered bleakly, had possessed him to think it was somewhere he could come and hide and try to forget? It seemed to him now that nowhere on earth was more likely to remind him of everything he had lost.

He cycled faster. The woman in the car had only delayed him further. He was late, much later than he usually was. This was entirely due to the advanced hour he had retired the night before, when he had been obliged to attend a tedious drinks reception marking his arrival as Master of Branston. It had been as exhausting as it had been wearisome and unexpected.

He had understood that, being one of the university's lower-profile colleges and in line with its – pretty crazy – appearance, Branston was less formal than most. But, no. An entire line-up of other college heads had been present, some, frankly, caricatures. The Master of St Alwine's, for instance, was as ludicrously anachronistic as the foundation over which he presided was rumoured to be. He'd been resplendent in black robes, gold lace and a floppy, feather-trimmed bonnet. Why, Richard wondered, had he gone into academia when he was obviously more suited to pantomime?

Possibly because the booze was better. As his puce nose attested, the Master's main interest appeared to be vintage port and, while vaguely aware Richard was a neuroscientist, he was clearly struggling to understand his new colleague's particular field, synaptic plasticity.

'Yes, I think my wife does that,' the Master had remarked after much thought. 'She's very keen on it.'

'Synaptic plasticity?' Richard masked his surprise. He had met the Master's wife earlier. She was goggle-eyed with a receding chin and had talked almost exclusively about her cats. She had not seemed interested in the frontiers of brain research.

The Master of St Alwine's had grabbed a passing sausage. 'Every Friday morning in the church hall,' he explained. 'She wears loose trousers. She says it keeps her fit.'

It emerged that he meant Pilates.

'Synaptic plasticity is about how the brain makes connections,' Richard explained through gritted teeth. The Master was patently making no connections whatsoever, apart from with more passing canapés.

He had been rescued by a kindly classics professor who had made strenuous efforts to connect her subject with his, but Richard, while grateful for her solicitude, was unable to pick up any of the many lines she threw him. He had lost the knack of small talk, which had always been Amy's department anyway. At parties she had flitted engagingly about, chattering brightly, charming all. Her ability to always say the right thing had consistently amazed Richard and sometimes, when examining slices of brain through microscopes in his laboratory, he had tried to spot this skill. It had been possible for some time to trace the physical process of thought, but charm, seen only in the eye of the beholder, left no such trace.

No one last night had seemed to find him particularly charming, unless you counted the junior research fellow, squiffy on the Branston house white, who had stumbled into his personal space and, over the thrusting cleavage, bursting out of her low-cut, red satin top, slurred, 'It's true what they say about you.'

He had met her unsteady gaze with his own, flinty one. 'Which is what?'

'That you're the sexiest neuroscientist in the business. Talk about *cortex interruptus!*'

Once, Richard knew, this would have made him laugh out loud. Now he merely gave her a freezing look. It did not, however, appear to register; either alcohol had dulled her senses or the skin so abundantly on show was a very thick one. It looked it, certainly.

'Well, Prof,' she said breathily, leaning confidingly into him. 'When you need a night off from the neurons just give me a call.'

Richard had strode away, appalled at the implication that he was somehow available and looking for love. That there could be anyone after Amy was unthinkable, least of all some inebriated postgraduate, pushing her flabby white breasts in his face.

The evening had ground on. There had been speeches to endure, then a terse reply of his own. Only then had Richard been able to escape.

He had bowed tightly at the assembled company and hurried off, knowing they would talk about him after he had gone. 'Poor man,' the women would witter. 'He's so closed-up, isn't he? Of course, you know he lost his wife a couple of years ago. Yes; didn't you know? Dreadful. Cancer. Mmm. She was quite young, too. They met when she was one of his students. Quite romantic, really. So tragic. No, no children.'

In his more philosophical moments, Richard felt that his situation as a widowed and grieving neuroscientist was an oxymoron. It was a contradiction in terms, a philosophical joke almost. More than most, he was aware that he and Amy's entire marriage, viewed from one angle, had been nothing more than a sequence of neurons firing in a particular way. They had both been mere collections of habits, preferences and impressions, all products of excitation and inhibition in the flabby grey computers they carried in their skulls. At one stage he had hoped that thinking of it like that would help him bear it. But now he knew it just made it more depressing. The only thing that helped him was his work.

Towards the labs he pedalled on amid the parting families. Under a Venetian-style bridge linking a pair of venerable college walls, a woman in a leopardskin coat and aubergine hair was theatrically hugging a girl with a bright pink fringe. A man with a beard, sunglasses and a grey woolly jumper waved from beside a nearby Dormobile covered in CND symbols.

Beside the gates of St Alwine's, a tall, beautiful but impassive-looking boy was clashing cheekbones like rock ledges with an elegant woman and distinguished-looking man.

'Bye, darling', the woman cried as they climbed into their shiny black car. The doors shut with an expensive clunk and the growl of an expensive engine followed. As the boy raised a hand in farewell, his signet ring glittered in the sun.

The atmosphere was one of carnival almost; every pavement seemed full of smiling, waving people, car doors slamming, engines starting, people hurrying back and forth with bags and boxes. Richard was unable to suppress a wave of misery so powerful it made his knees shake.

He changed gear and cycled faster, as if the physical effort would offset the dread suspicion that he had done the wrong thing in coming here at all. Perhaps he should have turned down Branston. He almost had, but at the last moment, after a particularly miserable New England weekend as the end of the summer term approached and when the sunshine, flowers and general golden youth had almost been too much for him to bear, he had got on a plane and gone to the interview.

England – why not? A change of scene would do him good; a change of continent even more so. Branston, in addition, enjoyed a location close to the internationally famous neurology department where his real interests lay.

The college, so glad to have him interested, had readily agreed to his terms, which were that he was there first and foremost as a research scientist. They could put him on their masthead, website and brochure if they wanted, but he would remain essentially uninvolved in the domestic and pastoral business of the college. After all that had happened, the last thing Richard wanted was to be hosting tea parties for undergraduates. Not least because, in the past, that was something Amy had loved.

At the ghastly drinks reception, some college heads had blithely described the lunch and dinner parties they gave regularly for their students. 'We aim to provide a family atmosphere,' one Master had cheerfully said about his teacake-and-toasting-fork gatherings in front of a roaring fire. Richard had shuddered. A family atmosphere was the very last thing he would be providing. Nor would he be spearheading attempts to drum up money, which, according to many college principals, was what they spent most of their time doing. 'We're basically just fundraisers,' one had said. Well, not him, Richard vowed. What money Branston needed, it could raise itself.

Admittedly, Branston had never mentioned such a thing. Nor had it said anything about teacakes. And the final point in its favour – the most important point of all, in a sense – was that the college had an almost unbelievably horrible garden, all dark trees and bald lawns, litter and weeds, positively emanating neglect and abandonment.

A garden, in other words, that could not remotely remind him of his wife. Amy had been a passionate plantswoman. It wasn't just that her fingers were green, every other bit was too. She had spent every spare minute in their garden at home. Selling the place after her death, he had held out for the right people, and had taken a lower offer because he could tell the buyers would look after Amy's back yard. She had particularly loved English gardens and at various points over the years he had trailed after her as she paced excitedly past Stowe's temples, through the white beds at Sissinghurst, by the fountains of Hampton Court, round the lake at Chatsworth, all the time exclaiming at eye-catchers, admiring ha-has, gasping at effects achieved by great sweeping avenues of beech and chestnut.

The further the plane taking him for the interview had got across the Atlantic, the more certain Richard grew that the college gardens would be a deal breaker. Those of the university were famously picturesque. In the taxi to Branston his dread had reached its peak, merciless images of roses against old stone, time-worn, wisteria-framed doorways had filled his imagination. He had considered turning round, there and then.

But the taxi had stopped before something that looked like a nuclear reprocessing plant – the only plant visible, from what Richard could see. He had stepped out in disbelief – and relief. Branston's brutal, unromantic appearance, so at odds with the ancient grace and gorgeousness of the rest of the university, struck an instant chord. It looked every bit as bleak as he felt; exactly the kind of featureless box he wanted to lock himself away in.

When the Assistant Bursar, an oppressed-looking woman who seemed permanently welded to her clipboard, said something disparaging and apologetic about Branston's grounds, he had surprised her by saying they looked perfectly OK to him. They were looking for a new gardener, the Assistant Bursar had confided. Richard hoped they wouldn't try too hard.

Chapter 4

Branston's porter did not conform to the traditional college servant stereotype. He did not have a moustache and bowler hat. He was burly, bald, wore an Arsenal T-shirt and sat behind the sort of sliding glass screen usually found in hospitals. He looked as if he worked out a lot, but seemed friendly enough.

Bent under her rucksack – heavier even than she remembered – Isabel paused at the pigeonholes in the college foyer, a framework of wooden boxes nailed to the wall. Each student had a named one in which their post was put.

The one with Isabel's name on held a flyer for the freshers' fair and a bundle of English Faculty instructions. A pigeonhole nearby, however, was bursting with thick cream-and-white envelopes upon which glimpses of beautiful italic handwriting could be seen. They were obviously invitations, and smart ones at that. There was even a bunch of roses stuffed in there. Isabel felt sorry for the flowers, shoved in as they were, without any water.

Curious, she read the name above the pigeonhole: the Hon. A.R.S. Piggott. Isabel's thoughts flicked instantly back to the *Brideshead* conversation she had had with Olly, about the university not being that sort of place any more, and Branston especially not. The Hon. A.R.S. Piggott rather seemed to belie this. He or she – she, judging by the roses – also sounded vaguely familiar, but Isabel could not think why. She didn't know anyone with a title.

But she had other matters to concern her, such as finding her room. The *Gesamtkunstwerk*, Isabel now discovered, was designed inside like a huge wheel. The lifts and lobbies formed the centre and corridors spoked off at regular intervals. As a design concept it was no doubt groundbreaking, but finding your way round was a challenge. The fact there were no windows was disorientating. You could be in outer space, or on a journey to the centre of the earth. Which corridor was which? They all looked the same with a strip of orange corridor carpet and rows of shiny beige-coloured doors with brushed aluminium handles and numbers and names slotted into holders.

Isabel pressed on. She passed a closed pair of pale wooden doors which, together, formed the shape of an upright egg. They each bore one half of a simple brass cross and she realised she must be at the spiritual heart of the *Gesamtkunstwerk*, the Branston College chapel. Pushing open the stiff, rather awkward doors Isabel saw an egg-shaped concrete chamber whose grey walls tapered to a rounded cone.

Was this what an unhatched chick felt like? Was it some sort of metaphor? The chapel had no windows and was entirely unadorned apart from a few pale wood benches and, at the cone end, a wooden table supporting a tall, thin, figureless crucifix. One's faith would have to be strong, Isabel thought.

Her rucksack was pressing heavily on her shoulders now and, panting under the weight of her burden, Isabel went on, only to find herself back in the foyer. She had gone round in a circle, it seemed. She could not help noticing that, in the time she had been absent, A.R.S. Piggott had received yet another bunch of flowers.

She adjusted the straps digging hard into her shoulders and set off again, in the other direction. This time she passed a couple of perfectly globular concrete meeting rooms and the closed door of the college bar. A neat sign read, 'Branston Bar'. Someone had written underneath, in crazed marker, 'The Turd'.

Isabel grinned, remembering what Olly had said about the place.

Quite suddenly, there it was: Room twenty. Miss I.J. Murray.

The key was in the door, a metaphor not lost on Isabel. She took a deep breath, then turned it. She opened the door and, heart racing, stepped inside.

Her first impression was that everything was pale. The carpet and curtains were beige, the desk was of blond wood and its chair had an oatmeal padded seat. It was small, but no smaller than her own room at home. Between the desk and the small bed opposite there was just about room to edge through sideways once she had closed the door and placed the rucksack against it.

Isabel looked round. The cream walls were a blank canvas. She realised she could put up what she liked, be who she liked in this room. Who would she be? She stooped to stare at herself in the thin mirror fixed to the tall, slim cupboard by the door. Her own eyes looked back at her uncertainly. What now? they seemed to be saying.

She put her head outside. The corridor was quiet and empty and Isabel felt a sudden loneliness. Was no one else coming? Perhaps they were lost in the wheels and spokes of the *Gesamtkunstwerk*, as she had been. She paused to read the name of her next door neighbour.

A Miss E.S.M. Grey was in twenty-one, to the left. A cool, ladylike-sounding sort of person, Isabel thought, noting the three initials and reflecting that while she had never consciously thought about it before, she had imagined one middle name only to be the rule. But it was she, plain Isabel Jane plus surname, who was the exception here. On the other side, she experienced a faint stab of recognition. The Hon. A.R.S. Piggott. That name again. Why did she feel she knew it?

A commotion at the end of the corridor made her jump. Someone was coming. Seized with shyness, Isabel darted back inside her room and closed the door softly.

A light, breathy, girl's voice, sounding relieved: 'Oh, look; *here* it is! Mummy! Daddy! Room twenty-one. It's here!'

Room twenty-one, Isabel was thinking. So this was Miss E.S.M. Grey.

The sound of a turning key echoed in the concrete corridor.

'Where do you want this box, Ellie?' A man's voice; the father, Isabel guessed. She suppressed a sudden wave of longing.

As an adopted child, Isabel was not in the habit of thinking of her birth parents. It felt disloyal and, besides, there was nothing to think of, no peg to hang anything on, no picture, no sound. Only Mum was real and she hadn't let her come. As the waves of self-criticism rose once more within, Isabel stared at the door and felt that she never did anything right.

The door was slightly ajar and she could see movement outside. Figures. After a few assorted glimpses, Isabel could put together the following: a girl with long fair hair in a long blue cardigan, skinny jeans and Ugg boots; a man with claret cords and a blue pullover; and a woman – the mother, presumably, who seemed to have dressed up more for the occasion – in a brown-printed wrap-dress and sandals with aquamarine heels. Isabel heard her, now, exclaim, 'The Hon. A.R.S. Piggott! She's got the room next-door-but-one to you, Ells. You don't think it could be *the* Amber Piggott, do you?'

'Amber Piggott? Never heard of her,' the father said.

'She's been in the papers all summer. She's an heiress, got an incredibly rich father; he owns department stores, I think. She's a sort of "it girl", very glamorous, kind of the new Tara Palmer-Tomkinson, but even more so, if you see what I mean.'

'How awful,' said the father uncharitably. 'The old one was bad enough.'

Ellie's door closed now, and Isabel was unable to hear anything else. She sat back on the bed and stared at the creamy blankness of the opposite wall.

So that was who the Hon. A.R.S. Piggott was. She remembered the woman's tabloid on the train, the picture of the glamorous blonde laughing in the limo and something about her starting a degree in literature somewhere. She would never have imagined it was here, Isabel thought. But being spectacularly rich and glamorous didn't mean you couldn't be clever too.

Voices out in the corridor broke into her thoughts. Ellie's parents could be heard saying goodbye, but Isabel did not look through the hole again; goodbyes really were private.

She busied herself with unpacking. She could hear the faint thumping of music through the walls. She thought she could hear Ellie's voice too, singing along, and there were busy scraping and thudding sounds as if she were arranging her belongings as well.

Isabel's rucksack contained mostly clothes and once they been put away the room looked similar to how it had when she had started. She decided to strike out, find the kitchen and explore the bathrooms. The bathrooms were at the end of the corridor; she remembered passing them on her way down.

Opening her door again, she set off along the soundless corridor. It was odd how dead and strange concrete felt beneath one's feet, even concrete under a carpet.

The kitchen was at the end, as seventies as the rest of the décor, with rather battered off-white units containing water glasses, plain white plates and mugs. There was a large steel sink with a ridged draining area and a white metal stove with round black electric rings scuffed and faded in the middle as if they had seen a great deal of use over the years. There was a window with a view over the college gardens; they looked rather scrubby and unloved, Isabel was thinking. Someone was working out there, though: a woman in a funny-looking purple hat . . .

Someone entering the kitchen from behind made her turn round suddenly. A girl in skinny jeans, Ugg boots and with one hand plunged deeply into the pockets of a long, baggy pale blue cardigan: Ellie, obviously.

She swished her long fair hair and smiled. 'Hi,' she said in the light, rather insubstantial voice that Isabel already knew. 'I'm Ellie.'

'Isabel.'

'Oh, you're the girl next door,' Ellie smiled. 'Fancy a coffee in my room?'

Ellie was reading history. Her room was a revelation; she seemed to have eradicated all institutional touches. The bare bones were the same as Isabel's, but it could not have looked more different.

'Oh, I've had years of practice; horrid girls'-school bedrooms and all that,' Ellie said breezily, as Isabel, clutching a steaming mug with the BBC logo admired the colourful embroidered cotton throw on the bed and the fringed, sequinned and patch-worked Indian cushions piled on top amid a couple of teddies, evidently worn by love and time. One had an eye missing, the other lacked an ear but they were, Ellie had rather touchingly confided, her absolute favourite possessions.

She had strung pink fairy lights along the top of the wardrobe and customised the biscuit-coloured shade fixed to the centre of the ceiling with magenta tissue paper. The general restful, souk-like atmosphere was completed by a thick, white, scented candle glowing on the desk and emitting a delicious citrus smell. Inhaling it, drawing in the general rosy comfort and warmth, Isabel wanted to lie down on the glittering bed amid the teddies and surrender to exotic dreams. Or else hear about Ellie's gap-year stint as a BBC intern. Her godmother worked for Radio Four, Isabel's favourite station. 'Jenni Murray?' Ellie said absently. 'Oh, she's really sweet. Anyway, here's my travel blog.'

Her smart new laptop was open beside the scented candle on the desk and she was busy scrolling through a sequence of colourful pictures.

After the BBC, which Isabel would much rather have heard about, Ellie had gone to work for various charities abroad. She had helped in the favelas of Brazil and on a women's collective farm in the Congo. She had also taught English in India and helped build a school in Mexico.

'Where did you go for your year off?' Ellie asked brightly as she prodded the buttons from time to time, to change the image.

Isabel felt the sudden urge to giggle. Working in 'Bide A Wee', the Lochalan café, hardly compared to Ellie's altruistic globe trotting. She had been saving up for uni, not saving the world. The only social difference she had made was to persuade Miss Macpherson, the café's somewhat conservative owner, that a patisserie range consisting entirely of shortbread was somewhat limiting and carrot cake could be introduced with no loss of life or limb.

'Oh, nowhere amazing,' she said with perfect truth, quickly turning the subject back to Ellie again. 'That school sounds wonderful.'

'It was,' Ellie sighed, pulling a rueful face. 'I know this sounds a bit much but I really did feel privileged to help these poor children; realised just how lucky I am and all that.' Her face flushed, but then she grinned. 'But it wasn't all like that,' she added, launching into a description of a holiday in Thailand with two schoolfriends called Milly and Tilly, both now at Exeter. 'It was sort of like our last fling,' Ellie reminisced wistfully. 'They were my absolute besties.'

Isabel examined the photos on the blog of Ellie and her absolute besties. The besties had long hair, just like Ellie, although, being thinner, they were better suited to the gap-year uniform of strappy black vest top and safari shorts. In the picture, the three of them were sitting under strings of fairy lights holding pastel-coloured plastic cups the size of large plant pots, bristling with straws. 'Thai buckets,' Ellie explained, her voice fond with remembrance. 'You can dance all night after one of those. Actually, I did some fire-eating.' She giggled.

'Fire-eating?'

'Mm. I'd seen a couple of girls from Australia do it in Koh Jum. I really wanted to do it and it was quite easy, actually. The lighter fuel in your mouth doesn't taste half as bad as you expect.' Ellie was giggling. 'Tills and Mills thought I was an absolute maniac.' She sighed and looked suddenly serious. 'We had such fun. I wish they could have come here too. I miss my besties.' She turned to Isabel anxiously. 'But we can be friends, can't we?'

Isabel nodded in delight. She was more than happy to fill the bestie gap. She'd never really had a bestie before.

'That's that then,' Ellie said, pleased. 'Maybe we could go to the Incinerator together later?' She was rearranging a few things on her desk, including the large pinboard covered in invitations, postcards and notes that she had had since she was thirteen.

Isabel stared. 'But I've hardly got anything in my bin yet, I haven't been here long enough.'

Ellie was giggling. 'The Incinerator's what they call the dining hall.'

Isabel had not yet visited the dining hall and had been prepared to accept the official prospectus description of its being 'a great, white, light-filled circular space occupying the central position beneath the college's distinctive dome.' But, according to Ellie, it looked like an industrial plant crossed with a hospital mortuary. 'And not in a good way.'

'And afterwards we could go to the Turd – that's the bar, you know . . .' Ellie continued.

'Yes, I know,' Isabel interjected, keen to dispel the impression she knew absolutely nothing about anything.

'And then we come back here and watch a film on my laptop. I've got loads of romcoms.'

Ellie had it all mapped out, Isabel thought, happy to be bowled along in her slipstream. Bars and romcoms. It wasn't the life she was used to, not at all.

Outside, in the garden, Diana was getting tired. Gardening was so exhausting when you did it all day. You ached all over, your extremities numbed. Hopefully she would get used to it; she would have to.

Perhaps she was overdoing it, working on Sunday when, officially, her first day was tomorrow, Monday. But the thought of sitting at home when there was so much to be done was impossible. There were issues with her new home that she chose not to face just yet: the neighbours, mainly.

Diana hastily reminded herself that, even in the wealthy part of London she had lived in, there had been neighbour problems. Different ones, perhaps. Her old neighbour, Sara Oopvard, she of the Queen's gardeners, had been particularly ghastly. It seemed almost incredible, now that money was so tight, to recall how freely Sara had spent it – and no doubt still did – on services of such marginal necessity as the professional from the London Zoo aquarium who came to clean out the fish tank. Or the fashionable interior designer who, each December, came to 'theme' the Oopvard Christmas tree.

Sara, English wife of a rich Dutch banker, had been the first to drop her like a hot brick once divorce loomed, Diana remembered. But that had actually been a relief. Rosie need not, any longer, go for playdates with Milo, the Oopvards' spoilt son.

Flashing now into Diana's mind came the memory of Milo at his last birthday party. 'Mu-um! Cassius and Ludo've dressed as Buzz Lightyear as well. They've copied me! You got me the same costume as everybody else. I *hate* it!' He had ripped savagely at the Velcro on his spacesuit front. Diana felt a warm sense of relief that she never had to see the Oopvards again. However bad the new neighbours, they could not be as bad as the old.

Gathering her gardening tools, she pictured Sara in the gym, or on Twitter, or donning paper pants for a spray tan. Or competing away – and definitely not eating – in some fashionable organic café against other aimless and wealthy wives in the same boat – or yacht. Or perhaps having the muslin-covered fingers of a Hungarian facial specialist rubbing creams into her Botoxed forehead. Or as one of a privileged coven complaining around skinny lattes about Svetlana's calling Moscow whenever she felt like it, or Imelda's inability to manage the six-ring burner. Rosie's own nanny, Hannah, had been a large, slow-witted creature employed solely because everyone they knew had such 'help'.

Diana, who had long wanted to look after Rosie herself, had been secretly glad to see the broad back of her.

Divorce had given her this opportunity. At first, accustomed to leaving the details to someone else, Diana had constantly found herself in sudden rain without a coat for her daughter, in a muddy park without a change of clothes. She had never had a bottle of water when Rosie was thirsty. She had not understood the importance of frequent loo breaks. Or how dips in sugar levels triggered mood swings.

Gradually, she had broken through. Among the things Diana now knew was that Rosie preferred crisps to chocolate and, while hating broccoli, would eat carrots. Rosie liked to draw and loved to swim. So far as books were concerned, she preferred Malory Towers to St Clare's, Just William to Horrid Henry and, while she liked Harry Potter, she preferred Lemony Snicket's ill-starred Baudelaire family, especially the baby, Sunny. She also loved Sherlock Holmes. Each new insight was a source of joyful fascination to Diana, mixed with guilt. She should have insisted Hannah went long ago. The person she was now would never allow someone else to take such a primary role in Rosie's life, even if money was no object.

Diana looked carefully about to make sure no tools had been left. She could not afford to lose a single one. Then she walked over to where Rosie was reading in the back of the car.

Diana's afternoon had been punctuated by near-constant glances over to the battered blue banger, which contained the single thing most precious in the world to her. But Rosie had not moved.

'You won't be bored?' Diana had asked, anxiously.

'I'm OK, Mummy, honestly,' Rosie said, smiling and shaking her light brown curls. 'Don't worry, Mum,' she added reassuringly.

Rosie had been as good as her word, Diana reflected now. As good as gold. Autumn gold.

There were a couple of mature beeches overlooking the car park. Diana admired them as she carried the tools towards her car boot. She loved beeches, especially at this time of year, their formerly rich green leaves turning slowly through gold to burnished copper. Sometimes, to show off, one tree did all three at once. Whereas the poor old elms, so stately in the summer, lost their leaves like men lost their hair: the top was the first to go. Simon's early-onset baldness had been a source of agony to him. Perhaps, Diana reflected, it was that which had made him vulnerable to predatory women. She blinked, recognising a sea change. She had been, up to this point, too angry with her ex-husband to care in the least about his motivation.

It was getting colder. There was a nip in the air, tweaking the tops of her ears and tightening the end of her nose. Diana felt glad of her hat, however unflattering. What did it matter if only stupid people like the cyclist saw it?

She opened the boot and placed the tools carefully in. Rosie was sprawled on the back seat placidly reading *In The Fifth At Malory Towers*. It took some time, even after opening the door and speaking to her several times, to catch her attention.

Diana got in, her heart sinking slightly at the mess. The front passenger seat was awash with battered cardboard boxes, empty plastic plant pots and plant markers. The days of valeted limousines were over, she reminded herself. And, on the whole, unlamented.

Apart from in one respect, possibly. It was not enough, Diana thought, that she herself had survived her own change in circumstances. Rosie's great test was yet to come. None of what had happened was her fault, but was she about to suffer for the folly of her parents?

Diana could hardly believe how Rosie seemed amazingly happy, in spite of everything. She was sure she must be pretending in some way, and yet, Globe acting lessons notwithstanding, would a nine-year-old be so accomplished a dissembler? Nonetheless, she had worried herself sleepless that Rosie would miss her old lifestyle, her princess bedroom, her riding lessons, her friends and their birthday parties that seemed to get more elaborate and expensive every year. One of the last Rosie had attended involved stretch limos and party bags containing DVDs and Dior make-up.

More than anything else she had worried about how Rosie would cope with school. It was her first day at her new one, Campion Primary, tomorrow. Diana's secret terror was that her daughter would be bullied. Would she be picked on for her refined manners and accent? For the fact she had come from a different world?

Smart's Preparatory School in West London had occupied a white stucco town house with a portico. Rosie had worn a blazer and a stiff-brimmed straw boater. The school's website was slick, as was the silver-fox headmaster, whose blog successfully balanced amusing with authoritative. Among Rosie's fellow pupils, the offspring of media bigwigs, film stars, oligarchs, Cabinet ministers and royalty (both home-grown and European) had been two a penny. The school's narrow hallway had been, on a daily basis, a combination of the *Vanity Fair* post-Oscars party and the *Newsnight* greenroom, as high-end TV presenters pushed past Westminster power brokers. Less-rich parents, it was said, took out mortgages in advance of the summer fête. This was so they could bid for raffle prizes ranging from trips in other parents' private planes to walk-on parts in their films.

Meanwhile, Campion Primary was a state school of some two hundred and seventy pupils and had seemed, to Diana's panicking eyes, a shanty town of prefabricated and temporary-looking units set on broken tarmac and cracked concrete. Of the notices stuck all over the walls, the emergency, anti-bullying and Childline numbers were the ones that leapt out. The acting headmistress, during their brief meeting, had seemed a severely harassed woman mainly in the business of crowd control.

To make things worse, the first term of the year had already started. Friends, Diana fretted, would have been made, alliances formed. It was into this alien world that Rosie would walk alone tomorrow. And yet she seemed utterly unruffled. Diana urged herself to feel the same.

'I love this film,' Ellie sighed joyfully. 'It's the best bit, too.'

Isabel, snuggled amid the teddies and the cushions on Ellie's bed, felt almost ridiculously happy. Uni was bliss, as Ellie herself might say. Dinner at the Incinerator had been great fun, despite all the hard concrete surfaces making for a deafening noise of clattering plates, clashing cutlery and voices. But Isabel had loved looking about at all the other new students from the safe haven of Ellie's companionship and thinking how alone and vulnerable she would have felt without her.

The food had been, at best, unremarkable. 'We used to have something like this at school; we used to call it "Dead Man's Leg",' Ellie said, poking the unidentifiable meat about her plate. 'And that pudding of yours is just like one we used to have at St Mary's. "Nun's Toenails", we used to call it.'

Isabel had laughed. Even the bad food at Ellie's school sounded fun. In the Turd, afterwards, she had sat against the blue-lit, curved concrete walls and – after Ellie's example – drunk vodka while her companion assessed the romantic possibilities. 'Not great,' was Ellie's conclusion after a swift scrutiny of the available talent. 'Fat hippies, mostly, and Goths in guyliner.' Isabel wasn't sure what guyliner was, but there was no disagreeing with the rest; large, shambling long-haired types in black T-shirts seemed overrepresented in her view.

'No one to practise my snogging skills on,' Ellie lamented, then giggled at Isabel's expression. 'You looked so shocked! But that's pretty much all we learnt at school: how to snog and how not to get a hangover.'

Isabel stared at the vodka in her hand and felt she didn't have much of a clue about either. She felt lumpishly unsophisticated in comparison. But Ellie must have learnt something else at school, surely, or she wouldn't be here.

They went back to Ellie's room and set up the laptop.

'We spent our lives watching DVDs at school,' Ellie said.

Isabel was beginning to feel she had attended Ellie's south-of-England girls' school herself. Perhaps she just wished she had been part of the jokes, the camaraderie, the communal atmosphere. It certainly seemed more real to her than the far-distant lochside where, right this moment, her mother would probably be sitting alone in front of the TV. Isabel pushed the thought away – she would ring tomorrow – and tried to concentrate on the film, *Dog For Christmas*.

'Two lonely people who, after hilarious misadventures, misunderstandings and mistakes, are brought together by a loveable mongrel just in time for the festive season.'

Isabel, feeling warm and woozy after the vodka, was conscious of missing various crucial plot twists because of her eyelids drooping. She tried, now, to concentrate as a bespectacled actor of the handsome geek variety and a dark-haired actress of the pouting temptress variety were making passionate love on a sofa. A blonde actress of the wholesome-but-beautiful variety was coming in the door.

'What's going on?' Isabel muttered.

'It's the scene where the heroine walks into her flat to find her boyfriend at it on the sofa with the sexy neighbour,' Ellie explained. 'And this is the bit when they all shout at each other and the relationship's over,' Ellie popped open a tube of Pringles without her eyes ever leaving the screen.

The film's blonde heroine now lay on a sofa, sobbing while a woman with a long nose, pink hair and electric-blue leggings was tottering about unsteadily in lime-green high heels.

'The heroine's wacky flatmate,' Ellie snorted. 'This is the bit where the flatmate tells the disappointed-in-love heroine that she's just gotta get up off her ass and get out there, that there are plenty more fish in the sea.'

Right on cue, a high-pitched, nasal, female American voice filled the room: '. . . just gotta get up off your ass and get out there. Plenty more fish in the sea, babe,' the flatmate added, with a toss of her pink hair.

The camera cut to the woman on the sofa. 'Yeah, but all I ever get is plankton!' she sobbed.

Isabel roared with laughter, but then a terrible thought struck her. The excitement of the evening, of making friends with Ellie, of discovering the college in her company had completely eradicated all thought of Olly, who had been so kind to her; who had, in fact, been the first to befriend her.

The vodkas now curdling in her stomach, Isabel sat bolt upright amid the cushions. 'And this,' she gasped, her voice shaking, 'is the bit where I remember I was supposed to be meeting someone, *hours* ago, for a drink.'

Chapter 5

Olly, waiting in the gathering cold and dark outside Branston, had imagined at first that Isabel was simply late. Any moment she would emerge, smiling and full of apologies, from amongst the knots of students and their parents coming in and out of the farty-sounding doors. But the minutes went by, and with it the file of shambling youth with plastic bags of teabags and milk cartons – the latter, Olly knew, destined to sit outside on the windowsills of their rooms until they curdled or fell off. And still Isabel did not appear.

He occupied himself in studying Branston's architecture. It was possible that he had judged it unfairly, inasmuch as he had ever thought about it at all. It was not by Wren, admittedly, but Christopher Wren had been a modern builder himself once, and the builder of Branston might well be the Wren of the future. Although, as Olly's eye ran along Branston's boxy front, where the pale grey concrete was streaked black and green with age and weather, he rather doubted it.

After half an hour had gone by on the large red digital clock above the main entrance, Olly could no longer discount the possibility that Isabel was not coming. He struggled to believe it. She had not seemed the flaky sort – anything but, in fact. Had she not tried to help the old lady on the train? A good-hearted act, if ever there was one. And there was an innocence about her, a wide-eyed capacity for surprise and delight that seemed somehow at the heart of her charm.

He had thought she liked him, too.

He wondered if the pale concrete of the college building, oddly visible despite the darkness, was actually luminous. It was, he thought, just the kind of trick some crazy sixties Swedish architect might pull. What had been his name again?

His own T-shirt was luminous, Olly noticed with mild interest. He had gone casual for the date and, while this T-shirt wasn't ideal, it was the only clean thing he had and better than the shiny suit. At least, unlike the suit, it was intended to be a joke. He'd bought it at a festival the preceding summer; it had accurately captured the view his then girlfriend's father had of him. Olly had not realised until now that, if he stood in a completely dark corner, the words 'I Am The Antichrist' would appear to hang in midair.

Claudia, the girlfriend, a North London princess and brilliantly clever, was clearly intended for greater things than a failed student actor entertaining dim hopes of local journalism. They had parted amicably enough and Olly wondered what she was doing now. Not standing outside Branston College in the intensifying cold and shifting from foot to foot, that was for sure. He decided he might as well go.

But not without venturing into the college interior first and inquiring after her. A great Muscle Mary of a porter flatly refused to let him in and seemed to take particular pleasure in confirming that no, no message had been left.

In a violent spasm of embarrassment and self-disgust, Olly retreated. Isabel was not interested – no doubt thought him a pretty pathetic specimen. In a nasty suit. She was the Antichrist, not him. She was rude and ungrateful. How could he have been so mistaken? He was losing the ability to judge people along with the rest of his faculties. He resolved to dismiss her from his thoughts, but she bounced back immediately, with her long smile and brilliant red hair.

The path back to the road was through shaggy rhododendron bushes, lit by futuristic, triffid-shaped streetlamps that were presumably part of the *Gesamtkunstwerk*. They didn't seem to Olly to work all that well; it was oddly hard to see.

He walked slowly, musing on the immediate future. He would return to the small terraced house where he had rented a room all summer. It was a hideous room, cold and draughty, and with some other student upstairs who banged his huge feet on the floor in time to the start of *EastEnders*. Leaving it would not be a wrench. But leaving town altogether would.

There had been more riding on Isabel than she could ever have imagined, than he himself had realised, perhaps. The thought of their date, of perhaps striking up a relationship, was all that remained to tether Olly to the town where he had spent the last three years. He had no money. There was no prospect of a job. The lease on his room was at an end. All that lay before him was the train back home. It was a ghastly thought, made all the ghastlier by the suspicion that his parents were dreading his return every bit as much as he.

Mooching along, staring at the ground, his hands plunged into his jeans, Olly now cannoned straight into someone else not looking where they were going either. It was a thin man with a wispy beard and a baggy hound's-tooth jacket that had clearly seen better days.

'Ooof!' exclaimed Dr David Stringer, deputy head of the Branston English department, as his books and papers exploded all around him. To his incalculable relief Stringer saw that the person he had collided with was a student and not, as he had feared, the terrifying Professor Green, his boss.

Gillian Green was in a state of panic at the moment and lashing out at all her subordinates. The arrival of the new Master had spread terror like a contagion throughout the college. And yet Richard Black seemed to David to be at pains to avoid his colleagues, rather than launch inquiries into their departments as Gillian seemed to fear. She was, he knew, about to haul him over the coals for 'inappropriate internet representation', but that was largely her fault. It had been she who insisted, when the American Master was first mooted, that David get himself a Facebook page in an effort to seem more 'with it'. And now someone – he had no idea who – had put neon devil horns on all the photos of him and there were hairy bottoms on his personal wall.

'I'm really sorry,' Olly said, guiltily peeling close-typed sheets of A4 from the dirty tarmac. 'These are all muddy now.'

'They were muddy anyway,' David said scathingly. 'In terms of argument,' he added. He had gathered the papers up and stood looking regretfully down at the muddied knees of his cords and the scuff marks on the front of his suede desert boots. Professor Green, he knew, would not be impressed.

Would she sack him? Gillian had made it known already that she wanted someone younger, sexier and above all better known to do the appearances on *In Our Time* that David had come to regard over the years as his own. As his mirror confirmed on a daily basis, he had a good face for radio. And he had always got along well with Melvyn Bragg.

He looked speculatively at the youth before him. He was clean, fair and pleasant looking, but seemed anxious. He wore a T-shirt that said, 'I Am The Antichrist'. The anarchic spirit of this appealed immediately to David, who felt that too many of today's students were hopelessly conservative. 'How very interesting; I've always wanted to meet you,' he said, feeling skittish despite everything.

Olly was nonplussed. 'Sorry?'

'The T-shirt,' David explained, smiling. 'I've read about you in a variety of texts, of course: *Paradise Lost* and so on. But it's fascinating to meet the devil in the flesh.'

Olly felt as if he were going mad. After everything that had happened – and everything that had not – a surreal conversation with an obviously deranged don felt like yet another last straw. 'I'm not the Antichrist,' he said between gritted teeth. 'I bought this T-shirt as a joke. I know it's not very funny. I'm actually a failed-actor-failed-writer-failed-journalist former student who's just been stood up and I'm going to have to go back home now.' He stopped, feeling suddenly, mortifyingly, as if he might burst into tears.

'What's so bad about home?' asked David, wondering at the note of suppressed despair. Student accommodation now was a lot better than in his day.

'I mean *home* home. Parents. Old bedroom. Harry Potter books. Dinosaur posters.' Olly groaned. 'I can't afford to do anything else.'

'Oh dear,' said David. 'I see what you mean. Ignominious return of the prodigy and all that.'

'You don't know of a job?' Olly asked, encouraged by the sympathy. 'I'll do anything.'

David knitted his brows and looked hard at Olly. He had enough experience of students to be able to tell wheat from chaff at a glance. He sensed that this youth had a kind heart; he had helped him with the papers, after all. He also had an open, trustworthy face and looked – T-shirt notwithstanding – reasonably respectable.

'I even tried to get work cleaning, but . . .' Olly's voice trailed away as he remembered the fierce Zambian lady and her scathing opinion of writers.

Cleaning. The word had set the cogs in David's brain whirring. Actually, he did need a cleaner, rather badly. Neither he nor his wife, Dotty, were any good at housework, which was compromising the plan of letting out their attic room for money. David had, some weeks ago, been to see a contract cleaner: a terrifying African lady who had almost laughed in his face when he said what he could pay for her services. The cost, David worked out, would more than absorb any extra income the room might generate in the first place.

'Cleaner,' he repeated, thoughtfully. He and Dotty had then tried Plan B, which was to get their teenage daughter on mop-and-bucket duty. But Hero could hardly be prevailed upon to get dressed in the morning, let alone shoulder the housework burden. 'Well, we do need one, as it happens,' David said slowly. 'But it's rather a big house, one of those old Victorian places down by the station, you know. And it hasn't been cleaned for some time.'

'I'll do it for a room,' Olly burst in excitably. 'And if you don't have a room, a cupboard would do,' he added. 'Under the stairs, if you like. If it's good enough for Harry Potter, it's good enough for me.'

A weak light was shining into the worried interior of David's head. It would be useful to have a resident cleaner. Some of the more difficult mothers whose children Dotty taught violin to remarked on the mess from time to time and, given the way things were with the faculty, he couldn't risk any of his students taking similar complaints to Professor Green. A cleaner would help, definitely. It would actually be an investment.

He stared at Olly. 'You'd really rather live in a cupboard in my freezing hovel of a house than go back home?' Then, as Olly nodded, he asked, 'Just how bad *is* your home?'

Olly managed a smile. 'It's not bad. It's like you said – the going back. I'd feel like a failure.'

David nodded. He knew all about feeling like a failure. 'OK,' he said. 'It's a deal. You can move in as soon as you like.'

Chapter 6

'The name's Allegra Trott,' barked the voice on the other end of the phone. 'I'm a City director and I've just been given an enormous bonus.'

Richard tsked under his breath. It was Monday morning, he had briefly stopped in his office on the way to a meeting and he had no intention of being held up by this obviously misrouted call. 'Congratulations,' he said sardonically. 'But—'

'So,' Allegra cut in, in a commanding tone Richard could well believe brought boardrooms to their knees, 'I thought I'd ring up the old pickle factory and ask if there was anything I could do.'

She paused meaningfully. The appropriate neuron now leapt over the synapse and the connection in Richard's brain was made. She was offering money. Fine. He now knew to route the call to the development office. Fundraising was their business. He was not here to drum up money for Branston.

That was the job of Flora Thynne, development head. Richard had met her during his first few days in his new post. Tall, as thin as her name and with a long, mournful face devoid of make-up and wispy dark hair caught up at the back, she had made no attempt to disguise how enormous, even hopeless, was the task heaped on her frail and slightly sloping shoulders.

Whatever principles and influences its architect had in mind when designing Branston, it seemed that the British climate was not among them. Over the years since, the freezing cold of winter had cracked the concrete. The frequent and plentiful rain all year round had collected on the flat roofs and caused damp patches to spread in the rooms beneath. Simply keeping the college standing soaked up money, Richard learnt, and that was before any of the grandiose plans for new library wings, extended bursary schemes and academic chairs were gone into. There was the entire roof to replace, too.

Well, now here was Allegra, who might just do it.

Putting the call through, Richard reflected tersely that Flora should arrange to have 'The Allegra Trott Memorial Roof' spelt out on it in tiles so it would be visible to passing aircraft. The American institutions he had worked in would have done it without hesitation. Their tiles would, moreover, have glowed in the dark.

Shortly afterwards, Richard left his office for the meeting with the college council. Hurrying down to the college's front entrance, he almost collided with Flora Thynne, emerging from the development office. 'Did you,' he asked her, 'talk to that Trott woman?'

Flora trained a pair of sunken, hopeless eyes on him. 'She asked me,' she said in her dreary voice, 'to put something in the post.'

'And have you?' Richard was half-annoyed with himself for even being interested. It was not his business. He may be the Master, but first and foremost he was a scientist. It was up to Flora to grasp any opportunities she was presented with, and Allegra Trott was obviously an open goal.

'I'm on my way to the porter's lodge with this now.' Flora raised up her right hand, which held a small sheet. Richard read it in disbelief. It was for the list of Branston merchandise available at the office in the main entrance: Mugs, £5.99. Tea towels, £3.50. Postcards, 25p each or 80p for a set of four.

Burying the urge to ask her whether this really was the best she could do, Richard went on his way. He was not going to get involved. No more than he was going to get involved in the forthcoming college council meeting.

The thought of it was irritating, nonetheless. While he had been assured he need make only the most cursory appearances at official gatherings, just for the sake of the minutes, he had cursorily appeared at enough recently to know that nothing could safeguard him against the inevitable tedium.

He entered the meeting room abruptly and sat down immediately, so swiftly that the others were still struggling respectfully to their feet while he opened his notebook and clicked his pen expectantly. They sank down again and there was a clearing of throats and a flutter of paper. The Bursar smiled round in avuncular fashion. 'Shall we begin?'

Outside in the gardens Diana was trying to stave off her worries about Rosie's first day at school. Her stomach was rumbling with a mixture of tension and hunger. Her own breakfast had been scrappy, so intent had she been on making sure Rosie finished her cereal and ate her banana. Her nervousness about her own 'proper' first day had been subsumed in worry about her daughter's, but Rosie had maintained her savoir-faire. 'Of course it's a much bigger school than my old one, Mum,' she had said cheerfully to Diana's tentative efforts to inure her to prospective shocks. 'But more children means more people to make friends with, doesn't it?'

The rather dull, grey, heavy quality of the day pressed on Diana's spirits. It was cold and rather sulky weather, the flipside of autumn's dazzling copper-tinted face, the sort that might dissolve into heavy, relentless rain. Diana took a plastic bag from her pocket and spread it out on the path for a kneeler, wishing she had plastic to cover the whole of the rest of her too. Finances did not yet allow the purchase of the heavy-duty waterproofs she would surely need soon.

She began pulling up some dandelions and thinking that, had she started a month or two later, the worst would have been over, weather as well as weeds. The dry winter frosts would have killed them off and in places it would have been as simple as turning over a spade. Now, of course, just after the fierce growth of summer, the weeds were at their most rampant. Settling on her knees, Diana tried to concentrate instead on the rewards of weeding – the clean dark soil, the piercing pleasure of feeling a well-anchored dandelion root finally give and slide out.

And, of course, once the weeds were gone, she could really start on the ideas she had. Diana glanced over to the small circle of stagnant water, which might be a pond if it were cleared out and planted round the edge, the scabby, bald patches beneath the trees, which could be transformed with bluebells and cyclamen.

The neglect of Branston's gardens had its benign aspects; beneath the weeds and the crisp packets were the tiny, glowing petals of many an ancient species. She was surprised to see, this late in the year, a few scattered red and yellow bird's foot trefoils, and even a couple of yellow tormentil, and that little purple one, the little circular flower head with turreted purple petals, called 'self-heal'.

She had already decided to create a wild-flower garden at Branston. Diana loved wild flowers, the names especially: viper's bugloss, bats-in-the-belfry, priest-in-the-pulpit, hairy tare, frog-bit, water soldier, policeman's helmet. Lady's bedstraw, once used as a mattress stuffing. Rest harrow, which is what grew if one rested one's harrow, presumably. Periwinkle, or 'joy-of-the-ground', because it bound itself to the earth with nodes from the trailing stems. There was some in Branston's garden and Diana crouched by it now, marvelling at the history of the dark purple flowers. In Italy it was known as '*fiore di morte*', flowers of death, because heretics had been led to the stake wearing garlands of it. Periwinkle was planted on graves in the belief it protected against evil. Uprooting it was said to cause nightmares and haunting.

Diana tackled a buttercup root. Buttercups were so deceptive, that delicate yellow enamelled flower belying the tough and vicious root system beneath. You had to get all your fingers underneath, difficult to do properly in gloves. Apart from really freezing weather, or when picking up litter, Diana never wore them. She preferred to handle nature directly; nature returned the compliment by ruining her nails and ageing her hands.

About to pull up another plant, she paused. A delphinium, it looked like: weedy, yellowish, the plant dying off, but those fringed leaves were unmistakeable. It gave her a wonderful idea. She imagined the stained concrete walls which so abounded at Branston transformed by row upon row of great blue floral rockets ranging from deepest violet blue to palest forget-me-not. What a sight it would be: a jump of blue joy that would hit anyone entering the garden right in the eye and in the heart.

Her thoughts swung back to Rosie and she felt apprehensive once again. How was her daughter getting on? How was she finding the school? How was she coping with going from one extreme to the other, from the private and exclusive with education individually tailored to the child and delivered by committed professionals, to . . .

Diana pulled herself back from sliding into wholehearted panic. Well? she demanded of herself, To *what*? Who was to say that the education at Campion Primary wasn't delivered by committed professionals? She hadn't given them a chance yet.

She had weeded so fast and frantically her bucket was full. Standing up to get another, Diana spotted a small coil of brown dog poo under a nearby bush. Her nose wrinkled in disgust. One of the few advantages of Branston's garden was that it seemed relatively free of animal faeces. Certainly there was nothing akin to the horror stories she had heard about London's prestigious garden squares, whose gardeners could encounter anything from aggressive tramps to Coke bottles filled with taxi drivers' pee, tossed out of the cabs as they drove by.

The poo looked new, Diana thought, rummaging for a plastic bag with which to remove it. But she had seen no dogs at Branston. They weren't, or so she understood, allowed.

* * *

The session with the council, at a table of Arthurian roundness in one of Branston's peculiar circular concrete meeting rooms, was proving even longer and drearier than Richard had feared. So far he had thought mostly about his ongoing experiment, tuning in only occasionally. The first time he did this the Bursar was being congratulated for employing such a cheap new gardener, at a salary half of that enjoyed by her predecessor.

'A gardener?' Richard put in, suspiciously. Any effort at improving the grounds was a sinister development, in his view. He had hoped the college would not find one; who in their right mind, after all, would wish to tackle such a wilderness? Who could?

He felt slightly relieved to hear the person chosen was a recent graduate of horticultural college, and a woman. He pictured someone very young and slight, someone whose impact on the wholesale wreck of the Branston gardens would surely be minimal. With any luck, she'd resign after a week. 'And a single parent,' the Bursar had added, shaking his head. 'A sign of the times, I suppose.'

At this, all Richard's liberal neurons sparked at once and, for a second, the temptation flared to demand what exactly the Bursar meant by that. He desisted, however; the college officials were quite curious enough about his personal circumstances as it was and he had no intention of positively inviting their attention. He dismissed the college gardener from his thoughts. But instantly, perhaps inevitably given the topic, they routed to Amy and a huge, hopeless wave of longing swept over him.

He lowered his eyes; such private thoughts in a public place were doubly difficult. He tried to remain scientific and detached and examine this fascinating close personal evidence of how mere patterns in the brain folds could produce such intense physical misery. But the scientist, as always, was instantly overwhelmed by the man, and mental images of cortices were replaced by pictures of her soft brown hair in the sun, the scent of her skin, how happy they had been together.

'. . . look to alternative sources of funding and ways of raising the college's profile . . .' the Bursar was intoning in his fruity voice.

Richard, now drowning in memories, realised the agenda had moved on. He battled his way back to the surface. This could not continue. He must find a permanent way to cope.

Last night a bottle of cough medicine spotted in the bathroom cabinet had reminded him how drinking the whole lot would produce a neuronal blockade detaching sensory information from meaning. But he knew also that the effect would be short term and it would eventually become reattached. Harder drugs like heroin, mimicking as it did the chemicals produced by the brain to alleviate suffering, was another potential source of comfort. But he would hardly be solving his problems by becoming a drug addict.

He forced himself to think of the labs, of work, and felt the coiled spring within him give a little. Amy was gone, he was far from home, but at least he had his research. If he could ever get to it. The temptation to kick his legs against this ridiculous round table was almost irresistible. Would this meeting ever end? Looking at the agenda, he couldn't work out where they were. There was an item called 'Amber Piggott' – was that a person?

The college admissions tutor, a combative-looking woman with claret hair and purple glasses, was expressing her hope that one of the new students might attract some of 'the right sort of attention' to Branston.

They were discussing this Amber Piggott, Richard realised. She seemed to be a person. She was very rich and, for some reason, famous.

'An "it girl"?' he echoed, puzzled.

The Bursar leant over. 'Goes to lots of glamorous society parties.'

This made no sense to Richard. 'What sort of societies?' His frame of reference was firmly academic and none of the societies he could think of was remotely glittering.

'Oh, you know,' the Bursar said vaguely. 'Nightclubs with Prince Harry, that sort of thing. She's always in the gossip pages.'

Richard's frown deepened. 'And she's coming here?'

'When she deigns to turn up,' put in the head of the English Faculty, acidly. She was a woman mountain, Richard thought. Her booming tremolo voice seemed to come from some deep cavern within, like that of the Delphic oracle.

Purple Glasses now leant forward and explained Amber Piggott had been allowed into Branston as part of a profile-raising effort.

For all his intention not to get involved, Richard found indignation stirring. 'Does Branston really need to resort to that?' he asked. 'We're part of one of the most famous universities in the world.'

'Yes, my dear Master,' the Bursar replied evenly. 'But we're struggling for funds, even so. We need publicity.'

Richard drew himself back. It was up to them; he wasn't going to get involved. He was here as decoration only. Nonetheless, he found himself thinking that there were better ways to raise money and profile. The American universities he had worked in had had alumni offices that had hunted down former students without mercy and squeezed every last shekel out of them. They had organised ring-rounds with current students calling old students, set up alumni dinners. Amy had been involved with some of it. Perhaps he should mention it; Branston didn't seem to have a clue about that sort of thing, to judge by the list of merchandise Flora Thynne was sending to Allegra Trott.

Oh, whatever. It was their business. Abruptly, he stood up. 'I have to go,' he announced.

The day's early dullness had, most unexpectedly, melted into a glowing October afternoon. Autumn's fiery wand had transformed even Branston's beleaguered acres into a coppery blaze and wherever she looked – so long as it was not too closely

– Diana saw radiant trees with light bouncing off every leaf and grass with a hovering layer of gold atop the green.

She was working near a long, low box of grey concrete with a long slit close to the top, which went across the entire width of the building and made it look like an enormous postbox. In the unlikely event that anyone even noticed it, they might have assumed it to be a garage, or perhaps the room where all the electricity cables were gathered. In fact, it was the Branston College Master's Lodge and the long slit was the building's main window, although the influx of light was severely compromised by a dangling growth of red-tinged Boston vine, which fringed the edge of the building's roof. This meant that, for all the building represented in cutting-edge constructional thought, the effect within was, Diana imagined, not dissimilar to the gloomiest of Dark Ages fortresses. She was trimming the vine.

As she worked, she became aware of a growing commotion at the garden's other side, in the area nearest to the college entrance. Formerly empty, it now held a considerable number of people, mostly men in casual, dark clothes, jostling to get a glimpse of something she could not see. They were calling out and brandishing large, long objects with glass pieces that caught the light: cameras, Diana realised. She recognised the furry things swinging about as sound booms – and wasn't that a film camera there? What or who were they filming?

The possibility that it was the new Master flashed through her mind. She knew nothing about him, neither his name nor what he looked like. But he seemed the most likely contender.

Drawing near out of curiosity, Diana saw the crowd part suddenly and a beautiful blonde girl came striding through. She wore a mortar board and a dark scholar's gown with high heels and stockings. And nothing else, a bemused Diana saw. Except some very skimpy underwear, revealed now as, with a dazzling smile, the girl opened the gown wide. There was a roar of approval and the whirr and click of cameras.

Diana, clippers in hand, could only stare. It seemed most

unlikely that this girl was a student. This must be some sort of fashion show or something.

A small white fluffy dog was pushing its head out from under the black gown. It appeared to be clamped under the girl's arm. As Diana watched, she pulled it out, thrust it into the mortar board and, striking another pose, held it up for the photographers. There was another roar of approval.

A liberated man at last, Richard was striding towards the bike racks to the rear of Branston and considering the next likely move of the worms he was using in his research. The experiment involved associating smell with colour, and what that revealed about the brain. The worms, exposed to a certain smell, were supposed to head for a certain colour. So far, however, they were refusing to play the game and match any one colour to any one smell. Perhaps, Richard thought, strapping on his helmet, it was just that these were particularly stupid worms. He brightened. Were some worms more intelligent than others? Another whole new field to explore, potentially.

He swung his leg over the saddle, looking up at the Branston dome framed by autumn trees as he did so. It looked rather uncharacteristically picturesque and Richard was conscious of a brief burst of something almost like affection for the place. Why couldn't they leave it alone? He could still almost hear the Bursar banging on about the financial challenges Branston faced. Challenges which Amber Piggott's rich father could potentially help with. There was, apparently, a very brilliant Scottish first-year English student the college was funding. But more such bursaries were needed across all subjects to attract top students who might otherwise go to more prestigious colleges. Wobbling off, Richard almost groaned aloud. If only Branston would just get over it. Unprestigious was good. Drab was good. It was great there was nothing happening at Branston, that it was a quiet place, a backwater.

Or was it? As he wheeled past the college entrance, he was

surprised to see a crowd of people standing in front of it. Men, mostly, dressed in dark padded coats and jeans. They looked too old to be students and were shouting and gesturing to someone Richard could not see. There was an aggressive, rather wild atmosphere.

'Amber! Over here, Amber!'

'Give us a smile, Amber. Thassit, girl. A bit more leg; yeah, that's right.'

A loud whirring, clicking sound accompanied these exhortations. Cameras, Richard now saw. Above the heads of the shouters, a slim brown hand, flashing with jewels, could be seen turning slowly in the air.

Half of Richard wanted to go on his way; it wasn't his business, after all. But the other half shoved his way towards the back of the crowd.

Whatever was going on, he didn't like the look of it – or the shouty, raucous sound of it. Why did these people have long lenses the size of drainpipes swinging about? There were a couple of grey and furry boom microphones too, as well as what looked like a TV camera. A small, bossy-looking girl was striding about with a clipboard. What on earth was happening?

'Over here, Amber.'

'Work that mortar board, babe!'

There was a roar of lascivious approval at whatever action this had elicited. Richard had elbowed his way to the front now and could see, in front of the excitedly opening and closing college entrance, a heavily made-up blonde in a black bikini accessorised by high heels, a black scholar's gown and navy blue fishnet stockings.

He blinked in amazement.

Her legs were placed wide apart and she was holding the mortar board over the front of her bikini bottoms whilst bending forward to give the assembled cameras the full benefit of her cleavage. Under her other arm was clasped a small white dog. It caught Richard's eye and started to yap loudly.

He rubbed his eyes. His ears were buzzing. He reached for his mobile phone. Fighting through the throng to the main doorway was out of the question and it was anyone's guess in which part of the ludicrously over-complex building the Bursar might be now.

When finally he was located, he sounded smoothly unperturbed. 'Yes, Master? How can I help?'

'There's some kind of underwear shoot going on at the entrance,' Richard gasped. 'You've got to stop it.'

He was surprised to hear his colleague chuckle. 'On the contrary, my dear Master.'

'*What?*'

'I rather imagine,' the Bursar said in a tone of rich amusement, 'that you're seeing Amber Piggott arrive to begin her studies.'

Richard was a man of few words, but rarely was he speechless, as he was now.

'We have to do what we can,' the Bursar was saying. 'Even if it means agreeing to be the setting for a fly-on-the-wall documentary about Amber Piggott's first term.'

Richard nearly dropped the phone. He cleared his throat to collect himself. 'I'm obviously hearing things, Bursar.' He gave a nervous chuckle. 'I just thought I heard you say "fly-on-the-wall documentary about Amber Piggott's first term"!'

'I did say that, Master.'

Chapter 7

'It's fine,' Isabel assured her mother. 'Yes, everyone's very nice.'

'You sound a bit – well – flat,' came the voice from the other end of the mobile.

Actually, Isabel felt irritated. And tired. And probably a bit hung over still – vodka was not her usual tipple; nothing was.

The long journey of the day before had caught up with her, as well as the late night in Ellie's room, watching films. After *Dog For Christmas* had come *Hide The Sausage*, a tale about romance in a provincial butcher's. This had been followed by *Happy Accident*, where a female doctor with a broken leg fell for a male nurse. For Isabel, yawning amid the sequins and feeling mildly overcome by the powerful scented candle, they had eventually all merged into one.

'Really, I'm fine,' she insisted. Then, changing the subject, 'How's Lochalan?'

Her mother launched into the expected sequence of anecdotes. 'The minister's wife's doing her alternative therapies again; she's at loggerheads with the doctor, apparently . . .'

Isabel chuckled. Mrs Craig, the vicar's wife, had caused a sensation in Lochalan with her sudden espousal of New Age beliefs and holistic treatments. Those who had experienced the latter, reported that the front room of the manse had been given over to beanbags, whale music and joss sticks.

'Mrs Robertson's run out of midge spray . . .'

Isabel smiled. That, from July to November, the hardiest and most macho of Highland stalkers and gamekeepers splashed themselves liberally all over with a sweet-smelling beauty lotion called 'Skin-So-Soft' before stepping foot out the door was one of Scotland's best-kept secrets. And that Mrs Robertson, who ran the supermarket, had run out of the stuff would be nothing less than a local crisis.

As her mother chattered on, Isabel closed her eyes and there was her home village, spread before her like a painting. She was driving into it, on the familiar rain-slicked black road, the bordering grass glowing greedily green in the limited light. Past the white chapel with the pointy windows, past the ancient graveyard with the green-furred mossy stones, past the pitch and putt, past the garage, past the village's one, rather stern looking, hotel. On the other side was the silver loch stretching to the west and the sea from the shawl of familiar hills, hills covered with thick, green misty heathland broken here and there by secret mountain lochs, or dotted with the occasional high, lonely lodge. There were deer up here, stags and does, as well as tiny flowers with honey-sweet scent and, above it all, wild birds crying and riding the sweeping winds.

Her mother rang off eventually and the feelings of dissatisfaction that had plagued Isabel through the day returned. Partly this was due to Ellie, although things had started well in that respect. She had knocked on Isabel's door first thing in the morning, fresh faced and all smiles as a bleary, headachy Isabel, dressed in her bedtime T-shirt, stared through her tangled hair.

'If you're not doing anything tomorrow,' Ellie suggested, 'we could go to the freshers' fair.'

Isabel had beamed back. 'I'd love to,' she said warmly. But – tomorrow? That was twenty-four hours away. What was Ellie doing today?

She soon found out. 'See you later.' Ellie had danced away down the corridor. 'Gotta run,' she had sung over her shoulder.

'Where are you going?' Isabel called after.

'Seeing some friends in other colleges,' was the blithe reply.

Isabel had closed her door feeling crushed. Ellie had never mentioned friends in other colleges. If she had so many, why ask Isabel to be her bestie? Had she not meant it, after all? No doubt all these other friends were from St Mary's, Isabel thought forlornly. They would know how to snog and avoid hangovers.

Alone, tired and out of humour, Isabel spent the day getting her bearings round the college. After all the excitement and movement of yesterday, the day seemed flat and dull. She had felt shy and awkward and had scurried back into her room when anyone else appeared in the corridor.

She went alone to the Incinerator at lunchtime but felt intimidated by the others without Ellie to jolly her along. She stared fixedly at her plate of macaroni cheese and contemplated the disaster that was her date with Olly.

Oh, what must he think of her? He was the real root cause of her bad mood, Isabel knew. She was furious with herself. He would have waited last night; he would have thought she was not coming; he would think she had stood him up, and after all his kindness too. How appallingly rude and ungrateful she must seem.

In fact, she had rushed out from Ellie's room to the college foyer and hurried about the tarmac entrance outside, peering round every sulphurically lit corner. There was no Olly, however. Then she had asked the porter, but no message had been left.

What could she do to make amends? She had no address for him and he had said he would be leaving town altogether soon – thinking the absolute worst of her. She felt hot with shame.

Towards the end of the dull, tired, heavy afternoon, Isabel decided to have a bath. The panacea for all ills, Mum always said. A tub of hot water, swirled about with a little scented oil, never failed to lift the spirits and soothe the soul. She collected her towel and washbag and set off.

There was a figure outside the bathroom door, a short, rather squat one, wearing nothing but a towel and not a particularly large one at that. She looked oddly familiar to Isabel.

As she got closer, Isabel realised it was Kate, the girl she had met at interview.

'Hey!' Kate exclaimed, her small face alive with pleasure. 'Good to see you!'

A sense of triumphant relief filled Isabel. Here was another potential friend. She need not rely entirely on Ellie, after all.

'Are you queuing for the bathroom?' she asked.

Kate reddened with annoyance. 'I shouldn't be,' she grumbled. 'I've been out rowing this afternoon and I was running a bath. I went in my room to get undressed and then I came back. And, guess what? Someone's in there.'

She cast an annoyed glance at the bathroom door behind her, behind which could be heard vigorous splashing. 'My washbag's in there, my bath stuff, my bath towel and everything,' Kate complained.

A loud, throaty female voice could be heard from within. 'Whaddya mean, you don't know what happened? I'll tell you what fucking happened. It was all going like a dream until that guy turned up.'

Isabel stared at Kate. 'Who *is* that?'

Kate rolled her eyes. 'Can't you guess? Amber Piggott, resident celebrity supermodel genius whatever. Something went wrong with her close-up, by the sound of it.' She hammered on the bathroom door by way of a reply. 'Hey! You've nicked my bath!'

'I don't care if he *was* the Master,' the voice inside yelled. '*You* said it had been green-lighted.'

'Is she talking to you?' Isabel asked, puzzled. She wondered when Amber had arrived. But, as she had spent the day avoiding people, it was hardly surprising she had missed her.

'To some sort of manager, would you believe,' Kate said crossly. 'On her mobile. What sort of student has a *manager*? Apart from a bank manager?' She took a deep breath and roared at the door. 'And you're not supposed to smoke in college buildings!'

Isabel now noticed the strong scent of cigarettes.

'Oh, sod it,' Kate growled. 'I'm going back to my room. I'm bloody freezing out here. See you in the Incinerator?' she added to Isabel. 'We could have supper together.'

'That would be lovely,' Isabel said eagerly.

'Not sure that's the word. You've seen the food, have you? Anyway, I'll come and get you. What number room are you?'

As Kate stomped decisively off, Isabel, about to follow, heard the locks on the bathroom door slide back. A strange, sudden urge to go, to avoid the inevitable meeting, fought with the urge to finally see this creature she had heard so much about. She hesitated. Then, remembering Kate's scorn and deciding to go after all, she started down the corridor. It was too late, however. The door was open.

A cloud of scented steam billowed out, its flowery aroma mixed with cigarette smoke. A spectacularly good-looking blonde lounged in the doorframe.

'Hi,' drawled this vision, flashing Isabel a smile of the same dazzling whiteness as the bathrobe dangling open about her. All traces of her recent fury seemed completely gone. 'And who are *you*?'

'Isabel.'

'Amber.'

She had a very direct, appraising gaze and there was something fidgety and impatient about her. She leant against the lintel, flicked her damp blonde hair and gave another high-wattage beam. Isabel, feeling anxious and somehow trapped, could only stare back.

'Oh, we're out, are we?' came an annoyed voice from behind.

Isabel glanced round to see Kate hurrying up the corridor, still in her towel. Held helplessly in the Piggott force field, Isabel admired the fact Kate seemed just as cross as before.

'That was *my* bath,' she said accusingly to Amber.

75

Amber took a long drag of her cigarette and exhaled in Kate's direction. 'Seriously? That horrible cheap bath stuff was yours?'

Kate's mouth opened and shut. She recovered herself quickly, however. 'Smoking's banned,' she snapped. 'It'll set the fire alarm off.'

Amber took another slow, defiant drag. 'No, it won't. I've deactivated it.'

She grinned conspiratorially at Isabel, who reddened guiltily. Kate had of course seen her talking to Amber outside the bathroom; did she think they were friends?

Something pale at floor level shot out of the bathroom and cannoned into Kate's calves. It was a small, fluffy and rather damp white dog, which began to yap agitatedly. It seized the corner of Kate's towel in its teeth and started to tug it.

'Coco! Do get off that, darling. You might catch something.'

Kate glared. 'Is that your dog? Pets aren't allowed in college.'

By way of reply, Amber picked up the animal and held it defiantly to her semi-exposed bosom. 'Don't listen to the nasty lady being horrid to Mummy,' she cooed into its fur. The dog did not look especially abashed, however. It regarded Kate with eyes as glittering and triumphant as Amber's own.

'I'm going to report you,' Kate threatened. Ignoring Isabel altogether, she turned on her heel and stomped away. Isabel wanted to follow but Kate's fury held her back.

Amber, unrepentant, grinned at Isabel, finished the cigarette and, turning with a whirl of hair, threw it expertly into the lavatory bowl in the bathroom behind her. 'Come for a drink?' The low-pitched tones clearly did not expect refusal.

Isabel regarded her uncertainly. Amber was wearing only a bathrobe, after all. Did she normally entertain in towels? All Isabel's instincts were telling her to put as much distance as possible between herself and this alarming stranger. 'Er . . .' she began.

'Come on,' Amber wheedled. 'Coco needs cheering up. She hates scenes. Poor darling.' She nuzzled the dog's small, bony head.

'Is it a poodle?' Isabel asked.

Amber clutched her pet and gasped in horror. 'Nothing so ten minutes ago. Coco is a Maltese.'

As Isabel searched for a reply, something glittering beneath the dog's fur caught her eye. A white-leather, jewel-festooned collar. 'Darling, isn't it?' Amber beamed. 'A little present from me for being such a clever dog and going to university.'

Isabel eyed her uncertainly. Was Amber serious? It was difficult to tell.

'Come on then,' Amber urged, turning on Isabel the most dazzling of smiles. 'The champagne's on ice.'

Isabel chuckled. This was definitely a joke. Amber meant coffee, had to. No student had champagne in their room. Or fridge.

'Thanks,' she said. She would stay five minutes, Isabel promised herself. Then she would make her escape.

Amber and Coco were already stalking ahead down the corridor. Feeling slightly hypnotised, Isabel followed in their wake.

Isabel wondered if she had ever seen so messy a room as Amber's. The plain college furniture was invisible under the tidal wave of clothes engulfing it. The boutique bags on the floor with their silken rope handles were a roll call of every expensive label Isabel had heard of and many more she had not. One patent ballerina flat lying alone on its side had 'CHANEL' printed on the inside of the sole. Coco, having been unceremoniously dumped on the floor, was now scrabbling frantically about in all of this. Looking for something to eat, Isabel suspected.

Dominating the bed was an enormous oblong trunk covered in leopardskin. Its lid was open and more clothes spilled out of here to join the mass on the floor.

Isabel looked longingly at the door, wondering if now she could make her escape. But, apparently impervious to Isabel's presence, Amber had just almost completely shrugged off her bathrobe. It dangled precariously from her shoulders. Opening the door would expose her entirely to anyone passing by.

Isabel tried to avert her gaze but noticed nonetheless that Amber's breasts were small but perfect with large dark nipples. What looked like a coat of arms was tattooed on one of her smooth brown shoulder blades. The shield depicted a mediaeval war helmet with the lid down, combined with some bags of money. The motto on the rolling scroll underneath said, '*Fronti nulla fides*'.

'Put no faith in appearances,' Isabel murmured.

'What?'

'The motto on your tattoo.'

Amber sniffed. 'Is that what it means? I thought it was something about full frontals. It's an old boyfriend of mine's family crest.' She shook her head. 'Silly thing to say though, don't you think? I *always* judge by appearances. I'm quite staggeringly shallow.' Her eyes ran up and down Isabel speculatively. 'You're bright, aren't you?'

It seemed to Isabel a strange remark. Possibly even a trick one. All the students here were bright, surely. 'No more than anyone else,' she parried.

'Brighter than me, definitely,' Amber grinned. 'I hate work. I'm here,' she exclaimed suddenly, whirling nakedly round in the mass of dresses, 'to have fun!'

It was obvious by now to Isabel that her idea of fun was different to Amber's. What with the champagne, the dog, the dresses and all. That, apart from the subject they were studying – the same, she had discovered – they had nothing whatsoever in common, seemed very likely. She longed to leave and took a tentative step towards the door.

Amber's sudden euphoria seemed suddenly to have faded and her large brown eyes were flashing angrily about her room. 'I've got shoeboxes bigger than this,' she said petulantly. 'I'm thinking of hiring a hotel suite in town to keep my clothes in.'

Despite her concern for her wardrobe, she seemed not to have noticed her dog ripping it to shreds. It was currently tearing concentratedly into a dress of thick black silk with a Victoria Beckham label in the back.

Isabel bent and pulled Posh Spice's handiwork gently away. A pile of bulky brown Amazon packets was exposed. 'The Hon. A. Piggott, Eaton Square, London SW1', Isabel read on the topmost one. This had been crossed out and 'Villa Piggott, Mustique' written over.

'You've bought a lot of books,' she remarked.

Amber shot her a white blaze of smile. 'You know, I'm actually really hopeless on accents. I can't understand a word you're saying. Are you Scottish or something?'

Was this rude? Isabel wondered. It was difficult to say, with that dazzling beam. She repeated her question.

'Oh, the books! That bloody reading list,' Amber cackled. 'Haven't had a second to look at it. And neither has *naughty* Coco.' She shot an indulgent glance at the still-scrabbling animal. 'Have you?' she asked, swinging her gaze back to Isabel.

Isabel reddened, to her own irritation. There was no shame in having done the work.

'You've read them *all*?' Amber's face was blank with astonishment.

Just below the sea of dresses, Isabel now noticed, was what looked like a small fridge. It had been dumped at a careless angle and had a glass door through which gold-foil-topped bottles could be seen. Only gold-foil-topped bottles. Her eyes widened. The champagne *was* on ice, after all.

Coco, meanwhile, was whining and scrabbling still harder. Amber flung the dog an irritated glance.

'She might be hungry,' Isabel suggested. 'Or thirsty.'

'I had something for her somewhere,' Amber muttered, peeling up a couple of dresses.

Surely there wasn't a plate of dog food beneath; Isabel winced.

Whether there was or not, Amber now abandoned the search. She opened the champagne fridge, grabbed a bottle and twisted the cork with an obviously practised movement. It exploded, sending the dog cringing into the corner. A white surge of bubbles dripped on to some of the clothes on the floor. As Amber did not seem inclined, Isabel lunged to the rescue again, whipping some Chloe and Stella McCartney out of the way just in time.

Amber had found an ashtray from somewhere, slopped some champagne into it and held it out to the dog. 'Here, Cokes!'

'She drinks champagne?' Isabel blurted.

Amber giggled. 'She should. She's Mummy's pooch de luxe, aren't you, Coco? Oh well, suit yourself,' she added carelessly as Coco cautiously dipped the black tip of her nose into the frothing liquid before cringing backwards.

'I've got some water in my room,' Isabel said, grasping the opportunity to escape. She had reached the door when she saw, striding up the corridor in a manner that betokened no nonsense, the burly, T-shirted college porter from the front hall. Behind him, fairly hopping with agitation, came a vengeful-looking Kate, now fully dressed. 'Which room did you say it was?' the porter was growling.

Isabel, remembering what Kate had said about pets not being allowed, shrank back inside. 'The porter's coming,' she gasped. 'He's looking for Coco, I think.'

A kind of panic was filling her. Isabel, who had never been in trouble the whole of her educational life, hated the thought of being caught with someone breaking college rules on her very first full day at university. Being caught by Kate in Amber's room was hardly less of a disaster.

Amber, however, just laughed. She picked up the still-trembling Coco and shoved her under the bed. A heavy fist now sounded on the door. Isabel felt sick with terror. But Amber's eyes were shining with excitement.

'Your bathrobe!' gasped Isabel. 'It's nearly fallen off!'

'Silly me!' Amber exclaimed, waggling her tanned shoulders so the towelling slid finally to the floor. 'Come in!' she trilled, arranging herself invitingly on the bed as the door swung open.

The porter now got an eyeful that turned his meaty face pale with horror. He then flushed a violent purple and made a choking sound before fumbling wildly for the handle and slamming the door shut.

Amber's lack of embarrassment was absolute, it seemed to Isabel. It was even possible that she was enjoying it. She raised a playful and perfectly plucked eyebrow at Isabel and called out, 'Can I help you?'

The porter on the other side of the door was clearly struggling to compose himself. 'I've been told,' he managed after some seconds, 'that you may have a dog in there, Miss.'

'*Definitely* has a dog in there,' Kate crisply corrected.

Amber was shrugging on her bathrobe. But it still hung open slightly as she opened the door and beamed at her accusers. 'Dog?' she echoed, her eyes stretched wide and her eyelashes batting innocently in the face of Kate's hostile glower and the porter's embarrassment. Even the tips of his ears were hot with shame, Isabel saw from her vantage point within the room.

'Yes, dog,' Kate hissed, as the porter seemed once again incapable of speech.

'There's no dog in here,' Amber sang, waving a white-towelled arm backwards into the room. 'Is there, Izzy?'

It took a couple of beats before Isabel realised this was directed at her. She blinked, realising she was being asked to lie. Amber had turned and was staring at her meaningfully, and beyond her were the burning eyes of Kate and the burning ears of the porter.

Isabel hesitated for an agonising minute before stammering, 'Er . . . no,' into the inquiring silence. She saw Kate toss her head in furious disbelief and Amber flash her a triumphant beam.

'Ha!' Amber exulted, once the footsteps of the interrogators had died away. She was sloshing the foaming liquid into a pair of glasses she had produced from somewhere. More wine was dripping on more clothes.

As Amber slithered into a tiny silver dress – 'Zip me up, would you, darling?' – Isabel stared at the tiny bubbles surging inside her glass. She had rarely drunk champagne, although Mum had splashed out on a special-offer bottle at the supermarket the day she got her university place. She didn't feel much like celebrating, not with Kate's angry face in her mind's eye. There had been the promise of friendship there, before Amber had appeared on the scene.

That there was the same promise with Amber seemed doubtful. Already she seemed to have forgotten Isabel's existence. She had shoved some of the clothes aside to reveal an enormous mirror propped sideways on the floor. She was staring at herself in it, twisting the hair at the back of her head up with one hand and, with the other, pinning it carelessly into place. It made all the difference. Amber had been lovely before with her hair flowing over her shoulders but now she looked stunning, her mane a pile of massy gold atop a flower-like face, balanced on the slenderest of necks.

'Open that, could you, babe?' Amber rummaged under some underwear and pushed a large, padded hot-pink leather box in Isabel's direction. Lifting the lid, Isabel saw a flashing, glittering tangle of jewels.

'My diamonds?' Amber asked airily.

'Are you going somewhere?' Isabel asked, handing them over.

Amber was dabbing something behind her ears from a tiny bottle. An indescribably wonderful scent rose into the air. 'With Jasper. Jasper De Borchy,' she volunteered. She was shoving thin brown feet with blue-painted toenails into strappy jewelled sandals. 'Know him?'

'I don't think so.'

'You'd know if you did.'

'Yes, it's quite a name,' Isabel said, slightly archly.

'Norman French. They came over with the Conqueror,' Amber stated. 'They go way back.'

Isabel felt impatient. *So what?* she wanted to say. *Whose family didn't?* She cared less about Jasper De Borchy's pedigree than the fact that Coco was staring silently and sadly at her mistress from her corner. 'Don't you need to feed the dog first?' she ventured.

Amber paused at the door. '*Would* you? That's so sweet of you!'

The next second she had whirled out of the room. Isabel was left standing in a cloud of perfume and a froth of champagne-soaked clothes, looking uneasily at a contraband poodle.

Chapter 8

Diana glanced at her watch, which had smears of dirt over the silver Cartier casing, one of the few remaining reminders of her old life. She could see, nonetheless, that it was time to fetch Rosie from school. Or from the after-school club, rather. The fact that Campion Primary ran both a breakfast club and after-school facilities with, it seemed, the sole purpose of helping working parents, was a very strong point in its favour, whatever other doubts she might entertain.

But how had Rosie fared? Please, Diana prayed, don't let me turn up to see her standing shunned and alone in the playground. She stared hard at the earth to stop the agonising picture forming.

The bald, tilled, weedless black earth she had worked on slightly soothed her agitation. It had been a long first day, and a tiring one, but a satisfying one ultimately. Apart from the extraordinary episode with the girl and the film crew, she had worked undisturbed. She had not seen the end of the shoot – it seemed to have broken up acrimoniously. There had been a lot of shouting and Diana had hurried away. The person shouting had been male and American – familiar, somehow.

She had made progress in the garden, anyhow. Where there was chaos, she had brought order. Perhaps gardening, ultimately, was all about control. Therapy, too. The business of planting and tidying brought succour at a time when there was little to be had anywhere else. Plunging her fingers into the earth, Diana felt she was nurturing and creating, even as all she had valued – Rosie excepted – had withered and died.

She drove off. The evenings were drawing in now and there were some spectacular sunsets. But the flaming clouds billowing across the sky were also a reminder of oncoming winter. Cold weather, Diana suspected, was expensive. In her former life, she had turned up the thermostat without a second thought.

Soon, Diana was drumming her fingers on the steering wheel, her progress impeded by a temporary traffic light. A hole surrounded by cones yawned to the side of her.

Drawing up, finally, beside the Portakabins and wooden shacks of Campion Primary, Diana took a deep, galvanising breath before getting out. Hands in the pockets of her green gardener's gilet, she hurried towards the red school gate.

She looked about for a little figure standing alone. None could be seen, however. Then, with a rush of pure relief, Diana realised that the small girl running about in the middle of a crowd of children, yelling the loudest of them all, was her daughter.

'Darling!' Diana waved at her. Rosie paused, looked at her beseechingly, then ran over. 'Mummy! Don't call me "darling"!'

'Sorry!' Diana whispered.

'I'm hungry, Mum.'

Diana had promised her daughter a first-day-at-school treat for supper. Anything she wanted. Now she was bone tired and bone cold too, Diana rather regretted this. Hopefully it would not be too labour- or time-consuming. 'What would you like for supper, darling?' Then, catching Rosie's chiding eye, 'Oh, sorry!'

'Toad in the hole, please. And it's tea, not supper.' Rosie cast a wary eye around at her new companions, all of whom were being marshalled by their mothers and not listening anyway. Diana could not help noticing that they seemed quite obedient, more so, certainly, than Rosie's former classmates at Smart's who routinely ignored the nannies pleading to take them home from parties and playdates.

'Tea. Right.' Diana passed a hand across her forehead, trying to remember if she had the ingredients. Eggs, milk, flour, sausages. Did she have flour? Possibly not. And she definitely didn't have sausages. They would have to call at the supermarket on the way home, park, stand in a queue; most of all, they would have to spend money.

Budgeting carefully to within a specific sum was a new and tricky skill to master, involving a new familiarity with the supermarket 'basics' range and the 'damaged' shelf. Rosie adored the 'damaged' shelf; always full of things they never usually bought. 'They're only 20p,' she would sing, grabbing a ragged jelly box or a packet of bashed boudoir biscuits and putting them in the basket Diana now always chose in preference to the trolley, which could so easily and so expensively get filled up.

And yet, despite the 'damaged' shelf, and for all the 'basics' ranges, Diana always ended up spending more than she meant to. That there had been a time when she had not kept a running total, had handed over the credit card without noticing the bill at the end, had flung whatever she fancied into the trolley on a whim, now seemed amazing.

'Sure you don't want beans on toast?' Diana now bargained. She had bread and beans at home.

Rosie's eyes lit up. 'Ooh, yes. I'd love beans.'

'OK,' Diana said, relieved.

'*With* the toad in the hole.'

Diana smiled resignedly. There was one thing at least to be said for the stop at the supermarket. It would delay the return to their new home.

The sun had set while they were in the supermarket and it was properly dark when, forty minutes later, they wound up through Fourth Avenue on the Campion Estate.

The semi-detached that was number thirty-six was an unlit

box, its pebbledash and its scabby garden looking bleak in the glow of the streetlamp. By contrast, light poured from every window of the house next door. As Diana, clutching her shopping bags, shut the car door with her foot, fear slithered coldly through her stomach.

When first she had come to look at number thirty-six, with a view to long-term rental, the denizens of number thirty-eight had been out. While Diana, moving from room to room, had noticed the cardboard-thin walls, the lack of carpet and the general stony chill, she had been glad of the apparent peace. And the patch of ground outside, while unloved, overgrown and full of rubble, definitely had possibilities. She could imagine a vegetable plot, see sweet peas and nasturtium splashing colour among the beige and grey palette of concrete and asphalt. A further source of encouragement was the estate's being named after the little pink campion, the ubiquitous hedgerow flower that grew from late spring onwards. While she had yet to see a single example of the flower in the vicinity, Diana the born-again gardener had signed on the dotted line.

Money was, after all, extremely tight and renting in the area expensive. Until she got financially back on her feet, a former council house would do very well.

But then, on hers and Rosie's first evening in the house, a continuous booming sound had accompanied the unpacking of boxes. Going outside into the darkened garden, Diana had seen that the neighbours were in and, at number thirty-eight, on the partition wall between the two houses, was mounted the biggest, loudest and flattest television she had ever seen. Booming TV voices, raucous laughter and pounding pop music had continued late into the night. On the camp bed that was substituting until she bought proper furniture, Diana had lain, fists clenched, staring at the blade of streetlight slicing between the thin curtains across the Artex ceiling. As the television had pounded, her mind had pounded too, with angry, indignant phrases she planned to deliver first thing in the morning.

Until, next morning, she had seen her neighbours lumbering out of their own garden gate. They looked big and fierce: a huge man, an enormous woman and two large, puddingy teenagers. Diana, whose build was wiry and whose stature was short, had felt her arguments – along with her courage – melting away. She had watched them stop and look at her car, exchanging what appeared to be disparaging remarks about it, before climbing into a very large, new and shiny people carrier, parked further down the road.

Now, as she approached her front door, Diana gazed with despair at the giant illuminated rectangle of the plasma TV screen in the neighbours' sitting room. Tanned faces, sheeny hair and improbably white teeth jerked about against a zinging background. A game show was evidently underway. Even from the car, the noise of canned laughter could be heard.

Diana pressed her lips together. For Rosie's sake, she must pretend that nothing was amiss. Rosie, in any case, had not complained about the noise any more than she had complained about the school. As her mother tossed and turned, Rosie had continued to sleep peacefully at nights in the camp bed beside her. Her daughter, Diana thought, was making a much better fist of the lifestyle adjustment than she was herself.

She heaved the bags through the battered gate and up the broken concrete path to number thirty-six. Plonking her shopping down on the front steps, she searched for the key to the front door. Rosie, she saw, had edged along the dark garden and was staring through the window of number thirty-eight, at the television. Diana could see its reflected colours on her daughter's fascinated little face.

'Rosie!' she said sharply.

The child hurried to her side, deftly sidestepping the broken bricks and other rubbish in what might once have been a border. And would be again, Diana vowed to herself, once she had cleared it out. It was full of stones and pieces of glass; the previous occupant of number thirty-six seemed to have drunk enough to sink a brewery and his idea of recycling was to fling them all straight into the garden. Bottles were buried everywhere. Patiently, with thick gloves on this occasion at least, Diana had been removing them. It was painstaking work, but the earth left behind was of far better quality than she had imagined. So the two balanced each other out.

The insubstantial door of number thirty-six rattled open. Diana switched on the bare bulb in the hall and lugged the plastic bags into the kitchen. In her old life, she had used jute recyclable ones, but there was no spare money now to spend a pound on a bag which was invariably left in the car boot anyway.

Before tackling the toad-in-the-hole batter, she switched on the electric oven. She had scrubbed this free of its clinging grease on the first day, but it seemed to her that it still had an air of rancidity about it.

Using things that other people had used before her – and not too respectfully, either – was something else she had had to get used to. In her old life, appliances had been ordered from John Lewis and delivered by a cheery man in a dark green van.

'Rosie?' Diana called, realising her daughter was not in the room. She hurried out of the kitchen, down the hall, her footsteps echoing on the unvarnished boards. There had been a carpet when she looked round but for some reason it had gone. The estate agent had been evasive as to why. He had been evasive about many things, including information about the previous occupant. The décor, if so it could be described, seemed to suggest an old lady, but the agent remained obtuse.

'Mummy?' Rosie looked up from where she sprawled on the beanbag before the gas fire in the front room. She had fished out her book and was buried in it once again, apparently insensible to the TV pounding through the wall from next door.

How *could* people behave like this? Diana wailed silently to herself. No neighbour in her old life ever had. Admittedly, the nearest had been several acres away.

She forced herself to smile at Rosie as she crouched to operate the gas fire. The flames sprang purple up the white asbestos ridging at the back of the heater and she was reminded of the delphinium idea for Branston College gardens. Feeling more hopeful, she returned to the kitchen and began to beat the batter, seeking relief from her feelings in the slap of the whisk in the mixture.

Later, they sat at the battered Formica table with its let-down flaps; Rosie, munching appreciatively, paused now and then to take a slug of milk. Diana thought longingly of the cut-price bottle of screw-top rosé she had permitted herself at the supermarket. She tried not to drink in front of Rosie, however; besides, in the undersized, underpowered and elderly fridge it would be nowhere near chilled yet.

The kitchen at number thirty-six was at the side of the house, overlooking, through institutional iron-framed windows, the planned vegetable garden. It was as far as any room in the house could be from the booming TV next door. And yet, now, there sounded a great burst of pop music.

Something within Diana seemed to explode at the same time. She had had enough. Perhaps Rosie's good day at school had given her courage. This could not, she decided, go on.

Smiling calmly, she rose slowly to her feet, not wanting, with any movement or expression, to alarm her daughter.

'I'll just be a second,' she told Rosie. 'I left something in the car.'

She felt strangely determined. Her entire existence could not be allowed to become a nightmare. She closed the rattly front door softly behind her and hurried down the broken path in the dark. She did not stop. The merest pause or hesitation and she would, she knew, be lost. Passing the gaping gate of number thirty-eight, she hurried up their path – in a worse state than her own – and hammered on the door.

There was no response; the blaring of the TV continued. Diana fought the nauseating surge of nerves and the desire to run; no one had heard her, after all; no one would be any the wiser. But then, remembering Rosie, who must be allowed a peaceful night, she raised her fist again and banged harder. Her heart galloped painfully as she heard shouts within the sitting room and noise within the hall, then a lumbering towards the door as if of some huge beast.

Diana's knees were knocking beneath her trousers. She cast a quick glance behind her; there was a heap of bricks and rubbish in the corner of the garden. She could, even now, hide behind that . . .

The door, after some tugging and cursing from within, rattled open. The burst of heat that issued forth was powerful enough to steam up the spectacles that Diana wore for driving and still hadn't – she now realised – taken off. The mist cleared to reveal, in the light of the hall – a bare bulb like her own – the huge young woman she had occasionally seen, but never like this. Her neighbour had clearly just taken a bath, or was about to. Her bulk was divided, sausage-like, by the belt of a pink towelling bathrobe. Her face was large, red and shiny with the heat and wore a belligerent, suspicious expression.

'Yeah?' she said, looking Diana up and down and evidently unimpressed with what she saw.

Diana forced a smile across her face. She was shaking with fright, but now she was actually here, facing what she most feared and resented, she felt a vague lessening of the tension that had dogged her. 'I'm your new neighbour,' she began.

To her intense surprise, the woman's expression changed. Before Diana's astonished eyes, it softened; the mouth changed direction and stretched sideways into what might have seemed, in any other circumstance, a smile. 'Oh,' she said, shuffling forwards in a pair of electric-pink fluffy slippers. 'So it's you, is it? We've been wondering. Well, nice to meet you, Mrs Whatever-yer-called.'

'Diana.' Diana was grateful for the ingrained instinct that now compelled her to hold out her hand. The woman looked at it in puzzlement at first, evidently unused to performing the ceremony, but then recognition dawned and she grabbed Diana's fingers in her hot, damp paw and gave them a convivial yank.

'Pleased to meet you. I'm Debs. Wanna come in?' The woman turned her huge pink bulk slightly to the side, stretching a large arm into the sauna-like interior behind her.

'Thanks, but I can't,' Diana gasped. 'My daughter's next door; she's eight . . .' she added, not knowing quite why.

The information quite transported Debs, however. In her sweaty face, her large eyes shone. 'Aaah, got a little girl, 'ave yer? Shanna-Mae could babysit for you, y'know, anytime.'

The name meant nothing to Diana; she had not heard it before. Was it male or female? she wondered before concluding that Shanna-Mae must be the large teenager she had seen getting into the people carrier. Female, then. 'Thanks, that would be great, but actually I came to ask you about . . . Well, Rosie's got school tomorrow,' she announced in a rush. 'She needs a good night's sleep and—'

'School? Where's she go to school, then?' Debs interrupted, warmly interested.

'Er, Campion.'

'Shanna-Mae goes there. To the senior bit. What's yer little girl's name?' Debs' head was on one side, inquiringly.

'Um, Rosie. Rosie Somers. Er . . .' The conversation was straying from the subject. In a moment, blindsided by Debs' unexpected friendliness, she'd lose courage altogether. As it was, the implied criticism was going to put a dampener on things. Diana swallowed and raised her chin. 'Er, I came about the noise,' she said.

'Noise?' Debs repeated in apparent surprise, over a burst of pumping music from the room next door, followed by televisual cheers and clapping.

'Um, yes. I'm really sorry,' Diana ploughed on, 'but because your TV's on the wall, we can hear more or less every word in our house and . . .' Her voice broke finally under the strain. She looked in dumb misery at Debs, who was staring back at her, her face a picture of puzzlement.

'You can 'ear every word? In your 'ouse?' she repeated incredulously.

Diana nodded, eyes locked to Debs' shiny face, expecting to see the fleshy mouth turn suspiciously down again and issue a robust and possibly aggressive denial, followed by the loud slam of the front door. Instead, Debs lurched away from the door and roared over her shoulder to persons invisible. 'Turn that bloody thing down! Next door can 'ear it!'

The noise halved in volume immediately.

'Sorry about that, love,' Debs said. 'Me 'usband can't function unless he's making so much noise it makes 'is face fall off. I'm so used to it, I don't notice.'

Diana was simultaneously trying not to cry and searching for the words to express her profound gratitude when the large husband hove into sight behind Debs' shoulder. In the confined space of the narrow hall he looked larger than ever, his belly straining under a black T-shirt bearing the legend, 'Are You Looking At My Cock?' under an image of a chicken.

Diana swallowed.

''Oo's that yer talkin' to?' he demanded, looking Diana up and down suspiciously.

'Next door,' Debs told him.

He shuffled closer. 'That your car outside, is it?'

Diana nodded.

'Bit of a wreck, ain't it?'

'Yes, I'm sorry. It *is* a bit scruffy.'

'Didn't mean that. Yer door won't lock, will it?'

Diana shook her head.

'Can't yer 'usband fix it?'

Diana reddened and looked away. 'I don't, um, have a husband,' she muttered.

'Aww!' murmured Debs, sympathetically. She looked expectantly at Diana, but Diana stared hard at the ground and did not elaborate.

The ensuing silence was broken by Debs' husband. 'Well,

y'don't want a car that don't lock. Not round 'ere.'

'There's nothin' wrong with round 'ere,' Debs put in quickly, indignantly.

'Well, no,' her husband agreed. 'But y'don't want a car that don't lock anywhere.'

'I suppose not,' Diana agreed, although there was little prospect of anything else. She should, she supposed, brace herself for the break-ins.

'I'll fix it for you, if y'like.'

Diana stared at him in delight. 'That would be . . . wonderful. Thank you.'

''S'all right. Might look at that exhaust too.'

Debs, arms folded, was looking at her husband in cheerful exasperation. 'But what she really wants is for you to turn yer telly down, Mitch. Why don't you take it off of the wall? Gives me neck-ache, looking at it up there.'

As Diana, her wildest dreams verbalised by the last mouth on earth she had expected, wondered if she were hearing things, Mitch shrugged his well-padded shoulders. 'Yeah, s'pose I could. The stand's in a box somewhere. S'pose we got used to next door being empty. Since . . .' He seemed to stop himself.

'Oooh, yeah!' Debs' eyes swung back to Diana, large with excitement. 'Old Mrs Minion! Four weeks it was before they found 'er, you know! Four weeks!'

Mitch, catching Diana's expression, laid a hand on his wife's shoulder. 'That's enough, love. Well,' he added, addressing Diana, 'I'll try and sort out that car for you tomorrow, if I can.'

'Th-thank you,' Diana stammered.

'Sorry about the noise,' Debs shouted as Diana swayed back down the path on wobbly legs. 'Just say if it gets too much, yeah?' she bawled cheerfully. 'Don't suffer in silence!' The door shut. Only a muffled noise came now from the front room of the house. Diana, looking up to the foggy, imprecise night sky, suffused with the orange glow of the streetlamps, sent up a silent and heartfelt prayer to whatever deity had overseen the exchange.

Her relief was overwhelming, and she felt triumphant too, having successfully defended her daughter and herself against what had seemed a hostile and uncaring world. As she reached Mitch and Debs' broken gate, Diana felt herself smiling broadly in the dark. She had prevailed!

Reaching out for the gatepost, she gasped in horror as her hand came into contact with living flesh. She recoiled, shocked and fearful. What new danger was this? Was it what Mitch had meant when he said that you didn't want a car that didn't lock round here?

'Rosie!' she exclaimed, realising that, after all, the figure was too small and slight to pose a danger. And that, also, it looked familiar. 'What are you doing here?'

Her daughter was clasping the gatepost, swinging on it. Her face, in the lamplight, was guilty.

'Were you listening?' Diana demanded, half angry and half inclined to be indulgent because the interview had gone so incredibly, unexpectedly well.

Rosie nodded. 'They sound nice, Mummy,' she said. 'The new neighbours.'

'Yes, they do, don't they?' Diana agreed, feeling suddenly exhausted by it all and thinking with sudden longing of the special-offer cut-price rosé. 'Come on, let's go in.'

'Mummy?' Rosie's precise little voice was thoughtful as they reached their own front door.

'Yes, darling?'

'What had old Mrs Minion being doing for those four weeks before they found her?'

Chapter 9

As Amber had not returned from her party, Isabel had been obliged to put Coco up for the night. She had considered turning the dog in to the porter after all, but the scene earlier in the evening not only made the prospect hideously embarrassing but also ensured she could not emerge creditably from the situation. She was stuck with Coco, a nervous and ill-trained animal who not only threatened to incriminatingly howl the place down if not the focus of absolute attention at all times but repaid her hospitality by peeing copiously on the carpet.

As a consequence, Isabel had missed supper altogether. She had been obliged instead to go out and find a corner shop where she could buy pet food for Coco. When she returned, slipping uneasily by the porter – who studiously avoided her gaze – the Incinerator had been closed.

Isabel felt resentful about all this, as well as hungry, but was uncertain about how she would tackle Amber when she saw her. Something about Amber made her feel rather out of her depth, as well as intimidated. Amber was unpredictable, dangerous even; she had been rude and aggressive to Kate and to whomever she had been shouting at on the phone in the bathroom. Isabel quaked at the thought of Amber speaking like that to her.

She felt she would like to avoid her, from now on.

Heavy eyed after a sleepless, worried night, Isabel had left

Coco asleep on her bed while, at the earliest possible opportunity, she went to find some breakfast in the Incinerator.

Inspiration had dawned as she ate her bacon and eggs. She returned to her room, picked up the sleeping Coco, bundled her into her coat and – again avoiding the porter's eye, although shifts had changed in the night, thank goodness – carried her out of the college front entrance and tied Coco loosely up to the bike racks with a piece of rope from her backpack. Here, within the bounds of the law, she could await the return of Amber.

Thankfully, it was a warmish autumn day and, even though Coco whined and shivered, the weather was as propitious as could be expected. Thankfully, too, no one was around to witness the deed. A relieved Isabel had returned to her room and left a note under Amber's door explaining the whereabouts of her pet. Hopefully Coco would not be left waiting too long. And that, she vowed, was the end of it.

Isabel wanted to forget about the whole thing. She wanted to rewind to what she was doing before Amber had materialised. She thought about the evening she'd spent with Ellie. They were scheduled to visit the freshers' fair together that afternoon. Ellie would be amazed to hear about Amber and what had happened. But then, Isabel thought, what could she say about the porter, Kate and Coco that did not reflect badly on herself? She had lied, even if she had been forced to. Whichever way you told it, it didn't sound good. Best, Isabel decided, to say as little as possible. She left a note under Ellie's door suggesting they meet at her room at lunchtime and go to the fair from there.

Meetings with new tutors filled up the morning. But, as the English group stood outside the office door of Dr David Stringer, tutor in metaphysical poetry, Isabel realised that forgetting would not be easy. She and Amber were studying the same subject and Amber should be at the meetings too, even if she hadn't turned up yet.

And then there was Kate, who of course was studying English as well. The meeting between her and Amber was hardly likely to be friendly and Isabel feared finding herself somehow caught between the two, as yesterday. How had everything become so complicated so suddenly?

Isabel stood miserably in the corridor, insides clenched in anticipation of the moment, any minute surely, when Amber would hove into view, heels clacking and hair swirling. But the minutes went by, the time for the meeting approached, and still she had not materialised.

Isabel was full of a wild hope that she wouldn't. Perhaps she had been caught with her dog and sent down already. The prospect was liberating, almost dizzyingly so. She could start afresh.

Kate seemed in no mood to let bygones be bygones, however. Her only response to Isabel's friendly greeting was to shoot her an acid look.

Isabel could hardly blame her. She longed to explain to Kate how the situation had come about, but it seemed unclear even to herself. Besides, Kate's fierceness at the time had frightened her almost as much as Amber's. Her efforts to set the record straight would be bumbling and nervous, and Kate might refuse to listen to her anyway. Perhaps, Isabel thought hopefully, Ellie might be able to help.

There were four others in the group: Paul, Lorien, Harry and Bethany. They seemed friendly and mercifully low-key, but Isabel was too conscious of Kate's simmering presence to make any overtures. She propped up the wall on the opposite side of the corridor from them and hoped they didn't think her haughty and distant.

They were too busy chatting to notice. Catching words like 'Prince Harry' and 'Mustique', Isabel gathered they were discussing Amber. Bethany, a northern blonde with a big nose, was grinning and waving a newspaper about and Isabel caught glimpses of the latest edition of the social page she had read on the train. It seemed like years ago, but was in fact just a mere two days. The main illustration was, as before, of Amber, this time clad in the silver dress Isabel had seen her putting on last night. She was beaming and holding a glass of champagne.

Paul, who had dark hair, glasses and the serious manner of the head boy he had only just stopped being, was reading out the accompanying paragraph.

'. . . *The demands of academia haven't, it seems, dimmed The Hon. Amber Piggott's famous party-going appetite. Last night saw her on – literally – glittering form in a shimmering minidress by aristo-eco designers GreenLady, at the launch of high-end stationery emporium Smootheson's Belgravia flagship store. Accompanied by fellow student, Jasper De Borchy, Amber trilled, "They're working me terribly hard at uni and a girl deserves a night off every now and then."'*

Harry gave an incredulous, high-pitched giggle. 'Terribly hard!' he snorted, while Lorien pondered, 'Can you actually *dim* an appetite? Is that the word?'

Isabel stared at the floor. She would have liked to join in the laughter, longed to be able to see Amber as the others did, as a joke. Had she really gone all the way to London for a party last night? Hardly surprising that she wasn't here; although where, Isabel wondered, did this leave the dog?

The door to David Stringer's room now flew open. 'Hi, guys! Come on in!'

He gave the group a friendly and slightly anxious smile. 'Hey,' he said. 'Isn't there another one of you?'

'Yes, but she hasn't turned up,' Kate said.

'Better things to do,' Paul added, as Bethany handed over the newspaper. David Stringer looked at it and frowned. 'What's a high-end stationery emporium?' he asked.

'Quite literally the opening of an envelope,' Kate sneered, shooting a nasty look at Isabel.

Stringer shook his head dismissively and closed the door behind them all. To Isabel's relief, he seemed disinclined to discuss the matter. In fact, Stringer himself was relieved; seeing the paper, he had imagined yet another flattering article about his archrival, Dan Bright. That it only concerned some stupid AWOL female student was good news – faculty discipline was Gillian Green's department.

Like all the tutors' offices at Branston, Dr Stringer's was circular and built of concrete. They sat self-consciously at a round table. The room was not terribly warm. 'All your supervisions will be in my house from now on,' Stringer told the group. Isabel, relieved, imagined cosy armchairs and a roaring fire. 'This is just a preliminary powwow.'

Dr Stringer was as Isabel remembered him from the interviews: thin, bearded and agitated. She liked him; there was something very warm and human, if chaotic, about him. He wore an ancient baggy T-shirt with the slogan, 'Will Power' in scratchy writing beneath a screen print of Shakespeare's head.

They talked through some verse and, in Dr Stringer's encouraging, enthusiastic presence, Isabel felt confident enough to launch a defence of a favourite poem against Kate's criticisms. Afterwards they made reading lists and took down essay topics. Isabel filed out last; about to close the door, she looked over her shoulder to see Dr Stringer beaming at her. 'You did very well there. Keep it up.'

Outside, Kate spotted Isabel's flush of pleasure. 'What did he say?' she asked suspiciously.

'Oh . . . nothing. Nothing,' Isabel assured her. If Kate was competitive as well as not liking her, things would be even more difficult.

The final meeting of the morning was with the director of studies. Gillian Green read the account of Amber's party going with thin lips. 'I'll keep this, if you don't mind,' she said to Bethany, pushing the tabloid into a large, book-stuffed woven bag at the side of her chair. The meeting then proceeded much as the Stringer one had but, at the end, Professor Green sent the others out and signed to Isabel to remain.

Left behind, Isabel glanced apprehensively up into the academic's handsome, high-cheekboned face. The fear that it was something about Amber's dog jabbed uncomfortably about her insides.

'I just wanted to say,' Professor Green said in her deep rumble of a voice, 'that we have expectations.' She gave a wintry smile. 'High expectations. You must work hard. Make the most of your time here.'

'I will work hard,' Isabel assured her in a daze of delight. Professor Green had high expectations! The world, she felt, was back on its axis.

The route back to her room took her across the front of Branston and near the place she had tied up Coco. Reluctantly, she decided to check on the dog's wellbeing. She was relieved to see that the bike rack to which she had tied Coco was empty. Amber had obviously returned from London, seen the note and retrieved her pet. It was perhaps unexpected that the piece of rope remained attached, but Amber had probably thought it was scruffy and rejected it on aesthetic grounds.

Isabel took a deep, relieved draught of air. It struck her, for the first time, how lovely the day was. From its mild beginning it had continued warm and now the air had a faint spicy scent of bonfire smoke and sweet decay. The sun filled each leaf with light so that it glowed.

Now to meet Ellie, Isabel told herself. Time for some fun, at last. Time to go to the fair, join the interesting-looking societies and make enough new friends to form a barrier between herself and Amber Piggott for the rest of her university life.

Turning into her own corridor, Isabel felt a stab of shock when she spotted, at the bottom of Amber's door, the small white tongue of the untouched note she had slotted under earlier.

The ghastly implications sank in. If Amber had not read it she did not know where Coco was. And Coco was no longer tied to the bike rack . . .

Isabel's heart boomed in her chest. Had someone stolen her? Had she run away? Had Isabel lost Amber's pet?

And Amber would be furious! A hot wave of horror broke

over Isabel as she imagined herself on the receiving end of Amber's formidable rage. Being required to replace Coco, even. She had no idea how much a dog like that cost. And then there was the collar . . . Were those jewels real?

In the middle of Isabel's panic, someone, suddenly, rounded the corner. As if in a living nightmare, she now saw, heading towards her, the person she least wanted to see. Without the dog she now most wanted to see. No small white canine head stared malevolently from under Amber's thin brown arm.

Her hair was tangled and her make-up smeared. A pair of silver shoes with red soles was tucked under one tanned arm. She was barking into her mobile – it had a pink, glittering case that caught the light. 'But *why* has it gone? It can't have!'

Isabel's stomach surged violently. Amber was clearly talking to someone about her dog.

'It's a *disaster*,' she wailed. 'It meant everything to me! What? The signal's going now.'

Isabel stared helplessly into the large, brown, dewy eyes. Tears hung like diamonds in the thicket of Amber's lashes.

'I'm so sorry,' she began, before Amber could say anything.

'It's a tragedy,' Amber cried.

'I don't know what to say,' Isabel confessed, truthfully.

'How dare they cancel it?'

'Cancel it?'

'I've just been talking to my agent. The bloody TV series has been canned,' Amber wailed. She stamped on the carpet with one bare tanned foot. 'A film crew was supposed to be following me everywhere during my first term,' she raged. 'Fly-on-the-wall documentary. Like *Made in Chelsea*, only about me starting at uni. But now some guy, the head of the college or whatever, has put a stop to it.'

Isabel was having trouble registering what she was hearing. 'I thought,' she stammered, 'that the tragedy was Coco.'

Amber's face was utterly blank.

'Your dog,' Isabel prompted.

Recognition dawned. 'Oh, yeah,' Amber said casually. 'My dog. I left her with you, didn't I?' Her attention was now back on her iPhone. 'Bloody agent', she was muttering.

Isabel cleared her throat. She took a deep breath. 'I'm awfully sorry, Amber,' she began, her voice high and rushed. 'But I'm afraid I've lost your dog.'

The first expression to cross Amber's smooth, brown face was of absolute indifference. But then came another, more speculative one. Then the lovely face darkened again, the eyes welled and the brows drew together in anguish. 'You've *lost* my dog?' Amber gasped.

'Yes, and I'm so sorry, Amber,' said the wretched Isabel. 'I don't know how I can ever make it up to you.'

Amber was weeping again, heartbrokenly. She looked up through her tumbling golden hair. 'There is one way,' she sniffed. 'I don't suppose that you could fill me in on those books, could you? The reading-list ones.'

'Fill you in?' Isabel repeated the phrase slowly, weighing its meaning. 'You mean – tell you what was in them?'

'Seriously, would you? That would be absolutely angelic.' Amber was smiling broadly, apparently quite recovered from her grief. 'I've been madly busy all summer, you see. I helped build a school in Mexico.'

Surprise filled Isabel at this unexpected evidence of altruism, especially as Amber had, according to the newspaper, spent the summer in Mustique. Ellie had built a Mexican school too, of course. Isabel was about to say so, to remark on the coincidence, but a brown arm shot out and grabbed her own.

'So you absolutely promise me?' Amber pressed, her face very close, her expression demanding.

'Promise you what?'

'That you'll write me a bluffer's guide to the reading-list books?' Amber's eyes seemed to be getting ever larger, her pupils drilling into Isabel's.

'But why?' Isabel asked, curious despite everything. 'Why

don't you just read them? Who are you bluffing, anyway?'

Amber was fiddling with her hair. Through the golden strands, she darted Isabel a sly look. 'Prof Green. She's demanded to see me. Assess my motivation, or something.'

Isabel looked down, suddenly fearful. Amber was asking her to help fabricate a fraud. Another one.

'Look,' Amber impatiently broke in. 'I *would* have read them, OK? But with this school thing taking up all my time, what could I do? I couldn't leave the poor little things with the place half built, could I?'

Isabel said, leadenly, that she supposed not.

'Good,' Amber said briskly. 'You'd better start now then. I need it by – ooh, let me think – four thirty?'

Isabel's mouth dropped open. 'Today?' To give Amber some idea of what she needed to know would take hours. She could not possibly set aside that amount of time. Not when she was going to the fair with Ellie. 'I'm very sorry but I can't do it right now,' she said, trying to sound firm despite the fact her hands were shaking.

Amber glared. 'Izzy! You promised, you *promised.*'

Isabel stuck doggedly to her guns. 'I've arranged to go to the freshers' fair with my friend.'

Amber's expression became scornful. 'But how unbelievably dreary. I mean, why bother?'

'To see if there are any societies I want to join,' Isabel replied, with spirit.

'Well, of course there won't be,' Amber sneered. 'They're all ghastly. You don't need clubs, anyway. I'm your friend now, aren't I? I'll introduce you to everyone who's anyone.' She put her head on one side. 'You have to help me,' she wheedled. 'I'll probably be sent down otherwise. And you *have* lost *darling* Coco. You owe me.'

Isabel had almost forgotten about Coco. Yes, she had lost the dog. But . . .

She raised her chin in the air. 'You did leave Coco behind,' she pointed out, rather desperately. 'And you didn't say you weren't coming back.'

The Piggott nostrils flared. The eyes flashed, then narrowed. '*You lost the dog,*' Amber reiterated, through clenched teeth.

Isabel's heart was thumping. She was not used to confront-ation, particularly with someone like Amber. She wasn't sure how much longer she could keep this up.

'Have you any idea what a dog like Coco costs?' Amber hissed, mercilessly pressing home her advantage.

Isabel thought quickly. She would square it with Ellie somehow. She must. Perhaps they could go to the fair on another day, or later on that evening. And, anyway, Ellie might sym-pathise, once she heard about Amber at the Mexican school.

Her heart, even so, sank at the thought of all the work ahead of her. She could hardly recall what was in some of the books herself. And the arguments were complex, not easy to précis. And perhaps this would just be the start of it, there would be more demands, Amber would keep holding her to ransom. All because of the dog . . .

If only she could find it. How, Isabel wondered, did one set about finding a lost poodle?

As Amber drifted off, singing, towards her room, Isabel went to find Ellie to break the news.

'Come in!' Ellie was sitting on her bed, cross-legged, humming along to a CD. She turned it down as Isabel came in. 'Look!' she said excitedly, holding out a notepad. 'I'm making a list. I'm going to join the cordon bleu society, if they have one. I was president of the one at my school. I'm desperate to get cooking. Oh, and the wine ones, of course . . . What's up?' she finished, noticing Isabel's unhappy expression.

'I've got some work to do,' Isabel began, awkwardly.

'Fine, we can go later,' Ellie sang. 'It's open until five, I think. Do you think there'll be anyone from the Bullinger there?'

'What's that?'

'That secret society. Haven't you heard of it? A friend of mine from school had a brother in it. They have wild parties in stately homes where they pour champagne over each other.'

'What?' Isabel was surprised enough to be distracted for a moment.

'With dwarves,' Ellie giggled. 'And strippers.'

'You're joking,' Isabel said. 'That doesn't really happen here. Not any more, surely.'

Ellie put her head to one side. 'You don't think so?'

Isabel bit her lip. All this, of course, was beside the point. 'I'm so sorry, Ellie. I can't come later either.'

The eyes from the bed were wide, uncomprehending, disappointed. 'Why not?'

Isabel explained in a miserable monotone about Amber and the reading list, citing the school in Mexico as the excuse. She left out the dog; it was all too complicated and incriminating.

She saw the sympathy drain out of Ellie's face as she listened. The soft, pink-and-white features became hard. 'Amber's lying,' she told Isabel in a tone which brooked no argument.

'I know it sounds a bit unlikely,' Isabel agreed. 'But she says she didn't have time to read the list; she was working at this school for poor kids in Mexico on her gap year. Just like you! It might even have been the same place!' She looked brightly at Ellie. But Ellie's expression was even stonier than before.

She rubbed her face and stared at Isabel through splayed fingers. 'It was the same place.'

'Really? So you knew her, before you got here?'

'You could say that. Although I have no intention of renewing the acquaintance.'

Isabel was puzzled at Ellie's bitter tone. 'But – Amber *did* help, she *was* there?' She wondered why Ellie had not mentioned it before, during the night of the DVDs, for instance.

Ellie looked scornful. 'Yes,' she said, 'for about five minutes. Literally that. Just long enough for her photographer – she actually brought one with her – to get some pictures for her audition reel, she said.'

'Audition reel?'

'For some TV programme about compassionate celebrities, or something,' Ellie said caustically. 'She seemed desperate to get into telly. Not sure *that* one ever got past first base, though.' She shook her head, irritated at the digression. 'The point is, Amber was using what we were doing for her own ends.'

Isabel bit her lip. She'd got the point.

'She stayed on the school site five minutes and didn't pick up as much as a trowel the whole time. Oh, actually, that's not true.'

'Isn't it?' Isabel asked, hope leaping within that there might be some redeeming aspect.

'No, it's all coming back to me, she brought her own spade with her. It was painted pink and she posed with it on the building site whilst wearing a leopardskin bikini. Raised the morale of the construction workers, if nothing else,' Ellie added dryly.

Isabel had closed her eyes. Could it get any worse? Yes, it seemed.

'Then she said she had to go, she was going to visit some friends nearby,' Ellie said. 'We thought they must be Mexican, to do with the charity, but it turned out they were on Mustique. Just up in the West Indies, a hop, skip and a jump by private plane. Needless to say, she never came back.'

Isabel swallowed nervously. 'Oh dear,' she said, confused. 'I don't know what to say. Or do.' She looked at the other girl in dismay. 'But I promised her.'

'Yes, but you had an arrangement with me before that.' Ellie's tone was stern.

The dog, Isabel thought. The dog. If only I hadn't lost the dog.

'Amber's a notorious liar,' Ellie said shortly. 'Or manipulator, I should say. It's all about her; nothing else matters. As you'll find out, I daresay,' she added darkly. She stood up. 'Well, I'm going to the freshers' fair, even if you aren't. See you later.'

Thus dismissed, Isabel trudged back to her room and stared

bewildered at the wall. What was happening to her? She had tried to do what was right but had lost not one but *two* possible friends as a result. Three, if you counted Olly.

Her throat hardened and her eyes pricked. She blinked hard; she would not cry. But everything was going wrong, and just yesterday things had seemed so wonderful, to be going so well.

Chapter 10

It was just after nine o'clock in the morning and Olly was rummaging for some boxer shorts in the battered chest of drawers against the wall. He found a T-shirt and pulled on the jeans that had been lying crumpled and stiff with cold on the floor. He winced as the metal belt buckle touched his warm, white and tender belly with a cold shock as piercing as electricity.

Being chilly was something Olly had got used to during his three years as a student. He had only spent a week as David Stringer's lodger but only now did he feel he understood what cold weather really meant.

It seemed, like Narnia, eternal winter inside the Stringers' vast Victorian semi-detached villa. 'Just stick another jumper on if you're cold, Olly,' David's wife, Dotty, would sing cheerfully from above the shrunken Fair Isle straining across her unsupported chest. She teamed this with a claret beret and Afghan knee-length knitted slippers.

Dotty was teaching now; Olly could hear the thin wail of violin. Below his boxroom was the upstairs sitting room in which Dotty conducted her violin lessons. Sometimes he lay enchanted as waves of rippling notes rose through the thin blue carpet. Sometimes the tuneless scrapings had him out from under the duvet more effectively than any alarm clock.

Dotty was incurably curious on the subject of his love life. She professed to find it impossible to believe that the girls weren't queuing up to ask him out. 'Some day your princess will come,' Dotty would say. Sometimes she would even play it on her violin, the melancholy waltz tune rising up through Olly's floorboards and making him roll his eyes in exasperation.

Of course his princess would not come. Isabel had not even bothered to step outside the college sliding doors. He had not mentioned the episode to Dotty, partly from lingering resentment and embarrassment at being stood up and partly because there was a possibility that, as David taught English at Branston, he might well come across her. Olly had no wish for Isabel to know that his career had now reached the dizzy heights of being David's cleaner. He had tried to feel cross with her but what he really felt was a remote longing, as for the lovely, unreachable heroine of a novel. His novel, possibly. He had chucked the *Brideshead* idea and had now started a sweeping Scottish romance with a red-headed beauty at the centre.

He was still working on his book. His routine at the Stringers' was to clean in the morning and spend the afternoon writing and looking for proper employment. Cleaning was rather more fun than he had imagined, the Stringers' standards being just above the level of their own gritty floors. Olly had not appreciated that university academics lived like this. He had imagined them all in handsome town houses with patinaed furniture and oil paintings. But the Stringer house was an incredible mess, with papers everywhere and towers of boxes blocking the light from the dusty windows. Olly, however, had found he rather enjoyed snapping on yellow rubber gloves and squirting the Cillit Bang around. It was strangely soothing; you got instant results, which was more than could be said either of the novel or his quest for work. And the Stringers were touchingly appreciative.

Dressed, Olly headed down for breakfast, passing Hero Stringer's bedroom on the way. Her pine bedroom door was plastered with warnings: 'No Entry' and 'You Are Entering A Nuclear Facility'. As this implied, and as Olly had discovered, the daughter of the house was a moody teenager who treated her parents with disdain and who went to school only when she felt like it. She never, from what Olly could tell, felt like it. Hero was rarely glimpsed outside her room, where her activities were a mystery, although, to judge from the smells seeping under the door, they included smoking and eating takeaway burgers. Olly supposed the latter a double whammy aimed at her parents, enabling Hero both to avoid eating with them whilst ostentatiously buying into the mega-corporations they despised.

The usual thrash metal thumped from Hero's room; eventually, Olly knew, either David or Dotty would crack and go upstairs to shout at their daughter to get ready for school, an instruction Hero invariably ignored. He wondered why she was so rude to her parents. They seemed perfectly all right to him; better than most, in fact. They were, admittedly, slightly bonkers, but kind nonetheless and Olly appreciated the slightly rackety musical-academic, colourfully Bohemian atmosphere.

He shuffled into the kitchen now to find Dotty breakfasting alone at the varnished pine kitchen table. The violin lesson was evidently over. She wore a burgundy beret plonked over her unbrushed henna curls and she looked him up and down with interest. 'Oh,' she said brightly. 'It's you, is it?'

'Yes, it's me,' Olly muttered.

'I didn't realise,' Dotty said, shoving a spoonful of muesli between lips coated heavily with purple lipstick.

'What didn't you realise?' Olly asked tolerantly, looking for a bowl. Dotty said strange things sometimes, not always to the person in the room.

'That you were the Antichrist,' Dotty said agreeably through a mouthful of oats.

'What? Oh.' Wearily, Olly looked down at his T-shirt. He really should get rid of it; he was sick of people commenting on it. On the other hand, had he not been wearing it, David would never have invited him here. So perhaps it was lucky.

He reached for the jar of muesli and they munched for a while in silence, broken only by the thumping of Hero's music from upstairs. Dotty did not appear to notice it, although surely she hated it, Olly thought. He had seen her alone in her music room, unconscious of the door being ajar, playing *The Lark Ascending* to herself on the violin. Her eyes were closed and there was a rapturous expression on her face.

Olly was beginning to suspect that Hero's music, like most other things Hero did, was a calculated attempt to irritate her parents.

David now burst into the kitchen. He was wild-eyed, clutching what looked like a list, and wore a tight Shetland jumper whose sleeves barely reached his skinny elbows. Olly had learnt early on not to give any of his laundry to Dotty. It came out either unrecognisable in colour, or fit only for a dwarf.

A muscle worked in David's thin cheek and he pulled agitatedly at his skimpy beard. He was glancing fitfully at the ceiling, through which the music continued relentlessly to thump. 'We agreed to just ignore it,' Dotty reminded him soothingly. 'That's our new approach,' she said to Olly. 'The "hands-off" parent. Non-intervention.'

Olly nodded. During the seven days he had been here, Dotty and David had tried three previous new parenting approaches, each more ineffectual than the last.

'We're letting her anger run its course,' Dotty elucidated brightly, glancing at her husband for corroboration.

'But what's she so angry about?' Olly asked, feeling this was the nub of the question.

Dotty's chest heaved in a great sigh. 'She says she's angry about everything. About society. So she's taking a radical position and staying in her room.'

Up until now, Olly had not appreciated that university academics could be like this. The ones he had been taught by at St Alwine's had been suave, self-confident, superior. But Dotty and David were all over the place.

David was indeed in a state of high anxiety. His fears for his career had intensified since Olly's first encounter with him. The interview with Professor Green had not gone well and she had apparently cut some of his responsibilities. He was sitting now, at the table, muesli untouched, staring at the diminished list of students.

'Never mind,' Dotty said comfortingly. 'The fewer students you've got, the more you can concentrate on them.'

'I know it's because of that Facebook page,' David fretted. 'But Gillian refused to believe me when I said I couldn't upload anything, even a towel on a shelf.'

Ah yes, Olly thought. The Stringer towels. They hung stiffly on the chipped rail of the downstairs shower room – worn, thin and of a cardboard rigidity. Using them was like rubbing yourself all over with sandpaper.

He decided to beat a retreat. 'I'll start the cleaning,' he said brightly. Minutes later, he was bumping the Hoover up the stairs. It was an ancient machine, like something out of a museum, with a proper old-fashioned bag to take the dust.

He Hoovered the upstairs hall, staring at the bookshelves as he did so. Books were everywhere in the Stringer house. Neither Dotty nor David possessed the ability to pass a charity shop without buying an armful of paperbacks. The range they had collected was enormous: Greek myth and picaresque, dense volumes of Wordsworth and Thomas Carlyle, histories of architecture and music, and biographies of everyone from Voltaire to Field Marshall Blucher. There were also many children's classics, each in several editions; enough *Wind in the Willows* to constitute a howling gale and a *Garden of Verses* stretching as far as the eye could see. Even the loos – one up, one down – were bursting with books: *1000 Places To See Before You Die*, *1000 Paintings To See Before You Die* and *1000 Buildings To See Before You Die* loomed at Olly whenever he entered. This fat-spined mixture of death and compunction could have an arresting effect, although Dotty's signature dish was obviously the answer to that.

Olly had a shelf in the fridge and another in the cupboard but was welcome to eat with the family if he wanted to. He was not sure how much he wanted to. He had discovered on the first night of residence that Dotty's organic chilli con carne rather emphasised the chilli and the result was altogether too brisk an experience for his insides. And David's fondness for very smelly French cheese – he seemed to actively prefer the rotten end of the spectrum – meant that opening the fridge was like encountering the breath of Grendel, the monster with halitosis in *Beowulf.*

Olly decided to do Hero's room next. He had never yet actually been in it but suspected it was fetid. She smoked in it, for a start, and as he never saw the takeaway boxes in the kitchen bin he concluded she either ate those as well, or shoved them under her bed.

He stood before the door, Hoover in hand. Thrashing guitars and hoarse, furious yelling blared out from behind the 'Nuclear Facility' posters.

He knocked.

'Go away!' Hero shouted, much as expected.

Olly put his head round the door. The curtains were drawn and the lamps were on. Hero's long, skinny form stretched out on the bed looking longer and skinnier than ever in her tight black jeans. Her eyes in her white face were ringed with black and her lips and hair were the same colour.

'Oh, it's you,' she said, without enthusiasm.

He was about to advertise his intention to clean the room but the powerfully vinegary scent of stale cigarettes made him cough. He waggled the Hoover pole at her instead.

'No way,' Hero said. But Olly had none of her parents' fear of this trenchant teenager and advanced into the room, the soles of his trainers crunching over the crisps in the carpet.

'Can we turn that down a bit?' Olly bent to the volume control. 'What are you're listening to?'

'Wanker.'

'Thanks a lot.' Olly pretended to be offended.

Hero rolled exasperated eyes. 'No; the *band*'s called Wanker, you . . .'

'Wanker?' Olly supplied, good naturedly.

'Actually, according to your T-shirt, you're the Antichrist. Ironic, is it?'

'No, I am the actual Antichrist,' Olly said, ironically. He was peering into the stinking darkness under the bedframe. 'How long is it since you cleaned under here?'

'What's the legal position?'

'Eh?' He was looking for the plug socket.

'If someone decided to kill you.'

'Why would anyone want to kill me?'

'Your T-shirt. Someone might think they were ridding the world of a great evil. Imagining they were killing the Antichrist. It might be a defence, you know, against a murder charge.'

Olly was, despite himself, impressed. He had gathered from David and Dotty that Hero had, before nihilism descended, once contemplated law as a career.

He plugged the device in and poked the end of the suction pole under the bed. There was a zapping noise and, when he pulled it back out, a Happy Meal box was attached to the end. He detached it with dignity, pulled out the black bin-bag he had shoved into his belt, shook it open and dropped the box in. Then he stuck the pole under again. Five more Happy Meal boxes followed, some in the advanced stages of decay.

That, Olly decided, was enough. He extracted the Hoover pole. Whatever else was mouldering under the bed could wait until next time, although there was a fair chance that by then it would have got up and gone of its own accord. He dragged the duster out of his jeans pocket and began flicking it around gingerly among Hero's collection of fantasy figures with coloured glass eyes and vampire wings.

'Do you mind?' Hero shouted as he started to pull the curtains. 'I like them shut, yeah? This is *my* room.'

'Yeah, and you should be out of it and at school,' Olly retaliated.

'Yeah?'

'Yeah. You learn things,' Olly said. 'You pass your exams; you go to university. You find out what you want to do in life. Get a good job.'

'Yeah,' Hero smirked. 'Like you have, right? How's the novel coming on?'

Olly regretted ever having mentioned this to Hero. It had been in a weak moment, probably immediately after the chilli had struck.

The laptop was open on Hero's Twitter page, he saw. Her address was @GothGirl and the photo was of a pair of black lips up close. She had a smart laptop, Olly saw, and a scanner as well. Her parents had obviously tried, at one stage, to appease her with computers.

Hero had turned up Wanker again. 'This one's called "Arse to Everything",' she announced.

Olly decided to take the hint.

Dotty was still at the kitchen table when he came back downstairs with the Hoover. 'That dog's there again,' she observed. Olly followed her eyes out of the kitchen window. The white poodle that had first turned up a week ago was staring in through the pane.

Olly had spotted it first. He had seen its nametag – silver, with 'Coco' engraved on it in swirling script – and attempted to make friends with it until a couple of vicious nips on the hand had curbed his enthusiasm. Dotty had wondered whether the jewels on the collar were real. They had given it food and water. It had left the chilli but responded eagerly to Hero's somewhat unexpectedly giving it leftovers from her burgers. She was the only one of the inmates it hadn't bitten, but perhaps it didn't dare.

It was David who made them get rid of it. He was allergic to canines as well as everything else at the moment and insisted the creature was best off at the local dogs' home. Dotty had taken it there some days ago, so the fact it had returned was unexpected. Olly eyed it apprehensively.

'Still,' Dotty sighed now, meeting Coco's somewhat crazed black eyes through the glass, 'it's nice that someone seems to like me.'

'I like you, Dotty,' Olly said comfortingly. He did, too. She was, he felt, impressively cheerful in the face of her difficult family and he particularly liked her lowbrow streak, the way she loved nothing better than to have a bowl of pasta – or the dreaded chilli – on a tray in the sitting room with David and watch *Strictly Come Dancing*.

He had found it hard to believe that Dotty, the passionate violinist and Royal College of Music graduate, could take anything but the most ironic interest in the likes of *X Factor*, but after sitting next to her on the battered sitting room sofa as she clenched her fists, shouted at the television and wept copiously as the fat lady who cleaned the council loos belted out a heart-stopping – or, as David wryly put it, Harpic-stopping – version of *I Will Always Love You*, Olly realised that her interest was genuine. He realised, too, that after a day spent teaching certain pupils of hers, and dealing with certain mothers, such undemanding downtime was essential for Dotty's sanity.

A strange, grinding noise interrupted them: the doorbell, Olly realised. Dotty glanced fearfully at the clock. 'Oh no,' she said. 'It's the Lintles.'

Limited though his time in the Stringer house had been, Olly was already aware that Lorna Lintle was Dotty's least favourite client. Most of the mothers whose offspring she taught sat outside the house listening to Radio Two in their cream-leather-lined four-wheel drives and ordering the weekly shop from Waitrose on their iPads as little Ottilie or Jasper scraped the catgut inside. But Lorna not only sat in on the entire lesson, but looked as if she grew her own vegetables and wove her own clothes out of hemp. She was a terrifying, grey-ponytailed harridan with an unrelentingly cultural focus and in this powerful and unflinching spotlight squirmed Alfie, her son. He was small, skinny, thickly bespectacled and being groomed to genius by every means to hand. He had two lessons a week and they always arrived outside Dotty's house with something improving like *Peter and the Wolf* booming from Lorna's battered, claret-coloured Volvo.

'What instrument was playing, Alfie?' Lorna would be shouting as she dragged him up the path.

'Er . . . trombone?'

'Alfie!' his mother would explode. 'It was a *bassoon*. Honestly, Mozart had written several operas and done a world tour by the time he got to your age.'

Olly felt powerfully sorry for Alfie because he had Lorna as a mother, and powerfully sorry for Dotty because she had Hero as a daughter. He had not expected merely renting a room to give such insight into the complexity of family relationships. He wasn't sure he wanted this insight; life at the moment was tricky enough. As the bell rang again, louder and more insistently, Olly beat a hasty retreat back upstairs.

As he did so, he could hear the poodle barking outside.

Chapter 11

It was all his own fault, Richard knew. He should never have got involved. He should not have taken any notice when Allegra Trott rang up and told him that, if sending her a list with six-pound mugs on it was the best Branston could do, she was going to blow her bonus on shoes, handbags and a part-share in a racehorse.

He should certainly not have considered this alongside the presence of the ghastly Amber Piggott and concluded that the college was going the wrong way about raising money. And, even if he had reached such a conclusion, he should have left it at that. He should certainly not have gone along to Flora Thynne and told her that Branston needed a bigger idea, a bolder vision and the courage to carry it out. But he had; he had done all this and now he was sitting in the meeting that Flora had called with the college high command in order to tackle what she called his 'issues'.

The Bursar was there, looking furtive and flustered, plus a couple of people whose names he couldn't remember, and Gillian Green. The chair opposite his was occupied by Flora Thynne. To her left sat an extraordinary creature.

He was male, mid-twenties, plump and his powerfully sweet-smelling aftershave overwhelmed Richard, seated several feet across the table. He wore glasses in exuberantly thick black retro frames and had spiky, gelled-up hair. He had been slightly late to the meeting and, as he had entered, Richard had been afforded a view of his trousers. These, while skintight round his plump thighs and solid calves, bagged off his generous bottom in a manner reminiscent of a full nappy, and exposed most of his underwear. The effect was completed by a heavy silver chain belt.

Flora did the introductions. The apparition, Richard learnt, was called Clyde Bracegirdle and was a freelance public relations expert. He had formerly headed a local firm called Gobstopper PR whose clients included a manufacturer of llama ice cream. Richard tried not to groan as, emitting gusts of violently scented aftershave, Clyde invited ideas from round the table for 'a mega-brainstorm to chuck ideas around for re-engaging the client in the Branston story.'

Richard felt he might scream soon in frustration. 'I thought,' he said, 'that *you* were supposed to be the one with ideas. That's what we're paying you for, isn't it?'

Clyde acknowledged that he was and it was. 'OK; let me level with you. Let me introduce you to . . .' he paused, theatrically, before adding, extravagantly, 'the Big Branston Ring-Round!'

In the absence of a reaction from anyone else, Flora coughed politely.

The basic idea, Richard gathered, was that groups of current Branston students were corralled to ring up alumni and chat to them in a jolly, informal fashion about what life in the college was currently like. In theory, the person rung up would be seized by nostalgia and would subsequently seize their credit card, eager that this idyllic way of life and learning could be perpetuated.

Richard stifled a yawn and passed a weary hand over his eyes. None of this was new to him. He'd heard it before, many times. American universities had been doing it for years. Probably lots of British ones had too, although the way Clyde was looking triumphantly around the table he was evidently expecting to be credited with the invention of it.

'Just running it up the flagpole to see if anyone salutes,' Clyde beamed.

Richard drummed his fingers on the table. 'Fine by me.' He glanced at Flora, who looked terrified. 'Think you can get some students together?'

There was a spasm in her thin throat as she swallowed. She nodded.

How difficult, Richard thought irritably, could it be? He'd seen it done a dozen times. All she need do was produce a poster saying, 'Your College Needs You!' offering free booze and tack it up on the student noticeboards alongside the ones about safe sex, jazz concerts, internet grooming, services in the egg chapel and auditions for *Huis Clos*. His mouth opened to say as much, but then he closed it again. He was not here to micromanage Flora Thynne. He was here to work at his research, and that was where he was going now.

'Good,' Richard said, rising abruptly to his feet. He had done his bit – more than his bit. He would now retire from the whole fundraising business and leave it to the experts.

As he pushed back his chair, he glanced out of the meeting room window into the garden. He felt something like a grim relief that it looked as bad as ever. That woman gardener had either not yet penetrated these drearier areas, or, with any luck, might already have packed in the job. From what the Bursar had said about her wages, he would not blame her.

A movement caught his attention; someone was working at the far side of the scabby lawn. The gardener? She had been camouflaged before; her soft brown hair and faded green jacket just smudges in the general autumn picture. There was something about her which drew the eye. He watched as she pulled up dandelions and tossed them into a bucket. She had wide eyes and a wide mouth stretched in a dreamy smile.

Richard felt something thud into his chest, as if someone had hit him. He recognised her; it was the woman from the car – the woman he had almost collided with on his bike. But more than that, he recognised her smile. She smiled just as Amy had. To see her, smiling like that, whilst working in a garden . . .

He looked away hurriedly, heart crashing in his chest. Heat and chill surged after each other through his body. He wanted to leave, get out and get away, but his feet would not move. It was as if something was compelling him to stay.

For a time after Amy's death, hard-nosed scientist even though he was, he had read messages from her in the appearances of various birds, in sightings of butterflies, in the pictures formed by clouds. It had taken time, a long and miserable time, to accept that none of this meant anything, that she really had gone, that he would never see her again in any form. So, to see someone so similar, now, in the last place on earth he had expected it, was a horrible shock. To have to face, presumably daily, something so painful in the place he had hand-picked in order to avoid such pain . . .

Someone, he realised, was talking to him. The voice was coming from what seemed a long way away. Gradually, he recognised the fruity tones of the Bursar.

'Master? Do you feel quite well? You look pale. Permit me to help you back to the Lodge . . .'

Richard cast him a wild look before crashing his way out of the room. Go back to that concrete hellhole? He wanted to get out of Branston, reach the sanctuary of the labs and never have to look at that woman again.

Unaware of the sensation she had caused, Diana, in the garden, was feeling almost cheerful. She was heaping leaves from a barrow into a wire cage at the back of the college. It was satisfying work: the smell of the mulch, the drier leaves exploding beneath her wellingtons like pistol shots. A robin, hanging around her in the hope of worms, skittered back at the alarming sound.

Things were working out unimaginably well. Rosie's positive first day at school had been followed by a second, and a third. Days had now turned to weeks and still she seemed fine, doing well even, despite the fact that every day seemed to bring a new supply teacher with it. For all her good intentions, Diana could not help wondering if discipline was affected.

'Oh, no, Mum; it's very disciplined,' Rosie assured her breezily. 'The teachers spend the whole time trying to get people to behave.'

As for the Campion Estate, Debs and Mitch had been as good as their word about the TV noise. The levels had remained within the bounds of bearability ever since. *And* Mitch had fixed the car door, resplendent in a T-shirt that said, 'Single Man, Double Vodka' on it.

Diana had been able to do little in return apart from pay in kind and put a few flowers and plants into Debs' garden, as well as some clematis montana.

'Thanks,' Debs had said gratefully. 'I like a bit of colour. Nothing like a nice-smelling clitoris round the door.'

Diana had bought the plants from a local market. Debs had told her about it. It was a revelation. It looked a cheerless enough place from the outside, a great prefab hall built of stained concrete in an unglamorous part of town.

On her first visit, Diana had felt rather vulnerable – intimidated, even – but the prices soon helped her to relax. Written in thick black marker on thick white card, they had seemed to Diana almost incredibly low. You could get half a sack of carrots for a pound, a great shovelful of mince for two. The butchers stood behind bleeding mountains of steak, buttressed by foothills of liver and chicken. They looked out at the crowd, amused, bantering. 'All right, duchess?' they called to Diana. It was hard not to laugh, and Diana had not resisted.

The second time, a Saturday, she had brought Rosie. The child had loved the place instantly, fascinated by the bustle, noise, irreverence and air of unquenchable life. She loved in particular the CD stall at the entrance that played mournful country and western at great volume. She loved The King of Bling, a shop selling cheap and very sparkly jewellery, and found the funeral flower shop fascinating with its morbidly theatrical arrangements on frames spelling letters and words: 'World's Best Nan'. Naturally she loved the sweet stalls with their mountains of chocolate and humbugs, liquorice allsorts and midget gems in great heaps. She would also pause for ages at the clothes stalls, examining gaudy sequinned dresses and Justin Bieber T-shirts while Diana dived in and out for serviceable tops and plain tracksuit bottoms that were much better made than the equivalent in the supermarket.

There was more. There were bakers' stalls where, for next to nothing, bagsful of broken biscuits – perfect for cheesecake bases – and great flat breadcakes could be bought in vast quantities. There were soft furnishing stalls selling very cheap cushions and fleece throws that, while not designer cutting-edge, were at least plain and therefore tasteful. Diana bought as many as she could afford to brighten up the Fourth Avenue sitting room. Another stall sold cheap white crockery at bargain basement prices. There was also a hardware stall that occasionally sold gardening equipment; Diana had picked up a zip-up mini plastic greenhouse at a fraction of what she would have paid at B&Q. It was here, too, that she bought the clematis, bought great sackfuls of narcissus bulbs for Branston's gardens too. It was, Diana felt, scarcely believable that she had, in the past, spent more on scented candles than the people in the market would earn in a year.

She finished the leaves, and went on to the next job, planting the pheasant's-eye narcissus. Considering the effect they would have when they came up, a shimmering row of scented, crisp whiteness, she felt quietly happy.

Clearing the ground for the bulbs, Diana now smelt something. A strong, clear, almost medicinal fragrance was wafting up from the soil. She realised, with excitement, that the plants she was pulling up were scented. She stopped, lowered her nose: curry plant, cicely, sweet sage and rosemary. Diana sat back on her heels, delighted. Who would have thought it? It seemed that once upon a thyme, as it were, Branston had had its own herb garden.

Or had it belonged to something earlier? Such an old-fashioned thing as a herb patch seemed unlikely, given the foundation's forward-looking principles. Perhaps the plants, some clearly long established, with leggy, woody roots, belonged to whatever garden had stood here before the college. All gardens, after all, were palimpsests, the earth had been written on many times . . .

'You look miles away!' she heard someone exclaim.

Diana glanced up in shock to see a young blonde woman in an apron smiling down at her.

'I'm Sally,' she said. 'I'm the college head housekeeper.'

'Oh. Yes . . . Hello . . .' Diana recognised her now. She had seen this cheerful, rosy face beaming out from the staff handbook.

'We're all taking morning break in there,' Sally jerked her ponytail towards the concrete walls of Branston. 'Come in for a cup of coffee.'

Diana was sorely tempted. Sore because she had been working hard and tempted by a shot of caffeine. Possibly a biscuit, too. She started to rise.

'We're dying to know more about you,' Sally added cheerfully. 'What brings you here and so on.'

Diana sank slowly back on her heels. That was the price, of course. Coffee and friendliness would need paying for with information about her background. And it was all such a mess, it was all so sensitive, and so awkward too, not just about the way she had lived in such a wealthy place and now lived on an estate, but also about Simon leaving her and the financial skulduggery of it all. It was all so embarrassing and it reflected so badly on her. Who would believe she was unaware they couldn't afford any of it, when she could not, even now, believe it herself?

She looked up ruefully at Sally. She was obviously a good woman, and friendly, and perhaps one day Diana would tell her all about it. But not just now.

She glanced at her watch, surprised at what a good actress she was. On the other hand, she had acted many times in recent months, usually with Simon in front of Rosie, maintaining the illusion she could stand the sight of him.

'I'd love to come for a coffee,' she said, with what really was genuine regret. 'But I've got a meeting.'

Would Sally believe her? Diana never had meetings, apart from occasionally putting her head round the door of the Assistant Bursar and asking for small advances on materials, like the bulbs.

Or would Sally be offended, recognising that she intended to keep herself apart?

To her surprise, rather than looking offended or suspicious, Sally's eyes shone with understanding. 'It's him, isn't it?' she exclaimed. 'Isn't he awful?'

Did she, Diana thought in shock, mean Simon? What did this woman know about her divorce, her ex-husband?

'I can tell by your face,' the other added as Diana dropped her head to hide her furious blushing. 'He's having that effect on everybody.'

Diana lifted her head fractionally. Sally's use of the present tense didn't quite add up.

'The new Master.' The housekeeper was rolling her eyes.

'I haven't met him yet,' Diana told her. 'What's he like?'

'Rude,' Sally said, with feeling. 'Short.'

Diana hoped not. Short and rude did not sound good. Diana imagined an irritable, undergrown, red-faced old academic limping over to criticise her planting. If she saw such a figure in the distance she would keep out of his way.

She returned to her work, and was absorbed in it again when another movement caught the tail of her eye: something red; she half-imagined it to be the robin that followed her everywhere these days, greedy for worms. Looking properly though, Diana saw now that it was the tall redhead. The one who looked so unhappy.

She had first noticed her some days ago: tall, pale, always carrying books. There was a heavy air about her, for all her slenderness. The sight of her, always alone, had brought Diana's maternal instincts to the surface. The girl was obviously miserable; possibly lonely and far from home. Diana thought of Rosie, in the future, in just such a situation. She thought of how she would appreciate some friendly type, like herself, offering to help.

On the other hand, Diana told herself, I'm ancient. As old as her mother. She's hardly going to want me to interfere. All the same, as the girl disappeared through a door, back into the college, she resolved that she would, next time – if the girl didn't look happier.

Chapter 12

'How's it going, love?' Mum asked. 'Making friends?'

Isabel closed her eyes and took a deep breath. 'Oh, yes,' she exclaimed in a voice full of forced gaiety. 'Lots of them.'

'Good,' Mum said warmly. 'But don't have too much fun, will you? You're there to work, remember.'

'Oh, I'm working all right,' Isabel said grimly. It was the first truth she had uttered in the whole conversation. 'And what about you, Mum?' she added, swiftly changing the subject. 'How are things?'

'Fine,' her mother trilled, perhaps too airily, before going on to catalogue the local gossip. The doctor had a new dog, which was keeping the entire street awake at night. Bookings were down at the holiday cottages. The new headmistress of the primary school had stopped her outside the dentist's to talk about Isabel: was one of the school's former pupils, as she had heard, really at such a prestigious university? 'I was so proud, telling her,' Mum said, her voice so full of love that Isabel could hardly bear it.

'I'd better go,' she muttered. 'Got an essay to write . . .'

'Yes, of course. Don't let them work you too hard!' Mum sang, merrily contradicting her earlier message as she rang off.

As if there was anything else to do, Isabel thought gloomily, given the wholesale disaster of her social life.

Since the day of the freshers' fair, she and Ellie had hardly spoken. Partly because Ellie was avoiding her and partly, Isabel suspected, because she had joined various clubs at the fair and was busy with new activities, new friends. Isabel would have loved, somehow, to join in with all this but Ellie looked right through her when, as was rare, they met. And each time they did, Isabel felt less confident, less inclined to stop her and beg for a minute to explain herself. As with Kate, who ignored her as well, she was unsure what exactly she would explain. Everything that had happened was so complicated. It all appeared partly her fault, albeit inadvertently. She had only herself to blame.

So Isabel had only Amber to call a friend. Although Amber clearly didn't regard her as one. Any hopes that she might be grateful for the help Isabel had given with the reading list were dashed as soon as Amber emerged – triumphant – from Professor Green's lair.

'How did it go?' Isabel had asked, emerging from her room at the unmistakeable sound of Amber in the corridor.

'Fine,' Amber returned coolly. 'The prof was surprised by my grasp of things. Said she thought I'd made some good points.'

Isabel beamed. She had spent a lot of time rehearsing Amber, giving her three really strong things to say. She looked expectantly at Amber; some thanks was due, surely. But Amber simply let herself into her room and shut the door.

From then on it seemed to Isabel that Amber had forgotten all her promises of friendship. She had said she would introduce her to everyone who was anyone and, indeed, a sequence of giggly, colt-like girls and tall, pink-cheeked young men filed in and out of Amber's room at all times of the day and night. Music could be heard, honking laughter, the pop of champagne corks. But Isabel was never invited to join in.

Only once had the sound of Amber's door opening been followed by the sound of knocking on her own. Wild with hope, Isabel had wrested it open to find herself looking into the rather wild eyes of a tousled-looking Amber.

'Izzy, darling! Don't have any milk going spare, do you? You do? Sweet of you; just leave it outside my door, could you?'

Meanwhile, whenever she went through the foyer, Isabel saw the invitations exploding from her neighbour's ever-full pigeon-hole. Amber was quite clearly the university's most popular girl while she . . . Well, the less said about that, the better.

She was not, of course, alone in being abandoned by Amber. Coco the dog had suffered the same fate. Nor had Amber made the least effort to find her. Isabel had, herself, conducted a couple of desultory searches around the college and looked about in the streets of the town. But neither hide nor hair of the hound had she seen. She was now of the view that this was not altogether a bad thing; the way Amber had treated Coco, the dog was best out of it. Hopefully she had been taken – or found – by someone who would treat her better. It seemed unlikely they would treat her worse.

As a result of all this, Isabel was making increasing use of the Branston library. She did not particularly enjoy working in it, but it was better than sitting in her room by herself, unvisited by either Ellie or Kate, and hearing Amber's lively social life going through its shrieking, door-crashing and giggling motions next door.

The library was vast and futuristic, the librarians' area of operations looking like the control centre of the Tardis. The towering metal bookstacks moved by means of hand-turned wheels like something in a submarine. The noise of this was distracting but Isabel did her best to block it out.

Working was difficult in any case. Isabel was beginning to find that, no matter how early she ordered them, the volumes she had hoped to read had all already been checked out by someone else. It didn't take long to find out who. One day she turned from the gap in the bookstacks where the books she required should have been to see Kate at the Tardis, taking delivery of those same books, evidently pre-ordered, from the librarian. She then disappeared with her haul.

It seemed ever more impossible that she and Kate could ever be friends again. And yet they saw each other all the time, at

133

supervisions. There would be one this morning, with Dr Stringer – their first at his house. Isabel could already picture the awkward group standing around, the others giving them space and talking amongst themselves because they could sense the antagonism towards Isabel coming off Kate like black smoke. The only good thing was that Amber was hardly ever present. Hopefully before long she would be sent down, although things were so bad now Isabel doubted this would improve her situation. She must just ignore it all and carry on doing what she had come here to do, which was work. Get high marks. Distinguish herself and make Mum proud.

Isabel walked into town for the Stringer tutorial. As usual, she was alone. She was becoming used to feeling solitary, invisible even.

Passing the gates of St Alwine's, Isabel thought about Olly, as she often did. It would have been nice – especially so now – to have had him as a friend, but that was another relationship not meant to be; the first that had gone wrong, in fact. How long ago that seemed now. She wondered how he was. Had he got a job on a newspaper yet? Had his novel been accepted? She smiled, recalling some of the things he had said, and this once-familiar movement of her lips felt strange .

She glanced into St Alwine's quadrangle, screened from the street by the ancient gate, and could not help but feel a thrill at the picture presented. The college seemed to spring straight from a mediaeval manuscript. Pale spires, carved and elegant, reached up into an impossibly blue sky. There were gilded shields, mullions, stained glass and all the rest of the rich panoply of age. The trees were a blaze of copper and gold, the lawns a rich green.

A tall and beautiful blond boy was talking to a girl. His face was turned towards the street and his idle eyebeam crossed Isabel's.

She started, violently. It had been a mere split second but it was as if a flashgun had fired at her. His image was branded on her retina: the long, narrow eye, the red lip, the curving cheek faintly flushed with pink, the level brow, the golden curls.

Ears thumping, heart racing, Isabel hurried on towards the tutorial. In her dizzy state she even took a couple of wrong turns but found it at last, one of several large Victorian semis on the road to the station.

Her excitement drained from her the second she saw the English set waiting outside the house.

Kate was looking her up and down as she approached. 'I see Her Majesty Queen Amber's not with you this morning,' she observed snarkily.

As Paul and Bethany looked at her, possibly sympathetically, Isabel felt her cheeks fire up. 'No,' she said, quietly. 'I don't know where she is.'

Kate gave her a bright, sarcastic look. 'And there's me thinking you were her best friend.'

Isabel raised her chin. 'I don't know where she is,' she repeated.

Kate grinned. Delving in her backpack she produced a newspaper and shoved it at Isabel, who recognised the newspaper gossip page – recognised, too, another photograph of Amber in a tiny party dress. It appeared, from this distance, to be transparent.

'*The See-Through Ball*,' Kate said, reading from the newspaper. She looked up and her small dark eyes locked on to Isabel's. 'Everyone wore something transparent, apparently. Well I guess that's appropriate. Amber's pretty easy to see through – if you've got the brains to, that is.'

'See-Through Ball?' Bethany was pondering. 'I don't get it. What's it for?'

Kate gave her a supercilious smile. 'What are any of these events for? Charity, on the face of it. Although, of course, there's only one cause Amber's interested in: herself.'

Paul cleared his throat. 'Come on,' he said in his best head-boy voice. 'Let's go in.'

Kate knocked at the scabby front door. A skinny, black-clad

135

and heavily made-up teenage girl answered it and scowled. The group shuffled in. From the far upper regions of the house came an unearthly wailing, as if of someone in terrible pain.

'What on earth is that?' Paul asked, concerned. 'Sounds like someone's being disembowelled.'

The girl looked at him stonily. 'Mum's a violin teacher.'

Paul's hands flew to his face. 'Oh, no. Sorry.'

Lorien regarded her with friendly interest. 'Oh, so you're Dr Stringer's daughter?'

Sardonic eyes, heavily rimmed with kohl, met hers. 'Don't remind me. Dad's in there, anyway.' She waved with black-painted fingernails to a door at the end of the passage.

Someone else was coming down the stairs. Isabel glanced up at the banister, curious to see the violinist. There were footsteps, a pair of trainers appeared, then some jeans and then a face Isabel recognised.

'Olly!' she exclaimed, and felt a burst of happiness, as if somehow she had been rescued from something. 'Oh, Olly,' she added, a second later, her voice a groan of apology. 'I'm so sorry. I overslept, you know. I couldn't believe it when I woke up. You must think I'm so awful . . .'

It was difficult to go on because he was smiling at her and it made her want to burst into tears of relief. Far from looking cross, which might have been expected, Olly actually looked glad to see her. She realised how lonely she had been, how sad, how hungry for a friendly face, and the resulting wave of self-pity was hard to hold back.

Olly was delighted. He had written off his chances of ever seeing Isabel again and there had seemed no point in chasing her. He felt rather dazzled at this unexpected materialisation, not least because, probably for peace-of-mind reasons, he had forgotten just how lovely she was. She looked as beautiful as ever, although perhaps a bit paler and thinner. Working too hard, he guessed, staring like one transfixed.

'I didn't realise you were a violinist,' Isabel said, unable to suppress a deep Scottish chortle in her throat. 'And why are you wearing rubber gloves?'

He had been cleaning the bathroom. Olly stared at his hands. 'Violin?' Then, amid the confusion, the penny dropped. 'Oh, you mean the noise? That's not me. It's this poor child called Alfie Lintle.'

So thrilled had Isabel been to find a friend that she neither knew nor cared that the others were following this fascinating exchange. But now the door at the end of the passage opened and David Stringer's haunted eyes peered out above his bearded chin. 'Why don't you come up and see me afterwards? Room at the top.'

'I'd love to,' Isabel beamed at him as she followed the others through Stringer's door.

Olly used the intervening hour to prepare his room for Isabel's visit, scooping up piles of clothes, wiping the condensation off windows, straightening the duvet and, for some reason, brushing crumbs off the sheets. Realising he was doing this, he stopped, blushing. Just what did he expect? He'd asked her for a cup of tea, not full sex, and anyway she didn't fancy him. He could not allow his hopes to rise by believing what she'd said about falling asleep.

Sooner than he was expecting, footsteps were heard on the attic stairs. A rich flash of auburn poked through his doorway.

Olly imagined his room through her eyes, still looking rubbish despite his efforts. Crimson with discomfiture, he set about trying to fill the tiny plastic kettle at the equally tiny hand basin. It took an age to boil and made a fearful noise while doing so. He saw with a flash of horror that the mugs weren't clean. Hands shaking, he rinsed them in the undersized sink. They clashed deafeningly against the taps.

What was the matter with him? His heart was beating and his ears were rushing. Perhaps it was the kettle.

'How was Stringer?' he asked her in a voice strangled slightly by his contorted windpipe. At least, thanks to his efforts, the don's messy study was better than it had been.

'Freezing,' Isabel said. The expected armchairs and roaring fire were conspicuous by their absence. There had been a small and exceedingly smelly gas fire, but Stringer had been more or less sitting on top of that with the result that no one else could feel it. 'The room was so untidy it was unbelievable,' Isabel added.

Olly stared at her indignantly, his shyness evaporated. He had worked long and hard on that sitting room, peeling mouldy newspapers from the floor. He had literally gone back in time; those at the bottom concerned the Paris uprisings of 1968. 'You should have seen it before,' he said, warmly.

Oh, but she was lovely. Her profile – even against the damp patch on the wall above the bed – was exquisite. Suddenly his humble room seemed exotic, warm and alive. With her long, flowing red hair, she looked like a Pre-Raphaelite model – in the tatty studio of an impecunious artist; that bit was right, certainly.

'What's that noise?' Isabel asked, suddenly.

Olly's head was filled with nervous rushing, but he could make out a familiar, strident voice. 'It's Lorna Lintle,' he said.

'Who?'

Olly explained, and about Alfie. 'Mother love,' he said flippantly. 'It takes some strange forms.'

Isabel wondered, as often she had lately in her bleak, dark hours, about her real mother. She felt a pang so powerful she almost cried out. Fortunately, Olly did not appear to have noticed; he was still talking about poor Alfie.

'Dotty's supposed to coach him to leadership of the London Symphony Orchestra. At the very least. Preferably by the end of next week.'

Isabel giggled, perhaps harder than the remark merited, and was able to hide her red face and shining eyes that way.

The problem was, Olly explained, that, according to Dotty, Alfie wasn't really orchestra-leader material. He wasn't violinist material either, even at the most basic level, and accordingly she was trying to release him from the musical bonds he so obviously hated.

'She's trying to stop the lessons?' Isabel précised.

Olly nodded. 'But it's an upward struggle, I gather.'

The kettle had now boiled and, passing Isabel her mug of grey water in which a grey corner of teabag bobbed like a jelly fish, Olly could hear Lorna downstairs, huffily receiving the news that Alfie probably wasn't grade-one standard *quite* yet. The voices, from the landing below, floated up the attic stairs and in through Olly's half-open door.

'Why on earth not?' Lorna could be heard snapping. 'He's been having lessons for ages.'

The listeners in the attic looked at each other, then back to the half-open door. 'Wow,' Isabel whispered, wide-eyed. 'I see what you mean.'

Dotty: 'I'm, er, well, not *entirely* persuaded he's going to pass it, Mrs Lintle.'

'Dotty's being very brave, I think,' Isabel hissed.

'Well, he can keep trying until he does,' Lorna said flatly. 'Failure is not an option for Alfie. On *any front*,' she added, ominously.

'I don't think he will pass it, though. Ever.' Dotty's tone was almost pleading. 'Really, I would consider withdrawing him, Mrs Lintle. It would free up his Wednesday lunchtimes. And Friday evenings. Yours too.'

Olly could picture Lorna Lintle's pursed lips. As the pursuit of leisure time was clearly not one of her goals, she would resent any inference that it was.

'He doesn't seem to me to be enjoying it much,' Dotty added, daringly.

Isabel, listening intently, clenched a white fist. 'Go, Dotty!'

Lorna would be staring at Dotty now, Olly knew. Through those preternaturally clean wire-rimmed glasses of hers. What, she would be thinking, did enjoyment have to do with the pursuit of Art? 'Are you saying Alfie should stop his lessons?' she demanded.

'Er . . .'

'He's simply taking his time,' Lorna's voice boomed up the stairs. 'Many famous people exhibited similar traits. Did you know that Einstein was ten before he could read?'

Isabel and Olly stared at each other. 'I want to laugh,' Isabel muttered, 'but I can just imagine poor Alfie standing there staring at those dusty floorboards . . .'

'Dusty!' interjected Olly, mock-indignant.

'. . . and wanting to disappear right through them. Sssh!' she added, raising a warning white finger as Lorna started to speak again.

'So,' she concluded brightly, 'I think if you can keep faith with Alfie a little longer, you'll find it's worth it.'

'No!' Isabel urged quietly from above. 'Don't give in now, Dotty!'

But Olly, who had a better idea of the pressures his landlady was under, could almost hear Dotty's resistance flicker and die. 'OK, Mrs Lintle,' she sighed. 'I'll put him in for the exam.'

Alfie and his trials, painful though they were, had conclusively broken what ice remained between Olly and Isabel. They talked, after that, for the rest of the afternoon. Isabel, starved of conversation for what seemed like years, had endless impressions to disburse, from the rock cakes in the buttery to the mysterious Master of Branston College who nobody ever saw. Olly listened with such concentration that Isabel, interpreting his fixed expression as boredom, brought her monologue to a sudden halt. 'Just listen to me, banging on about myself non-stop.'

'It's fascinating,' Olly assured her, with perfect truth,

'But what about you?' she said, flustered. 'How's the, um, novel going?' He shook his head in comic despair.

'No one understands my genius,' he sighed, reaching into the dusty shadows under his bed and pulling out the latest handful of rejection letters. 'You're supposed to send in the first three chapters and a summary, but I'm wondering now about sending in the last three instead and working it back from there.'

'You know the ending already?' Her wide, green, disingenuous eyes, focused so intently on him, made Olly suddenly feel the world had somehow slipped a little.

No, he didn't know the ending, he said silently, passionately, back to her. This was just the beginning. Aloud he said, smiling, 'Of course. The good end happily and the bad unhappily. That—'

'Is what fiction means!' Isabel chimed in, completing the quote.

Olly looked at his watch. He was surprised to see how much of the afternoon had gone by. She would be going soon, he realised, and he didn't want her to. Yet what was there for her to stay for? Supper with David and Dotty, watching *Strictly*, or supper in the kitchen listening to them watching *Strictly*? 'Er, fancy a drink?' he suggested, standing up. 'There's a pub round the corner.'

Isabel glanced at her own watch in surprise. 'It's only five,' she pointed out.

'Exactly,' Olly said boisterously. 'Happy hour.'

'I was going to go back to the library.'

'All work and no play makes Isabel a dull girl,' Olly countered. 'Come to the pub.'

Isabel, about to refuse, hesitated. Why not? It was about time she had some fun.

'It used to be ordinary but it's been gentrified,' Olly warned as they approached the Duchess of Cambridge a couple of streets away. 'Like the woman herself, I suppose,' he added.

Isabel giggled and glanced up at the pub sign, painted with a grinning Kate Middleton, teeth blazing and dark hair flowing, accurate right down to the heavy black eye make-up.

They stood at the bar with its real ale pumps and blackboard behind featuring an array of wines by the glass. 'Pint of Pippa's Bottom, please,' Olly called to the barmaid. 'What do you fancy?' he asked, turning to Isabel.

'A glass of Chateau Carole, if that's all right. It's white, isn't it?'

'As her teeth,' the barmaid grinned.

Olly piloted her towards a distressed leather sofa overlooked by a photograph of the eponymous Duchess in a yellow dress with her skirt blowing up. Facing it was a portrait of Prince William thundering down a polo field.

A feeling of wellbeing filled Isabel. The relief and happiness of seeing Olly again kept exploding within her like small fireworks. Their reunion struck her as a small miracle.

Isabel, habitually so shy, was amazed at how much she had to talk about with this virtual stranger. Seemingly interested in her every thought and impression, he asked her endless questions. And the glasses of Chateau Carole and pints of Pippa's Bottom kept coming. 'How's the job hunt going?' Isabel eventually managed to slip in. 'Been for any more interviews?'

He had been hoping she wouldn't ask. He had kept bowling her questions partly because he was interested and partly because of the licence her answers gave him just to stare at her face. But he was also reluctant to admit his utter failure to get a job. Talking about it – even thinking about it – made him bitter, and bitterness was not, he knew, a good look.

His chest heaved in a sigh. 'Actually, since I saw you, I've been to the *Thongsbridge Gazette*, the *Cripplesease Enquirer* and the *Slack Bottom Times*. I made that last one up,' he added. 'But the others are real.'

She giggled. 'So how did they go?'

'Gone,' Olly said ruefully. Like the *Chestlock Advertiser*, and owned by the same company, both were about to go weekly and were shedding staff rather than hiring them. 'Same old story,' Olly told Isabel. 'The parent company is renegotiating parameters and streamlining their platforms.'

The newspaper-owning De Borchys, in other words, were frustrating his every move. It was hard, especially now, on his next Pippa's Bottom, not to succumb to the bitterness he felt. 'It's just so unfair,' he heard himself moaning. 'One very rich family owns all these papers and they're throwing lots of hard-working and underpaid people out of work. Meanwhile, their horrible, overprivileged sons at university throw dwarf parties and smash windows and guzzle champagne like it's going out of fashion.' He ripped open a packet of Nobby's Nuts to relieve his feelings and to stop himself ranting. He had managed at least not to mention Caspar De Borchy. He didn't intend to give that oaf the oxygen of publicity.

Isabel watched him, the ends of her mouth twitching. She recognised the reference to the Bullinger Club and remembered Ellie had said something about dwarves and strippers. As before, she only half believed it.

The Chateau Carole, slightly greenish in its chill-beaded glass, was having a soothing effect. Isabel felt very relaxed. The pub had filled up a little, although discreetly, just enough to create a pleasant surrounding buzz. The jazz soundtrack, previously decorously low, was now turned up, the barmaid keening along in a rasping approximation of Nina Simone.

'So, back to you,' Olly said, sitting back and forcing a relaxed tone into his voice. 'It's going well, you say – your first term?'

He could hardly keep his eyes from the fantastic length of her legs, the fire of her hair, those bewitching eyes.

Alone with her now, her porcelain face glowing under the soft lighting, he felt under some sort of spell.

He was glad she was happy, as Isabel had insisted she was. She had been careful to give everything an upbeat spin, emphasise the positive, much as she did to her mother. He had accepted it all, unquestioningly; for a goddess like Isabel, it made sense. Life, perforce, would be easy. Only now did he notice that she had gone rather quiet, that she had not, in fact, answered him.

'What's the matter?' he asked her gently.

Her face was twitching strangely, he noticed. He thought at first that she was laughing but then he saw that her eyes were wet and that the opposite, in fact, was the case. She was about to cry.

'Another drink?' he suggested, hastily.

Isabel made a stupendous effort to control herself. 'Oh . . . yes. Thanks. I didn't realise I'd drunk that so quickly.'

'It's the nuts,' Olly said diplomatically. He got up and went to the bar.

Left behind, Isabel stared hard at Prince William wielding his polo mallet and tried to reel herself back in. The tears had come from nowhere. Well, nowhere she had planned to talk about, anyway. But now it all came pressing in on her: Ellie's indifference; Amber's trickery; Kate's jibes. She had not, up until now, allowed herself to recognise the full extent of her misery.

'Better?' Olly said, heaving cautiously into view and proferring yet another glass of Chateau Carole.

She nodded. 'Yes . . . thanks.'

'So tell me,' Olly said, setting his pint on the table and clasping his hands. 'Tell me all about it.'

Isabel took a deep breath and told him. She was gratified to see his head shake as she described Amber.

'Awful girl,' he said.

'You think so?' Isabel was amazed that any male found Amber less than bewitching. All the boys who came to her room seemed besotted with her. 'Let me in, you gorgeous thing!' they shouted, banging on her door.

'I've had to read a lot of papers for all these interviews,' Olly explained, 'and she seems to be in all of them. All the time.'

'I can't imagine why she's here,' Isabel said, 'at university.'

Olly felt he might have an idea. He had waded through endless Sunday supplements in which people like Amber regularly featured. 'I suppose,' he said, 'that being a rich-girl model who's at a grand university distinguishes her from all those rich-girl models who aren't.'

'You may be right,' Isabel allowed. 'It seems extreme, even so. Didn't she get any attention at home or something?'

'Or homes,' Olly put in. 'I imagine she must have a few.'

'Well, she's got all the attention she could want in Branston,' Isabel said. 'The newspaper pictures of her in her underwear are

Sellotaped to almost every male student's door.'

Olly shook his head. 'How very progressive. I read somewhere she was even going to be given her own column.'

Isabel rolled her eyes. Amber's life was an endless sequence of opportunities. Exit the TV series, enter the column. How did it all happen? She remembered the shouting in the bathroom; an agent, presumably. She had never even dreamed there were students like this, so aware of their market value, so willing to exploit it. 'But what will she write a column about?' she wondered.

'Piercing political analysis, I expect.' Olly's mouth was twisted ironically. 'Or maybe the latest scientific breakthroughs.'

'Or maybe pet care,' Isabel snorted. It was an introduction; she was nearer now than she had ever been to telling anyone about the dog, its disappearance, the continuing hold over her that its absence gave Amber, the lie that Amber had made her tell. Perhaps Olly would understand, would give her absolution.

'Pet care?' Olly's shrug was kind, but she could tell he didn't think it a very good joke.

She drew back. There was no practical reason for telling him, after all. It was unlikely that he would have seen Coco. And having just found him again and re-established their relationship, perhaps even moved it on a bit, she was unwilling to risk Olly thinking badly of her. She gave one last despairing shake of her head about the column then pushed Amber and all her works determinedly out of her thoughts.

As she sipped her third – and then her fourth – glass, Isabel felt her appreciation of Olly growing. He wasn't classically handsome but his regular, blunt features were pleasant and reassuring. She liked the broad strength of his build, his open face, his large, candid eyes. Here was someone who would never treat her badly, never deceive her, never reject her. She could tell all that just by looking at him.

Outside the Duchess of Cambridge, as Olly drew her towards

him under the streetlight and began, at first with delicious deliberation, then with increasing fervency, to kiss her, Isabel surrendered enthusiastically.

Olly pulled back, battling to control the passion within. It felt like attempting to put out a house fire with a thimble, but it was the only decent thing to do. He could tell she would have surrendered, was keen to, even, but he didn't want to take advantage of a woman who was clearly tiddly and vulnerable into the bargain. The last thing Isabel needed after what she had endured was to wake up amid the crumpled sheets and condensation-soaked windows of Station Road. With a hangover, and with the likes of Alfie Lintle letting rip in the room below.

When it happened – if it happened – it should be in a scented meadow with a blue sky above, or in a punt with champagne. Although that, depressingly, was months ahead, and there was a whole winter to get through first.

'Can I see you again?' he asked her, clasping her hands fervently, as if she might slip away and be lost to him. He realised too late how formal this sounded, almost ridiculous. He felt awkward, like some sweaty curate hopelessly importuning the heroine of a Sunday-night-TV, bonnets-and-shawls drama.

Something of this had transmitted itself to Isabel. She was blushing as she collected herself. The sharp, chill air outside was sobering; she felt rather shocked as she realised how nearly, how willingly, she had surrendered herself. 'That would be very nice,' she said politely.

Then they looked at each other and giggled.

'I'll walk you back,' he said, smiling, his breath clouding in the sulphurous orange light under the lamppost.

'It's OK,' Isabel assured him. 'I'll get the bus. I came down on it.' All those hours ago, when she had felt so alone in the world. 'It goes from the end of the street.'

He walked her there instead, and the bus came almost immediately. As she disappeared up the road, a waving arm silhouetted in the mud-spattered rectangle of light at the rear of the vehicle, he walked back to the Stringers', his insides glowing with the fire of her hair, the warmth of her smile, the flash of her eyes. Was this, then, how love felt? A sort of divine central heating?

Something small and white was skittering about the front door, waiting for him. Return of the poodle, Olly thought. Escaped from the animal home, yet again. Happy from his recent experiences, ignoring the painful lessons of the past, Olly allowed himself feelings of generosity – pity, even – for a fellow creature out in the cold. He went so far as to put his hand out. 'Here. Coco.' It was Coco, wasn't it?

Seconds later, the still end-of-October air rang with his sharp, angry cry. 'You bastard!' Olly seethed. 'You're going straight back to that bloody dog pound tomorrow.'

Chapter 13

Flora Thynne had failed miserably. Richard had difficulty understanding quite how. In his experience, offering students free alcohol invariably resulted in a stampede of willing helpers. But Flora's recruitment drive for the Big Ring-Round had not produced the required result. Very few students had come forward.

Secretly, Richard blamed the fact that Flora had lobbied them all online, through their personal e-mails. He knew himself that he hardly ever bothered with e-mails from Branston College, preferring always to read ones from scientific colleagues first. And if he didn't look at them and he was the goddamn Master, why would the students bother? And that was always supposing Flora had got the e-mail addresses right, up-to-date and the rest of it. It seemed unlikely to Richard. That Flora was not a details person was obvious from her unbrushed hair.

A simple poster on the noticeboard would have been best, but both Flora and Clyde Bracegirdle had deemed this old-tech and insisted that viral approaches were better.

So much better, in fact, that the staff were now doing the Big Branston Ring-Round instead. Richard had protested at this, surely the whole point of the exercise was the eager youthful voice at the other end of the phone drawing the alumnus gently back down memory lane to golden times when the world and hope were young.

'Indeed it is,' Flora had concurred. 'But no eager youthful voices have put themselves at our disposal, unfortunately.'

There was, Richard felt, a certain grim satisfaction in the way she said this, as if she had never expected any of them to and now she had been proven right.

Each member of what Flora called 'the senior administration team' had been given a wedge of print-out bearing the names and contact details of hundreds of past students and were urged to work through it in their spare time. Richard, handed his – 'There you go, Master!' – had considered shoving it straight in the bin but the knowledge that he – and Allegra Trott – had set this whole process in train stopped him. So, OK, he would make a few calls – but no more.

As he had been given names from *S* to *W*, Richard flicked through the pages to Allegra Trott. He would start with her; Branston's new pro-active fundraising approach would presumably accord more with her swashbuckling views. She would, hopefully, hand over a fortune on the spot – the fortune she had been intending to hand over in the first place – and that would be that. Job done, Richard thought, stabbing the telephone number-pad. Then off to the labs.

The number on his list, however, connected to a secretary who explained that Allegra had left the company. She was on gardening leave and unobtainable. Branston had conclusively missed the boat.

It was not an encouraging start. But no scientist can afford to be put off by early defeat and Richard accordingly pressed on. His next call was to one Tenebris Hasp who had arrived at Branston in 1987, left three years later and was now living at an address in South London.

The phone rang and rang and Richard was just about to replace the receiver in relief when there was a crashing sound at the other end, accompanied by scrambling noises and a distant curse, as if someone had dropped the phone and snatched it up again.

'Buster, don't do that!' the someone screamed. It was a male voice, very harrassed. 'Django!' it now yelled, with the under-breath appendix, 'Oh, Christ, these kids. Buster! Django!'

'Hello?' Richard said briskly, keen to get the damn call over with. 'Is this, um, Tenebris Hasp?'

There was an intake of breath and a change of tone. 'Look, I appreciate we've slightly overborrowed but if you could just extend the overdraft again . . .'

Richard frowned. 'It's not the bank,' he said. 'I'm calling from Branston—'

Tenebris Hasp interrupted. 'Oh, piss off!' he roared into the Master's eardrum. 'Just go away!'

'I'm sorry,' Richard said stiffly. 'I can see this is a bad time.'

'I was talking to the kids,' Hasp muttered. 'They're driving me round the effing bend. My wife thinks we should home-educate them but frankly it's like trying to teach a couple of dogs to read and write . . .' He stopped himself and took another deep breath. 'Um, where were we? Oh yeah, you're my personal business advisor, right? Look, extending the overdraft wasn't the plan but the organic nappy delivery service business just didn't take off as we imagined and—'

'I'm not from the bank!' Richard shouted.

But then came another crash, more distant cursing of invisible children. Tenebris Hasp's attention was clearly else-where.

Richard had had enough. He put down the phone and shoved the alumni list aside. Grabbing his jacket from the back of his office door, he strode out into the corridor, bound for his bicycle and, afterwards, the labs. He had discovered a new short cut across the garden that would get him to the bike racks quicker. It would claw back only a few minutes of the time he had wasted, but it was something.

Diana, in the garden, was musing on her delphinium bed. It wasn't yet the time of year to plant it but she could still think about it – plan it in relation to her designs for the garden in general. She felt that her original idea for the college front was still best. There it would stand full in the sunshine, a tiara of blue flowers, their colours from palest violet to deepest indigo working wonderfully against the plain grey concrete building.

That decided, Diana walked slowly back across the lawn. She noticed a movement and glanced up to see a tall, dark-haired man about her own age coming rapidly towards her over the grass. He seemed deep in thought. Diana muttered a polite, 'Hello.' He looked up, and she was surprised to see shock flash across his face. Alarm, even.

Diana looked back at him doubtfully. Something about him was familiar but she could not place him. She came across few tall, dark, spare and supercilious men in the normal course of things. 'Hello,' she said again, doing her best to smile. 'I'm Diana Somers. I'm the Branston gardener.'

The dark and brooding brow pulled even closer together and his mouth became thinner. 'I see. Well, I'm Professor Richard Black. Master of Branston College.'

Diana recognised the voice immediately, and the abrupt manner. Here was the man she had almost collided with on her first day at Branston. Rude, Sally had said. Short, she had said too, although Diana had taken this to refer to height. Perhaps, had Sally not used that word, she might have guessed earlier. Been better prepared.

She fought to claw back lost ground. 'Perhaps,' she suggested, trying not to appear flustered, 'you'd like me to show you round the garden? Explain what it is I'm trying to do. I've just been thinking about my delphinium border . . .'

He clenched his fists, took a deep breath. 'If you must,' he growled, ungraciously.

'He *hated* all my ideas,' Diana wailed to Debs afterwards. 'He hated every single thing I was doing.'

Debs' response was to tut and hold out the plate of biscuits.

'Doesn't he like gardens?'

'Obviously not,' Diana groaned. She sniffed hard as the tears pressed her lids. He had loathed her ideas. He did not want her scented climbing roses, or the jasmine and orange blossom, which Diana had planned to cascade over the walls like a peal of bells and radiate perfume on summer evenings.

He had waved away her plans for a white border of campanula, foxglove and valerian. Her introduction of roses and primulas to the pond edge was something else he wanted to stop in its tracks. But far more hurtful even than this was his derailing of her delphiniums. It emerged that, of all the plants in world, they were his least favourite.

'So what,' Debs mused, biting into a Bourbon, 'did he want?'

Diana snorted so hard it hurt her nose. Richard Black's ideas, she explained to her neighbour, were as dark and miserable as his name. He didn't even want the bulbs she had ordered – the pheasant's-eye narcissus, the sapphire and pink-tinged hyacinth, the golden tête-à-tête. He wanted all that cancelled and a new one put in for acidic daffodils and uncompromisingly scarlet tulips, a combination reminiscent of municipal planting in the nineteen-seventies. 'The only amazing thing,' Diana groaned, 'was that he didn't ask for a floral clock.'

'Have another biscuit,' said Debs, proffering the plate.

He had gone over the top, Richard knew. He hated himself. He had been uncharitable about her ideas, downright rude in fact, and the reasons were not her fault. She could not have known that delphiniums were Amy's favourite flower and that it would be painful for him to see them. Or that anything suggestive of the planting schemes she liked – soft colours and scents – were out of the question. Brash, basic flowers were all he felt that he could bear.

He went into the hallway of the Master's Lodge, wondering, not for the first time in recent days, what was different about it. Perhaps it was that he could see. Thanks to the vine dangling over the one long, high window, entering the hall had been like entering a mine. Now, however, you could actually make things out. The white walls of the room were suffused with something soft and pink – light, basically. He could see the graphics on the cover of *Scan,* one of many neurological publications he subscribed to and which lay in its plastic wrapping on the low, modernist hall table.

Ex tenebris lux, Richard thought. Yes, someone had definitely trimmed the ivy. That woman gardener, presumably. What did she say her name was?

He stared into a corner of the newly exposed, ultra-simple sitting room fireplace, his dark brows drawn together and his long lips pressed tight. Yes, whichever way you looked at it, he had definitely been rough on that woman.

He went to the window. He could see why the newly admitted light was pink; a spectacular sunset was raging behind the darkening façades of the carved buildings, like black lace against the evening sky.

The beeches across the lawn had lost their leaves now and an explosion of fiery opal exposed the dark silhouettes of the naked tree branches. Richard thought again of his wife, who had adored rainbows and sunsets and would have loved this one, streaked and patched like a fantastical silky cloak of dusky purples, coral oranges, greeny blues and lemon yellows.

Diana. Her name slipped into his mind so suddenly it surprised him. While he knew it had emerged as a result of various neuronal and synaptic impulses, the impression lingered that someone had said it aloud. Had Amy, from wherever she was, spoken it? He blinked. But why would she? What on earth had made him think that? Was she, from wherever she now was, coming to the defence of a fellow gardener?

This was fanciful, ridiculous. He had to stop thinking like that; it would drive him round the bend. Stop thinking at all, come to that. He went into his office and tried to concentrate on his e-mails about his research, from colleagues all over the world.

But Richard was tired after a day at the lab and the letters and symbols danced meaninglessly before his eyes. The one still thing he could see was Amy's reproachful face, a ghost-memory of it, transposing itself between him and the screen. Alternating with it was Diana's, her eyes wide with disappointment as he attacked her delphinium border.

Eventually Richard stood up, walked to the window and pressed his brow to the cool lead of the panes. He had got the message. He must seek Diana out and say sorry. When he could bear to, when he had gathered the courage necessary to face her. But until then he should be more pleasant to everyone.

Chapter 14

Isabel hummed happily on her way back from the library. Since meeting Olly, the world seemed transformed, her heart immeasurably lightened. She had hardly noticed when Ellie cut her dead, as usual, when they passed in the corridor, or when Kate, also as usual, was hogging all the books she wanted. Let them carry on with their petty little girls'-school cruelties, she did not care. They could not touch her now; she had a friend. In time, perhaps, more than a friend.

She turned the corner of her corridor and viewed without interest someone trying Amber's doorknob. One of the tall, handsome boys, she registered vaguely, but she did not seek to meet yet another blank, uninterested stare. They always looked right through her, these glamorous friends of her neighbour. Not that she cared any more, of course.

All the same, as Isabel approached, she kept her eye level to his hand, a long, pale hand with a ray of light bouncing off the gleaming gold signet ring.

He turned suddenly and she glanced, involuntarily, straight at him. As he met her eyes, Isabel felt something sharp and piercing in her lower abdomen, as if a bullet was ripping through it. It was *him*: the one she had seen in the quadrangle of St Alwine's on her way to the tutorial with David Stringer.

The feeling of being dazzled came back. It was as if everything stopped – not only her breath, but time itself. There was something about this boy not entirely of this world: yellow-blond hair with a metallic gleam; broad, lean shoulders; pink-swept summits to his cheekbones. His eyes were unusually light – yellowish, even – their line and length emphasised by thick black lashes and broad, straight brows. She gazed into them, hynotised.

'Hi there,' he said, and the sound shot around the inside of her ear as if no one had ever spoken to her before.

'H-hi,' she managed in response. She knew she was staring but she could not help it. He was straight from a stately-home ceiling, the sort of figure seen writhing with gods and goddesses and lit by rays of fantastic light. Instead of a scrap of silk, he wore jeans, almost falling off his narrow hips, and a baby-pink gingham shirt tucked half in, half out.

He pushed a hand through his bright hair and took a step forward. 'You don't know where Amber is, do you?' His voice was expensive, warm and low.

Isabel shuddered, rather than spoke her negative. Her voice sounded strange to her ears. Amber could be anywhere, after all. She seemed to remember a loud, imperious voice shouting something about Paris and a private jet, although it had been the middle of the night and she could have dreamt it.

He was leaning against the corridor's exposed brick wall, arms lightly folded, looking at her. With nervous, birdlike darts of her eyes she gathered details: festival wristbands, an expensive watch. Pictures tumbled into her mind: a summer of rock concerts, nights under the stars, laughing girls with long legs, perfect teeth and shining hair. She felt a powerful twist of envy.

'Couldn't scrounge a coffee off you, could I?' he asked.

She nodded and muttered and, with a shaking hand, unlocked her door. He followed her in, his tall, lean frame stooping. He seemed to fill the room. She plugged in the kettle; the noise, as it roared to its conclusion, seemed deafening.

'I'm Jasper,' he told her. 'Jasper De Borchy.'

'Isabel.' Why was everything she said coming out in this silly, gaspy voice?

Jasper De Borchy. She knew the name. Amber's escort for the first party – the one with the silver dress. Amber's boyfriend, probably, although so many came and went it was difficult to tell and she was not in her neighbour's confidence.

What must it be like, being kissed by this god? She could not suppress the question, although it wasn't formed of words, but pictures. She looked down, chest pounding, cheeks scorched.

'You've got very beautiful hair, Isabel.'

It was an easy compliment, just a pleasantry. In her rational mind she knew this. A bit cheesy, even, possibly. But that didn't stop her looking up, red face and all, and her insides dissolving as he smiled. The sound of her name on his lips set the blood thundering round her body. Her hand shook as she measured out the Nescafé.

'Thanks,' he said, tawny eyes boring into her as he took the mug – as if he could see what she was thinking. As their fingertips touched, Isabel suppressed a shudder.

But then, through the pounding in her eardrums, came the unmistakeable, gravelly sound of Amber's voice: loud, honking and right outside the door. She was on the phone.

'Amber!' Jasper called. 'In here!'

Isabel stirred her coffee, hard, trying to stir away the wish that he had said nothing. That they had sat here in a silent conspiracy, waiting for Amber to go away again. What was the matter with her? That had never been likely.

Isabel's door slammed back on its hinges, sounding like a pistol shot. The familiar figure lounged in the doorway, face plastered in make-up, long blond hair streaming about her shoulders. 'Jasper!'

He shot to his feet, Isabel noticed longingly. A gentleman. Manners were so sexy.

Amber flung herself at him. There was a prolonged kiss, the suggestive murmur, a giggle. Isabel turned away, feeling unaccountably sick inside. What had she expected, though?

'Who were you just shouting at?' Jasper asked. Isabel, listening intently, thought he sounded amused.

'My absolutely *foul* agent,' Amber exclaimed. 'Really on my case about this hideous newspaper column; seriously wish I hadn't agreed to do it, but I've spent the money now.'

'Oh, well,' Jasper said easily. 'Plenty more where that came from.'

'Except that I've blown all my allowance already this month,' Amber groaned. 'I need to do this column, really.'

'Why? How much does it pay?'

The sum she mentioned was so incredible it made Isabel gasp.

Jasper, however, merely looked amused. 'What's this?' He pulled at the ragged hem of what was obviously yet another party dress.

Amber giggled. 'You like my shredded chiffon?'

So the dress was supposed to look like that. Isabel had assumed it was Coco's handiwork, dating from before the dog's disappearance. Even that didn't seem so terrible now, with Olly on her side.

Although, now she came to think of it, the idea of Olly seemed less wonderful than it had . . . Now that Jasper was smiling at her.

'Isabel looked after me,' he was telling Amber. 'In your absence.'

'Couldn't help it, darling. When Karl calls, we all drop everything.'

Amber, surely, had been conscious of her all along. But it was apparently only now that she really saw Isabel, really focused on her. She gave her a huge, beautiful and apparently genuine smile. 'Darling! Haven't seen you for *ages*! Where *have* you been?'

A host of caustic replies sprang to Isabel's lips.

'Come next door for a drink,' Amber commanded, cutting her off. Isabel knew she should refuse. Did she want to re-enter the web? But it took just one honey flash of Jasper's yellow eyes to change her mind.

Amber's room, as before, was a sea of shoes and dresses and the jewellery box lay upturned. Pearls were tangled in the twists of a skull-printed scarf.

Pop! A small explosion. Amber brandished a bottle, the foaming wine spilling down the gold-foil neck.

Jasper sat on the floor, his long legs crossed before him, his back against the clothes-heaped bed. His eyes were on Isabel and seemed full of suggestion, somehow. Her insides twisted in excitement.

'Here,' commanded Amber, shoving a glass at Isabel. 'Sit down,' she added, waving towards the tangle of clothes and jewellery. Isabel lowered herself, gingerly. Amber made room for herself, throwing up a pair of transparent heels and catching up a ruby bracelet on the end of one of them. It flew through the air like a ring of fire.

Isabel had gulped more of the wine than she meant to. Sheer nerves had made her do it. Now she felt giddy. The champagne had hit her empty stomach like a lit match hitting petrol. Her limbs felt shaky and her cheeks burned hot. Jasper was still looking at her, a thoughtful smile playing about his mouth. She could almost feel the little sparks of electricity jumping between them. Amber and her complaining voice seemed suddenly far away.

'And now I have to write this wretched column,' Amber was lamenting. She took another slug of champagne and plonked herself down beside Jasper, wriggling companionably beside him. They both stared at Isabel and she felt exposed, inadequate. There was something detached and pitiless about such beauty. It was like being in two very strong spotlights.

'What is it about?' Isabel asked, remembering what Olly had said about piercing political analysis and trying, suddenly, not to smile.

Amber gave a careless shrug. 'Oh, you know. My life at university.'

'But you're never at university,' Jasper pointed out, flicking a conspiratorial look at Isabel. 'You're always at parties in London.'

'That's crap!' Amber tossed her hair. 'Actually, I've just been at a shoot in Paris.'

Jasper caught Isabel's eye again. This time she smiled back, but looked down quickly. Her heart thumped in her ears.

'They're going to call it "Blue Stocking" and have a picture of my legs in navy fishnets across the top,' Amber was adding, yawning.

'Deep stuff, then,' Jasper commented teasingly. He was trying to make her laugh, Isabel knew, and she stared at the carpet, squirming with the fierce urge to oblige him.

'Fuck off,' Amber squeaked. 'My agent says this column is, like, a potential breakthrough for me. There could be a novel deal, a film deal – you name it. And there better be, after the fly-on-the-wall got—'

'Squashed?' suggested Jasper, a gleam in his yellow eyes.

Isabel felt her shoulders begin to shake.

But now Amber was laughing too. She was beaming, her eyes dancing. 'But I've just had the most wonderful idea!' she exclaimed in her throaty rasp. 'Darling, sweet, adorable Izzy, *you* could write my column for me, couldn't you?'

'What?' Isabel's ability to react quickly had deserted her, along with any idea of what to say. She looked helplessly from one to the other. 'But . . .'

'But you weren't there?' Amber supplied brightly. 'You don't live my dazzlingly exciting life? No matter, babes. I'll tell you all about it. Well – the printable bits!'

This was not the way things were meant to go at all. Isabel looked appealingly at Jasper. He could rescue her from this situation with one word. She sensed that Amber was in awe of him, his cool authority.

But Jasper's golden eyes, meeting hers, were encouraging. 'I would,' he said. 'Shut the old tart up.'

Amber squealed in mock indignation as she elbowed him, diamonds glittering on her wrist.

'But . . .' Isabel said again.

The look Amber now turned on Isabel was mournful. 'And of course,' she said, 'Coco's still missing . . .' Her face fell; she pushed out her plump lower lip.

Feeling the familiar screw turn, Isabel looked resignedly down at her hands. It's only once, she thought. And if Jasper wanted her to . . .

'OK,' she said, looking up and being rewarded by two dazzling smiles. At the exact same moment, the mobile in her bag beeped.

'Message!' Jasper said. 'Boyfriend, is it?' His eyes twinkled suggestively.

Isabel reddened – for the millionth time, it seemed. 'I don't have a boyfriend,' she muttered.

Olly was putting his suit on and thinking of Isabel. Had she got his text? he wondered. She had not yet replied; she was in the library, probably. That she was mad keen on her work was obvious. Keener than he had ever been himself. He'd been sufficiently inspired, the next day, to ask David for some tips on metaphysical poetry, which seemed Isabel's particular favourite. The deeply erotic verse his landlord had given Olly to read had intensified the situation. His ardour was now a blazing fire.

Well, he'd better forget all that for the moment. Roving hands, melting souls and all that. Today he must concentrate. He had an interview with the *Hagworthingham Chronicle,* a regional newspaper in Lincolnshire which seemed the last one in the country not to be owned by the De Borchys and therefore not about to shut down.

After slipping on his trusty suit, carefully inspecting it for marks, he went downstairs. Thumping music could be heard from Hero's room. Another day off school, he guessed. As he passed her door, he noticed the addition of a row of 'Help For Heroes' stickers and, perhaps because of this new activity – or the noise – the black and yellow radiation sign had slipped to reveal something beneath.

He peered at the small white china plaque with 'Hero' in flowing black script positioned next to a tiny pink rose. It was the sort of nameplate little girls had on their doors and this blast from the past, evidence of the child Hero had been, struck Olly as oddly moving. That she had ever been anything other than a furious black-clad teen, scowling through smoke rings, seemed incredible.

He knocked on the door, ignoring the usual obscenity. Hero was lying on the bed, as usual, staring at her laptop and smoking.

'Shouldn't you be at school?' Olly shouted through the noise and the acrid swirl of cigarettes and joss sticks.

'Whose side are you on?' Hero blasted back. 'You sound like my effing parents.'

Olly opened his mouth to say that Dotty and David did a better job of being parents than Hero did of being a daughter. He shut it again, however. It wouldn't help.

'You're wasting your education,' he told her.

'So what?' Hero returned. 'What's education ever done for you?'

'As a matter of fact,' he informed her with dignity, 'I've got an interview.'

This news was sufficiently astounding to make Hero prop herself up on one elbow. 'Really? Don't tell me,' she added scathingly. 'Editor of the *Daily Telegraph*?'

'Better than that,' Olly flipped back. 'The *Hagworthingham Chronicle*.'

Hero cackled and returned to her laptop.

Dotty was at the kitchen table, gazing into space over a coffee mug with 'Doubt Everything' printed on it. She looked as if she was taking the advice literally. Her mouth was turned down and her forehead wrinkled. She looked, most uncharacteristically, devoid of hope.

'What's up, Dotty?' Olly asked, abandoning the idea of breakfast after one look at the kitchen clock. It was later than he had thought; he would buy something at the station. 'Lintles due, are they?'

Dotty shook her head and gave a wry smile. 'Martin,' she said. Olly nodded. Martin was a management consultant: tall, middle-aged and meaty, with rimless spectacles and a bald head beneath his cycle helmet. Helmet off, he looked like a short-sighted egg. But, according to Dotty, he was as electric an interpreter of Bach as they came. He had, she added, only started playing again a year ago, after more than a decade of not even looking at his bow. It was never too late, Olly remembered her saying.

He saw her now raise her eyes to the kitchen ceiling. The thumping upstairs had intensified. 'I don't think the "Hands-Off" approach is working.'

'Poor you.' Olly began to sympathise. 'I'm sure—' he began, intending to say something comforting.

'But it doesn't matter,' Dotty cut in, with spirit. 'No,' she added, slapping the sticky pine table and standing up, 'it doesn't matter at all.' Determination flashed in her small, dark eyes.

'Doesn't it?'

'No.' Dotty's face was positively burning with resolution. 'I've got a whole new approach and I'm going to start it today. The Commando Parent.'

Olly grinned. 'You're not going to wear underwear?'

Dotty gave him a shove with something of her old high spirits. 'It means I'm in charge and I have natural authority.'

He could not help but admire her. She had persistence. 'Gosh, Dotty. You don't give up, do you?'

She looked him in the eye. 'How can I?' Dotty asked bleakly. 'She's my daughter.'

He felt suddenly, quite powerfully moved.

'Well, good luck with it, Dotty,' he said in a voice thick with emotion as he headed for the door. 'I do hope it works.'

On the way to the station, his mind went back to Isabel. He felt sure the forthcoming interview would go well, that he would finally have a job, that she was his lucky charm.

Chapter 15

The robin was back, hopping around, clockwork head jerking busily. He fixed Diana with his bright round black eye, darting forward occasionally when a tempting flash of worm revealed itself. 'You can't have them all,' Diana told him. 'They do some good work for me. Airing the soil, turning it over. Very good gardeners, worms.'

She realised, as she was speaking, that she was not alone. A pair of ankles in tan tights was standing before her. Diana looked up, heart sinking slightly. It was Sally again, the over-curious college housekeeper. She held a mug in her hand. 'As you never come in for a break,' she said, brandishing the mug, 'I thought I'd bring you one out here.'

Diana smiled up at her. 'That's very kind of you. I've got a flask –' she gestured at her backpack, somewhere in the distance – 'but thank you.'

'Fresh is better than flask,' Sally said stoutly. She dug in her apron pocket and produced a plastic-wrapped packet. 'Brought you a biscuit, too.' She held the packet out and squinted at it. 'Viennese crunch.'

'Thanks.' Diana turned back to her bulbs. Sally's ankles remained where they were, however.

'Funny bugger, isn't he? Professor Black?' Sally remarked, her tone sufficiently indulgent to arouse Diana's suspicions. She looked accusingly at Sally. 'You thought he was awful before.'

'Well he seems to be making a bit of an effort now. Bit of a charm offensive, maybe. Some of the others even think he's quite sexy.'

Despite herself, Diana made a discreet exploding noise, which could have been a cough or a disbelieving guffaw and was in fact a combination of both. She had seen the offensive. But none of the charm.

'Quite Mr Darcy-ish,' Sally was continuing.

'Mr Darcy!' Diana plunged her fork hard in the ground to relieve her feelings.

'He's quite famous you know,' Sally went cheerfully on. 'Some sort of super-scientist. The brain's his speciality, I gather.'

'Is it?' Diana murmured, wishing Sally would go. So far as she could see, the Master's speciality was rudeness.

'Of course, you know his wife died,' Sally added casually.

Diana looked up, shocked.

'Oh, yes,' Sally said, gratified by the effect and the attention. 'He lost her a couple of years ago. You didn't know, really? Dreadful. Cancer. Mmm. She was quite young, too. They met at – where was it? – Harvard, is it? She was one of his students, apparently. That's why he moved to England; couldn't bear to stay in America. We all think –' she waved a hand in the direction of Branston's concrete bulk – 'that it's quite romantic, really. Gives him that sort of sexy tragic air, doesn't it?' She paused before adding, theatrically, 'No children.'

Diana was sitting back on her wellied heels, staring. She had a sense of things whirling in the air, slowly, then settling back down in a different pattern altogether.

'I didn't know that, actually,' she admitted quietly. 'I had no idea.'

The ankles shifted. 'I'll leave you to it, then.' Bestowing upon her a conspiratorial wink, Sally went back inside.

Diana finished her digging and moved to a more secluded part of the garden between the pleached pears. She had planned clumps of hyacinths here but now, resolutely, she emptied out the bag of scorchingly scarlet tulip bulbs destined for the area instead. She handled them carefully; they were still flowers in the making.

Her mind was running on the Master. To lose your wife was a terrible thing, and to have no children, either. How alone he must feel, especially having moved continents. She at least had Rosie to show from the wreckage of her own relationship. Perhaps she should be nicer to him from now on. Rude he might be, but it was the grief speaking.

A few hundred yards away, in the Branston College development office, Richard was doing his level best to control himself. He wanted to explode with frustration, but he was fighting the urge hard.

He loathed the fact that, along with others, including the Bursar and Professor Green, he now had to sit in the development office to make the Big Ring-Round calls. And he had to do it between nine and ten in the morning, just the time he would normally be setting off for the labs. All, apparently, Clyde Bracegirdle's idea. 'He thinks that we need to create a bit of an *esprit de corps*, do it together, daily,' Flora Thynne had explained earnestly.

Flora's own contribution was some home-made scones – 'wholemeal and not too sweet' – which she placed before the telephoners with a rehashing of Napoleon's remark about armies marching on their stomachs.

Richard reflected grimly that he had never yet seen Flora pick up the phone and that marching the entire length of France, as Napoleon had, in order to re-seize a throne was nothing beside the task of working through the Branston alumni list. This, definitely, was the last time he was doing it. He would pull rank – else pull the receiver out of the wall.

Miss Sarah Salmon had been at Branston between 1984 and 1987 and was now deputy editor of a national broadsheet. Her phone was picked up by a haughty-sounding young woman who asked Richard, disdainfully, who he was. Disdainful himself, he told her; more disdainfully yet, she returned in her clipped tones, 'Miss Salmon's in conference. You'll have to call back.'

Richard marked time by phoning a few more names on the list. Graham Trowell had been at Branston thirty years ago, 'I wonder if my room's still the same,' he thought wistfully. 'There was a stain on the ceiling the exact shape of a naked woman. I used to lie there for hours looking at it.'

When Richard called Sarah Salmon back he was put straight through.

'Richard?' cooed a voice. 'So lovely to hear you.'

Richard's hopes rose. This sounded like money to him. And he wouldn't let her get away, like Allegra Trott had.

'Necker was divine this summer,' went on the voice, dripping honey, 'wasn't it?'

He had no idea what she was talking about, except that it was at cross-purposes. 'I'm Richard Black. Ringing from Branston College,' he began. Clyde had instructed, via Flora, that college staff should not give their titles. This was, Richard understood, to preserve the illusion that students were calling. Very mature ones, presuambly.

An angry exclamation from the other end. 'But Sasha told me you were Richard Branson.'

'Well, I'm not,' Richard said levelly. 'I'm Richard, *ringing* from Branston.'

'Branston?' said Sarah Salmon. She sounded choked.

He began his spiel. Flora had originally written one out on a card, but it had been so bad he preferred to improvise. 'We're doing this big fundraising ring-round. Perhaps, as such a distinguished alumnus, and possibly because you feel Branston helped get you where you are now, you might want to contribute.'

A strange sound was filling the spaces between his words. It was coming from the other end of the line. *Huh huh huh*, it was going. Richard stopped immediately. 'Sure I'll donate to Branston,' Sarah said lightly.

He need not have feared, Richard realised, satisfied. 'Well, that's great . . .' he began.

'But only,' Sarah Salmon went on, 'if the whole place is knocked flat, renamed and rebuilt in the style of the Palace of Westminster.'

She slammed the phone down after that.

Richard rose to his feet. 'That's me done. I'm going.'

He strode rapidly over the garden, his accustomed short cut towards where his bike was parked. He caught his breath and slowed down as he saw, in the distance, Diana – talking to someone.

Goddamn it, and he hadn't apologised to her yet. He hadn't seen her for a few days; he had been hoping, he realised, that she might resign before he had the chance to say sorry and save him the necessity. The instructions he had given her, after all, had obviously gone down badly. She had not complained, not in the least, but her eloquent face had said it all. She was busy, anyway. Perhaps he could sneak past, before she saw him.

Her heart was so light, Isabel thought as she wandered across the lawn, it had gone up into her throat; it was bobbing there. Was it Olly? But no – it was Jasper. At the mere thought of him she felt filled with sunshine. She felt she floated above the ground; the sky was blue; the clouds were white; everything was beautiful – even Branston's garden, which had previously looked so scabby, so unloved. No, but it had really improved. It looked attended to. Saved. Brought back to life.

And here was the gardener, a nice, smiling, friendly-looking woman.

Diana raised an earth-encrusted hand and waved. 'How's it going?' she asked the smiling red-headed girl. What a difference! She looked transformed.

The auburn hair shimmered out as Isabel happily swung it. 'Great!'

'Good for you,' Diana said warmly. The girl's shining eyes

said it all. Something good had happened, obviously. She felt relief; the girl's situation had weighed on her, she now realised. She had been actively worrying.

Isabel now noticed the robin pecking about in Diana's barrow. 'Oh! Look at him! He's so tame!'

'He's stalking me,' Diana grinned. 'Just watch this!' She bent and turned up a clod under which, as she had guessed, a fat, ribbed, shiny-pink earthworm writhed under the sudden exposure. She placed it near the robin, now watching proceedings from the safe distance of a bush. As the women watched, he hopped out, grabbed the worm and scurried away triumphantly.

'Not much of a contest,' Isabel observed. 'The worm had no idea what was happening, poor old thing.'

Diana smiled up at her. 'That's nature for you. Predator and victim.'

Isabel felt suddenly sober. Was that how it was? Did you have to be one or the other?

The bird had flown away and, as Isabel said goodbye and hurried off on pale colt legs, Diana looked after her. She was so lovely, so eager, so full of life. So happy now, obviously, thank goodness. But was there something fragile about her too?

She mused on this, sitting back on the heels of her wellies while the red net of bulbs lolled in her hands. A shadow fell over the grass, sharp and sloping in the low light, making her jump. She looked up, startled, into the sharp black eyes and closed expression of Professor Richard Black, the Master of Branston College.

'I'm sorry to disturb you,' Richard said stiffly. She looked, he realised, frankly horrified. Was he really such a monster? He felt even guiltier than he had imagined.

Diana, too, felt uncomfortable. Sally's words about his widower status burned into her memory. She was uneasy, knowing so many painful, private things. Her warm heart was already going out to him, not entirely with her permission.

'I just,' Richard struggled on, 'wanted a quick word about the garden.' He had tried to force a friendly tone in his voice, but it was coming out gnarled and strangled. Apology was not something he had much practice in or natural affinity for.

'The garden?' While her hackles had risen and her defences were up, Diana nonetheless sensed something conciliatory in his manner. She realised it was possible that his stiffness of expression was not personal coldness, only inability to communicate.

Richard cleared his throat. 'I just thought . . .' he began, then stopped. Oh, this was difficult. Why was he doing it? As his defensive instincts started to bunch together, forming the usual curtain wall, he shouldered his way through, forcing the words out. 'A misunderstanding,' he began. 'There's been a misunderstanding.'

'A misunderstanding,' Diana nodded. She wanted to encourage him, as one would a child. As she listened, a sense of unreality began to creep over her. Was he really saying that she could put in her delphinium border after all? She gazed up warily into the narrowed eyes in which something else lurked, something that she could not read. 'Really?'

He was calming down. She wasn't all that similar, up close. Her wide, clean face lacked Amy's freckles, her nose was smaller and her hair curlier, tangled, blow-away. It shone as the breeze affectionately ruffled it. So long as she did not smile, he would be OK. But how would he stop her – he was about to give her what she wanted, after all. He must keep his voice discouraging, grumpy even.

'The delphiniums?' Diana repeated. His tone was so unpromising she had to check.

'The delphiniums, yes.'

Now Diana could not help a great beam of pleasure flooding her face. He looked down, unable to bear the impact of *that smile*. She could not know the sudden stab to the heart this gave him.

'I'm so pleased,' she said, glowing. 'They'll look wonderful, I promise.'

He was talking again, in more of a rush now, as if whatever obstacle had held the words back earlier had eased itself. She frowned to follow what he was saying about having given more thought to her idea about drifts of crocuses across the lawns.

Diana butted in excitedly. 'And the roses? I'd picked some wonderful ones. Madame Hardy, Buff Beauty, Bengal Crimson, William Lobb, Pierre de Ronsard . . .' She went on, unable to stop. 'Of course, you never get more than three really perfect blooms at once, and one breath of the scent is never enough but it's just so . . .' She stopped; he was looking at her with a strange expression.

Richard blinked, brought up short. He had been watching her mouth – full, generous – and enjoying the feeling of being swept up and away in her pleasure. It was some time since he had seen a woman talk with such passion, on that particular subject.

He cleared his throat. 'Yes, roses, great, that's fine. My . . .'

No. He would not bring Amy into it. He looked at the ground, collecting himself. Resisting. He took a deep breath and looked at her. 'And I believe you had some plans for wild flowers too . . .'

The warmth of her gaze was something he could almost feel; a strange, new, sensation of heat was spreading through his insides. 'Can we walk round again?' she asked him, eagerly. 'Just to go through it again? Just to make sure?'

She had caught his arm – unconsciously, it seemed – and yet he was very conscious of it himself. Her fingers, light as they were, seemed to weigh on the outside of his fleece. 'Don't you think?' she was saying, her face turned inquiringly up to him like a flower towards the sun.

He hadn't heard a word but nodded eagerly, keen to seem all attention. Now he made himself listen, as well as look.

She was reiterating her plans. As he agreed and confirmed, Richard found himself admiring her certitude. She had a great ability to visualise. He could see, as she described it, how a sun-warmed wall to the side of the unlovely boiler room would look with honeysuckle and orange blossom tangled against it.

Diana was confused by such absolute attention. She had never known a man who followed what she said so carefully. The change, given how he had behaved before, was bewildering. He listened intently, eyes narrowed in concentration, nodding gravely, and then occasionally, and sometimes unexpectedly, smiling. There was something about his smile, Diana thought. It was slow, sensual, rather mesmerising. She could almost see what Sally had been talking about. Even if she had never particularly warmed to Mr Darcy.

'Over here I thought, by the pond,' she added hurriedly, 'we could have primulas . . . Lots of colours, quite vibrant, because reflected in the water they'll be gorgeous . . .'

Gorgeous. Yes, he thought, staring at her.

'Thank you . . .' she was saying now. Her eyes were brilliant, wide and warm.

He swallowed. 'I feel I ought to make it up to you in some way,' he said, quickly, helplessly. 'I was so rude before.'

'Oh, that.' She flashed him a smile. 'Let's forget it.'

'No, I was very rude. Completely unjustifiably.' He paused. 'Perhaps,' Richard found himself suddenly adding, 'I could take you out to dinner?'

Driving home later, with Rosie, Diana wondered if she had imagined the whole of the exchange. Had Richard Black really asked her out? She relived the conversation over and over again, Rosie's chatter going over her head. It was not until she reached home that she realised Rosie's tone had become more urgent and exclamatory.

'Oh, Mummy!' she was gasping. 'Just look!'

Mitch and Debs' house had come alive. When Debs had mentioned, casually, a day or two earlier, that they were putting up Christmas lights, Diana had envisioned a line of bulbs along the roof or around the window or doorway. The kaleidoscopic-kinetic outer carapace their home had now acquired was something she had never imagined. It was completely covered in a flashing, multicoloured framework of exuberant illumination. Outside Oxford Street or Piccadilly Circus, Diana had never seen anything quite like it. Not an undecorated inch remained. The lights were all colours, not only edging doors and windows, but arranging themselves into tableaux, spelling out messages, continually restless, flashing, rippling, strobing and pulsing. It made Diana tired to look at them.

Stars throbbed. The roofline dripped with running blue flashes. Various red-dot, rolling messages of seasonal goodwill scrolled, headline-like, endlessly along an invisible frame. A three-dimensional plastic Father Christmas, complete with sack and illuminated with an inward bulb, had been attached to the edge of the roof, apparently en route to the chimney. In the space between the sitting room and bedroom windows was a framework of lights on which a wildly flashing sleigh, complete with reindeer and crammed with presents, switched to three different succeeding positions before returning to the start of the sequence. On the wall by the front door, a pulsing Christmas tree flashed down through several diminishing, multicoloured versions of itself before beginning again.

'But,' Diana breathed, 'it's only the beginning of November.'

'Can we go round?' Rosie was pleading. 'Shanna-Mae's going to paint my nails for me.'

Diana drew in her breath, then let it out again. In the old days she would have refused without a second thought. Nine-year-old girls had no business with painted nails. But Shanna-Mae, as determined a character as her mother, intended to open her own beauty salon one day and practised on anyone who would let her. What Diana had seen of her handiwork – and face-i-work and hair-i-work, come to that – was impressive and it now it flashed through Diana's mind that she could use some of Shanna-Mae's skill with cosmetics for the forthcoming date, not to mention the cosmetics themselves. She hadn't worn make-up since the divorce.

'OK,' she said, 'but you have to do your homework before any manicures.' Especially Shanna-Mae manicures. She went the full nine yards, with crackle polish, stuck-on gemstones and the lot.

'I will,' Rosie said. 'Mrs Biggs won't let Shanna-Mae do anything before she's done hers, anyway. You know how strict she is.'

Diana grinned as she nosed the car into a parking space. Debs *was* strict, certainly. Her belief in the importance of education made her every bit as much a tiger mother as the ambitious West London women Diana had left behind.

She and Rosie went up the path to Debs' house. After the first shock, the lights were rather growing on her. That they looked cheerful there was no denying. And the successful juggling of colours and balancing of design represented, in its way, a considerable artistic triumph. It had inspired others, Diana could see. A few houses up the street, someone had created a vintage motorcar in coloured lights, its spoked wheels rolling. Someone else had a big plastic nativity scene in the front garden, glowing from within and complete with flashing halos for the Holy Family.

People had clearly been busy. But no one had reached the heights and ambition of Mitch and Debs.

'Like it?' Debs grinned, opening the door to Diana's somewhat muffled knock. It had been difficult to find a space to put her fist amid all the plastic holly.

'It's amazing,' Diana said truthfully, stepping inside, which, illuminated as it was by the one bare bulb, seemed infinitely less luxurious than the outside.

Debs explained that they budgeted all year in order to afford the electricity bill, that the vintage car two doors up had been there last year but that the nativity scene was new.

'Like to put on a good show, we do,' Debs said proudly. 'Cheers everyone up, it does. People can get low, this time of year. I like to think of it as our present to the street.'

Diana smiled, but felt inwardly slightly ashamed. The class prejudices with which she had arrived in the street had not been borne out. Life on a council estate was not in the least what she had expected. It was not as it looked in the tabloids, or on the TV news.

What she had not expected was the old-fashioned sense of community. The estate's children played outside constantly, in all weathers, watched from a distance by an informal and revolving rota of benign adults. Relations between the adults, meanwhile, were supportive. People exchanged information, ran errands for each other, helped each other out.

All this seemed amazing to Diana. Her previous experience of neighbours had been the Oopvards in London: Sara Oopvard, with her aquarium cleaner, Christmas-tree themer and Olympic-level social ambitions. She had wanted not so much to keep up with the Joneses as to annihilate them. But on the Campion Estate, the Joneses actually got helped.

Debs had offered, from the start, not only friendship and company, but help of the most generous and practical kind. If Diana was delayed at work, or in traffic, Debs would happily take Rosie home from school with Shanna-Mae. While the good words that Debs put in for her with other mothers on the Campion Estate smoothed Diana's path from the start in the school playground. She had never stood there as an awkward new mother, just as Rosie had never felt like an awkward new girl.

Diana was deeply grateful. It seemed to her that, to far greater positive effect, Debs was a social force to rival her ghastly former London neighbour, Sara Oopvard.

She did what she could in return. Mostly this was – with Rosie's help – work in Debs' garden. But, even as she dug, she was aware that there was something else Debs wanted.

While obviously curious about Diana's past, Debs' innate good manners prevented her from prying. Diana had told her little more than the fact of being divorced but, just as Debs obviously secretly longed to know all the details, Diana secretly longed to give her them, to unburden herself more fully, preferably over a glass of wine or three. Perhaps she even ought to. Only after admitting what had happened, and to someone she trusted, could she really come to terms with it and move on.

Once or twice she had been on the brink of disclosure. But then her natural caution stepped in and warned that the financial details of her divorce were too sensational not to weigh down the fragile foundations of such a short friendship.

'Wine?' Debs asked, pressing a plump finger on the tap of the wine box in the kitchen. Diana nodded gratefully. In the sitting room, Rosie and Shanna-Mae frowned over their exercise books.

'How's the love life going?' Debs wanted to know. 'Not got yourself a nice new man yet?'

Diana had not been intending to tell Debs about Richard. It was not long, after all, since she had sat in this very kitchen and excoriated him. But now she felt herself blush. And she could not, after all, keep everything secret.

Debs stared at her for a moment, then punched the air with her powerful arm. 'You've got a date? You go, girl! Who's the bloke?'

'He's called Richard,' Diana said carefully.

Debs peered at her again. 'Not him from the college!' she cackled. 'The one you said you hated?'

Diana dipped her head and stared at the floor. It did all sound rather unlikely. Ridiculous, even. Perhaps there was no point. She had nothing to talk to him about; she knew nothing about neuroscience.

'I wouldn't worry about that,' Debs said comfortably. 'He might know all about brains but you know all about gardening. Ask you a question about plants and you can go on for hours.'

'Are you saying I'm boring?'

She noticed that Debs sidestepped the question. 'Just because he's a top scientist doesn't mean he's got common sense,' her neighbour sagely added. 'Knowing your arse from your elbow, that's what matters in the end.'

'He's only asking me out because he feels guilty,' Diana fretted.

'Well, what if he is?' Debs chuckled. 'Dinner out in a fancy restaurant's my sort of guilt.'

'He didn't say it would be a fancy restaurant,' Diana pointed out.

'Bound to be,' Debs returned cheerfully. 'Master of the college. Hardly going to take you to McDonald's, is he? Probably take you somewhere new and posh.'

'Lecturer,' Diana said, having read an advertorial about it in a freesheet only that morning. It was the latest luxury boutique hotel.

Debs looked amazed. 'You didn't tell me that.'

'Tell you what?'

'That he was a lecherer. He sounded like a nice bloke.'

Later, when Rosie was in bed – newly decorated nails spread carefully out over the top of her duvet – Diana was jerked from dozing over her gardening magazine by her mobile ringing. Who could possibly be calling at this hour?

'Hello? Diana?' The voice was a woman's. Crisp, entitled and obviously used to getting its way. Diana struggled to place it.

'Sara Upward, darling.' There was an impatient note in the voice now.

Upward? Oh, Oopvard. Of course. Pronounced Upward, not inaptly. Diana narrowed her eyes. Why was she calling? Sara had cast Diana into the outer darkness, had she not?

'Hello Sara,' she said evenly, unable to resist adding, 'Long time no hear.'

'Sweet one, I've been longing to get in touch but I lost your number,' Sara cooed, not particularly convincingly. 'But let me get to the point— Oh, that's the doorbell . . . Give me two secs, will you, darling, while I find someone to open it . . .'

Diana imagined her former neighbour clacking about her gracious home in her high heels, checking her extensively remodelled face in any one of many large mirrors as she sought one of her numerous domestic helpers.

Sara's voice – high-pitched and breathy but with unmistakeable steel beneath – came back to the phone.

'So, Diana, darling. Congratulate me. I'm a free woman.'

Diana considered this. It was not entirely clear what was meant. Free, certainly, is not how Henrik would describe his very expensive wife. Then, a shaft of insight. Surely not, though? 'You're leaving Henrik?'

The golden goose? Henrik looked like a goose, now Diana came to think of it – pale, and with a long neck. For Sara to leave him was unexpected, even so.

'No, Henrik's leaving me, which is much better.' The voice on the other end was loudly exultant.

'But why?'

Sara sniffed. 'Turned out he was putting rather more than messages into the inbox of a certain female colleague. But who cares? It's all worked out wonderfully. My lawyer's squeezed poor old Henny till the pips squeak. I've got the house and everything. Oh, and Milo,' she added, the joy draining suddenly from her tone.

'How is Milo?' It seemed unlikely that time and circumstance had improved him.

'He's nine now,' Sara said briskly, 'and I want him to focus on where he's going in life.'

Does anyone, at the age of nine, know where they're going in life? Diana was about to say. The idea seemed preposterous. But then she stopped herself and asked, instead, 'How do you mean?'

'Well, obviously, after Smart's he'll be going to St Paul's. Or Westminster,' Sara announced confidently. 'And one of our ancient universities after that. So I just wanted to show him one, you know. Focus him a bit. So that's why I thought we might come and see you. Stay for a few days. Have a look round.'

Diana's heart sank. She had better things to do than waste her time being Sara Oopvard's tour guide. She determined to brush off the responsibility. This woman had done nothing to help her, after all. 'You want me to recommend some hotels?'

'Of course not!' Sara trilled. 'We want to come and stay with you. Catch up! It's been ages! Milo's missed Rosie so much!'

Diana blinked. Sara Oopvard, chatelaine of one of the finest houses in one of West London's most expensive areas, wanted to come to her council estate? Surely not. The idea was ludicrous. Perhaps she had the address and thought she lived on another sort of estate: one with a long, tree-lined driveway and stables.

Then Diana remembered how mean Sara was. Gnats' arses had nothing on the grasp she had on the Oopvard finances. Diana almost felt sorry for Henrik. Experienced on the international money markets he may be, but there would only be one winner on the domestic front.

'So, if you could put us up for a bit, that would be great,' Sara pressed.

Diana struggled for the words. 'Look, Sara, honestly, I don't have the room . . .'

'We'll squash in with you! We love to be cosy!'

'A hotel would be better,' Diana insisted. 'There's a new one just opened, a boutique one, called Lecturer . . .' She enunciated the name carefully. It really wasn't a brilliant one for a restaurant, even one in a university town.

'Boutique hotels are out,' Sara cut in. 'I'm a divorcée now, after all. Have to watch the pennies. *You* know all about that, of course . . .'

Diana let this pass. 'When are you coming?' she sighed. She was tired; she accepted the inevitable. She knew Sara Oopvard of old. Even if she, Diana, refused, Sara would still turn up. The brass areas of Sara's anatomy were not confined to the neck. She had a brass everything.

Chapter 16

The Hagworthingham Chronicle had been a disappointment. Yet another waste of time, Olly felt. He had been told by the interviewing panel – specifically, a pompous, brassy blonde in a too-tight dress – that a great many well-qualified people had also applied for the position and that it was therefore unlikely he would get through to the next stage. Should that be the case, he would be contacted by letter. He was already sure, as he left, that he would not be.

It was hard not to feel bitter. Especially as the newspapers he had read on the way to the interview seemed full of the by-lines of former student contemporaries. And most papers that morning had run in their diary column the fact that Jasper De Borchy – despite the fact he was supposed to be studying at a university some hundred miles to the north – had been voted, at a recent gathering of great social minds, London's most eligible male. He had, naturally, been accompanied on this auspicious occasion by Amber Piggott.

Olly had glared at the accompanying photograph of the handsome, self-satisfied face. 'Currently setting all undergraduette hearts aflame,' read the sidebar. 'And setting other things aflame as well, if the club of which Jasper is a member – the university's exclusive Bullinger Club – is living up to its notoriously destructive reputation.'

Olly soothed his ragged nerves by thinking about Isabel.

Jasper De Borchy might have looks, money and influence. But he didn't know Isabel. She was, Olly felt, and despite the *Hagworthingham* setback, his guiding star, so cheerful a prospect it was impossible to feel depressed. He had texted her a few times, hoping to meet up when he got back, but she had not yet replied. Possibly her mobile had run out of juice. Or she had lost it. He would go up to Branston tomorrow, Olly decided happily. Cut out the middleman. Much better to see her in the flesh, anyway – and what flesh it was!

In the meantime, tonight, he would make good use of his time. Get on the internet. Start looking again for a job.

It was raining and Olly's suit was wrinkled and soaking by the time he got home. He winced at the thought of dry-cleaning costs. Not that he was likely to be recalled to the presence of the pompous, brassy blonde.

The house, when he let himself in, seemed oddly silent. He had the distinct feeling there had just been a row; there was a still-ringing quality to the quiet, as if the shouting had only just stopped. Even Hero's music was not thumping as usual. He crept upstairs, not wanting to disturb the peace he imagined had only just fallen. Although now, as he approached his room, he could hear a noise: behind Dotty's music-room door, a softly keening violin was winding up into the cold air of the staircase. It sounded sad; he wanted to burst in, share with Dotty some of his own good cheer. But perhaps he should leave her to herself; besides, he was soaked through.

He shrugged off his wet clothes, unable quite to rid himself of the sense that someone had been in his room in his absence. Yes. His laptop was missing. Suspecting Hero, Olly immediately went down and banged on her door.

She was on Twitter, as usual, sitting cross-legged on her black-covered bed, tapping the keys with long black nails. The light from the screen glowed blue on her dead-white face.

'Who are you following?' He could not help but be interested. She looked so intent.

'I told you. Amber Piggott. And her friends.'

'You're wasting your time,' Olly told her. 'On my bloody laptop, as well. Where's yours, anyway?' Hers was much better, after all.

The panda eyes narrowed and the black-painted mouth twisted. 'She –' Olly knew this meant Dotty – 'threw it out of the window.'

'That window?' he glanced at the window of Hero's bedroom, or the eternally drawn, black curtains, which covered where the window must be. He had never actually seen it. But it was there; he could hear the rain hurling itself against the glass like a handful of pebbles.

'No, the kitchen one,' Hero said sullenly.

'Why?'

'Said I shouldn't tweet at the table. Just eat.'

'Well, good for her,' Olly said, taking his laptop and turning to leave for the fresher air of the landing.

'Whose side are you on?' Hero shouted furiously after him as he closed the door.

Olly was nonplussed. He did not recall ever telling Hero she could use his laptop. He carried on downstairs. He was hungry; he had a packet of noodles somewhere and a couple of cans of lager that had been on special offer at the corner shop. A modest feast indeed, but the thought was unexpectedly cheering. He felt, at the moment, that nothing could depress his spirits.

A noise in the hall made him glance down. His eyes met the top of Dotty's magenta beret and a shabby black and white tweed coat with big black plastic buttons down the front and on the epaulettes. David, opening the front door, looked strained and dishevelled in a creased navy cagoule.

'You going out?' Olly asked. 'In this weather?'

Dotty tipped her face upwards and gave him a smile that barely struggled past her nostrils. 'Parents' evening at the school,' she said, with a little twitching movement of her lips.

Olly now realised what the feeling of dreadful doom was all

about. And the rows. Perhaps they'd decided to have them in advance, get them over with. Or they might have been a warm-up.

'Good luck,' he said, sincerely. 'Still being a commando parent, Dotty?'

She raised doleful eyebrows. 'I'm leaning towards being a cheerleader one now,' she said wistfully. 'It's all about praising your child's achievements.'

'What achievements?' David groaned from the doorway.

Dotty turned on him furiously. 'Your negative mindset hardly helps, David.'

He held up both palms in a gesture of defeat. 'Look, can we just go and get it over with?'

Like condemned men, they went out into the rain.

Olly ate, drank and went back upstairs. He looked for jobs on various websites. One site, SkintStudent.com, offered to match the person to the job and Olly typed in his details, citing 'Desperately' and 'Anything' in the fields for how much you wanted work and what you were prepared to do. The match it made for Olly was with something called Petting Zoo. It supplied animals to children's parties and required handlers. No experience was necessary, as full training would be given. Due to what was described as a temporary technical hitch, there were no pictures and Olly, typing in his details in the 'Fancy A Job With Us?' bit, imagined rabbits and white mice.

This done, he went down for another beer and was rootling in the alien glow of the open fridge when, from the distance of the hall, the outside door banged.

This was followed by the bang of the sitting-room door as Hero, who, in the absence of a laptop, had made a rare trip downstairs to watch the telly and had been immersed in some gloomy Scandinavian murder mystery all evening, shot back up to her room.

David, his face ashen, stomped into the kitchen.

'How did parents' evening go?' Olly inquired as he peeled the tab off a lager can. A surge of foam shot out and ran coldly over his fingers.

In reply, David just stared at him with haunted eyes. Olly raised the can. 'Want one of these?'

With a sort of strangled growl, David shook his head and lunged for the cereal cupboard, at the back of which, Olly knew, reposed the whisky bottle.

Dotty came into the kitchen now, looking distraught. She said nothing to Olly, just dragged out a chair with a screech of legs on floor, sat down hard and covered her face with her hands. Olly diplomatically left the kitchen. He did not want to intrude on private grief.

'No time like the present,' Amber had said, as Jasper, with one last look at Isabel, had drifted out. 'Let's get the wretched thing over with.'

This was the introduction to hours of work on Amber's column. The first item was the award for London's most eligible singletons, which Jasper had won.

'I'm sure that won't surprise you,' Amber had said, glancing slyly at Isabel from the bed where she lay dictating.

Isabel said nothing. She wondered why Jasper wasted his time in this way; on the other hand, Amber could be difficult to resist and perhaps they were a couple, they certainly looked right together, although the situation was otherwise hard to read. But the real surprise, Isabel felt, was the amazing extent of Amber's extracurricular activities. She hardly ever seemed to be in college. University was, of course, designed so people could run their own lives: enormous freedom combined with relatively few formal obligations. But even so, Amber seemed to be pushing it.

In the past seven days she had topless-modelled jewels for an in-flight magazine and been to Paris and Venice. She seemed to use private jets like other people used buses. 'You bet!' Amber crowed when she mentioned this. 'The first time we flew scheduled, I turned to my mother and asked her who all the other people on the plane were.' Hysterical laughter followed this witticism.

'Shouldn't your PR be doing some of this?' Isabel asked when, after the column had been sent to the appropriate newspaper supplement, Amber rounded off the session by demanding Isabel tweet for her.

'Probably, but she's sacked me,' Amber said carelessly. She looked up and gave Isabel a bright smile. 'But now I've got you!'

Isabel felt a sort of panic rising. 'Look, Amber, I can't do any more for you. I've got essays . . .'

'Don't tell me about it!' Amber groaned. Her expression became speculative. 'You couldn't run up a couple for me while you're doing yours, could you?' She pushed out an entreating lower lip. 'I'm getting some *vewy cwoss* letters from the English Faculty.'

Isabel felt something in her snap. She remembered Olly's warning about not allowing Amber to exploit her. Olly. He had been sending texts like crazy. She must reply, see him again, although possibly she might not mention the afternoon's activities. He was certain not to approve.

'I'm sorry,' she muttered. 'It's out of the question, Amber. I simply don't have the time.'

She had expected Amber's face to change to thwarted fury, not the ecstatic delight she now saw registering on her adversary's perfect features. But Amber's eyes, Isabel realised, were focused elsewhere, on someone who was apparently behind Isabel in the doorway.

'Jasper!'

He was back. Isabel could not look. The merest glance would betray her, she knew. He stepped into the room; his mere proximity made her stomach flip over.

'Finished?' he asked.

'Not quite,' Amber huffed. 'Izzy doesn't want to do any more. I asked her for just a tiny wee bit of help with some ickle essays but she says, "No, No, No . . ."' She stuck out her lower lip, either in a parody of babyish behaviour or babyish behaviour in reality; it was not clear which.

Isabel looked at him, her gaze guilty yet pleading for understanding. He *couldn't* want her to do all Amber's work for her. He *must* be able to see how unfair it was. His answering gaze was level, however. Not quite critical, but not exonerating either.

'Izzy!' he said, softly chiding. 'Surely you can help Amber a little bit? We don't want her to be sent down now, do we?'

Isabel felt suddenly helpless. She wanted to please him more than anything else in the world. Olly and his warnings melted away, then dried up completely in the overwhelming blaze of heat and light that was Jasper.

She turned slowly to Amber. 'OK. I can help you with the next couple. But no more.'

Jasper was beaming at her; she felt a powerful burst of happiness. She decided, all the same, to get out of the room before she agreed to anything else. She rose to her feet, stumbling slightly, and muttered her farewells. Amber merely tossed her hair; that she had already banked the favour was obvious.

Outside the door, fighting an overwhelming sense of being exploited, Isabel realised she was not alone. Jasper had followed her; he was standing close, looking down at her.

'Are you free on Saturday night?'

She stared at him in spellbound surprise. Was he asking her out on a date? But . . . were not Jasper and Amber a couple?

There was an expression in Jasper's lingering, golden-syrup eyes that suggested otherwise. Or at least that things were less cut and dried than might be supposed.

She looked away. Looking at him was like looking at the sun. It made her want to screw up her eyes. She found her voice at last. 'Yes.'

'I'll see you then,' he smiled. 'Meet you outside the main entrance, seven-ish.'

'Branston?' Isabel croaked.

'Oh, sorry. My college, I meant. St Wino's.'

Isabel felt a faint twist of disappointment. The delicious vision of both Kate and Ellie watching as she tripped off on the arm of the gorgeous Jasper had leapt to mind. But it was not to be. Then something else he had said filtered through.

'St Wino's?' She frowned. 'Is that what you call St Alwine's?'

He grinned. 'My dear innocent, it's what everybody calls it. On account of the *outrageous* decadence of its inhabitants!'

She wasn't sure whether he was joking, nor did she care. A slow smile was spreading along Jasper's mouth like a spark along a fuse.

Isabel's whole body felt rigid with the promise in this smile: a sensual, silent promise. She felt she could not wait for Saturday.

Olly felt restless and worried. It was Isabel's fault.

It was Saturday; he had expected to fix up a date with her by now, but she had not been in touch. Her failure to reply to any of his text messages was making him jumpy. She could be vague, of course – falling asleep and the rest of it – and the mostly likely explanation was that she had lost her mobile. But the possibility that she no longer wanted to see him could not be discounted either. She had form, after all, in that respect.

And yet, Olly told himself, she had seemed keen enough outside the Duchess of Cambridge. Would he have been quite so much of a gentleman had he known he would only get one chance?

The week wearing on without any contact wore down his confidence. He shelved his plans to surprise-visit her at Branston. She would have a supervision with David Stringer next week; she would come to the house. He would see her then, but he had not imagined having to wait that long.

He thought the same thoughts so often, he imagined their well-polished grooves in his brain. Was Isabel testing him? She had not seemed the tricksy sort. But, of course, you never knew with women. He tried to tell himself that, given his impecunious circumstances, there were advantages to the delay, if delay it was.

He would have taken her somewhere smart, somewhere spoiling.

But now, instead, he would have to satisfy himself with a trip to the High Street. One or other of the posh men's shops was sure to be having some sort of sale.

He needed a new shirt, desperately. His old ones were either worn out or bore the unmistakeable after-effects of Dotty's attempts at laundry. In the unlikely event that he got asked to another interview, they would lose him the job before he opened his mouth and lost it himself – always supposing it hadn't been lost before he got there, by another De Borchy platform-restructuring.

The employment outlook was truly dire. The few savings Olly had were by now almost exhausted and, as the bank of Mum and Dad had stepped up to the plate yet again in the past week, he dared not ask them for more. The hundred-pound cheque that had arrived, unexpectedly, from his father had touched Olly more than he could say, although he had tried to say it in his thank-you letter. 'Got a few irons in the fire,' he had also lied cheerily. It was, he knew, what they wanted to hear.

Preoccupied with these thoughts, going down the stairs, Olly spotted Hero drifting back to her room from the bathroom. As usual, and despite his low spirits, he felt the urge to laugh. There was, to him, something inherently comic about Hero's teenage fierceness and the seriousness with which she took herself.

'A rare sighting outside the natural habitat,' Olly intoned now in a mock-David Attenborough voice.

Hero, outraged, whirled round and scowled at him. Outside the confines of her bedroom, in the more everyday surroundings of the landing, her eyes looked blacker and her face whiter than ever.

'You could do with some fresh air,' Olly told her. 'Come into town and help me choose a shirt. You're not doing anything else, are you?' It was Saturday, so no school, not that that was usually a consideration with Hero of course.

It seemed to Olly that, since the parents' evening, Dotty and

David had given up on their daughter. They had stopped nagging her about her education and and had, it seemed, given up on the idea that she should eat with them even occasionally. Whenever they coincided in the kitchen these days, no-one spoke. A pall of despair seemed to hang over the house. Olly wished he could do something about it. He had tried. But his efforts always failed, as they were doing now.

'Piss off,' Hero said, consigning his latest diplomatic effort to the dust, 'I don't want to be your personal shopper, OK? I hate shopping. Retail's a conspiracy to disempower the proletariat.'

Olly sighed. 'Do you hate absolutely everything?'

Hero answered in the affirmative.

'Even your parents?'

Hero's eyes flashed. '*Especially* them.'

'You quite like that dog, don't you, though?'

Coco had been back and forth from the animal shelter to Station Road several times in the last few weeks. Hero now wanted to adopt it but Dotty – showing rare determination – had drawn the line, saying that a dog was the last thing the family needed, and why it was drawn to one as blighted as theirs, she could not imagine.

'The dog's all right,' Hero conceded, twisting the handle of her door and stepping back into the dark.

The day outside was rich and golden. It seemed such a shame to miss it. At the very least Hero could do with the vitamin D. 'Oh come on,' Olly cajoled. 'It's cold, but it's a nice day.'

'Not for me, it isn't,' Hero snapped back. 'Why are you so cheerful, anyway? The ecosystem's fucked, the bankers have everyone by the balls, mad dictators are developing nuclear weapons. What's good about anything?'

'Love?' Olly asked, intending to shock her by giving vent to the subject most on his mind. He had meant to sound ironic, or at best ambiguous, but it came out sounding incriminatingly sincere.

Hero stared at him in malicious delight. 'Love!' she repeated, her black lip a curl of contempt. 'You mean *you're* in love?'

'I might be,' Olly said, embarrassed at his outburst but sticking to his guns nonetheless. 'And what if I was? At least it would be real, with an actual person, rather than just one out there in cyberspace.'

'Think so, do you?' Hero flashed back. 'What's so real about real people, anyway? You never really know someone, not their innermost thoughts. Why's that so different from following some illusion on the internet?'

So amazed was Olly at this evidence of profundity that he could not, for a second, frame a reply. The reflection that eventually made it through the backwash of surprise was that love was the main reason Hero's parents tolerated her appalling behaviour and there was nothing illusory about that. But it was all, Olly decided, getting a little heavy. He'd only asked her to go shopping, after all.

'You know, Hero –' he grinned as he continued down the stairs – 'you're quite pretty under all that black make-up and scowling. If you smiled, you'd make someone a lovely girlfriend.'

His answer was Hero slamming her bedroom door behind her.

Half an hour later, Olly was shopping in earnest. It was only November, still, but Christmas had well and truly arrived on the High Street. Tinsel and baubles coiled loosely round the packets of shirts in the windows, and the shirts themselves had a festive slant: horrid, shiny grey tight-fitting ones, with contrasting black collars, suitable for the office stud; crazy stripes for the firm's clown. And, to go with them, novelty cufflinks featuring tiny enamel Minis, Union Jacks, pints of beer, even women's breasts and bottoms. It was, Olly thought, the type of crass sexism the Bullinger Club thought amusing. He turned away. None of this was any use to him.

He wandered into the shopping centre where Slade was,

somewhat inevitably, raucously inquiring of everybody whether they were hanging up their stockings on the wall. As always, and despite his efforts not to notice the lyrics, Olly was struck by the suggestion. As a child, he had left a rugby sock at the end of the bed on Christmas Eve. His father would have been furious if, as the song seemed to be suggesting, he'd hammered it into the wallpaper.

The shopping centre was festooned with lengths of pine needle-effect rope: fat, green, sprinkled with berries and sprayed with artificial snow. Dangling on it and among it were oversized gold and red baubles. The Tannoy music changed to the nervy, repetitive electric piano introducing Paul McCartney's 'Wonderful Christmastime'.

Beneath the shopping centre's transept, the point at which its horizontal arms crossed with its vertical length, a number of living statues stood on polystyrene plinths of varying sizes. There was a centurion, a chicken, Queen Elizabeth II, Tutankhamun, Shakespeare and Elvis in sunglasses.

Olly had seen some of them around the town before, but all in separate places. Presumably they were all together under the shopping centre's seventies glass roof because of the cold outside. They made an odd sight; like, Olly thought, a line-up from one of those 'My Ideal Dinner Party' articles in which barely literate stars of reality TV told magazines they'd love to eat with Einstein and Julius Caesar.

Even so, Olly felt sorry for the statues. You must have to be really desperate to do that, and he could identify with desperation at the moment. He decided, in a spirit of seasonal generosity, to slip a few quid to the one he considered the best.

Tutankhamun, it had to be said, did not enjoy this distinction. He was swathed in shiny gold nylon and topped with a spectacularly poor reproduction of the teenage Pharaoh's famous death mask. Almost as bad was the Shakespeare 'statue'. Its clothes were caked all over with cracked grey paint, to resemble stone presumably, and it wore a grey plastic mask. 'The Queen's resemblance to her original, meanwhile, depended largely on a large white plastic handbag. Olly eventually decided to drop his two-pound coin into the terracotta dish at Elvis's blue-suede-shod feet. He, at least, was still. The Shakespeare, by contrast, was twitching all over the place. In response, the King bowed gravely in his direction.

'*Bastard*!' Olly now heard. A snarled whisper, coming somewhere from behind: '*Bastard*!'

Were they talking to him? Olly looked round. The crowds were passing through the shopping centre: families, gangs of girls, pairs of women chuckling ruefully to each other as they staggered along with several bags on each arm. No one was looking at him.

'*Bastard*!' the voice said again.

Olly realised now that the Shakespeare figure was beckoning to him. He went over. The Bard had climbed down from his plinth and was stepping out of his paint-stiffened breeches in front of Costa Coffee. As the grey plastic mask was lifted, Olly recognised the flushed face in surprise. Sam Bradbourne had been one of the more talented of the student historians in his faculty group. Had Olly thought about it – which, until now, he hadn't – he would have imagined Sam, after taking his first-class degree, waltzing straight into some well-paid academic position.

When, awkwardly, he said this, Sam snorted in an exasperated sort of way. He had thought that too, but it hadn't worked out like that. Didn't Olly know there was a recession on? Hadn't he heard about education cuts? 'And why didn't you put your bloody money into my pot?' he added crossly, emptying the plastic cup containing his takings into his hand. 'Fifteen bloody pounds and twelve pence. For four hours' work!' He shook his head despairingly. 'I knew I shouldn't have come in here. Too much competition from the others. That Elvis is a bastard. Whenever anyone's looking at you he wiggles his hips and gets all the attention.'

Olly chortled, then realised Sam hadn't meant to amuse. On

the contrary, he was looking at him bleakly. 'It's not really how I imagined,' Sam said. 'I thought I'd be at Harvard or somewhere by now, but instead I'm in a shopping centre in a pair of second-hand breeches riddled with fleas. And when I'm not doing that . . .'

Olly now listened as Sam described his other job. He worked in a tiny café down one of the town's more ancient and dark passageways. His area of responsibility was egg-mayonnaise sandwiches. Sam disliked eggs and his antipathy had only increased since being obliged to spend the mornings boiling enormous numbers of them and mashing up the results with a fork.

'Oh dear,' said Olly sympathetically. He wasn't especially fond of egg mayo himself.

'That's not all,' Sam said darkly. The café owner was a fanciful woman who believed that everyone was surrounded by different-coloured fairies, or auras. 'They look like small balls which float around people's heads. They're coloured depending on what sort of person you are. *Apparently,*' Sam added, heavily.

'Coloured?' Olly queried. He knew it was irrelevant but he had never seen that as a reason not to be interested in something. Perhaps that was where he had gone wrong.

'Well, bad-tempered people have black ones and happy people have pink ones,' Sam went on, with an ironic emphasis on the happy bit, as if this was never likely to apply in his case. 'Sad people have blue ones. *Very* dark blue ones in my case, she says.'

'Wow,' said Olly. 'That's crazy.'

The other shrugged. 'But it's a port in a storm, admittedly a sulphurous one. And it's better than working at a call centre.'

A flash of suspicion shot over Sam's face as he looked Olly up and down. 'Don't tell me *you're* a merchant banker or got a newspaper column or a part in a Hollywood film. I'll bloody kill you.'

Olly swiftly confirmed that he wasn't any of these, least of all the middle one. At the mention of the De Borchy family and its part in Olly's downfall, Sam pulled a face. 'Don't tell me. I've just seen Jasper De Borchy drifting past.'

'Caspar?'

'Jasper. The younger one. De Borchy minor.'

'I've never seen him,' Olly remarked, although of course he had felt his influence; that of the whole family, squatting like toads on his future.

'He's not a sweaty, purple-faced hog like Caspar. He's blond and sickeningly good-looking. Entertainments officer for the Bullinger, apparently.'

Olly pulled a face. 'Strippers,' he said. 'Dwarves.'

'And the rest,' Sam said. 'The word in the living-statue community is that things have gone up a gear under De Borchy minor. Nazis, dwarves, girls leaping out of cakes – you name it.'

'How do you know?' Olly was curious. Sam had been less gregarious than himself as a student. He had certainly not moved in the charmed and gilded circles of people like the De Borchys.

Sam waved a hand at his immobile colleagues. 'They're asked to do parties sometimes. There was a Bullinger one recently where they wanted the Queen in the nude.' He nodded at Elizabeth II.

'I was, how you say, not being amusing,' Her Majesty remarked in a strong Eastern European accent.

Olly glanced up at the shopping-centre clock. The afternoon was slipping away and he still hadn't bought his shirt.

'See you around,' Sam said. 'Well, you might be around,' he corrected himself. 'I tend to stay still, as you can see.'

As Olly walked off, a child was squirting Her Majesty with a water pistol and a tramp was installing himself at the foot of Elvis's plinth.

He went back out on to the High Street and started looking at shirts again. He had spotted nothing so far that would perform the three functions of improving his appearance, getting him a job and – should the opportunity arise – impressing Isabel. It seemed, suddenly, a fiendishly difficult choice to make. A white shirt might be a bit waiter-ish. While a striped one was a bit City-ish, a bit Bullinger, altogether too Jasper De Borchy. He sounded horrendous, Olly thought. Even worse than his brother, if that were possible.

He turned away from the window and looked down the busy street. The Christmas crowds were thicker than ever, a purse-bearing, bag-barging, shoulder-shoving, toe-treading river. Among the heaving mass he thought he recognised something. Someone. A flash of red hair. A glimpse of white cheek. Isabel! He felt a powerful leap of delight. Something beautiful amid all this tawdry grabbery; something he knew – and loved.

He stepped out to flag her down, calling her name. Her face, as she spotted him, seemed to flex in shock. He had expected a smile. Dismay filled him, but then understanding hit like a thunderbolt.

Something had happened. Something untoward. With powerful determination he shouldered his way through the crowds to her side.

'Olly!' Her voice was pitched artificially, nervously high. Her wide green eyes scanned his, her mouth stretched in something midway between a smile and a grimace. Her narrow body strained away as he held her thin shoulders in a greeting; her cheekbone hit his chin as he kissed her. He had the strangest feeling that she wanted to run away.

'Is everything OK? You haven't answered my texts,' he said solicitously, inviting her to confide all.

She seemed to draw in a huge breath at this, as if steeling herself to say something considerable. For a moment he held his breath too.

But all she said was, 'Sorry. I meant to. Been a bit, um, busy.'

It was as if, he thought, they had hardly met. And that hardly-meeting had been years ago. No one watching them would believe they had spent hours talking in his bedroom just days ago. And then gone to the pub, where she had all but begged him to sleep with her. Looking at her downcast face, he could hardly believe it himself.

He wondered if she was embarrassed. She was biting her lip awkwardly, avoiding his eye quite obviously. But she had done nothing to be embarrassed about – largely thanks to him. Or did she think he had rejected her? Women! Olly thought, with a flicker of exasperation. You were damned if you did and even more so, it seemed, if you didn't.

He must move to eradicate doubts, eliminate the lingering uncertainty with one brilliant blast of positivity. He fixed on her a radiant smile. 'I'm so glad to see you. The other night, in the pub – it was brilliant. I was hoping I'd see you again.'

She did not react. Perhaps she had misunderstood.

'I mean, not just see you, obviously I'm seeing you now,' he gabbled on. 'I mean, see you as in –' he shrugged – '*see* you.' He sounded like an idiot. He turned out his palms in appeal. She must have got the message, however imperfectly expressed.

She said nothing.

'If you wanted to,' he added, penitently.

Isabel looked up. Her large white front teeth were still pressed into her pillowy lower lip. 'Oh, Olly,' she said. 'I can't. I'm sorry.'

The world reeled. He recognised how much he had depended on a 'yes' from her. How all else was an abyss, the darkness. 'Can't?' He blinked, rapidly, helplessly.

She did not elaborate. Her glance slid away, back down to the pavement.

Olly picked himself up and prepared for another effort. 'Did I do something wrong?' His voice sounded, he knew, plaintive. But he couldn't help that. He felt plaintive. He was panicking.

Her narrow chest raised itself in a sigh. 'It's, um, work,' she said vaguely. Still she was not looking at him.

He seized on it in violent relief. Work, after all, was not another person – someone else who had caught her eye. Although, was that likely, in such a short time? He sought to calm himself.

'Work?' he repeated, in as level a voice as he could manage.

The shining red hair nodded. Small curls at the end were thrown about. 'Essay crisis.'

He looked at her in anguish, plunged once more into doubt. He had believed work, but not this detail. For Isabel to have essay crises was uncharacteristic. She was much too meticulous, dedicated and well organised. It was something else, he was sure now – surer than before. He must talk to her, find out what.

'Come for a coffee?' he pleaded.

She turned to him, half her face hidden behind a fall of hair. 'Olly, I'm sorry. I can't miss this next tutorial.'

'With David?' He snatched at the possibility. They could walk back to the house together.

'With Professor Green.' It was, Isabel felt, frightening how easily lying came to her. She had hardly ever told an untruth before but this was the fifth in as many utterances.

Guilt churned within her as she saw how she was hurting him. Olly was shaking his head, smiling in his good-natured way, but a puzzled frown was puckering his broad brow.

'But it's Saturday. I thought we could go out tonight, somewhere.' There, he had said it.

'I can't.' Isabel swung her head down. 'I'm, um, busy.'

'Busy?' He said it pleasantly, lightly, but there was terror in his eyes, he knew. Thankfully she was not looking at them.

'Doing an, um, extra paper.'

Oh, this was hard. She could see his disappointment and bewilderment. She could have replied to his texts, at least. Put him out of what was quite obviously his misery. He deserved better from her; he had been nothing but good to her, behaved with impeccable politeness at all times, like a gentleman – although not one like Jasper, obviously. The thought of what she was really doing tonight now filled Isabel with a rush of hot excitement. 'Come out for dinner,' Jasper had said. 'Candlelight and spaghetti; little place I know; nothing fancy, but really sweet. Cosy.'

'Come on,' Olly pressed gently. 'A coffee will do you good.'

He saw now that her attention was no longer on him. She was looking over his shoulder, her eyes wide and her mouth slightly open. She looked rapt, like one seeing a vision.

Olly twisted violently round. She was, indeed, seeing a vision. Some feet above the stunted crowd, a tall god was approaching. He had shelf-like cheekbones and glinting gold hair. The smile on his face was that of the victor, not only in this situation but in life generally.

'Jasper,' Isabel gasped, from somewhere deep down in her throat. It was enough.

He experienced a violent understanding. As if he had been hit and, simultaneously, something inside him had exploded. The essay crisis. It approached and smiled at him with detached contempt.

'Jasper *De Borchy?*' He could not help repeating it. That there was someone else was bad enough, of course. But that that someone else was . . . him. The extra paper, in other words.

'And this is . . . ?' His long-lashed amber gaze, aloof, regarding Olly as if from a vast, unbridgeable distance.

Olly saw that Isabel was positively radiating adoration, Jasper coolly absorbing it. He felt sick with misery. He felt murderous. He felt he wanted to crawl away and hide under a stone – die there.

'This is Olly,' he heard Isabel say distantly. 'He, um, lives in the house of one of my tutors.'

Olly pulled himself together. He could not just walk away and leave Jasper De Borchy to take the field, with his cruel beauty, his cold smile.

He could tell that Isabel didn't realise. Couldn't, possibly. He spoke in a low, urgent whisper. 'Honestly, Isabel, you don't know what you're letting yourself in for, the way the De Borchys treat women . . . Honestly, I've seen it, I've heard them and their sort talking . . .'

She couldn't hear properly, but enough to get the gist. All the conflicting awkwardness, guilt and febrile excitement within Isabel now exploded into a great anger. What made him think he could tell her what to do?

'He's a member of the bloody Bullinger; have you any idea what they do? Dwarves, strippers, you name it . . .' Olly looked at her exasperatedly. 'Drugs . . .'

It was the final weapon in his arsenal. He had heard rumours, that was all. But, as the Bullinger was a byword for any number of vices, there seemed no reason not to chuck the kitchen sink at it.

Isabel listened to him stammering out his words, but none of them really went in. Her eyes were fixed on Jasper. He was looking at his watch now, looking around, yawning. Dear God, don't let him just walk off. Terror twisted within her, sharpening her annoyance with Olly. Just because he had helped her with her bags, just because he had taken her for a drink, Olly thought he owned her.

Even as this crossed her mind, she recognised its unfairness. But there was, nonetheless, a truth within that could be twisted to suit her purposes.

'. . . the whole De Borchy family, just poisonous . . .' Low-pitched, fervent words were streaming out of Olly. 'They own all the papers I've been trying – *trying* –' he rolled his eyes ironically – 'to get a job with . . .'

Isabel felt desperate. What did she care, now, when Jasper was blazing away in all his magnificence mere feet from her? She wished that Olly would go away. Leave her. He was embarrassing her. It was her life; she was a grown-up. She had navigated herself perfectly well up to now.

She bit out the words. 'I can look after myself.'

Desperately, he played his last card. 'But he's a member of the Bullinger!' Olly's eyes searched hers, begging her to understand, for the old Isabel to come back and replace this new, cold, superior one.

'What if he is?' she snapped.

He swallowed, trying to compose himself. 'You can't. You just . . . can't,' he repeated desperately. 'Please, Isabel. You've no idea . . .'

'Come on,' Jasper De Borchy was suggesting. He took her arm – her slim, white, beautiful arm – and turned to Olly. 'Best leave her alone,' he suggested with a cold smile. 'Out of your league, don't you think?'

Olly felt as if he were falling. He stumbled off before either of them could hear or see the great howl-sob rolling up from within.

Chapter 17

Richard was in the labs. It was the end of the day and outside the metal-framed, thirties windows the sun was setting. Great glowing salmon streaks of light were painted over a duck-egg blue sky. It had been a beautiful day, glowing, golden and warm, although admittedly he hadn't seen much of it. He had been crouched over his experiments, making up for the time lost in all the endless development meetings of late.

The most recent had been called by Flora because of what was apparently being referred to in the development office as 'the Bursar's breakthrough'.

Working his reluctant way through his section of the alumni list, the college financial controller had desultorily dialled a former student in New York. He had had an unexpectedly electric effect.

An American modern languages graduate from 1968 called Mary-Beth Baumengartner had, it seemed, gone on to forge a successful career in the haulage business and marry multiple times, latterly and most recently to a hugely wealthy businessman called Chuck Snodgrass III. Mary-Beth seemed surprised and amazed to hear from her old college and a cheque was apparently in the post. The Bursar was triumphant.

Richard now got to his feet and began pacing about the labs. He stopped at the noticeboard to read the laminated set of laboratory rules he had put up there himself. Number four: 'Never assume that your work can be completed in the bare minimum of hours required by the faculty. Successful careers in neuroscience demand at least double this commitment and in many cases even more.' He had told it like it was, Richard reflected. No point beating about the bush. After all, he wasn't asking anything of them that he wasn't willing to do himself – had done himself, for that matter, and for many years too.

The large, strip-lit room was empty, nonetheless. For all the double commitment required of them, most of his research colleagues had by now gone home. It was Saturday night, after all; even science nerds had places to go and things to do. As had Richard, although the place he had to go and the thing he had to do was a prospect that filled him with terror.

Tonight was his date with Diana and the first time he had dated a woman in years. What had possessed him to ask her out? It had been completely unnecessary and over the top, a mere apology for his behaviour would have done. No doubt she thought he was mad; perhaps he was.

Richard returned to his own experiment. The wall at his end of the room was covered entirely with a great many illuminated Perspex boxes, all fitted closely together in a way that had stretched the department's maintenance staff to their limits, accustomed as they were to unusual requests. From a distance, as Richard approached, it looked like a contemporary art installation, glowing rectangles of red and blue with a number of worms in each one.

He stopped and stared at them, almost fondly. The worms had definitely got with the programme now. They were beginning to firmly associate certain shades with certain smells that he was able to release into the boxes, and they would respond in certain predictable ways to certain combinations. That you could influence the brain through colour seemed not just likely but definite.

Richard, regarding his colour-sensitive worms with deep

absorption, didn't want to leave. It was so pleasant here in the quiet lab with his work going exactly the way he wanted it to. He could easily spend another couple of hours here. Instead, thanks to a moment of madness precipitated by guilt, he had to waste his time in a restaurant with a woman he didn't know. It was all so illogical and impulsive. Absorbed, he pressed one of the buttons to send in another one of the smells and shuffled on his seat, fascinated, as the invertebrates began to react.

Shanna-Mae was an artist with eyeliner, Diana thought. As Debs' daughter stepped back, brush in hand, Rosie's mother leant forward and stared at herself in the mirror. Her eyes looked huge, her lashes long and feathery, her eyebrows, lightly plucked, appeared level and groomed. Her weather-beaten skin, concealed by a layer of foundation, looked dewy and youthful. She looked as if she were going to the Oscars, not spending Saturday night in a local hotel restaurant.

It had been she, in the end, who suggested Lecturer. It had been on her mind since the conversation with Sara – who, mercifully, had not shown up yet and hopefully never would. The hotel did at least have the virtue of being new and people were talking about it; although, from Richard's guarded reaction, she guessed he was generally not a fan of new places that people were talking about. She wasn't either, usually, having had a lifetime's worth during the London years. But old habits died hard, she had been unable to think of anywhere else and he had obviously been unable to think of anywhere at all.

Of course, it was only dinner. Nothing more. All the same, Diana concluded, it was months, if not years, since she had looked this good. She shook out her hair, on which Shanna-Mae had worked more miracles with her straighteners. It rippled over her shoulders in a silky sheet the colour of milk chocolate, with occasional flashes of red and green from Debs' hysterical light display next door.

'You look great, Mrs Somers,' Shanna-Mae grinned.

'Yeah, Mum,' Rosie echoed from where she sat on the bed, watching. 'You look wicked.'

Shanna-Mae had a vast array of kit: rolls of make-up brushes, bottles of different-coloured foundation, tubes of lip gloss, eye-shadow compacts the size and shape of toolboxes and containing a dizzying selection of colours. She had, Diana learnt, saved up for it all over years of birthday and Christmas money and through doing odd jobs in between.

As she had worked on Diana's face, Shanna-Mae had spoken knowledgably about the make-up artists she admired, the brands and equipment she rated and had outlined her professional plans, the courses she intended to take, how she would finance her business and where it would be. Listening, Diana's admiration had risen. She had no doubt that, in even less than the ten years Shanna-Mae estimated it would take her after leaving school, her neighbour's daughter would be right at the top of her very competitive game.

Diana was, all the same, guiltily aware of how, once, she would have judged this girl. Shanna-Mae, for all her skill in beautifying others, was far from glamorous herself. At fourteen, she was almost the same generous size as her mother, a size which she insisted on drawing attention to by wearing the tiniest of denim miniskirts teamed with opaque black tights. She habitually wore an enormous amount of make-up and her hair, dyed a bright yellow-blond, was cut by Shanna-Mae herself in an unflattering – but, Diana gathered, wildly fashionable – asymmetrical wedge which covered half her eyes.

'This is for you,' she smiled, slipping a ten-pound note into Shanna-Mae's hand. 'Buy yourself those eyelash curlers you were talking about. Don't tell your mother!'

Debs had been adamant not only that Shanna-Mae did the make-up for Diana's big night out, but that her daughter's services were free. Shanna-Mae took the money gratefully, but Diana saw doubt in the small hazel eyes ringed thickly with mascara. 'What's the matter?' she asked.

Shanna-Mae bit her lip. 'I can't not tell Mum,' she confessed. 'I tell her everything.'

'You tell her then. I don't think she'll mind.'

To go with her smart face, Diana had found a pair of black cigarette pants and a thick, cream silk fitted blouse: both relics from wealthier days, although never had they looked so good. Both were considerably looser than they had been. Walking miles every day round Branston's gardens lugging buckets of weeds was succeeding where many a smart West London gym had, over the years, failed.

Diana took a deep breath and watched her pale and powdered nostrils narrow. She twitched up the corners of her glossed and painted lips and noticed the hollows deepen under her cheek-bones. She wondered what Richard would make of her look. He had only ever seen her with her hair everywhere and smudges of dirt on her face. But what did it matter, anyway, what he thought? He was only taking her out under duress.

The hotel was near the centre of town, so Diana parked in the staff car park of Branston and walked the short distance. It was misty – one of those dense and weighty autumn fogs that occasionally present themselves as an alternative to the blaze and glow. Students muffled in scarves and woolly hats laboured past on bicycles or hurried in and out of college entrances. Across the road, the Georgian windows of the closed gift shops looked blankly back. Across the city, the age-old sound of bells rolled and drifted like ectoplasm.

Couples were walking; groups were lurching. There was the occasional distant shout. College chapels were lit from within, presumably for some concert or practice. The effect was strange; stained glass glowed through the vapour like lights from an alien spaceship and the faint sound of singing could be heard.

Lecturer was at the end of one of the mist-swirled main streets. It was a small and elegant Georgian red-brick manor with windows picked out in white and a fanlight over the portico entranceway. It looked comfortable and tasteful and so it was a shock for Diana to find, once over the broad stone steps of the threshold, that the restrained nineteenth century gave way abruptly to the contemporary at its most moronic. As the framed birch canes lining the walls and the receptionist in a mortar board attested, Lecturer was a hotel with an academic theme. She looked around, horrified. She had had no idea.

Seized with panic – what would the caustic Richard make of all this? – Diana tried not to look, as an elderly waitress dressed as a schoolgirl crossed the wooden-panelled foyer.

'Can I help you?' the mortar-boarded receptionist asked, her hauteur undiminished by her headgear.

'I'm meeting someone,' Diana muttered. 'Professor Richard Black. Is he here yet?'

The mortar board clicked a mouse and peered over half-moon spectacles at the screen. 'No,' she said, as if she enjoyed it. 'Would you like to wait in the bar?'

She waved Diana towards a doorway above which was a small, framed blackboard with 'Bar' scribbled on it in chalk.

Diana went hesitantly through. Perhaps Richard was late because he was cycling here. But would he? In this weather? He might be knocked off. He might not come at all.

Inside, the floor was wooden and the bar tables were those small, old-fashioned desks with lifting lids and small holes for long-vanished inkwells. All were set at incongruously companionable angles, each with its inhospitably hard chair and a bar menu which looked like a maths exercise book. The walls were white and fixed to them were dark-wood frames displaying the periodic table, a British Empire-era world map and some handwriting exercises. There was a bookshelf with a number of battered old books and age-spotted paperbound collections of O-level papers from the nineteen-seventies and eighties.

The bar, inevitably, was equipped with a chalk board on which the wine list was scribbled and, while there was no barman around, his recent presence was signalled by the mortar board lying on the bar top.

'You're late!' someone suddenly snapped from behind. A male voice. Diana turned, heart in mouth. It didn't sound like Richard, but who else would speak to her like that?

It was a tall youth in an academic gown. 'One hundred lines!' he thundered at Diana. She stared at him, confused and not a little scared. Then his stern face melted into a professional smile. 'But now you're here, what can I get you?' It was, she realised, flustered, the barman.

'J-just a tap water, thanks,' Diana stammered.

'I can't interest you in a glass of champagne?' the barman said, baring his teeth and gesturing at the wine cooler on the bar. It contained several magnums of champagne, the unopened bottle tops bristling out like the spikes of a hedgehog.

'No,' Diana said firmly. She certainly couldn't afford it herself and to order it would send out all the wrong messages to Richard.

He rolled his eyes huffily and said, 'Whatever, Madam,' with such rudeness that, briefly, Diana had a good mind to retaliate, but decided to retain her dignity.

He sloppily poured out a glass of water from a jug on the counter and shoved it sulkily towards her. 'Economising tonight, are we, Madam?'

Diana looked him in the eye. This was one step too far. 'Is my drinking tap water a problem for you?'

'Not at all, Madam.' Acidly.

Diana now did her best to ignore him and, such was the hostility in the atmosphere, she felt relieved when he crammed on his mortar board and flounced out.

Registering his departure with relief, she hardly noticed someone else come in.

'Hello,' said Richard, rather stiffly.

His physical presence, materialising so unexpectedly, sent a powerful jump of excitement through her. She stared at him, reddening and flustered and feeling somehow exposed, as if revealing a shameful secret.

He was carrying a cycle helmet, which answered one question.

But he looked less bedraggled than the conditions outside suggested. The faint sheen on his skin, the flush in his cheek, the sparkle in his eye was becoming. He looked alive. Fit. Vital.

How had she not noticed before?

His hair, close-cropped in the Caesar style, was dark but flecked with grey. His face was as long and lean as the rest of him and there was something of the wolf about the long nose and piercing greenish eyes set slightly aslant beneath dark eyebrows.

He unzipped a smart short dark-blue raincoat – not a graceless cagoule – to reveal a crisp white shirt, new from the packet by the look of it. He had achieved what she would have imagined impossible – elegance, despite a bike ride, and a wet one at that. A cufflink flashed as, awkwardly, he held out a hand to grasp hers. Obviously a kiss would have been too forward, too intimate, but the very fact he hadn't done it made her wonder what it would have been like. His hand was brief, firm, dry. 'Diana. Good to see you.' His manner was businesslike without a hint of interest.

The barman now reappeared and aimed a loaded sneer-smile at Richard. 'Would sir care to join madam in a glass of tap water? Or would sir prefer something else?' His bony, reddened hands seemed to Diana to be wringing with suppressed violence.

Richard, ordering two glasses of champagne, did not appear to notice this, which only seemed to annoy the waiter more. He flounced theatrically off.

Richard looked around. 'Weird place.'

Diana's heart sank. 'Maybe I shouldn't have suggested it.' Was the evening ruined already?

The mortar-boarded barman was back, ferociously gripping two flutes of champagne. 'Your table's ready now,' he said with an acid mock-playfulness. 'Hurry and sit down if you don't want six of the best.'

Cheeks burning, Diana followed Richard to the dining room. She was expecting the worst. Long communal forms, possibly, and a retro-horrid school food menu featuring deep-fried Spam and Manchester tart.

Richard, for his part, was by now aware of the 'Dead Man's Leg' and 'Nun's Toenails' served in Branston College's Incinerator. He had realised with a growing disbelief that a certain breed of Englishman strongly identified with bad institutional food. Presumably this place catered to just such types.

They sat down in silence. The waiting staff, incredibly, were dressed like schoolchildren from the nineteen-fifties and had been picked without any apparent preference as to size and age. Or perhaps the university town, with its plethora of restaurants, offered a seller's market to waiting staff, because those on show this evening seemed either too old or too wide – and sometimes both – for what they had to wear. That corpulent middle-aged sommelier, for instance, was probably having his human rights infringed in the tight shorts and straw boater he was required to affect.

Richard met Diana's glance. There was something very strange about her face. As if she were struggling with something. Boredom? He felt his insides, which had relaxed somewhat, shrink into themselves and his backbone stiffen.

She made another strange noise, into a napkin this time. He thought for a fearful moment she was having a seizure and then, with a rush of relief, realised she was trying to control hysterical giggles. He glanced around, saw the shorts and boater and felt something rising within him: a strange sensation, one he had not felt for a long time – had almost forgotten, in fact. After a few puzzled seconds he realised that it was laughter.

Chapter 18

That evening, Jasper was not outside his college when Isabel arrived. She waited restlessly in the mist, uncomfortably aware of a pair of St Alwine's college porters hovering at the entrance in their purple-banded gowns, watchful that no undesirables or undeserving got through the hallowed portals.

'Isabel!' It was a male voice, hailing her from behind, but not Jasper's light, low drawl. Almost reeling with disappointment, she turned – to see the smiling faces of Paul and Lorien in whose eyes a certain shy pride flickered. They had just started being a couple and were, they now explained, going to a *Star Wars* all-nighter at the Arts Cinema.

'What are you up to?' Lorien asked with a smile. 'Lurking outside Bullinger Central in the mist!'

'Meeting a friend,' Isabel replied, to their obvious amazement. As they said goodbye and hurried off, she looked down and tapped her foot. They could think what they liked; Jasper was not the usual St Alwine's – St Wino's, whatever – boor. And what business was it of theirs anyway?

She wished they had not mentioned the Bullinger, even so. Why was everyone so fixated on it? Whatever it was, she didn't believe the half of it, personally – despite what Olly had said this afternoon. Although she hadn't consciously listened at the time, Isabel could hear him now and was finding it hard to shut out his anxious face, his pleading voice. She wanted to forget that whole

215

hideous episode in the High Street. She had ignored every text he had subsequently sent, left his calls unanswered. How dare Olly say what he had said? He had made Jasper sound like a monster. 'Go easy on him; he's only jealous,' Jasper had said. 'And who wouldn't be?' he had added lightly, bending to kiss her nose.

To distract herself, she stared into the misty college court and the ancient bulk of the college chapel, gargoyles *à-gogo*, its dark, east window split with mullions. The lights were on; someone was practising. The sound of an organ added to the Gothic atmosphere.

Isabel imagined how the chapel would look inside. There would be a soft smell of wood, of chill, of age. Gold would gleam on the altar, and memorials of various sizes and shapes would hang heavily on the walls. There would be ragged flags, presumably from some long-ago battle. Now Isabel imagined smoke, yells, the boom of cannon fire, men screaming.

The stained glass of the east window looked Victorian; its central figure was Jesus, flanked by saints. One was John the Baptist. In line with church convention, he looked short-tempered and scruffy with messy hair. He contrasted with a nearby St Sebastian who had smooth, shiny salon-fresh locks and looked, again as convention dictated, completely unmoved despite being chock-full of arrows. St Andrew looked surprisingly cheerful, despite standing there holding the cross to which he would shortly be nailed.

Only Jesus broke the usual mould. He was extraordinarily buff, with simply enormous muscles and a rippling chest. Had he not been the son of God, Isabel thought, he could easily have had a career as a bodybuilder. The thought made her smile and lifted her spirits, but these plunged downwards again once she heard the college clock – its lacy gold face invisible in the gloom – strike seven fifteen.

Either Jasper was not coming, or he was, for some reason, late. Had Amber held him up? Physically? Suspicion ripped through

Isabel, not for the first time. Jealousy was as completely new to her as infatuation and just as powerful, she had discovered. Whatever else happened this evening, she was determined to find out the truth about Jasper and Amber. What exactly was their relationship?

She had been meaning to ask him this afternoon, but then had come the scene with Olly. Amber, meanwhile, had been evasive all week. The sum total of Isabel's contact with her over the past few days was the appearance of some indecipherable scribbled notes about various parties, which had been shoved under Isabel's door when she was out. From which, presumably, she was expected to concoct a publishable piece.

To please Jasper, she had managed it, cobbled together the detail from what existed in online newspaper gossip columns, whose representatives had been at the parties too. It had been a lengthy and irritating process and, throughout it, the question of Jasper and Amber had pressed upon her ever more heavily. Were they a couple? Was he just asking her, Isabel, out as a sop, to guarantee her cooperation with his girlfriend?

Her mobile shrilled suddenly into these seething thoughts. Jasper? She positively snatched it from her coat pocket.

'It's just that you've been a bit hard to reach, lately.' Her mother's voice was strained, and not only, Isabel guessed, because it was coming from several hundred miles to the north.

'There's nothing to worry about, honestly,' she said, trying to suppress a note of irritation. Jasper, after all, might be trying to get through. This very moment.

'Everything's fine? You're having fun?'

'Oh, yes!' She could be honest about this, at least. '*Lots* of fun.'

'Working hard as well, I hope?' There was a nervous note to her mother's voice.

'Er, yes. Actually, Mum,' Isabel's gaze lingered longingly on St Alwine's escutcheoned gateway. 'I have to go. Ring you later. Bye!'

She switched the phone off. Mum might call back and she didn't want to risk being interrupted during the precious time with Jasper – time ticking away, even as she stood there. Had he forgotten? It was as bad a thought as his being with Amber.

Not knowing was unbearable. If he wasn't coming out, she was going in. She approached the door of the St Alwine's porter's lodge and stopped, surprised. The scene through the age-swirled panes of Georgian glass was one of another time. The small office, lined with dark wood and boasting a grate with a small but roaring fire, contained two porters. One was cradling a large tea mug and the other was reading a newspaper spread on the polished oak counter. Both wore dark waistcoats and bowler hats and had similar fleshy puce faces with bushy moustaches. As she opened the door, they looked her coldly up and down.

'I'm looking for Jasper De Borchy,' Isabel nervously told the porter with the paper.

There was something knowingly horrible about the smile he gave her. 'Mr Farthingale,' he said, addressing his colleague in tones reminiscent of a music hall comedy act. 'This young lady here is looking for the Honourable Mr Jasper.'

The porter with the tea looked up and seemed to straighten, as if in anticipation of amusement. 'Is that so, Mr Scavenger?' he replied in a similar 'I say, I say, I say' voice. 'The Honourable Mr Jasper, eh?'

'The very same, Mr Farthingale. High-spirited young man, our Mr Jasper. Mind you, so was his brother, the Honourable Mr Caspar.'

'And his father, Mr Scavenger. Don't forget his father.'

'Ah, yes. The Honourable Mr Jasper's father, Lord Edmund. Had to fish him out of the fountain a few times, I can tell you, Mr Farthingale.'

Isabel wondered how old they were, in that case. It was difficult to tell. Time inside this porter's lodge had apparently stopped somewhere around 1912. Mounted above the fireplace was a circular Bakelite clock with thick black hands; that it seemed to be going forward was almost a surprise.

She folded her arms. 'Is he in, anyway?'

'All in good time, my dear lady,' Farthingale chided. He slid himself along the counter to consult a board on the wall. It was of the same dark polished wood as everything else and contained a list of names carefully hand-painted in a beautiful white italic hand. At the end of each name was the word, 'Out' or, 'In' with a small black-painted wooden slide covering whichever didn't apply.

'In,' Farthingale said.

Isabel didn't like the porters, but felt grateful for this inform-ation. Farthingale lifted up the polished oak flap and loomed pucely before her. 'I'll escort you to Mr Jasper.'

'If you just tell me where—' Isabel began, before the other porter cut in.

'We don't allow unescorted females to enter the college,' he said meaningfully. She felt him appraising the backs of her legs as she went out, hurrying after Farthingale as he disappeared into the swirling mists of the Tudor courtyard. The cobbles pressed painfully up into her thin soles, but the beauty of the place was evident even in the foggy darkness. Like a building in a mediaeval manuscript illustration, she thought – airy towers, oriel windows, carved beasts and shields. They stopped before a small arched corner doorway.

'Top floor,' Farthingale said. The door creaked as she opened it and an ancient chill greeted her from a shadowy staircase twisting upwards like a stone screw.

Feeling rather like the heroine of a particularly fanciful Victorian poem, Isabel crept up silently. Across the door at the top was painted, 'The Hon. J.A.G. De Borchy' in neat white italic on black, like the board in the lodge. Isabel wondered what the A and G stood for. She wondered, too, if Jasper was alone.

She felt suddenly, horribly nervous. The prospect of seeing a mocking, beautiful Amber parading around in a skimpy towel, in Jasper's pyjamas, even in the nude, seemed suddenly, horribly likely.

She forced her shaking hand to knock, and felt a violent jerk of fear as the old wooden door, gloss-painted in shiny black, gave a brittle rattle in reply. She had barely recovered from this when the door opened entirely and then, suddenly, all was well.

Jasper's long, beautiful face appeared, exploding a bomb of pure joy within her. If its initial expression was irritated surprise, she missed it; it turned instantly to smiling apology in any case. He held up one long finger in warning, pointing at the mobile shoved to his ear. 'Sorry,' he hissed. 'Running late!' He gestured to her to come in.

She had already established that he was alone, and relief had joined the joy. As well as surprise. Her eyes were flying everywhere, clutching at the details. So this is how people lived in St Alwine's. St Wino's was a misnomer. It suggested disarray, degradation even. But this was . . . paradise.

The room was old and beautiful. It had armchairs, Isabel saw. Her room would not have fitted one in, and yet here were two big ones, upholstered in soft, faded red, and with a long red sofa to match. Large lamps with pale shades lit walls undulating with age, but did not penetrate far into the great, carved fireplace with the mirror over it. Or through the half-open door revealing the end of an unmade bed. The rumpled sheets looked thrillingly intimate. Her heart was galloping again and Isabel looked away.

Jasper had not seemed to notice her consternation. He was pacing before the fireplace, murmuring into the mobile. The conversation from his end just seemed a series of affirmatives.

She felt somehow untethered, as if she had left her normal self outside St Alwine's gate; as if she had been shaken up inside like a little snowstorm ornament and everything was whirling and glittering within. Was this love?

'No!' Jasper's voice cut harshly into her dreamy state. She blinked, struck by the violence of his tone. But then he smiled at her and the flakes began to whirl again.

'I've got to go now,' Jasper was saying. He shoved the phone in his pocket and strode over to her. She held her breath, half-closed her eyes, hoping he would touch her, pull her to him. She was surprised to feel an almost sluttish abandonment, it was almost as if she were drunk.

But instead of taking her, as she half hoped he would, and flinging her on the bed, Jasper merely kissed her nose. 'I'm starving. Come on. I know just the place.'

Diana now thought that Lecturer hadn't been such a bad idea. Its ridiculousness had been a breakthrough. She was enjoying herself – really enjoying herself. By mutual agreement, they had left the hotel after the champagne and were now sitting happily in a noisy Italian restaurant with steamed-up windows and tablecloths of red check oilcloth. Behind them was a noisy family party singing 'Happy Birthday To You' as a pair of gawky waiters carried in a traybake stuck with sparklers.

The iceman had gone. A beguiling warmth was revealing itself beneath Richard's stern outer carapace – especially when he spoke about his work. Everything reminded him of his research, even the restaurant napkin; shaking it out he held it up and told her it was about the same size and shape as the brain's cortex, if it was ironed out flat and not scrunched up. As he described the 'Halle Berry neuron', identified in the brain of a young man because it fired repeatedly when shown pictures of the attractive Hollywood actress, Diana no longer had to fight her urge to giggle. 'I've probably got a delphinium neuron,' she said.

'Undoubtedly,' he agreed. He was, Richard thought, having an unexpectedly good time. His interest in food, along with his interest in anything except his work, had died with Amy. Or so he had imagined. But the pasta with buttery home-made pesto sauce had resuscitated something within him.

Diana had, she now realised, been concentrating on Richard to the exclusion of all else. With a prick of guilt she wondered how Rosie was, with Debs and Shanna-Mae.

'What are you thinking about?' She found herself looking into a pair of friendly, curious dark eyes.

'My house,' Diana muttered, hoping not to explain further. It wasn't the estate so much as the circumstances that had brought her there that she wished to avoid revealing.

Richard, however, had seen the shutters come down. He was now relaxed enough to be curious, and to give some of that curiosity expression. He was not a top research scientist without knowing which questions to ask and how to ask them. That she was divorced he already guessed; the Bursar had said she was a single mother, but her circumstances had obviously recently changed, and quite dramatically. That there had been a husband, and a wealthy one, he was sure, despite the fact that she had scrupulously avoided mentioning a partner. Within a couple of minutes he had established she lived on a local council estate, an admission which seemed to fluster her. He moved to put her at ease. Lifting the carafe of house red and pouring a dark stream into her glass, he said, lightly, 'I know all about social housing.'

Diana flicked him a look, half-nervous, half-sardonic. He was making a reference, she assumed, to those social-economic studies that colleges like Branston conducted in an effort to solve the mystery as to why students from poor backgrounds failed to apply there. She doubted Richard's knowledge had, in that case, much depth. Until he added, completely unexpectedly, 'I grew up in a trailer park myself.'

Diana lowered the fork she was raising to her lips. 'A *trailer* park? But . . .' She trailed off. She had imagined him the son of American old money, the side-parted scion of a pillared and porticoed white mansion overlooking miles of green lawn. Privately educated, his progress one of seamless privilege from prep school to the gilded doors of Yale.

'Not at all,' Richard said. 'Nothing private or privileged about it.'

'You knew what I was thinking?' She felt alarmed. Could brain specialists actually read minds?

He grinned. 'I can't see inside your brain, no. Those thoughts were written all over your face.' He added, impulsively, 'It's very expressive, you know.'

Diana looked down. Her heart had suddenly picked up speed.

She looked up to see him gazing into the candle flame. 'Yeah, I grew up in a trailer park,' he said. 'Before we went up in the world . . . to the housing projects.' He gave a rueful snort. 'My dad left my mom to raise me alone.'

'That must have been hard.' Her voice, Diana thought, sounded like it belonged to someone else, not to her: high, strained.

'For her, it was. She had to do everything for me and hold down about three different jobs at the same time. You know?'

Diana felt herself nodding. Yes, she knew all right. She knew all about being a single mother. She was about to say, tell him everything – about the divorce, Simon's deceit, everything. There was something in his face, in his eyes to be specific, that she knew she could trust. He would understand; he would not judge her; he knew about the harder side of life, and a much harder one than she knew. His wife had died, after all. Diana opened her mouth, suddenly desperate to unburden herself; she would, if they were to see each other again, have to tell him at some stage.

As with Debs, not long ago, she felt it was important to get it out in the open. If she were to move on, to flourish, she must not conceal things from those close to her. Every day she cleared dead leaves and rubbish from around the roots of her garden plants so that they could breathe and grow. She must do the same for herself.

But then, again as with Debs not long ago, caution placed its strong, firm hand over the wavering one of impulse. What might Richard think? He might not react the way she expected. She did not know him, after all, certainly not well enough to open this most delicate and intimate of subjects. What reciprocal guarantees did she have? He had not, for his part, even mentioned his wife.

He was fiddling with a fork and frowning at it. It was obvious that his thoughts were very far away. Diana waited, suddenly sure that Richard *was* about to start talking about his wife.

She felt powerfully sorry for him. To marry someone, as she had done, and find they were not what you thought was hard. But she had Rosie to show for it; one truly wonderful thing had come out of it. But to love someone, lose them and be left with nothing . . . What must that be like?

Richard said nothing, however. She wondered if he was expecting her to ask, but what could she say? What business, frankly, was it of hers? Then he looked up and caught her eye and she had a sudden flash of insight that he was holding back in the same way that she was. And for the same reasons.

No. She would not tell him. Not yet. Not ever, perhaps. It wasn't as if she would see him again, in this intimate kind of context, anyway. Their next meeting would be in the Branston gardens – a distant wave across the lawn, probably.

The silence stretched between them, but now it was not uncomfortable. Reticence was, Diana felt, underappreciated. Not saying things had a lot to be said for it.

'Are you enjoying being Master of Branston?' she asked eventually, steering the talk back into safe waters.

Richard paused. He was about to say, *No*, but Diana worked for the college and, however inadvertently, his remarks might be passed on to others. Besides, dwelling on the dark side would bring him inevitably to the subject of his widowerhood. He searched for something light to say, something humorous.

He began to tell her about the Big Ring-Round, the Bursar and the impending visit of Mary-Beth Snodgrass. The development office was now arranging an entire alumni dinner round Mary-Beth's arrival. Flora expected him to attend and make a speech. The thought filled Richard with dread, but at least it made a good story. Diana was laughing.

Diana, amused and relaxed now, was eagerly drinking him in. His eyes glowed dark in the candlelight. His skin was dry, smooth. She could detect the cedary whiff of his aftershave. She dropped her eyes, aware she was staring at him.

But then, he was staring, too. She worried that it might not be for the same reasons. Perhaps it was the five different shades of eye shadow and two different blushers? Perhaps she should never have let Shanna-Mae loose. It was frightening, how good she had thought she looked. She must really be losing all sense of what suited her.

She had done something to her face, Richard was thinking. He had thought so at the start, but now he was sure. Something which enhanced the gentleness of her eyes, the faintly questioning arch of her brow, the generosity of her wide mouth. He hadn't realised she was this good-looking. He felt suddenly rather out of his depth and nervous.

Diana was asking him about the students. Did he know Isabel?

'Scottish girl?' Richard repeated, trying hard to picture who she meant. 'Tall redhead? Gorgeous smile?'

'She's a lovely girl,' Diana said. 'Seems to work very hard. Always going to the library when I see her.'

Diana seemed to know the students better than he did. The thought that she would make an excellent Master's wife came out of nowhere. 'Unlike some people,' Richard said. 'Going to the library, I mean.'

She knew exactly what he meant. 'You mean that girl, Amber? I saw her arrive. All cameras and boom microphones.'

He raised his eyebrows. 'Turns out she doesn't write essays – writes some newspaper column instead. Spends all her time trying to get modelling work. Wants to be famous, I guess.'

'So why's she here?' Diana mused.

'Search me. Maybe she didn't get any attention at home or something. Money's no substitute for lack of parental love, after all.' Richard smiled and ate the spaghetti.

What a father he would make, Diana found herself thinking, with blushing suddenness. She hid her red face, twisting up pasta in her fork. And he was right, of course. Look at Debs. Money was tight in the Biggs household, both parents finding work only intermittently in a depressed job market, and even then at minimum-wage level. But Shanna-Mae did her homework every night and had serious ambitions, which her parents encouraged. She had saved for every scrap of her make-up kit herself.

And then there was Milo, son of her erstwhile next door neighbour. Diana had shoved the Oopvards to the back of her thoughts, but now she recalled Milo's dark, scowling face, like an angry imp's. What had that anger been about, really? He had the finest teachers money could buy. Every material possession he could wish for was pushed on to him by his indulgent mother. But Milo lacked discipline; his rudeness went uncorrected; his aggressive tendencies had received no checks, except the financial kind. Sara was, essentially, uninterested in her son.

'Shall we have dessert?' He had not originally intended to encourage this, expecting to be desperate to escape by now. In fact, had the dinner been twenty-four courses, it would have been fine. More than fine. He hoped she wasn't the sort who didn't eat pudding.

'Yes, please.' As the waiter passed them the menus, Diana's eye flicked involuntarily away from the table and fastened suddenly, and altogether unexpectedly, on a familiar red-haired figure. A few tables away, in an intimate corner by the window, the shadows of the candles flickered over Isabel's lovely face. Diana sat up slightly, her eyes narrowing.

Isabel was sitting facing her, although she had obviously not seen her. Her attention was focused entirely on her companion, whose back was turned to Diana. He slouched in his seat, she noticed. His long legs, unseen by Isabel, jiggled impatiently beneath the table. He had bright blond hair with a wave in it and as, now, he yawned and put a long-fingered hand up to rake it, a signet ring flashed. Isabel's eyes were glazed and her mouth slightly open. She looked like someone under a spell. Diana, for no reason she could put her finger on, felt a tightening within, a twist of anxiety.

The spaghetti was wonderful, Isabel thought as she wrapped it round her fork. The whole place was perfect: a neighbourhood Italian straight out of central casting, right down to the red candles which were stuck – apparently non-ironically – in raffia-wrapped wine bottles.

The only thing that wasn't perfect was her. She could not seem to ask the right questions to get a conversation flowing. Perhaps it was nerves. She had imagined Jasper – so charming, so easygoing – would be easy to talk to, would open up at a touch. But there was something oddly restless about him; the way he glanced about, she feared she was boring him. Occasionally she could feel his leg jiggle impatiently under the table and from time to time he drummed his pale thin fingers on the base of his wine glass. A distance seemed to have opened up. What she really wanted to do was discuss Amber, but she had little experience in manoeuvring a conversation.

'What made you want to come to university here?' she asked him, rather lamely.

There was surprise, and a touch of disdain, in the yellow eyes. 'It's just – well – where everyone goes. Isn't it?'

Isabel, unsure how to respond, found herself nodding, as if it was indeed where everyone went. As Jasper began to talk about people she had never heard of, she steeled herself to slip in a mention of Amber. Did she, Jasper was asking in a bored sort of way, know Binky St Aldan? Chippy Crewell? Floppy Grimsby?

The names were silly enough to jolt her back to something like normal.

'Floppy? What sort of a name is that?'

'Poor guy's got erectile dysfunction,' Jasper replied, with an answering chuckle clearly meant to suggest it was not something from which he suffered himself. Isabel looked down, blushing suddenly.

She was relieved when the subject moved on and he began to talk about his car. Not only did he have one, he kept it at college, which seemed to Isabel extraordinarily sophisticated.

'It's a vintage Aston Martin,' Jasper went on. 'Used to be my father's when he was at Wino's. He left it here for us.'

'Us?' The impossible idea that some elderly aristocrat had left a vintage sports car for herself and Jasper to use spiralled wildly through Isabel's mind.

'My brothers and me.'

'You mean it's been here since he graduated?' A classic sports car, waiting at university for boys who would inevitably follow, suggested an amazing degree of self-confidence. Isabel recalled the Lord Edmund referred to in the porter's lodge, the one frequently fished out of the fountain. And Amber saying the De Borchy family had come over with the Conqueror.

She felt a kind of awe and realised that her former suspicion of such people had melted with one glance from Jasper's long yellow eyes. And with good reason, she told herself as the candlelight glanced off his signet ring. His being born into wealth and privilege was not his fault, any more than it was hers to be given by her mother to someone else as a baby.

It was, nonetheless, quite a contrast: the difference between knowing a millennium's worth of ancestors and knowing none at all. The security of such a past fascinated her, drew her like a magnet. She could not resist the inevitable conclusion, that it was somehow better than hers.

'Didn't really bother graduating, Pa didn't,' Jasper was saying. 'Had an estate to run and all that. Then the business. We have a few newspapers.'

Oh, yes. The newspapers. Isabel remembered Olly's uncharitable view of the De Borchy family firm. She had sympathised. But that conversation seemed to belong to some distant past, when she was a different person. Everything was different now.

Jasper yawned and stretched and the sudden fear that she was boring him shot through Isabel. He leant forward, placed his hand over hers. He was looking at her intently and the soft light flickered reverently over the delicate lineaments of his face. 'Let's go back to your room.'

'*My* room?' She was surprised enough to exclaim. His was nearer. And nicer. Why would anyone want to go to Branston when they had that?

He gave her one of his long smiles. 'Let's just say I dig that crazy sixties concrete vibe.'

Isabel was leaving, Diana saw. She was rising from her chair like a tall pale lily and following in the confident wake of the handsome blond boy. He was holding her hand loosely, walking in front of her – almost, Diana found herself thinking, as if he were leading her to some sacrifice. She blinked. Why on earth had she thought that?

As they passed, she tried to catch Isabel's eye, but she was obviously in another world altogether. Diana looked hard at the boy. Handsome, very handsome; a little too perfect, perhaps, his face so planed and chiselled it was almost flat. She noted the studied slouch, the creased look of his clothes. He must have sensed her looking because now he glanced at her and his eyes, as they slid across hers, sent an involuntary shiver through her. A cold shiver. A shiver of foreboding.

She reminded herself determinedly that Isabel was a grown-up – a clever grown-up at that. She herself was jumping to conclusions about someone she did not know, just as she had about Richard. And look how wrong she had been there!

'What's the matter?' she heard him say, behind her. 'You're in a daze.'

Diana twisted back to him, wrenching her frown into a smile. She would not explain about Isabel, even though they had mentioned her earlier. Had they been discussing any other subject she might have changed it. But they had been talking about Rosie, Diana's favourite topic.

'You were saying she was at a good school . . .' Richard prompted.

'Oh, yes.' And Diana plunged back in again.

The more questions he asked, Richard realised, the more he could gaze at her sparkling eyes and lovely face. Watching her mouth widening and puckering in reply, he found himself wondering what it would be like to kiss it.

'Rosie is lucky,' he said when she paused for breath.

'Yes, the school's great.'

'Not that,' he returned. 'She's got a great mother, was what I meant.'

Flustered at the direct compliment, Diana looked down at her plate. Something like a warm, slow explosion was taking place within. It was a long time since she had felt like this, if, indeed, she ever had before.

He leant forward. 'I'd like to see you again.'

She looked at him, startled.

'If you'd like to,' he added, quickly.

'I'd like to,' Diana said, unhesitating. 'When, do you think?'

She had expected him to say next week. Next Saturday night, perhaps. 'How about tomorrow?' was unexpected.

'Tomorrow?' she repeated, flustered but delighted. 'That would be . . .'

Wonderful?

Amazing?

Exciting?

Incredible?

All of the above?

'. . . fine,' she finished.

Isabel walked back to Branston with Jasper in a dream of happiness. Everything was all right again. Back to normal. After his fidgetiness in the restaurant, Jasper seemed to have calmed down. The wine, perhaps, she thought. Or maybe – this with a surge of excitement inside – something else?

He had his arm around her and his warmth flowed into her with tremendous force. It was as if he were possessing her. His attention was entirely focused on her now; his phone had rung several times and he had ignored it. Eventually he had taken it out and switched it off, which made her feel absurdly flattered.

She would have been entirely ecstatic had it not been for the fact she had had to pay in the restaurant. She had been prepared to pay half – and was careful to budget accordingly in advance. So when, with a dazzling smile, Jasper had carelessly pushed the plastic saucer containing the bill over to her side of the table and said that he was out of cash at the moment, so could she do the honours, it had been a shock.

Naturally, she had obliged without fuss, but not without secret worry. For all Branston's generosity, her term's budget was both a shoestring and a knife-edge; unexpected expense risked cutting the shoestring right through. Asking Mum to supplement it was out of the question. Isabel quietly resolved to make fewer trips to the Incinerator next week. You could never be too thin, after all. Or so Jasper had claimed, teasing her once about love handles. She had worried about it since, though she had never thought she was fat before. The opposite, if anything. 'Perfect figure', Mum always said, but perhaps Jasper had a different, higher, idea of what perfection was.

She felt nervous as they approached the porter's lodge – lair of the burly T-shirted beast – but Jasper breezed through without incident. She put this down to Jasper's manifest self-confidence and felt quietly proud, although the porter was on the phone at the time and had hardly looked up. Rather to Isabel's disappointment, there was no one about in the corridors to advertise the fact she was bringing back such a prize – Jasper would certainly have given Kate and Ellie something to think about. On the other hand, it was a relief not to encounter Amber.

Even as Isabel closed the door of her room, Jasper was standing on the bed, swiftly disabling the fire alarm. He put a finger to her lips as she started to protest, digging out a packet of tobacco and something wrapped in clingfilm with his other hand. She watched as he sat at the edge of the bed and quickly rolled a joint, steeling herself for the moment when he passed it to her. Isabel had never smoked marijuana; when the moment came, however, it was less alarming than she had imagined. Emboldened, she took a deeper drag, closing her eyes as she did so.

Her head spun suddenly and nausea blocked her throat. Her heart was hammering painfully. She opened her eyes wide and gripped the chair arms.

'You OK?' Jasper croaked over the ectoplasmic swirl of smoke he held in his mouth.

She nodded, fighting to right herself, to not seem pathetic and jejune before him.

He sat on the chair opposite the bed, his shod feet on the bedspread, looking at her steadily. The room was still spinning, but not so fast. Her hammering heart had slowed too and the furious jump and fizz of her nerves was subsiding. A heavy calm was spreading within her.

He smiled at her, a slow, unhurried smile, full of sensual promise. She smiled back, uncoiling herself from the hunch in which she had arranged herself, stretching her body out along the length of the bed.

She had fantasised about this moment, fantasised with no real expectation of gratification. Now it was here it was hard to believe. She watched the joint go slowly in and out of his mouth, mesmerised by the red glow at the end as he inhaled. She shook her head as he offered it.

'What's the matter?' he asked her. 'Don't you like it?'

Before she could reply he had ground it out in a tiny, antique porcelain sweet dish Mum had given her for her last birthday. The gesture knocked her off her stroke. She had been on the point of asking the Amber Question.

'What's the matter?' he urged, laughing.

'The Bullinger,' she found herself saying.

She felt as surprised as Jasper now looked. As a subject, it had flown out of nowhere. Or so she thought. Perhaps it had been waiting, and confusion had dislodged it from wherever it had lurked. Now, awful as it was, it was too late to unsay it. She could only look brightly back.

'What about the Bullinger?' he said lightly.

'Oh, you know . . .' She tried to match his tone with a flippant one of her own.

'What have you heard?' His voice was flat, yet there was a warning in it.

'Dwarves,' she said, keeping up the smile as if it were a joke, which hopefully it was. 'Strippers. Drugs. Tearing up fifty-pound notes in front of homeless people.'

He was looking away, perfect brows slightly knit. Her heart rattled with terror. Had she offended him?

Then, to her incalculable relief, he turned and smiled at her. 'Don't believe all you hear. We get a bad press. Mostly from people who are jealous because they haven't been invited to join themselves.'

His smile widened to something brilliant and she found her mouth stretching in response, desperate to smooth the waters she so regretted ruffling. Had Olly exaggerated about the iniquities of the organisation? Was *he* jealous? Must be, she decided.

'Besides, you know,' Jasper continued, 'I personally didn't have much choice. De Borchys have always been in the Bullinger. My brother . . . my father . . . Family tradition. You know.' He shrugged.

Isabel nodded eagerly, feeling another wave of longing for the patrimony referred to. Things like the Bullinger just went with the territory, she decided: rites of passage for the likes of Jasper. They meant nothing. All the same, she didn't want to know any more.

'It's OK,' she assured him, hastily.

He rose and bent down to her, pulling her tightly to him. She felt a surge of pure excitement. His fingers sought, then twined with hers: a dear, intimate gesture that moved her almost to tears. He was gazing at her, his beautiful face serious.

'Isabel,' Jasper said, 'I want you. I've wanted you since the moment I saw you. I've never felt like this about anyone before.'

Isabel did not trust herself to speak. It was all too wonderful to believe, too good to be true. She closed her eyes as he pushed his face into her hair. 'I need you,' he murmured, inhaling as if she were full of oxygen, saving his life, even. She felt a powerful rush of protectiveness, of pride. She had never been needed before. She, the vulnerable baby, the poor student, had always been the needy one.

Then he unwrapped her, slowly, like a present, and only when the tension and longing seemed about to explode within her did he slowly peel his own clothes off. Naked, he was the god she had always imagined, his body perfect and clean-cut: a Caravaggio lit by a desk lamp. She rose to him, her skin blazing against his. The world was whirling around her and she felt herself reeling backwards beyond the shoebox confines of the tiny room, into the infinite space behind the stars.

Chapter 19

A car was approaching the Campion Estate. In its driver's hand was clamped Diana's address.

Sara Oopvard had suspected that her former neighbour had slid down in the world. But never to this extent. Poor Diana! It was, Sara thought, marvellous to see that someone, at least, was worse off than she was.

Wild horses would not have dragged it from her, but it had been a tough few months since the divorce from Henrik. On the surface of it, she had scored victory after victory. Sara had hung on to the West London house with its basement swimming pool and penthouse home gym. Thanks to her divorce lawyers, she had amazing amounts of money, as well as custody of Milo, although this last victory was hollow, since Henrik, eternally at work, had barely seen his son, anyway. But something was missing; something that Sara, for all Henrik's money, could not buy. And that something was status. Only now she had lost it, did Sara realise how important it was.

As all her friends were firmly in the Henrik camp, the one with the money, the Provençal villa and, above all, the work-experience placements, she had learnt the hard way that a woman like her was only as good as the man she was married to. She was adrift in a sea of yachts owned by the important husbands of others, fringed by beachside villas in which were being held the smart holiday gatherings Sara was no longer asked to. She had spent much time brooding on this lack of social clout. How could she get it back again? Make people take notice? Most pressingly of all, how, when and where would she find another powerful man to marry?

Not in London, it seemed. Women she had lunched with now had their chauffeurs drive straight past her. Charities wrote to say that the orphans, heroes, homeless and others with compromised life chances, whose committees she had adorned, no longer needed her help. Milo was disinvited from a Wild West party with real bison and cowboys imported from the family ranch.

Life was becoming impossible, weekends in London even more so. Sara took every opportunity to stay with people in the country, particularly people, like Diana, who had not exactly invited her and were not necessarily expecting her.

Before turning into the Campion Estate, Sara had to stop at a zebra crossing. She waited, rudely revving the engine, her manicured fingernails tapping on the pale suede padding of the steering wheel. Normally she drove straight over crossings, especially those with shaky old people hesitating questioningly on the pavement at the side. But there were too many people mid-road to do this now. She watched in disgust as a thin man in a baseball cap loped over, several small and scruffy children scurrying in his wake. I bet none of them can hold a pencil, went Sara's burning thoughts. Their father included – if he *is* their father.

Across the road, a chip shop was enjoying a surge in custom. A row of large bottoms, their owners slumped against the pale blue counter, could be seen waiting in line through the plate-glass window. 'They should spend less time stuffing themselves and more time trying to get jobs,' the never-knowingly-employed Sara fulminated as a fat man with tattoos emerged, limping, from the establishment, passing a fat young woman, who was heaving a pram into it.

As, now, only a shaky old lady stood at the side of the crossing,

Sara stuck her foot down and roared off, in spite of the fact she had to turn almost immediately. With her usual screeching of wheels, she threw her large, white four-wheel drive into the estate entrance.

Then, as the first of the pebbledashed semis came into view, Sara felt her Manolo on the accelerator pedal rise up slightly. The car slowed. She felt tight inside. She had, she realised, never been into an actual, real council estate before – let alone as darkness fell.

She caught her breath, felt her heart pump harder, felt the adrenalin swirling round her system. She was going in! She knew exactly how a war correspondent must feel in a combat zone. She glanced in the tinted, heated, oversized driver's mirror at Milo in the back seat; he was, however, buried in a computer game, slowly eating doughnut after doughnut from the box intended as a house present, and evidently oblivious to his surroundings.

Sara raised her chin and flicked her eyes watchfully about, prepared at any moment for some armed and dangerous member of the underclass to come leaping out at her. Nothing happened, which was almost a disappointment. Driving into these badlands was giving Sara quite a frisson. A heat was rushing through her that had nothing whatsoever to do with the automatically warmed seat beneath her skinny bottom. The Campion Estate was the most exciting thing that had happened to her for months: an experience out of the ordinary; an exhilarating taste of the downmarket.

As Sara parked her white four-wheel drive outside the address she had been given, her soul lifted to see the Christmas light display on the house next door. It was a triumphant vindication in flashing neon of everything she had supposed and expected. The wall was absolutely covered! If people had money to burn on electricity bills in such quantities, the alimony-funded Sara raged to herself, why should the state support them by giving them houses? Parasites! There was one of them now, a fat woman, staring nosily out of the window. Sara glared back with all the outrage a top-rate-taxpayer-by-former-marriage could summon. She yanked on her handbrake with a crunch. 'Darling!' she trilled at her iPad-absorbed son. 'Switch that thing off, will you? We're here!'

Upstairs in the house, unaware of the impending visitor, Diana's eyes met Rosie's in the mirror. Her daughter had come up softly behind her and her face, too, now glowed in the sunset light from the window against which the dressing table was pushed. Rosie was changing, Diana saw. Her formerly round face was starting to lengthen, the plump cheeks melting to reveal ridges of cheekbone. Rosie's eyes, mere slits when she was a baby, had lengthened and thick black lashes now fringed the candid blue eyes. Rosie was growing into a beauty, her mother saw, her gaze suddenly wobbly with tears. Her snub nose with its cinnamon dusting of freckles remained, however, the same.

'What's up, Mum?' Rosie grinned. 'You look as if you're crying.'

'Just a lash in my eye, darling . . .'

'You're smudging it all,' complained Shanna-Mae, who had heroically offered to come and do her make-up again, as well as to babysit Rosie. Debs had insisted.

All things considered, there had been a lot of insistence surrounding this second date. Richard had insisted on picking her up, for example. He would be here soon, a prospect that knotted Diana's insides. All day, she had been running over the previous evening in her mind, unsure she had not imagined it. Could it really all have gone so well? Had she been drunk? But this morning, she had not had a hangover; on the contrary, she had woken with a wonderful sense of wellbeing, tinged only, perhaps, with a slight regret that she found herself alone in the bed . . .

But, as the day had worn on, so had her nerves. And with the approaching darkness, her fears had gathered momentum. She glanced out of the window now, eyes peeled for Richard's car.

Did he even have one, given his reliance on his bicycle? Perhaps, Diana thought, it would be a tandem. She shot a guilty glance at Shanna-Mae, whose handiwork might be all too soon crushed beneath a cycle helmet.

At a sudden noise below, Diana's eyes met Shanna-Mae's in excited alarm. It sounded like a knock – yes, here it came again; it *was* a knock. Her heart galloped in her chest. Richard was early.

She had not imagined – not in a million years – that the enormous white people-carrier she had just seen pass the window might contain him. But she had seen it park, although not who was driving. Shanna-Mae had been finishing her lashes just after that and she had been obliged to stare at a stain on the carpet. There were many to choose from.

'Watch it!' Shanna-Mae warned as Diana now rose to her feet, half her hair still in the straighteners. Snatched from Shanna-Mae's grip, they swung and hit her on the cheek. Diana hardly noticed. Her mind was a whirl of panic. Who was it that said you could never repeat successes?

Almost upsetting the dressing table, Diana hurried downstairs. She took a deep breath and smoothed her already-smoothed hair before reaching to the door-latch with a shaking hand and pulling it open.

The person standing outside, illuminated by the still-bare bulb hanging in the hallway, was not Richard Black. It was a skinny woman in improbable sunglasses – all the more improbable for its being dark now – and with long, highlighted blond hair, a tight, tiny denim jacket and very tight white trousers. She had on a fixed red-lipsticked smile, displaying dazzling white teeth. In one hand she held the handle of an enormous silver pod of a suitcase on wheels and on the other side stood a small, scowling boy of about nine. He was wearing a sweatshirt printed with neon skulls and clutching an iPad.

'Sara,' Diana said faintly. As she clutched the lintel for support, flakes of paint crumbled off around her fingers.

Two brown, clawlike hands, glittering with rings, came flying through the air and seized her shoulders. Two bony cheekbones crashed into hers. There was an overpowering wave of perfume. 'Darling!' exclaimed Sara Oopvard. 'Here we are!'

Diana, stunned, looked helplessly at the box Sara had shoved into her arms. It was a battered container that had once evidently held twelve Krispy Kreme doughnuts, but now held four. Various grease-marks and drips of icing marked the places once occupied by the others.

Sara was looking at her, head on one side. 'You were expecting me? Remember I mentioned it on the phone?'

'Er . . .'

'I wanted to show darling Milo here round the colleges. So he could choose which one he wanted to go to.'

Darling Milo did not even look up at this. He was frowning at his iPad, pressing it with his fingers and muttering under his breath.

'So lovely to see you!' Sara trilled. 'I thought the TomTom had got the wrong place at first!'

Diana's eyes flicked over Sara's shoulder to the great white four-wheel drive she had seen from the bedroom window. It glowed at the kerbside beyond the broken gate and seemed, in the streetlight, to have an electric pink sheen about it. The number plate read, 'SARA 1'.

'Very *different*, isn't it, darling?' Sara remarked in her drilling voice. She had pushed back her enormous sunglasses now and her sharp eyes took in the bare light bulb, the battered hall and the underfelt in the passage in one forensic swoop. 'Very, um, *understated*.'

Her bony profile – which looked even tauter than Diana remembered; her nose, certainly, was a different shape altogether – turned towards the small boy. 'Milo!' she urged. 'You remember Mrs Somers, don't you? She used to live next door to us in London, until it turned out Mr Somers was having an affair. And, when they got divorced, it turned out that they hadn't any money either; remember all that darling . . . ?'

Milo took no notice. He had activated his iPad now. The real world was a closed book to him.

Sara's words finally spurred Diana to action. 'Was that necessary?' she asked, her voice tight with anger.

'Of course!' Sara turned on her a surprised smile. 'So important to be honest with children, don't you think?' she said in syrupy tones. 'Terrible mistake, I always think, to brush things under the carpet.' She looked at the hall floor. 'Always assuming you have one, of course.' She accompanied this remark with the laugh, which instantly transported Diana back to her former home. It sounded like a burst of gunfire; you could hear it through the walls. 'I must say, darling, it's terribly *brave* of you to live here.'

'I like it here,' Diana said doggedly. 'My new neighbours are wonderful,' she added pointedly.

Sara's thin, manicured hand was at her mouth, as if pressing back amusement. 'Oh, yes. Your neighbours. That Christmas light display is very . . . How exactly shall I put it? *Special.*'

'Cheerful, you mean,' Diana said firmly, aware of Shanna-Mae on the staircase behind her.

Sara giggled. 'Well, it certainly made *us* laugh. Didn't it, Milo?'

Shanna-Mae gave an audible gasp.

Diana was thankful, at this awkward juncture, to hear Rosie now start to come down the stairs. To her surprise, her nine-year-old daughter now took effortless command of the situation.

'Hello, Mrs Upward,' Rosie said politely. 'You remember me, don't you? Rosie Somers. And this is my friend, Shanna-Mae, from –' Rosie left just the suggestion of a pause – 'next door.'

Sara had no intention of acknowledging Shanna-Mae – too obviously the sort who'd have five different children by five different fathers just to get a council house and never do a day's work in her life. Instead, she gave her entire attention to Rosie. 'Goodness! I hardly recognised you. Is that really a school uniform you have on? Say hello to Rosie, darling,' she urged Milo.

Milo took no notice. 'He's tired, poor little chap,' Sara cooed, patting her son's hair. He jerked his head impatiently. 'The sooner we get him to his room, the better.'

'His *room* . . . ?' Diana gasped. There were only two bedrooms; both were occupied. Panic swirled within her. Richard would be here any minute and that was nerve-wracking enough. But that Sara Upward and Milo had turned up unannounced within minutes of his arrival and required accommodation was nothing less than a nightmare.

'And then you can show me to mine,' Sara ordered in a brisk voice that had a hint of impatience in it. 'I could really do with a shower, if the en suite has one; but if not a bath will be fine.'

'Now, just hang on a minute . . .' Diana was about to tell Sara, in no uncertain terms, that they should go to a hotel, when her eye caught, down the road, a pair of slowly moving car headlights approaching. Someone was driving up, looking for something. An address? Was it Richard?

It seemed so. As the car slowed down outside her house, Diana wanted simultaneously to scream with frustration yet hide that frustration at any cost. The last thing she wanted Richard to witness was her rowing on the doorstep with Sara Oopvard. Sara was certain to be as obstructive and unreasonable as possible. Diana looked helplessly at her unwanted guest, not knowing what to say.

Sara unhesitatingly seized her chance. She now sailed into the hall, past an open-mouthed Diana, her high heels clacking on the boards. Milo followed her sulkily, shoulders slumped, staring into his screen.

Diana could see Richard – she was sure now it must be Richard – parking behind Sara's white and pink monster. His lights flicked off.

She shot into action. Bedrooms, bedrooms . . . She had a mere few minutes to settle in her guests, get them out of the way. Infuriating though it was, she would simply have to move Milo and Sara into her bedroom for the night. She would move in with Rosie. There was no time to do anything else; she had to go out. They would have to sort it all out in the morning. She thundered back up the stairs.

'Rosie!' Diana gasped from the landing as she rushed about finding towels and duvets. 'You can manage pesto and pasta for everyone, can't you?' It was Rosie's signature dish, rustled up by her on the many occasions when Diana had been too tired to cook.

'Of course, Mummy.'

'Pesto and pasta!' Sara shrilled in horror from the sitting room, where she had parked herself in the one armchair and produced a magazine from her bag. 'I'm sorry. I don't do carbohydrates.'

Rosie smiled sweetly. 'You could always have just pesto, Mrs Oopvard.'

Sara seemed about to issue a sharp reply when her open mouth closed suddenly. Her eyes had left Rosie and were now appraising, through the sitting room window, the person coming up Diana's garden path. In the limited light of the nearby streetlamp, he appeared both tall and good-looking – and dark, which especially appealed to Sara. Her last husband, that *bastard* Henrik, had been short and fair – in the hair sense, if no other.

Of course, this man probably lived on the council estate too – a neighbour, possibly. She was not interested in him in any serious way. And yet he could probably show a girl a good time, Sara thought, licking her lips and grinding her hips slightly into the seat cushions. He looked very fit and muscular. Not unlike some of the gardeners whose services she had enjoyed in the past.

And there was something else about him. Proud bearing, you might call it; a noble savage sort of thing. He might be on jobseeker's allowance, or whatever it was called, but he had practically the same air of authority she recognised from her former wealthy London neighbours. The high court judge and the newspaper editor, say.

He was a distressed gentleperson, perhaps. As he reached the threshold, Sara raised herself unsteadily and sailed towards him over the underfelt, armed with her most dazzling smile. 'Can I help you?' she inquired magnificently.

Overhead, Diana could still be heard thundering about, looking for sheets.

Richard looked in astonishment at the female in heavily maquillage, wobbling before him on ridiculously high heels. 'Do excuse me,' he said, alarmed. Of course. It made sense now. He was in the wrong street. That ludicrous car he had parked behind could not possibly have belonged to Diana. 'I'm in the wrong place,' he added.

'Aren't we all, darling?' Sara riposted with a giggle that sounded like gunfire. 'Personally, I've never been on an estate in my life, unless it's got butlers and stables. I expect it's the same for you,' she added in the spirit of social *esprit de corps*.

'Not really,' Richard said, surprised. What was this strange woman talking about? Hurriedly, he turned to leave.

'Hold on,' Sara gasped, batting her eyelashes wildly. 'Perhaps I can help you.' She paused for a few minutes before adding; 'Were you looking for someone?'

'I was looking for Diana,' Richard said stiffly.

'I thought so,' Sara said. 'And *poor* Diana does live here, actually. *Dreadful* business,' she added, shaking her head pityingly.

'Dreadful?' Panic leapt within Richard. Had something awful happened to Diana? Was that why this ghastly woman was here? He felt real worry and realised with surprise how passionately he cared.

'Absolutely.' Sara shook her head mournfully. 'Diana was my neighbour in West London,' she announced, pausing for this to sink in. He was, it had to be said, looking most satisfactorily surprised. 'But then,' Sara bent forward, lowered her voice and shook her head pityingly, 'her husband left her for his secretary.'

More fool him, Richard thought.

'And Diana got *nothing* in the divorce, absolutely *nothing*.'

'She got her child,' Richard pointed out. That there had been a divorce was no surprise, of course; he had guessed as much. But why was this woman – in those ridiculous sunglasses – talking about Diana in this way on the doorstep of her own house? Was she mad?

He was now seriously concerned. Where was Diana? He tried to look behind this woman, but she kept striking poses and tossing her hair about so it was difficult to see anything else.

'Her *child*!' Sara let fire another volley of mirth. 'What the hell use is *that*? She's got no money!'

Fortunately, at this moment, a pair of legs in dark trousers came running down the stairs behind. As Diana appeared, looking flustered, Richard felt a warm, powerful, wave of relief.

'Richard!' Diana exclaimed, her delight at seeing him so intense that nothing else, suddenly, mattered. She was glad of Shanna-Mae's foundation. The fact she was blushing furiously would be well concealed.

'You can use my room now, Sara,' she muttered to the figure in sunglasses who she vaguely sensed was behind her.

Sara, however, had no intention of going upstairs. She was standing in the hall alternately pouting at Richard and fixing Diana with a steely, inquiring beam. 'Aren't you going to introduce me?'

Diana braced herself. 'Richard, this is Sara Oopvard.'

'Upward?' Richard repeated incredulously.

'Oopvard,' Sara corrected, pushing her lips out suggestively. 'Oop-vard. It's Dutch. My husband, I should say *ex*-husband,' she went on, with an inviting smile, 'was Dutch.'

Diana interrupted hurriedly. 'This is Professor Richard Black.'

She had anticipated that Sara would nod, shake hands and go upstairs.

Sara nodded and shook hands, but she did not go upstairs. '*Professor*?' she repeated, evidently stunned.

'He's a professor of neuroscience and the Master of Branston

College, one of the university colleges . . .' Diana explained briefly, anxious to limit Richard's exposure to her ghastly and unwelcome guest.

Sara was thankful for the recent Botox injections enabling her to maintain a serene expression. This – this *dish* – who she had supposed a mere horny-handed son of toil, was actually head of a college? A more perfect solution to her difficulty could not be envisaged. She saw herself already, sweeping across the college lawns in a ballgown, her laughter tinkling into her champagne flute.

Hurriedly, she marshalled her forces. So what if he was here to see Diana? Prising him away from her would be easy. Diana had always been a drip, the way she'd let Simon walk all over her.

Even so, it had not escaped her notice that Diana, who had formerly erred on the plump side, now looked positively lithe and that her make-up, also formerly cack-handed and applied in a rush, looked positively professional. Ironically, considering her appalling circumstances, she looked the best she ever had. Had she looked like that for Simon, he probably wouldn't have left her in the first place.

Diana had her head down now, however. She looked the picture of embarrassed misery, Sara was satisfied to see. The professor, on the other hand, was looking at her with a steely glint in his eye. Sara fired at him a dazzling grin that he did not return.

'Ready?' Richard asked Diana.

Sara put her head on one side and shook out her glossy mane for Richard's benefit. 'Going somewhere nice?' she inquired breathily.

Diana looked nervously at Richard, who looked impassively at Sara. 'We're going out for supper,' he said flatly.

'Really!' Sara exclaimed, her eyes on Diana. 'And leaving dear little Rosie behind?'

'Shanna-Mae's babysitting,' Diana said, cross to be bounced into defending herself. What business was it of Sara's? The suspicion that Sara was up to something was growing within her.

'May I ask where you're going?' Sara beamed unwaveringly.

Richard's eyes flashed briefly at the ceiling. 'Out for dinner.'

Diana was growing increasingly anxious and irritated. Why wouldn't Sara go upstairs? Or even into the kitchen, where she could hear Rosie getting out the dried pasta and trying to chat to Milo. 'What's your favourite lesson at school?' she was asking.

'*Favourite?*' was the incredulous reply.

Sara seemed to follow Diana's thoughts. 'Pasta,' she said again, shaking her head. 'Carbohydrate's just the *worst* thing for my digestion. If *only* there was something else I could eat . . .' She shrugged helplessly at them both and Diana tried to suppress the feeling of rising dread, of impending doom.

'I *know*!' Sara added, with sudden, spontaneous excitement, as if the glad thought had only just occurred. 'Why don't I come out to dinner? With you?'

Chapter 20

Diana sat in the car, full of admiration for the cool way Richard had dealt with Sara Oopvard. No, she could not come to dinner with them, Richard had explained. He needed to be alone with Diana. He had something personal to discuss with her.

As even Sara could not argue with this, she had subsided, eyes spitting sparks of resentment. Diana was reminded of a snake settling back into its coil. And now, instead of making an unwelcome third at their evening together, Sara was spending the evening on the Campion Estate with Milo, Rosie and Shanna-Mae.

Diana felt guilty sympathy for her daughter and her friend. The two of them had been planning to experiment with making face cream in the kitchen; Shanna-Mae intended eventually – or perhaps next week, who knew? – to launch her own range of beauty products. They were also intending to hold make-up sessions in the bathroom where mirrored tiles – some cracked, admittedly – on the door and walls offered a range of viewpoints for various effects. Instead, as she and Richard had left, Rosie had been fighting for space on the kitchen table with Milo's range of hand-held devices while Sara had set about using all the available hot water in what would no doubt be a prolonged bath. Diana hoped Sara would spare her Penhaligon's bath oil, a rare survival from her old life and one of the few luxurious items she owned.

Diana darted a glance at Richard's profile – handsome, sharply cut, preoccupied – as they drove along. She felt a wild fluttering within. He was telling her that the car was not his, that it belonged to the Bursar and he had borrowed it for the evening. It smelled both unexpectedly and markedly of cigarettes, as if the Bursar spent long periods sitting in it, smoking furiously. Diana now fixed her gaze on Richard's hands at the wheel and wondered how it would feel to have them caress her. They were long, delicate, deliciously sensitive-looking.

Richard was staring straight ahead. He was babbling, he knew, about the Bursar, but something was bubbling within him and he felt – most uncharacteristically – almost chatty. He strained to stop himself before he told her what was at the very top of his mind: that he had hardly slept for thinking about her; that her gentle brown eyes, the shining folds of her hair and the soft, creamy curves of her face – as well as other soft, creamy curves elsewhere – had haunted what dreams he had managed. He had awoken with an ache he had thought long gone; he had imagined all desire in him to have died with Amy. But for the first time in many months he had wanted a woman – Diana, in particular. The thought of her had haunted him all day as well; so much so that he wasn't sure he had packed up his last experiment properly. This was unheard of; his concentration was usually absolute. They would have to call in at the labs before going to the restaurant, at any rate.

They were turning off the dark road, through a pair of brick gateposts. The headlights picked out the entrance to a car park. He swung into a space and switched off the engine. 'It's the labs. Just something I have to check on. Come with me, if you like.'

His tone was warm, excited. Diana smiled back. She was, she realised, being invited into the inner sanctum – the red-hot centre of his preoccupations. That he was far more interested in his work than in her was obvious, but his enthusiasm was such that she scarcely minded. She unstrapped her seat belt eagerly. 'I'd love to.'

He smiled, touched. 'Sure? It's only a lot of worms.'

'Worms?'

He expected her to look disgusted; instead, she looked something closer to charmed. 'I love worms,' Diana said. 'They're great gardeners.'

The laboratory was an older, more graceful building than Diana had imagined, with beautiful cast-iron Art Deco doors. 'Department of Neurology', read the sign on the wall next to them. Richard was already inside and she had to hurry to catch up. He threw some friendly words at the uniformed guard and Diana, scurrying after him across the expanse of marbled floor, shot an apprehensive look at him too. 'Evening, Madam,' said the guard, grinning and touching his white peaked cap. She blushed.

In the lift, Richard shoved his hands in his pockets and stared at the ceiling, his brows knit, evidently thinking of whatever it was he had come to do. Diana covertly examined his outfit; given the chaos of his arrival at her home, it was her first opportunity to do so. He wore a dark suit and a white shirt with a rich green scarf that looked like cashmere. A heavy, plain grey overcoat completed the look. The same rather distracted elegance as before, she thought, as if he had dressed in a hurry, but with unerring taste. His lack of vanity was very attractive. She felt a shiver of lust.

The lift doors opened; she followed him down a series of quiet, strip-lit corridors and, eventually, through a pair of doors.

He turned to her. 'Welcome to my world!' he said, with a touch of irony.

The room was large, empty and full of desks and computers. As they passed a large light box, Richard slowed. Ranged on the top of it were laboratory slides with what looked like pieces of wafer-thin brown meat on them, so finely sliced every detail of their marbling could be seen. 'That's a brain,' he told her. 'Look, here – that dot – that's a neuron. They change shape and size with use. The person studying these is trying to show how you can quite literally see someone's thoughts.'

Diana looked at the brown slices of brain. They reminded her of the smoked cod's roe carpaccio she'd had in a London restaurant once. The comparison made her snort. She realised with surprise that the unimaginable had happened: aspects of her old life now seemed funny.

Then, halfway down the laboratory room, something in a high-sided plastic box made her jump. 'Hamsters?' Diana looked down at the squirming bodies in the vivarium.

'Mmm,' Richard said absently. He was at the far end of the room, bent over a desk. 'One of my colleagues is looking at what makes them laugh.'

'Laugh?' Diana repeated. 'I didn't realise hamsters laughed.'

She grinned. Rosie was going to love that.

The wall before Richard was entirely covered with small, colourful, illuminated Perspex boxes. As Diana approached she saw each box contained several worms, their bodies glistening in the coloured light. She turned to him. 'Don't tell me. Worms laugh too?'

'Not exactly.' She listened hard as he explained.

'So,' she said slowly, when he paused to take a breath, 'you put a smell in the green-lit box that they don't like and later you take the smell away. They still stay out of the green box because they associate the colour with the nasty smell?'

'That's it.'

'So what's the point of that?' Diana asked, more bluntly than she had intended.

Richard stared. Scholars at his level tended to be left to their own devices. 'Well,' he began, struggling with his instinctive indignation. 'It's to do with how the brain can be controlled by colours.'

Brain control sounded worrying. Didn't it? Instead of nodding and subsiding, Diana forced herself onward. 'Is that – well – ethical?'

She half-expected he would shoot her down in flames. But instead he smiled.

'You're quite right. There are controversial aspects. But we're confining it to worms at the moment; the research is at a very early stage and will probably be used for mental health therapy in the end.'

Diana nodded seriously. She wondered, but didn't dare ask, what the point of the laughing hamsters was. Perhaps later.

The Bursar's car had not even disappeared around the corner of the estate before Sara had pushed Milo off the iPad and was on the internet researching Richard. Her excitement rose. On the various sites in which he appeared, the distinguished Professor Black was usually in his laboratory looking dark, handsome and thrillingly preoccupied by his high-powered and prestigious work. The only variation on this theme – clearly he had not exactly courted the attentions of photographers and, judging by some of his expressions, seemed rather to resent them – were shots of Professor Black looking impressive on a podium, addressing rapt students at various exclusive Ivy-League colleges.

The possibility – indeed the probability – that he was married had occurred to Sara. Not a problem. Married men were fair game, as the women who had snatched both hers and Diana's husbands had shown. Nonetheless, it had been a great moment when Sara discovered that Richard was a widower: a sitting target.

The ex-wife – who featured in some of the pictures, too – didn't look anything special, Sara concluded. Freckled face – unmade-up – with messy strawberry blond hair caught up loosely behind. Neither fat nor thin, although it was difficult to tell in the ancient jeans she had seemed invariably to wear. If that was what Richard Black had been used to, Sara had concluded, she herself could hardly fail to make a positive impression with her polished appearance, honed figure and blazing white teeth. Diana may have upgraded herself slightly and lost weight, but she was no match for the full gala Oopvard.

Sara's hopes soared. That such a prize had fallen into her lap!

Into Richard's, too, as he would soon grow to appreciate. A glamorous, metropolitan and sophisticated woman such as herself would be a considerable asset to him as he entertained, after all. As for Milo, growing up in a university atmosphere with an internationally feted neuroscientist as his stepfather was bound to have a positive impact on his up-till-now modest academic achievements. He would hardly be able to help becoming a towering genius himself.

All that remained was to bring Richard round to her plan. Sara decided to devote the rest of the evening to plotting how this might come about and drifted back upstairs to the bath she had abandoned earlier.

She was irritated to see that Diana's nine-year-old daughter, who had much too direct a stare for Sara's liking, was back up there, leaning over the basin with her fat friend. Make-up and brushes were perilously balanced on the top of the loo and along the edges of the tub.

They seemed to be discussing someone.

'I think he's nice,' Rosie was saying. 'I know Mum thinks so too. She's been excited about it all day, even though she's been trying not to show it. And she went all red when he got here, you could see it even under the make-up.' She chuckled.

'He's hot,' the fat teenager opined. 'For an old person,' she added, critically.

They were, Sara deduced, discussing Richard. *Her* Richard. Indignation mounted within her. 'Hey,' she said crossly, storming into the bathroom. 'I'm having a bath, OK?'

'Sorry, Sara.' Rosie backed away from the basin immediately. Sara could not help noticing that, even with only one eye made up, the girl already had a fawnish prettiness.

'We thought you'd finished,' Shanna-Mae said.

'Well, I hadn't, so scram,' Sara snapped ungraciously.

Rosie and Shanna-Mae collected their belongings and went downstairs. They surprised Milo in the kitchen, rummaging in the cupboards.

'What are you doing, Milo?' Rosie asked calmly.

He turned, his dark face twisted in a scowl. 'What's it to you?' He squinted to look at her better. 'And what's up with your face, anyway? Looks like someone's punched one of your eyes out.'

Rosie ignored these last remarks. 'If you need something in particular, I might be able to help you find it.'

'Looking for the Krispy Kremes,' Milo snarled, evidently unused to having to explain his actions.

'They're in the fridge,' Rosie said. 'There's one for each of us.'

An incredulous grin spread over Milo's face. His eyes, slightly lopsided, gleamed. 'No, there isn't,' he said. He opened the fridge door, reached for the plate and tore off almost half of a chocolate one with one bite.

'That's very mean of you,' Rosie said immediately. 'They were brought as a present for us and we don't get things like that very often. Any more,' she added, as an afterthought.

Milo looked scornful. 'So what?' he demanded. 'Your mum shouldn't have walked out on your dad.'

Rosie was white, her face incredulous. A black fire crackled in her eyes. 'Stop that!' she said in a low, dangerous voice.

Milo merely smirked in reply. 'Although my mum says that, if your mum had made more of an effort, your dad wouldn't have started screwing around . . .'

'Shut up!' Rosie screamed, and launched herself at him. Shanna-Mae, however, was too quick for her. Despite her size, she was unexpectedly fast on her feet and had grabbed Rosie round the waist with her powerful arms. Rosie was held, suspended, above the carpet, kicking and flailing, clawing the air as if to slash the skin from Milo's face.

'Just ignore 'im,' Shanna-Mae counselled, shooting a look of disgust at Milo. ''E ain't worth it.'

Rosie allowed herself to be lowered, shakily, to the ground. With a final glance of loathing at her tormentor, she left the kitchen. Milo looked after them, grinning broadly, his cheeks stuffed with doughnut.

With Shanna-Mae shuffling after her, Rosie returned to the sitting room. 'We can do our make-up here,' she suggested.

'OK,' Shanna-Mae agreed. Her plump face fell slightly. 'Shame about them Krispy Kremes. I've never had one before.'

Rosie beamed at her. 'Never mind, Shanna-Mae. One day, when you have salons across the world, you can have as many Krispy Kremes as you like.'

Shanna-Mae's small eyes lit up. 'Yeah – and have doughnut concessions in all my shops!'

Rosie giggled. They had just finished unpacking the cosmetics again when Milo entered the sitting room, a half-eaten doughnut in his hand. 'This is the last one,' he mocked. 'Watch me and weep, paupers.'

With an enormous effort, Rosie ignored him. She and Shanna-Mae began quietly talking to each other about the merits of the various eye shadows spread about them on the carpet.

Milo paced around them. Furious at being ignored, he began cavorting round the room's edge, executing huge and violent kicks at unexpected moments. He was clearly doing his best to aggravate her, just as Rosie was doing her best to ignore him. But after the trainered foot came to within a centimetre of her nose, Rosie could bear it no longer.

She looked up, exasperated. 'What are you doing, Milo?' she asked calmly.

The dark eyes gleamed spitefully. 'My karate.'

'Just ignore 'im,' Shanna-Mae urged.

Eventually Milo ended his physical exertions and lay, sprawled on the floor, with his console, either uttering curses or exclaiming with violent jubilation.

'What are you playing?' Rosie had tried to ignore him, but it was impossible.

Shanna-Mae flashed her a warning look.

'*High School Slaughter.*' Milo's narrow eyes sparkled with excitement as he gunned down victim after victim. 'Die, you bastard,' he muttered to himself occasionally as he virtually picked off another group of virtual schoolchildren with his virtual AK-47.

Shanna-Mae and Rosie looked at each other. By mutual consent they rose and returned to the kitchen where they resumed manufacture of the face cream.

For a while, all was calm. The girls were soon absorbed in their task and it was only once the ingredients had been stirred together and were cooking in a pan on the stove that it occurred to Rosie how uncharacteristically quiet Milo was being.

Not even the roar of simulated gunfire could be heard any more.

Shanna-Mae, dipping a finger in the mixture to check the consistency, looked up too. 'He's very quiet,' she said slowly.

'Too quiet,' Rosie agreed. Their eyes met.

'Let's go and have a look.' said Shanna-Mae.

Upstairs in the bath Sara was staring into the steamy mirrored wall tiles. Was her eyelid about to go next? She bent forward to inspect the newly loose and dangling flap of skin where all before had been taut and perfect. She was falling apart. Everything was falling apart. Richard Black had come into her life only just in time.

But the plan she had hoped to make, the plot to trap him, was taking its time in coming.

She had done everything to create a contemplative atmosphere. She had chucked in the water every last drop of some cheap old bath essence she'd found and piled up for post-bath use every towel she had been able to find in the whole house. But inspiration had not struck.

Sara stared into the mist and stirred her boiling thoughts. What she needed was some excuse to be alone with him. But what? Even if she were to stay here indefinitely in this horrid box of a house, Richard, if ever she saw him, would obviously only be here to see Diana.

The thought of them together, even now, burned and festered

within her. If only, she thought, there was some drama she could stage, some crisis which would bring Diana back and then, somehow, throw Sara and Richard together. But what? A house fire would only result in them all having to go outside – in that scrappy, crappy, little garden. In November.

Of course! Sara sat up excitedly in the bath. A medical emergency; something small-scale. She could pretend to have broken her ankle and have him take her to A & E . . .

The fires of excitement accompanying this inspired thought died down again, however. Richard would obviously have had medical training. He might be able to spot a feigned break. Perhaps she could sprain it instead. But Sara drew the line at throwing herself down the stairs, particularly stairs as nasty as Diana's. She would have to think again.

Sara was sinking back in her bath when a loud scream from below brought her bolt upright again. The scream repeated itself; there was blood in it, Sara felt – fury and vengeance. And now she could hear someone else as well; it sounded like Milo, yelling in terror: 'Mum! *Muuuuummm!*'

She rose out of the bath, grabbed one of Diana's towels and plunged downstairs. The noise seemed to be coming from the sitting room, if you could call something that size a room.

Sara peered round the doorway. An extraordinary sight met her eyes. Had the three of them been painting? They'd covered the whole room, by the look of it.

Everywhere there were smudges of colour: red, scuffed black, shimmery orange and violet. Blue, sticky varnish decorated the walls, as if it had been thrown there. Seeing a great pool of a greasy beige substance on the carpet, Sara realised that it wasn't paint – it was make-up; the make-up that Rosie and the fat girl had been using.

What had happened? Bits of compact lay here and there, broken glass glittering, their hinges wrenched and broken. Squashed tips of lipstick, open tubes of gloss and bent mascara wands were scattered about. Eye pencils and make-up brushes were snapped in two. Nail-polish bottle tops, detached from their bottles, stuck to the sofa cushions.

The fat teenager was rolling on the floor, screaming. 'You *bastard*!' she was yelling, pounding her fists hard into Milo.

He was pressed beneath, unable to move, thrashing his head from side to side and shouting. 'Mum! Muuuuuum!'

'That's right,' the fat girl cried hysterically. 'Shout for Mummy, why don't you? Coward!' She punched him again and Milo screamed anew.

Sara stepped into the middle of the floor. 'Just *what* is going on?' she shrieked. She lunged at Shanna-Mae with one hand, hanging on to her towel with the other. 'Leave my son alone, you great bully!'

She was aware that someone had taken her arm and was shaking it. She looked up and found herself staring into the wild gaze of Rosie.

'You've got it all wrong, Mrs Oopvard,' panted the little girl. 'Milo's done something really terrible. While we were in the kitchen, he took all Shanna-Mae's make-up and wiped it everywhere. He's destroyed everything she had. She saved for it for years; it's everything to her . . .'

Sara stared around, briefly awed herself by the extent of the wreckage. That Milo could unleash such chaos was impressive even by his standards. She gazed at her son, red-faced, rolling out from under Shanna-Mae who now stood up and, head in hands, sank on the sofa and began to sob bitterly.

Milo was loudly protesting his innocence. 'She hit me, Mum . . .' he whimpered.

Fury raged within Sara. She was staring at disaster. Defeat. They would have to go back home now. Even she couldn't brazen this one out; even Diana, wet as she was, would refuse to give them houseroom after this. And where would she be then with Richard? She felt like laying a blow on Milo herself.

'Get up,' she snarled at her cringing, snivelling son with such violence that even Shanna-Mae paused in her sobbing and peeped at her, awed, through her fingers. Fingers which, Sara found herself noticing, had long false nails attached, with elaborate patterns in diamonds on some of them.

A great flash of blinding light struck her. As Milo heaved himself upwards, wailing loudly at every beating and bruise he claimed to have suffered, she stepped swiftly forward. 'Is that,' she demanded, wrenching her son's sharp chin towards her, 'a scratch? From those *talons*?' She stared incriminatingly at Shanna-Mae's hands.

'Yes!' Milo screamed immediately. 'She almost murdered me, Mum. I bet she's broken some of my bones, Mum.'

Sara looked at him contemplatively. 'She might well have done, son. We'd better go and have you checked out.' She swung her glittering gaze to Rosie. 'You'd better show me the phone,' she hissed, suppressing with difficulty the exultation in her voice. 'I'm going to ring your mother. They'll have to come back and then Richard will have to take me and Milo to casualty.'

'Why can't you drive yourself?' Rosie challenged, shaken but not quite defeated.

Sara was outraged. What right did this infant have to question her, still less lay open the fact there was no reason beyond dividing Richard from Diana and having him all to herself. 'I should have thought that was obvious,' Sara snapped. 'I'm far too upset to drive. And someone needs to look after my poor little boy. Your horrible fat friend nearly killed him.'

Chapter 21

The evening was going wonderfully, Richard felt. Better even than the first one. The restaurant was a small French bistro recommended to him by the Bursar, who had spent a lengthy period in his office that afternoon complaining about the alumni dinner. It was progressing apace, Richard learnt. There was to be a welcoming drinks reception in the Turd and the final menu had been drawn up with the kitchen. The Bursar confided to Richard his doubts about the pudding – a sauternes jelly with grapes suspended within. 'Looks like dog food', the Bursar sighed.

'Dog food!' Diana snorted, as Richard repeated the story to her now. She seemed to find everything concerning the alumni dinner interesting and amusing and the idea of asking her as his guest was starting to bloom in Richard's mind. It would cause a stir in the college, he knew. People would gossip. But so what? Diana was a Branston employee, and besides, he liked her. Perhaps more than liked her. Certainly, he wanted to see more of her. And the dinner was coming up, and having her there would make it approximately one hundred times more bearable. Even fun.

Diana was amazed. Such a public announcement of the fact of their relationship was both thrilling and terrifying.

'You don't have to,' he said quickly, glancing over the bread roll basket towards her astonished face. 'I'll understand if you say no. It's just that I need someone to come with me and it would be great if it was you; we seem to get on pretty well . . .' He stopped himself before he could downgrade things between them any further. It wasn't coming out the way he meant it to, not at all.

'Er, OK,' Diana said quickly, hurriedly filtering and evaluating all this new information. *Seem to get on pretty well* – was that all? It wasn't what she had expected, when the second date had followed so fast upon the first. She had imagined – hoped – that it was the beginning of something between them.

'You don't sound very sure,' Richard said, but knew it was his own fault.

Diana did not contradict him.

'It's not the hottest of dates, I admit,' he added, then shut up again. He was in a hole and it was best to stop digging.

A sound caught her ear now: a muffled, insistent ringing from somewhere close. Diana's hands slapped the sides of her chair, searching for her bag. 'I'd better answer it. It might be Rosie.'

He watched her shake back her hair and reveal a small and delicate ear. She shoved the phone against it, her mouth half-open with anticipation. He saw her face disappear under a scrunch of frowns. 'Sara,' Diana said, flatly.

That monster in the make-up, Richard thought. She had just dropped in, Diana had said earlier. She had not offered anything further and he hardly wanted to ask. The least said about that creature, the better. He would have thought her to be miles away by now, on her way back to wherever her lair was, but he was alarmed, now, to see the colour drain out of Diana's ruddy face.

'An emergency!' Her voice was a choking gasp. 'A disaster in the house?' She was stumbling to her feet, wildly grabbing at her coat. 'Sara, I'm coming. I'm coming right now.'

They drove at top speed, Richard oblivious and uncaring as to the consequences to his career of being caught by the police.

Diana, next to him, had been sick with fear. Sara had given no details. An emergency at home was all she had said. The line had then gone dead and Diana had been unable to reconnect despite constant, frantic, shaky-fingered dialling all the way home.

The car had not even stopped outside Diana's house before she had torn open the door, raced up the path, burst in.

'Jesus!'

The hall looked like the aftermath of a bomb – a bomb in a cosmetics department. Bottles of foundation and nail varnish spilled beige or sparkling viscous liquid into the gritty underfelt carpet. Gaudy colours daubed the walls. The tops of broken eye pencils lay around like small gold bullets on the floor. There was a powerful smell of perfume.

Diana was too terrified even to think. For entire seconds the world whirled and blurred. Then it jolted back into focus as a small, white-faced figure appeared.

'Rosie!' Crushing the small body to her, Diana nearly collapsed with sheer relief. If Rosie was safe, she could face any catastrophe.

In her ears, the screaming silence of panic had been replaced by screaming and shouting from the sitting room. Still clutching Rosie, Diana staggered in its direction.

In the middle of a more intense and colourful devastation than that of the hall stood Debs. Her large face flamed red with anger as she shouted in her powerful voice at Sara Oopvard, who stood, hands on narrow, leather-clad hips, smirking. Behind her skulked Milo, clutching his face theatrically. Shanna-Mae lurked to Debs' expansive rear.

'Rosie? What's going on?'

Both women now turned and spotted Diana. There was a mutual intake of breath before Rosie's explanation was drowned in an explosion of competing tales. With difficulty, Diana pieced it together. The bottom line seemed to be that Milo had wrecked Shanna-Mae's precious collection of make-up.

'Just a few eye pencils, that's all,' Sara spat dismissively. 'Milo didn't mean any harm.'

Debs' nostrils flared like a charging bull's. 'Let me at her!' she yelled.

'Mum!' Shanna-Mae shouted, restraining the maternal bulk with difficulty.

Rosie's low, firm voice now took up the tale, explaining how, unsurprisingly, Shanna-Mae had retaliated with violent fury to the havoc wrought by Milo.

'She's gored him!' came Sara's interrupting shriek. 'Scratched him so badly he'll get tetanus if we don't get him to hospital!'

'*Scratch*!' Debs exclaimed. 'You can hardly bloody see it! I'll give *her* a bloody scratch, just let me near her—'

'Have you *seen* that girl's nails?' Sara hurled back. 'She's gouged him!'

'Where's the scratch?' Diana was asking when Sara leant to the side and addressed someone behind her. 'You'll take us to hospital, won't you Richard?' she purred, throwing him a look of pure feminine appeal.

Richard! Amid the whirl of action, the churn of panic, Diana had forgotten about him. He must have been standing behind her all the time, in the middle of all the mess, violence and hysteria.

What must he think of this bedlam? Of the way she lived, the people she knew? She turned to him in horror, her lips framing an apology.

But Richard, with a startled look back over his shoulder, was already being bundled out of the room by a satisfied-looking Sara, who was dragging Milo, who was clutching his iPad. As the door slammed behind them, it crossed Diana's mind that he was probably relieved to get away.

The others seemed to melt away too. The room that had been so full – of noise, of people – was now empty. The house seemed suddenly very silent.

Diana looked slowly around. She saw with dull misery how complete was the wreckage of her efforts to make a new home. The carpet she had scrubbed was filthy all over again, the cushions and throws she had chosen from the market were smeared and torn. Diana bowed her head, fighting the tears.

But then, as a glum-faced Rosie came back into the sitting room, she pulled herself together. As, slowly, they began to address the mess, Debs appeared in the doorway. She had evidently been in the kitchen with Shanna-Mae.

Diana leapt to her feet and rushed to her friend, intending to give her a consoling hug. But Debs turned away and Diana was startled. Of course what had happened was dreadful, but surely the good-hearted, sensible Debs could see it was not her fault?

'I'm so sorry, Debs,' Diana gasped. 'Of course I'll pay for the make-up, replace everything that's been ruined.'

She knew, even as she spoke, that it would not be that easy. Both financially – the collection was worth hundreds – and because Shanna-Mae had assembled it from many different sources over the years. But she would find the money, look for the make-up online if necessary.

Debs waved her apologies away, however. And not politely, either, but with angry cuts of the hand through the air. Diana looked with anguished appeal at Shanna-Mae, but she was leaning against the wall with her arms belligerently folded. It was obvious that the wreckage Sara had left behind was not only material.

Panic clutched Diana. She could not let the corrosive Oopvards ruin this friendship. Unhesitatingly, she threw herself on Debs' mercy. 'Please,' she began, desperately. 'Please. You must forgive me. Sara just turned up, tonight, out of the blue. I wasn't expecting her, I had no idea . . .'

Debs turned to her, face wrenched into an unfamiliar expression. With a shock, Diana realised it was deep dislike – loathing, even.

'You people,' Debs spat. 'You patronise us, you pretend to be friends, but all the time you're laughing at us, looking down on us. *Lying* to us.'

Diana's mouth dropped open. From somewhere in the sitting room now rose the sound of Rosie's quiet sobs. Diana shook her head frantically, holding her hands out to her friend in desperate appeal. 'Debs, that couldn't be further from the truth. I don't know where I'd be without you. You've helped me so much, from the minute I moved in—'

'Save your breath, Mrs High-and-Mighty,' Debs put in, violently. 'Your good friend there –' she jerked her thumb in the direction of the door – 'told us *exactly* how it was.' She was shaking with a sort of savage satisfaction.

Diana was electrified with a sudden alarm. '*What* did she tell you?'

Rosie stepped forward. 'She said . . . you know . . . about Daddy . . .'

The impact was almost physical. Diana belt double as if she had been punched in the stomach. She put her hands over her face as Rosie's little voice went on, through the screaming in her head. 'That he had been a cheat and lied to everyone, and that you had, too.'

Diana parted her fingers slightly. Debs and Shanna-Mae were staring stubbornly at the floor, however. It was obvious from their set faces, their folded arms, that no arrows of reason were going to penetrate their defences. But what could she say, anyway? The Simon part of it was perfectly true.

A furious misery welled within her, but no longer on her own account. What had Sara Oopvard thought she was doing? To lash out like this seemed a gross overreaction to the scuffle involving Milo in which her son, in any case, had inflicted the worst damage. And an appalling return on Diana's generosity in, however unwillingly, giving the Oopvards houseroom.

The fire had gone from Diana now. A feeling of absolute hopelessness overwhelmed her like a tide. She sank slowly down on the make-up sticky sofa, oblivious to the nail varnish soaking in to her best pair of trousers. As she pulled her daughter to her, the little body resisted only just enough to crank the handle of her pain still harder. But this was no time to feel sorry for herself. Rosie needed explanations.

Wordlessly, the other mother and daughter left, the latter clutching what remained of her make-up kit. Wordlessly, Diana and Rosie watched them go. As the door shut behind them, Diana pressed her face to her daughter's hair.

'Is it true, Mum, what Sara said?' The little voice was quiet, but steely. As the words came out, the small body in Diana's arms had tensed.

Diana hesitated. 'Well, what did she say exactly?'

'Well . . .' The child bit her lip. 'That Daddy spent money he didn't have.'

'Yes,' Diana admitted. There seemed no point in pretending otherwise. After what Sara had said, euphemisms were hardly going to help. 'But, actually, I didn't know about it,' she added. 'I should have. I should have known a lot of things.'

She shook her head regretfully. 'I should have told Debs about it too, when I had the chance. Better that she heard from me than from Sara. Too late, though, now.'

There was a silence. Diana waited, worriedly, for her daughter's reaction. After holding still a few minutes more, the little body slumped, the little arms clutched her and Diana felt a soft, warm cheek on hers. 'Never mind, Mummy.'

'No.' Diana held her daughter tightly and felt that, after all, she didn't mind. What could she do? What was done was done. Rosie was all that mattered.

'I'm glad they've all gone,' the small voice, sleepy now, came again.

'That's definitely something,' Diana agreed, with a glimmer of a smile. For Rosie, as ever, had accentuated the positive, even in a situation like this. Of course, the one bright prospect to emerge from the whole sorry mess was that they would never see the Oopvards again. Not even Sara would have the gall to re-enter the house after what had happened. When they returned from the hospital, it would be to climb into their white monster of a four-wheel drive and slink off, back to London. 'And now,' she said to Rosie, 'to bed.'

After many weary, wiping-and-mopping-up hours later, Diana's last act was to stuff her unwelcome guest's belongings back in her great gleaming case, drag it outside and lean it against her car. It was, she felt, a hint that even Sara Oopvard would understand.

As she drifted off to sleep, Diana felt there was another positive aspect to tonight's dramatic events. Yes, she had been wrong not to tell Debs about Simon and the divorce before. So Sara had got there first and given it the worst possible spin. Now she must learn from her mistake. She must, Diana thought, tell Richard about it at the first opportunity. Admittedly, on the back of all that had happened tonight, it was unlikely to impress him – the opposite, probably. Nonetheless, it needed to be done. She must come clean, and do it before that dinner he had asked her to; they could hardly discuss it there.

As she went to sleep, Diana felt a further disquiet; Richard, of course, had taken Sara to the hospital. But it was surely out of the question that her divorce would be discussed. Even Sara would draw the line at vindictive gossip while in A & E with her son. And Milo's wound was so slight they were probably finished now anyway and on their way back. Then Sara would see the suitcase, get in the car, return to London.

All the same, Diana felt, she must get to Richard as soon as possible.

'Of course, you know,' Sara said, turning to Richard brightly as they sat in A & E awaiting the attentions of a doctor, 'that Diana's quite notorious.'

Richard had been watching Milo critically as he lounged on the seat beside him, muttering violent imprecations at his computer game. It seemed to him that the boy was perfectly healthy. As the last few surprising words of Sara's sentence now sunk in, he turned to her in amazement. '*Notorious?*' Had he heard right?

But Sara was beaming at him, and nodding. In the hospital strip lights, her teeth were almost painfully white. 'Oh, yes! I mean, I hate to say this, but strictly *entre nous*, that's why she had to leave London.' She drew breath to launch into the tale. 'She and her husband—'

'Husband?' Richard jumped in, shocked.

Sara seized on it. 'Didn't you know she was married?'

He shook his head, gripped by a sudden misery. Of course, Diana had not said she was available, not in so many words. He had just assumed she was and, as a scientist, he should know how dangerous assumptions could be.

'Divorced now though,' Sara added. She was playing Richard like a cat would a mouse, or a fisherman a hooked fish, and enjoying the sensation thoroughly.

'Oh.' Richard's despair now changed to a rush of relief.

'Absolute crooks, both of them,' Sara went on with relish, noting with triumph how Richard's face fell again. For such a clever man, he was amazingly easy to read.

'Crooks?'

'Con men. Fraudsters. Borrowed like mad things, lived like lords and then declared themselves bankrupt when the bills came in,' Sara announced with all the moral outrage of someone who had married for money and never worked in her entire life.

Richard stared. 'I can't believe it.'

'Well, believe it,' Sara said brutally. 'There are details online, if you want to look at them. I bet she never said anything to you about it, did she? And you've been out a couple of times, I'm guessing.'

'No, but . . .' Richard began, before stopping and wondering what the 'but' was. They had indeed been out a couple of times and Diana had said very little about herself. At the time, he had thought this delightfully restrained.

'Well then,' Sara said, with an air of satisfaction, as if this concluded everything.

Richard passed a hand across his eyes. He was tired. This was all very unpleasant and confusing. 'She just didn't seem that sort of person,' he said, eventually, his tone almost pleading.

He could not believe that Diana was a cheat and a liar. Still less that Sara, who was actually staying with Diana, was saying things like this about her. 'Aren't you her friend?' he began, uncertainly.

'Absolutely!' Sara replied with disarming swiftness. 'And it's as Diana's friend that I'm telling you.'

He stared back into her popping eyes, wondering if he'd missed something somehow.

'Because she cheats about more than just money.' Sara was shaking her head sorrowfully, so strands of highlighted hair hung fetchingly over her face. 'Now that she's divorced, she's looking for a new man. But not just any man. She's very conniving. She wants you.'

'She does?' Her insinuating tone could not stop the flood of pleasure he felt.

'Yes,' Sara snapped. 'But only because you're a professor and have a high-status job.'

This winded Richard completely. As, in vain, he sought a reply, his eye caught Milo, sitting next to his mother. It was not, Richard felt, a suitable conversation for a boy of that age to be listening to, especially as it concerned his former neighbour. On the other hand, he was obviously not listening. He seemed deep in some cyber conflict, his face contorted in an expression of violent hatred. 'Die, losers,' he was muttering under his breath.

'Diana's desperate for status,' Sara purred, leaning confidentially forwards – so confidentially that, without even wanting to, he could see how her low-buttoned shirt revealed the divide at the top of her breasts. 'She's used to a lavish lifestyle. She used to have everything and now she's just a gardener.'

'She seems,' Richard weakly put in, 'to rather enjoy it.'

Sara's lips drew back in a mirthless laugh. 'Ha! That's a good one. She's never done it before, you know. Hates getting her hands dirty. She actually hates plants,' Sara added, in a moment of inspiration.

'*Hates* them?'

'Loathes them, absolutely. You should have seen her garden in London. Looked like a Californian desert. Hard core and cacti everywhere.'

She could see, to her annoyance, that he was having real difficulty believing this. She cast her mind back to the Branston website. There had been a small tab about the gardens, featuring an annoyingly flattering picture of Diana and an article in her typically breathless tone about some of her plans.

'She especially hates delphiniums,' Sara declared. To her joy, this had an immediate impact. He looked astonished.

'Hates delphiniums?' Richard repeated. He could picture Diana's face as she spoke of her blue border. Had that all been an act? Really?

'Loathes them. *Hates* gardening. But she wants you to think she's a cheerful, outdoorsy type, all berry cheeks and bright eyes, getting back to nature and all that.'

He *had* thought that, Richard mused. That exactly.

'She wants you to think she's got simple tastes and is happy being poor,' Sara went on, seeing with delight how every word was sinking in. Brain expert he may be, but she could play him like a piano. Well, perhaps not a piano. Sara couldn't actually play an instrument. 'So you'd never suspect she was a confidence trickster with millions of pounds of debt behind her.'

There was something illogical about all this, Richard was sure. But it was unfolding too fast and too confusingly.

Again, the breasts were practically in his face. 'That was why,' Sara told him brightly, 'I was trying to come along to the dinner with you both. I was trying to help you! Save you!'

To Richard's relief, the nurse now interrupted. The doctor was ready to see Milo. Still staring into his computer screen, he was led off. 'Want to come, Mum?' the nurse asked Sara.

She swept a bountiful, glittering hand upward in reply. 'Be my guest. He'll be fine on his own.' Waste a valuable seduction opportunity escorting her son to a completely unnecessary examination? Not likely.

'Won't he want you there?' Richard queried.

Sara turned on one of her dazzling beams. 'Not at all. I'd just cramp his style, anyway. Milo's bound to be there for ages, he's so interested in science. He'll be asking them all sorts of questions. I really think he'll be a doctor one day, or perhaps he might go into your field.' She batted her eyelashes violently. 'He's really interested in brains.'

'He hides it well,' remarked Richard.

Sensing she was losing ground, Sara took out her big weapon and prepared to use it. 'Believe me,' she added, 'Di's got you taped. She's researched you on the internet. You should have heard her when she found out your wife was dead . . . that you were, tragically, a widower,' Sara corrected herself swiftly as she saw Richard's horrified face, and realised how much deeper and sharper her shot had gone home than she could ever have hoped. Nearly there. One final painful twist should do it.

She took a deep breath and summoned anguish into her eyes; thinking of Henrik's mistress in her old house was one infallible method.

'Diana said to me, "Sara, he's a sitting duck. Got my name all over him. A world-renowned academic, Master of a college and, would you believe it, a widower!"'

Richard stared, speechless, at the floor. Such was the hurt and anger rising within him, the possibility Sara was lying never even crossed his mind.

Something touched his hand. He looked down at a brown, very thin hand, glittering with rings. 'I just had to let you know,' Sara sighed in a voice oozing with regret.

For a moment he was silent. Then, 'I'm grateful to you,' he said abruptly.

'It's nothing,' Sara beamed enthusiastically. 'I was happy to help – well, perhaps "happy" isn't the word,' she added hastily, assuming a suitably doleful expression.

She allowed a minute or two to elapse before approaching the open goal before her.

'But, as you *are* grateful, could I ask you a favour? Obviously we can't go back to Diana's now. Not after those feral neighbours of hers practically *murdered* Milo.' Sara widened her eyes and batted lashes solid with mascara. 'Perhaps we could stay with *you* until he's better?'

Chapter 22

Isabel laid down her pen and rubbed her eyes. She glanced through her fingers at the stack of books she should be studying, all critical texts on Shakespeare. 'Bird Imagery in *Hamlet*' had been the unpromising essay title suggested to her by the aptly named Professor Finch, who was taking the group for the compulsory Shakespeare paper. Perhaps the unpromising subject had been meant as rebuke; Finch was, Isabel knew, surprised she hadn't come up with an idea herself. 'Is everything all right?' he had asked her after the last session.

'Fine!' Isabel had said.

'It's just that you seem a little . . . distracted. Not as engaged as you have been.'

She could hardly tell him that she was engaged with something else instead. Something more fascinating even than Shakespeare.

She bent her head back over her books. Bird Imagery in *Hamlet*. 'I am but mad north-north west, when the wind is southerly I can tell a hawk from a handsaw' . . . 'I am pigeon-livered and lack gall' . . . 'I should 'a fatted all the region kites with this slave's offal'. The quotes came tumbling on each other; she had scarcely to think about them. The old magic was still there, Isabel thought with relief, reaching for her work pad and scribbling a few notes.

Well, that sort of magic, anyway. She knew now that it was not the only sort. Yesterday, it being unusually mild for

November, she and Jasper had lounged by the river in the late autumn sunshine. They had been on a walk – her idea – but the day had been so lovely. Through the carved colleges they had gone, along the flashing river, in ravishing gardens where drops of water sparkled on the grass.

She had seen it all before, but never properly, or so it had felt. Nothing, for some reason, seemed to have been real before. They had wandered into chapel interiors; everything had seemed hyper-real, her sensitivity so highly strung, so super-alert that the bursts of colour from the stained glass windows had almost hurt her eyes. She had almost *felt* the soaring pillars explode into lacy fan-vaulting as they hit the carved roofs.

Jasper, it had to be said, seemed less keen than herself on Tudor architecture. But no doubt he was used to it; his family home, from what she could gather through her eager questions, was pretty old and of course St Alwine's was a poem in stained glass and dreaming spires.

That, he claimed, was the reason he preferred the concrete corridors of Branston. But Isabel longed in secret for the cosy little room off Jasper's sitting room. Being in Branston, they risked encountering Amber.

Even though Isabel herself rarely saw her and seemed no longer required to write things, Amber was still very much around. Jasper, at the end of his visits, liked to pop briefly in to her room – for a chat, for old times' sake, as he said. Isabel, declining his invitations to go too, usually went off to the library. She did not want to appear neurotic and jealous, even if that was exactly how she felt.

In the library, Isabel sat and dreamed about Jasper. She was dimly aware of her coursework unravelling around her, but paid it no heed. She also chose not to worry about the supervisions she had missed, or that she was increasingly the recipient of irate notes from Professor Green. Once, Isabel knew, such notes would have filled her with dismay, but now she seemed oddly anaesthetised to them. Jasper, anyway, just laughed. 'Green-eyed monster,' he said. 'Dried-up old bat like that. She's jealous that you're having a good time.'

Isabel could hardly believe, now, that literature had ever been so important to her. For what was it but a pale imitation of reality? There were two great themes in literature, love and death, and now she was living them both. Love when she was with Jasper. Death whenever she was without him; then the world stopped and became an icy waste – cold, monochrome and muffled until she saw him again. She was hardly eating, but she hardly noticed. She hardly noticed anything not directly concerned with Jasper.

He had hit her like a speeding train. She had been unprepared for the impact, for the all-absorbing nature of passion. Light-headed with love, dizzy with sex, she had flung off the cloak of her old, hard working, conscientious self. She had imagined it would be heavy, like a carapace, but it was as light as gossamer, leaving no trace. She now felt like someone altogether different.

Even Jasper's continuing inroads into her savings was something she hardly noticed. What did it matter if she paid for the coffees, the trips to the pub or student bar, or dinners out in restaurants (Jasper could not stand student food)? Or even the rather more considerable lump sums he was increasingly asking her to lend him? They were all tiny outlays compared to what she received in return: the company of the most wonderful man in the world. And Jasper endlessly assured her he would repay her when his allowance came through; the debts she was vaguely aware of piling up would be settled.

The end of yesterday's walk had brought them to St Alwine's. A shiny red sports car was parked outside the college gate. 'Yours?' Isabel breathed.

'Like it?' He was stifling a yawn.

'It's beautiful.' Like, she thought, something from a Bond film. Apparently one of the porters had brought it round from the college garage. 'They do valet parking?' Isabel joked.

'They do anything you tell them to,' Jasper said, shortly. 'If you slip them enough cash, that is.'

If, now, on the edge of Isabel's mind hovered the question of what cash he was slipping them, exactly, and how he managed to pay for petrol given his apparent constant lack of means, she dismissed it immediately.

The car's interior had ridged seats in toffee leather and tiny triangular chrome-framed windows with little levers you twisted to push them out. It had spoked silver wheels and a leather-padded steering wheel. Jasper leapt in in a practised fashion, stretching his long legs beneath the dashboard.

They growled around town. Isabel half-enjoyed, half-shrank from the feeling of being stared at by the passers-by. She also dreaded seeing Olly.

It was very cold and the air stung and numbed her exposed cheeks. Golden leaves – the last of the year – blew on to the stitched seats of the car. Through the near-bare branches of the trees, the sky was a brilliant, clear cold blue. It was a richly beautiful afternoon and yet there was something profoundly melancholy about it too, something that, for all her happiness, dragged heavily within her.

Autumn always affected her this way; Isabel was not sure why. Lately it had occurred to her it might be atavistic, to do with the time of year she was parted from her real mother. Mournful autumn, the season Persephone annually parted from her mother to join the dark lord of the underworld. Appropriate, in a way, although Lochalan made as unlikely an underworld as Mum did a Hades.

Jasper broke into her musings by announcing abruptly that he had to see someone. He had, she gathered, glancing at him half-driving, half-checking his Blackberry, just got an urgent message. Could he drop her here? He would see her later, for dinner.

She found herself bundled summarily out at the next set of traffic lights, at the point the road turned back into town over one of the ancient bridges. As Jasper roared off, she stared after him, wondering at the sudden rush, his farewell kiss still buzzing on her lips. Then she looked down at the thick paste of fallen leaves on the pavement. How had Shelley put it?

Yellow, and black, and pale, and hectic red,
Pestilence-stricken multitudes . . .

Something now made her look up. Staggering towards her across the pavement was a familiar-looking figure.

'Amber?' Isabel said, uncertainly. She looked so different. Walked so different. That old, confident stride – what had happened to it?

Amber did not appear to see her. Her eyes seemed unfocused and wild, her gait, as she stumbled from foot to foot, unsteady. Isabel stared in amazement. It wasn't, of course, unusual to see Amber skimpily dressed, but even so, the denim miniskirt and black vest top she wore seemed wildly inadequate for a freezing day at the start of winter. A sudden wind had started up, sending Amber's unbrushed blond hair swirling about her. On the hand clawing it back, a diamond flashed like a warning.

'Amber?' Isabel asked again. Was she ill? Up close, her face was sweaty and pale, her cheekbones more sharply prominent even than usual, her clear blue eyes dull and bloodshot, underlined by dark smudges. Perhaps because her face was thinner, her nose looked bulbous and misshapen.

Amber looked terrible. How the mighty had fallen – or were about to fall; Isabel caught the other's cold, bare arm. Her heels skittered on the paving stones.

'Are you OK? Can I help?'

Amber's gaze slid over Isabel's and away into the distance.

'Shall I try and get Jasper?' Isabel was alarmed enough to suggest. They were friends, after all. He probably should know; perhaps she should call him; he couldn't be far away yet, after all.

But the other girl's unfocused eyes had narrowed and an expression of the utmost contempt came into them. The slack mouth twisted bitterly. 'Jasper? Are you *joking?*'

She had been wise, Isabel realised, to give her neighbour a wide berth. Amber was taking their relationship badly. Very badly. Violent fury was finding an outlet in alcohol; because the other girl was drunk, definitely. Deliriously, crazily inebriated.

All the same, she had to help her. She was not sure how, exactly. Branston was some distance away.

'Go 'way,' Amber was muttering, wresting herself free and teetering off at an angle. 'Don't wan' your help.'

'Careful,' Isabel gasped, moving to catch her again just in time. 'Look, can I call someone else, then? Some other friend?'

'Friends!' Amber spat, rolling her head from side to side and turning the whites of her eyes in a horribly bovine manner. 'I don't have any fucking friends.'

'Of course you have friends,' Isabel exclaimed. Had not hundreds of people come to Amber's room in the time she had lived next door?

'What do you know?' Amber snarled, her pupils boring suddenly, startlingly, into Isabel's. ''S none of your bloody business.'

'But . . .'

'Leave me alone, you swotty Scottish witch.'

Amber twisted away with a violent lunge. Isabel watched the skinny frame stumble and clatter off down the street. Should she pursue her? But she was sure to be violently repulsed.

The aggressive self-pity seemed further proof that Amber had been hitting the bottle. Could it really be because of her and Jasper? Isabel wondered, rather awed. She searched herself for a tiny gleam of triumph; given Amber's past treatment of her, it would not be unnatural. But she felt only that it had been both frightening and pitiable to see her in such a state. Amber would have one hell of a hangover.

Amber had disappeared now, round the corner. Should she go after her? But Amber really *did* have hundreds of friends. Whatever she said. Any one of them would help her if she needed it.

Later, in a candlelit corner of a riverside gastro-pub, Isabel described the scene to Jasper. His attention, she could not help noticing, seemed more on the rib-eye steak with hand-cut chips and the half-bottle of burgundy she had paid for. Isabel, clutching her tap water and disingenuously insisting she was not hungry, hoped he could not hear her stomach rumble.

'I wouldn't worry,' Jasper said lightly, dabbing a forkful of steak in a dollop of mustard and flashing her a mildly exasperated smile. 'She'll be fine. She's a survivor, Amber. Tougher than she looks.'

'But I've never seen her like that.' The memory of Amber's rickety progress down the wintry street endured. She had not seemed tough then. Isabel had never thought of Amber as vulnerable before, but now the thought would not leave her – and neither would the feeling that there was some sort of mystery about it all.

Jasper stabbed a chip. 'I have. Lots. Especially recently.'

'Really?' This was unexpected. Had Jasper not always assured her, after his visits, that Amber was fine?

'Pissed as a fart sometimes. She just likes her champagne, that's all. And *of course* she's got friends. Hundreds of them. Millions!' he declared, raising his glass to emphasise his merry overstatement.

'She has, hasn't she?' Isabel said, relieved. She paused, frowning again, wondering how to introduce the sticky topic. Jasper's own breezy tone seemed the best bet. 'She didn't seem to want to see *you* though. Have you had a row?'

Jasper rolled his eyes with an irritation that sent a flash of fear through Isabel. 'You know Amber,' he said. 'Touchy. Falls in and out with people all the time. I might have upset her, but I can't remember. Don't worry about her.' He reached to playfully tweak a lock of her hair. But there was nothing playful about his tone of voice.

Isabel stared worriedly at the floor. This seemed to irritate her companion.

'Look,' he said, laying down his knife and fork with a weary air, 'actually, last time I saw her, I might have told her to lay off the booze a bit.'

'You did?' Relief flashed through Isabel. 'So you were being a concerned friend, and she took it badly?'

'Precisely.' He applied himself back to his steak in a satisfied fashion; the subject, it seemed, was closed.

Isabel took a steadying breath. 'All the same,' she said quietly, 'I'll check up on her when I get back. I feel a bit worried about her,' she added, looking at him appealingly.

He was cross now, she saw. His gaze, as it met hers, was freezing. 'She wouldn't worry about *you*, believe me.'

Absolute panic now swept Isabel. 'I know she wouldn't,' she agreed hastily.

This seemed sufficient capitulation to pacify him. He smiled and stroked her cheek and she shuddered with pleasure at his touch. Her neighbour's far-from-tough, stumbling progress down the pathway faded from Isabel's memory. Drowning in that golden-syrup gaze, now mercifully warm and approving again, she could think of nothing else and no one else.

Chapter 23

Hard work, Dotty insisted, was the cure for heartbreak. She had, Olly felt, rather adopted him as a project, possibly to take her mind off her own problems. Her pupils were thinning out, unable to bear, Dotty said, the constant hypertension thump of thrash metal from Hero's room as a background to their musical efforts.

Martin the management consultant had been the first to go and Olly rather missed him. He had always liked the way, in the narrow hallway after his lesson, Martin would put his cycle helmet back on with fumbling fingers, the same fingers that had played so skilfully just before. He seemed to radiate embarrassment, as if being caught having violin lessons was shamefully self-indulgent and not something a man in his fifties should be doing.

Less of a tragedy was that Lorna Lintle had left too, claiming that the noise from Hero's room was compromising Alfie's efforts to connect to his inner Menuhin. 'Poor boy,' Dotty tutted. 'I do feel for him.'

And now she felt for Olly – unsurprisingly; it was to her, after all, that he had unburdened himself after the ill-fated shopping trip. He had vowed, stumbling back, not to show the pain he felt to anyone, to bear it stoically and secretly. But Dotty had been in the kitchen, rocking from foot to foot, eyes closed as she played something so sweet and melancholy on her violin that he had crumbled instantly. Over her kitchen table the whole tortured story had come spilling out.

'She doesn't want me, Dotty,' he concluded, head now sunk hopelessly into his arms on the table. 'But who would?' he added, as self-pity tightened its grip on him.

'Nonsense,' Dotty had said, galvanisingly. 'Lovely, charming, clever boy like you? Someone'll snap you up. You'll see.'

Olly raised his head and pushed back his hair. He felt a strange mixture of gratitude and resentment. Part of him wanted to slide beneath the surface, sink like a stone in the bog of his own misery and hopelessness. He swallowed, poised temptingly on the edge of the bog again. 'I'm no use to you here,' he told Dotty. 'I'll go home.'

'Go *home*?' Dotty's small, fine arm came flying over the table and held his wrist in a surprisingly strong grip – the result of all that sawing at the catgut, he imagined.

'You're doing nothing of the sort,' she instructed, with the same stern maternal solicitude she might have used on Hero, had Hero been remotely receptive to it. 'You can't go back there. You're heartbroken and going back's not going to help.'

Olly was struck by this. '*Am* I heartbroken?' It seemed a dramatic description. He had hardly known Isabel, really. But was that the point? It was what he had built around that slender acquaintance that he was mourning.

There was a feeling in his chest so dreadful and heavy it was as if something was sitting there. How was he to endure the future – tonight, the whole of the next day and the next day after that?

But gradually, under Dotty's sympathetic, cajoling, motherly influence – she seemed to be lavishing on him everything Hero rejected – he made an effort to re-engage with life.

He had to bring some money in, after all. Cleaning was all very well but Dotty and David needed more than elbow grease. Work, for David, was drying up.

Olly finally abandoned his novel – who was ever going to care about that? – and mechanically followed up every employment lead. Whatever it was. Anything. He was even thinking of joining Sam in the living-statue business. What difference did it make, really? He was going through the motions, that was all.

Then, out of the blue, he hooked a fish. Or some sort of animal, anyway. The crackling, practically inaudible message left on his mobile was something about a zoo and helping at a kid's party. Someone had dropped out and could he step in? He had called back the number – after playing the shouted message four times to make it out – and replied in the affirmative to the Orange answerphone service. Although, to what, where and when, he was still not exactly sure.

Frankly, it could be almost anyone. He had filled in so many online job application forms that they fused together in his mind when he thought about them. A children's party sounded harmless enough, though.

'Someone for you,' Dotty now shouted up from downstairs. Olly descended to find her standing, looking concerned, in the hallway. 'They say they're from the Petting Zoo,' she hissed.

A penny dropped in Olly's mind. Petting Zoo had been one of the party entertainer businesses he had applied to in one of his weaker moments. He brightened. After the miserable time he'd had recently, watching children and little animals would be some fun, at least.

'See you later,' he said brightly to Dotty. She gave him a look in return. It seemed to Olly a peculiarly doubtful look, and now he realised why.

Two men stood at the other side of the open door. One had dreadlocks, flesh tunnels and tattoos on his neck. The other was of a corpse-like paleness.

Olly reminded himself that he needed the money. He reminded himself that the rusting white Escort van beyond would contain only bunnies and mice. It was a children's party zoo, you didn't need to be David Attenborough.

Only after they had set off did Olly discover that the Petting Zoo dealt in reptiles and large exotic insects.

'What?' he yelped. Olly hated snakes and had a horror of large insects. One of the few benefits of his current lodgings was that the dampness discouraged spiders.

'Oh, yeah,' Tattoos said impassively. His name was Bill. 'Snakes are the new thing. And scorpions. We do all the posh parties round here.'

Olly had heard of children's party peer pressure. He had read many newspapers recently and this phenomenon frequently cropped up in the features pages. Rich parents spent vast amounts on stretch limos, designer party bags, pop stars and theatre companies to entertain their children. But killer snakes was a new one.

The party venue, in a gated road in the city's wealthy suburbs, was huge and carpeted throughout in zebra-skin-patterned carpet. It had purple walls, silver banisters and a security system that, Olly imagined, left the White House trailing in its wake. The drive was crowded with top-of-the-range four-wheel-drives, all polished to a dazzle and boasting incomprehensible person-alised number plates.

The hostess, the party girl's mother, was a much-maquillaged brunette whose loud, forced laugh could be heard at frequent intervals. The party girl – 'Tallulah', according to the vast castle-shaped birthday cake – was a pudding-faced eight-year-old. She had elaborate ringlets and, as Olly passed with his plastic boxes of lethal invertebrates, he noticed that her once-pristine white gauze party dress was already spattered with the contents of the chocolate fountain in the hallway.

As things got underway, Olly tried to control his panic. Bill had told him the animals were safe. 'It's all right, mate. Bin taken out, all the venom sacs 'ave.' But Olly was increasingly wondering whether this was true. How exactly did one remove venom sacs? Bill made it sound as easy as taking out a battery.

Pressing heavily on his mind was the fact he had seen no safety certificates, either concerning the snakes or the people. Did Bill and his sidekick, Rich, look trained?

He glanced across. At the other side of the great beige sitting room, Bill, with his brick-red face and long, matted hair, appeared positively diabolical with serpent's heads writhing around his meaty shoulders and forming living bracelets round his illustrated arms. While Rich, corpse-pale, skinny, his hair gleaming stickily with gel, appeared sociopathically unmoved as he passed pythons to toddlers.

Still, at least Olly hadn't had to handle the snakes himself. He had been told by Bill to watch the scorpion. The whole reason he had been recruited, Olly now knew, was because the scorpion's usual handler was struck down with flu.

Really flu? Olly now wondered fearfully. Or a killer bite?

What would he do if the scorpion went berserk? He had been told to drop a plastic box over it immediately if it showed signs of agitation. But what if he missed? What if the scorpion made a break for it?

Olly looked about him. The birthday girl's father was talking loudly about business start-ups to a couple of fathers impervious to the fact their children were covered in slithering pythons. Tallulah's mother, meanwhile, was swigging champagne and screeching with laughter as a tarantula, hairy legs almost buried in the striped carpet, ambled past, inches from her bare and painted toes.

'Say cheese, Ottilie,' another mother was instructing as she held up her iPhone.

The picture might come in useful at the inquest, Olly thought. He was certain he was staring death in the face. Oh, please, no. His existence was far from perfect, but he realised that, contrary to his recent assumptions, he wanted to hang on to it. He didn't want to die. Not here. Not now.

He reached for a plastic box and dropped it, clattering, over the scorpion. The horrible thing skittered around in its polythene prison, furious at the curtailment of its freedom. It even *sounded* venomous, Olly thought.

Feeling someone next to him, he looked up. A small boy stood before him, a vast python writhing evilly round his shoulders.

'Excuse me,' the boy said in a trembling voice. 'I don't like this snake. Can you get it off?'

'Sure,' Olly said, full of his new confidence. Nonetheless, sweat began to break out on his forehead. The boy's snake was, it had to be said, *absolutely* huge. He swallowed; his bowels felt loose. Desperately, he fought the urge to run away.

But he couldn't. A small and helpless boy needed him. He clenched his fists, set his teeth and approached the reptile on shaking legs.

The snake looked more terrifying than ever. Its yellow eyes bored mockingly into his. *Come on, then*, it seemed to be saying. *Come and get me.*

Olly slowly reached out his arms towards the writhing, glistening body. He shut his eyes hard as his fingertips made contact with the scales. The snake, to Olly's amazement, came quietly. From somewhere beyond the terrified thunder in his ears, he now heard the boy's piping voice thanking him.

'It's nothing,' he muttered, looking down at the reptile in his hands.

Then, he ran.

Olly had never moved so fast in his life. He felt he had a mere matter of seconds before the snake thought better of its docility and became a thrashing, rearing instrument of death. He almost flew to the side of the room and the unsteady stack of big polythene boxes the animals had arrived in. Removing a lid with one hand whilst holding the reptile with the other, Olly coaxed its head into the box and then summarily bundled in the rest of it. He shut the lid and grasped the windowsill, breathing hard and deep.

Around him, Olly realised, children were leaving. The party was over. Across the room, Bill was packing up the tarantulas. Olly stared at the champagne shagpile carpet and wondered if things could get any worse.

Chapter 24

The chaffinches were chasing each other behind the bushes, their unmistakeable chittering trill bubbling from their coral-feathered throats. It rang piercingly in the still autumn air, extraordinarily loudly given the birds' tiny size.

Diana sat back on her heels and watched them hopping about, tapping at tree-bases, rustling in piles of dry leaves, all the time watching her with their tiny, bright black eyes. Usually, she loved to look at them; they seemed so joyous, these little creatures, and yet they had so little – just grubs and worms, and they were vulnerable to the coming winter weather. They were, she knew, a lesson to her: cheer up; seize the day. But she could not.

It was the Monday after the dreadful Saturday. Something had happened to the weather. It was as if the unusually long, mild, bright autumn had suddenly realised it had overstayed its welcome and should long since have given way to winter.

From a bright start, the day had turned dull. It was approaching lunchtime almost as if it dreaded the encounter. Grey clouds sat like a lid on the sky and the atmosphere was heavy.

Diana felt heavier even than the weather.

Saturday night had been a dream that had turned suddenly into a nightmare. The intimate warmth of the dinner had been horribly interrupted by the cold blast of shock. Relations with Debs were shattered; her old neighbour had destroyed the friendship with her new one. But at least Sara had gone back to

London. On Sunday morning, Diana had been thankful to note, both the car and the case had disappeared.

Diana now got to her feet, put her hands on her hips and looked about her. Odd that there had been no sign of Richard. Mindful of her vow to see him at the first opportunity and explain her difficult past, she had called him repeatedly on Sunday. But the telephone did not seem to be working. She had tried to text, too, but there had been no reply. And so she had counted on the appearance, this Monday morning, of a familiar tall, dark, preoccupied figure coming to find her. But no such figure had yet appeared.

She had considered, endlessly, simply marching up to the Master's Lodge and knocking on the door. But she might be seen; the ever-vigilant Sally, for instance, might get wind of it and the news would travel like wildfire through the college staff. Diana hated the thought of being gossiped about. On the other hand, once they had appeared together at the dinner Richard had asked her to, all bets would be off. Everyone would know.

The thought of the dinner invitation cheered her. It seemed to guarantee that Richard would come to her as soon as he could. He was busy, that was all; his was the sort of research that took sudden, unexpected strides forward and she knew how he hated interruptions. Even from her.

On the other side of town, Richard was in the labs, bent over the small illuminated boxes containing his research worms. But, for once, he was not thinking of them. His celebrated capacity for investigation was bent on one train of inquiry only, and that was not in the least scientific.

Had Diana really taken him in? For all his initial wariness, his wealth of bitter experience, his vow that he would never become involved in a relationship again, had he been deceived?

The picture Sara Oopvard had painted of Diana as fraudster, as confidence trickster, as a woman knowingly living way above her means, had astonished and appalled him. As he had dithered about whether or not to believe in it, he had counted on hearing from Diana herself. She would surely ring and then the record could be put straight. But, incriminatingly it seemed, she had not been in touch. According to Sara, she was retrenching. Planning her next sly move.

His eventual decision to call Diana had been thwarted by general telephonic meltdown. First his mobile seemed to have disappeared. Then all the phones in the Master's Lodge developed a fault simultaneously.

Richard looked up from his work and raked both hands through his hair. He didn't understand any of it. He should have stuck with his worms and kept away from women. He had never intended to go near them again in the first place, of course. But somehow Diana had got through his defences.

The phone on his desk now rang. Richard was irritated by the interruption. 'Yes?'

It was the student welfare officer, a colourless woman Richard had always felt ill-suited to her job. But then, who at Branston wasn't?

'Sorry to bother you at the labs,' she said, apprehensively. 'But it's important.'

'My research is pretty important,' Richard said tersely. He hoped this was not about that straggle-bearded English don and his inappropriate internet representation again. Or yet another Branston student missing tutorials. What else could he do about it? He had agreed only this morning with a clearly exasperated Gillian Green that Amber Piggott would not be returning after the Christmas break.

That particular effort to raise Branston's profile had, Richard reflected bitterly, been a catastrophic failure. As, no doubt, the forthcoming alumni dinner would be. To which, as things stood, Diana was still coming.

'Master, I'm afraid it's rather bad news. The police have been in touch. They suspect that someone at Branston is dealing.'

The words, rather than the dreary delivery, made Richard wake up. '*Dealing?* Drugs, you mean?' He closed his eyes tight shut, willing it not to be true. A college head's worst nightmare. As if he didn't have enough on his plate.

'I'm afraid so, Master.'

Was it his fault, Richard asked himself. Had he not been sufficiently vigilant? But Branston students, Amber Piggott and a few other bad apples excepted, had always seemed serious and hardworking. Amber again excepted, there were no rich dilettantes. They hadn't seemed the drugs type, whatever that type was. Of course, it could be any type.

'Are they sure?'

'They're still trying to build the full picture, I gather. There's not enough evidence at this stage to justify a full search of the place, although that might come.'

'Something to look forward to then,' Richard said with heavy irony. But, even as he put the phone down, he felt guilty. It wasn't the poor woman's fault. She was only the messenger.

All the same, he had not spoken so snappily for some time. But he had not needed this, not after the Diana business. He felt heavy and weary. And cold, suddenly. The old disenchantment with life had seeped back, like a chill, into his bones.

He found himself wondering, as of old, what exactly he was doing here at Branston. Meetings with recalcitrant students, fundraising dinners, drug dealing. None of it was what he had signed up for. It had seemed so different when he had talked about it to Diana – almost fun, that immersion in college life. She, for her part, had talked eagerly about the students. He had, sucker that he was, even had a glimmer of her as the Master's wife. Walking, therefore, straight into the trap Sara Oopvard claimed had been set.

He had escaped it, anyway. Dodged the bullet. Hadn't he?

He pushed to the back of his mind the spark that had leapt between Diana and himself. It had been a moment of madness, some stray synapse; it meant nothing. He would avoid all women from now on, although there was that damned dinner with Diana, of course. How was he to get through that?

He could hear, once again, Sara Oopvard's sibilant voice. Her tones adhered to his brain-folds like Velcro. Part of him – the scientist in him – wondered whether, under laboratory conditions, it might be visible:

'Diana said to me, "Sara, he's a sitting duck. Got my name all over him. A world-renowned academic, Master of a college and, would you believe it, a widower!"'

Richard put his head in his hands and groaned.

Sara was not one to let the grass grow under her feet. She hated grass. In the old days, when she employed the same gardeners as the Queen, she had them yanking out handfuls of the horrid encroaching green stuff.

She had penetrated the Master's portals, and that was no mean feat. She had quickly decided that it needed a makeover: a few uplighters and sofas. A few clicks on Ralph Lauren Home and all would be well. They'd also need new phones.

Unplugging them all from the wall, she had deplored their being nasty, bog-standard grey BT ones, not the witty, zebra striped, retro trimphone ones she had introduced at home. Former home, she reminded herself, savagely. Richard's mobile, which she had confiscated without his knowledge, needed upgrading too. It wasn't even an iPhone.

All that was the easy part. And she had done the hard part too, or most of it.

To have turned the chaos of the evening to her advantage, as she had, was possibly her finest hour. The mental effort it had involved was exhausting. And yet Sara had slept badly that night on the Master's lumpy spare mattress. Her disquiet was born of ambition; she had a long way to go yet and had lain awake scheming into the early hours, bent on consolidating the victory.

Her opportunity had not been long in coming. She had, once Richard had left for the labs, lost no time in plugging the telephones back in. Should Diana call, Sara would be immediately able to inform her that she had been replaced in Richard's affections. Indeed, she was anticipating doing so with pleasure.

A call from a woman duly came, but it was not Diana. It was someone called Flora, and about a dinner she was organising in the college. Flora was writing out place cards and wished to check the spelling of the name of the Master's guest. 'Oh,' she said, when Sara told her. 'It's changed.'

'Indeed it has,' Sara agreed, a satisfied smile curving her gleaming, blood-coloured lips.

'Upward, you say? As in onward and—?'

Sara put her right and then, smiling, replaced the receiver. She paced about for a while, savouring her triumph, and then decided it was about time she went to visit the labs. Now she was to share his life – and there was no question that she was – she must share Richard's interests. It was certain to raise her in his estimation.

Some half hour later she swung her large white four-wheel drive into the small, tree-fringed car park before the elegant thirties façade of the neurology department. The car park was full apart from one empty slot, marked with a wheelchair.

'You're parking in a disabled space,' a youth clutching armfuls of folders pointed out as she eased herself from the car in her tight jeans and stilettos.

Sara gave him a withering look. 'So?' she flung back. 'There's no one disabled using it. Is there?'

Tossing her hair, she stalked towards the laboratory entrance. She felt supremely confident. She clacked up the wide stone steps into the laboratory's Art Deco foyer. The security guard behind the desk looked up from texting on his mobile phone. 'I'm here to see Professor Black,' she informed him loudly.

She spoke with such authority that the security guard, who was young and new, assumed that this was the eminent female neurologist down on the visitor list that morning. One of his colleagues, noticing her name, had made an approving remark about long hair and trendy clothes. The guard picked up the telephone. As always, it took a while to track Black down.

Sara tsked, shifted from teetering foot to teetering foot and rippled her nails along her folded arms.

Eventually the guard got through. 'Professor Black? Lady to see you.'

Richard, annoyed at another interruption, glanced in irritation at the clock. He had a visitor later that day, but was not expecting anyone now.

Then the thought that it might be Diana hit him like a lightning strike. She'd come to explain everything! All his doubts fell away and he felt flooded with a happy relief. Full of hope, he rushed out of the room, tapped his feet impatiently before the lift and then, once it had juddered with agonising slowness to the ground level, pushed open the heavy brass doors into the foyer.

'Richard!' Sara exclaimed, clacking forward over the marble. 'Darling!'

The professor, casting a glance of absolute astoundment at the guard, who shrugged and held up his hands, now found himself dragged into Sara's arms and soundly air-kissed on both sides. It was just at that moment that a pair of Richard's students entered the foyer, stared in amazement and nudged each other.

'Way to go, Prof,' said the more daring of them.

Richard felt Sara taking his arm. 'Now. We need to talk diaries.'

'Talk what?'

She fixed him with a glassy beam. 'Someone called Flora just called. About a dinner.'

Richard stared at her. A feeling of dread was squeezing him from within and not entirely because of the impending alumni event.

'I told her that I'd be delighted to come with you. It's on Saturday, of course.' She made an insinuating gurgling sound in her throat. 'But I'll be happy to stay on until then, to help out.'

'Er . . .' Richard said. He felt behind in some way, an unusual and unpleasant feeling for him. He was normally the one ahead of the field.

But Sara had turned on her heel, was pushing at the inner double doors leading to the labs. 'You must show me round your place of work! I absolutely insist!' she was exclaiming. 'I want to know everything about you! Now that I'm staying!'

Diana's trowel lay desultorily at the side of her. She had been digging fitfully for some time but now abandoned all pretence of work. The tight feeling inside her had twister tighter in the course of the past hour. Now she felt so constrained she could hardly breathe and there was, she knew, only one way to relax it. She must see Richard face to face.

She looked at her watch. Twenty minutes remained before it was time to get Rosie. Not enough for a full confessional, but she could make a start. Her pretext, she decided, would be to check the Saturday college dinner was still on. As she straightened and began to gather her tools, Diana felt better already. After all the hesitating and worrying, definite action was a relief.

She headed for the Lodge. No guarantee that he would be there of course, but she could always leave a note. Approaching the familiar grey concrete block, Diana felt again the tightening in her stomach. How would he receive her? Nervously she tucked her hair behind her ears and wished she had spent a few moments arranging her face. Such had her hurry been to get here that she probably still had smudges of soil on her nose.

The path before her was bordered by bare-branched beech hedges, behind which was a small car park. As Diana hurried along, she heard a vehicle swinging into it with a screech of brakes and a spray of gravel. She glanced involuntarily through the twigs.

The vastness and the whiteness was enough. She did not need the personalised number plate. Diana stood immobile while, within her, feelings of cold horror fought a sense of inevitability. Sara Oopvard had not gone home after all. She was here, at the Master's

Lodge. Diana swayed for a second or two. Even in the solid footings of her wellingtons, she felt suddenly that she might fall.

'Hey!'

The voice exploded into her thoughts and made her jump. Her scattered senses failed to identify it. Forcing her strained features into a semblance of normality, Diana turned slowly.

'Heard the news?' Sally panted up to her, grinning, her arms bearing a pile of scrunched towels. She had evidently just come from the Lodge.

'What news?' Actually, Diana could guess, but she needed the time to compose herself, the better to control her reaction.

'Some woman's moved in with the Master. Arrived last night, they say.' Sally's eyes were bright with agitation. She shook back her golden curls and leant forward, dropping her voice. 'I've not seen her,' she added with a confidential giggle. 'But the inside of that house is a real tip. Clothes everywhere. Underwear. Make-up all over the bathroom.'

Diana's eye, sliding down to the towel pile in Sally's arms, snagged on a bright red lipstick smudge. Her vision blurred and her self-control gave a violent lurch. 'Is that right?' she said tightly.

'Dreadful state!' Sally was fairly crackling with vicarious excitement. 'And she's totally mutton dressed as lamb, they say. Someone saw her going out this morning. Long hair. Leather trousers. Really high heels. Not the sort you'd think the Master would go for. But, according to Flora, she's going with him to the dinner on Saturday.'

Diana could not speak.

'Ooh,' Sally was gasping at her watch. 'I'm late. Must dash. See you later,' she sang. 'Have a lovely evening.'

Chapter 25

Olly could scarcely believe it. At last, a breakthrough. Life had come to feel like a dark pit in whose bottom he was languishing. But now a window had opened in the blackness above and through it, fluttering down into his eager fingers – or into the text message part of his mobile – had come a job interview!

The *Post* was a new paper, so new that it had not been launched yet; its address, an industrial estate on the outskirts of town. They had advertised for an investigative journalist. It was hardly the *Guardian*, but it was a start, especially as the *Post* wanted to see him so quickly. Immediately, in fact. Now.

'Get you!' teased Dotty when Olly descended in the shiny suit, which had failed to bring him luck in so many previous interviews. David, admittedly, had offered him the run of his crumpled, don's wardrobe, but Olly had tactfully turned him down. He felt he would rather take his chances with the unfortunate suit than appear before a prospective employer in baggy-kneed tweeds and jackets with holes in the elbows.

As Olly buttoned himself into his own suit, he hoped today would be an exception to the unlucky rule. Possibly, if he didn't see Hero. He remembered his interview with the *Hagworthingham Chronicle*; her withering remarks might have been what jinxed it, not the suit.

But Olly had seen little of Hero lately. She rarely appeared downstairs, at least not in daylight hours. It seemed she foraged at night, like a rat; according to Dotty, the kitchen looked as if a bomb had hit it every morning when she came down.

And Olly had been out a lot, in search of work, while Hero had been in, avoiding it. Although Dotty *had* reported a sighting outside, in actual daylight, with the vicious poodle that intermittently hung about the place. Hero and the poodle had struck up a friendship, Dotty said, clearly surprised and hurt that her daughter loved a dog – a mean dog at that – and not her own devoted mother. Yin and yang, Olly had said, to cheer Dotty up. Black and white. Goth and poodle. Dotty had not so much as smiled, however.

She seemed, Olly thought, to have lost all hope where her daughter was concerned. As had David. Olly wondered whether he should step in, but every time he summoned the will to tackle Hero about her attitudes, he never followed through with any action. He told himself that this was because he felt it was the family's business. Deep down, however, he knew he was afraid. Hero might bite him, like the dog.

'Good luck!' Dotty called encouragingly now from the sitting room as he passed the door. He smiled guiltily back at her.

On the bus, his excitement returned, even to the point of him jiggling in his seat. More than once, the grim-faced old lady in front turned to favour him with a belligerent stare. Olly didn't even notice. To ask him for interview, he was thinking, staring unseeing through the murky bus windows, the editor must have been impressed with the features ideas he'd sent. Very impressed, given the command that he present himself instantly.

Olly was especially proud of the suggestion that he become a living statue in the shopping centre for the day. Seeing Sam had given him the idea; the experience would make an amusing piece. The fact that he could return to his job afterwards and Sam had to return to his polystyrene plinth the next day was, Olly uncomfortably decided, a bridge he would cross when he came to it.

He wondered what the editor was like. His name was Alastair

Cragg, a most suitable one for an editor, Olly felt. It had an indomitable, unyielding, seeker-after-truth sort of ring to it, and was, of course, Scottish – self-evidently a good thing.

The bus ground up the road out of town, past new office buildings with cheap green glass fronts and new hotels that were indistinguishable from the offices. People were going in and out of both, no one looking very enthusiastic, and Olly felt a novel sense of his own enormous good fortune. The job he was going for was no boring grind, but both absorbing and exciting. He had no doubt that he would be good at it – if, that was, he was given the chance; but that looked likely. Why else ask for his immediate presence? It was very gratifying, especially as most other job applications had resulted in no acknowledgement whatsoever.

Yet, for all his optimism, Olly could not help his thoughts drifting to Isabel. They did so several times a day and even more frequently at night. His anger and indignation had been replaced by a nagging, growing worry. Why had she not yet seen through Jasper de Borchy? She was neglecting her work, too. He knew this because David was one of her tutors and he had waited whenever her group was due, duster in hand, heart in mouth, polishing madly on the stairs. But when she failed to turn up not once but twice, a faint inner alarm bell rang. That Isabel – the normal Isabel – would deliberately miss a session was out of the question. She was committed, enthusiastic. Or had been.

He felt shy about asking David about it, and David evidently had problems enough with his teaching career. The beleaguered tutor had been poring, in depressed fashion, over a list in the kitchen when Olly came in one day.

'Of course,' he was muttering, 'that ridiculous Piggott woman's being sent down. But I had thought better of Isabel.'

'Isabel?' Olly had been reaching for the teabags when he heard it.

'Haven't seen her for weeks,' David muttered. Olly would have asked more but the doorbell rang and David went to answer it, as Hero no longer performed even this small service for her parents.

While he was out of the room, Olly paused by the table. The list David had been looking at contained the names and home addresses of his students. There was Isabel's, in Scotland. Quick as a flash he took out his mobile and keyed the details in.

Now, on the bus, Olly wondered why. Some journalistic instinct, he concluded. Or perhaps a protective urge. At the very least, at some stage, he could send her a postcard.

The industrial estate that the *Post* was on was of a different vintage from the new glass ones he had passed on the way. It was a sprawl of damp-stained and rotting concrete and seemed largely deserted. The building he was to report to was easily identifiable because it was one of the few with cars outside, and not many at that.

Olly pushed open a stiff, cold metal door, crossed a deserted foyer and ascended three flights of stained, grey-carpeted stairs to a brown door on which someone had written 'The Post' on a piece of A4. The newspaper, Olly concluded from this, was not a very professional set-up. They would be glad to have someone even of his limited experience on board.

This impression, it turned out, could not have been more wrong. Olly had been only five minutes in Alastair Cragg's company when he realised he was hopelessly out of his depth.

Alastair had an impressively – terrifyingly – strong grip of current newspaper trends and technology and spoke at great length and in great detail about websites and reader interaction and online advertising. Olly followed as best he could; Alastair's intention, he gathered, was to produce both an online and physical daily newspaper.

'That's a lot of work,' Olly ventured timidly, then wanted to kick himself. He didn't want to give the impression of being workshy. 'Which is *great!*' he added, brightly.

Alastair flicked him a doubtful glance. He had close-cropped hair and, when he chose to display it, an engaging grin. He was not displaying it now, however. 'Lot of work, yes. And a hell of a lot of competition. And of course we don't have much money. Our only advantage is staff. I want the best staff.' Alastair stared hard at Olly, who tried his best to look as if he fitted this demanding bill.

Alastair looked unconvinced. He cleared his throat and picked up something from his desk, which Olly recognised as the letter he had sent with his features ideas. Including the living-statue one. He sat up a little straighter. Now he could get his advantage back. He reminded himself that he had been sent for immediately, which had to count for something. Although, increasingly, he could not see what.

'These ideas,' Alastair said.

'Yes,' Olly beamed, widening his mouth in an expectant smile. Alastair was surely about to say he liked them, then hopefully the offer of a job would follow. He felt a glow inside. He pictured himself rushing back to Dotty and David's with the news, perhaps picking up a bottle of champagne on the way, Dotty's shriek of joy, corks popping . . .

'Well, they're not very good, are they?' Alastair's words cut sharply into this pleasant dream.

Olly gasped.

'A lifetime in the day of a living statue in the shopping centre,' Alastair quoted from the letter. His eyes bored into Olly's. 'It's been done before.'

'Has it?' Olly faltered. And he had thought it so original.

'*Daily Telegraph*, to name but one,' Alastair sniffed. 'And most of the other stuff you've suggested here's been done too.'

Olly's spirits swung sharply downwards. He felt horribly disappointed.

'If the *Post*'s going to make its mark – survive, even –' Alastair's voice came through the embarrassed thumping in his ears – 'we need to build a reputation for news stories. Headlines. I advertised for an investigative journalist, not a features editor.'

A red spike of anger now joined the other feelings churning

round Olly's heart. If Alastair had thought the ideas in the letter so bad, why had he sent for him? Did he find humiliating people amusing? He raised his head and met the editor's eyes with a new feeling of hostility.

The evident change in his expression seemed to interest the editor. 'Tell me,' Alastair said, sounding unexpectedly friendly, 'what really drives you. What story you'd really like to do, if you could.'

Olly gazed glumly back. Apart from the reiteration of the discredited suggestions on the letter, his mind was blank.

The editor's fingers were drumming impatiently on an unassuming wooden desk that had struck Olly on arrival as being unexpectedly tidy. He had imagined newspaper editors to be surrounded by a chaotic sea of paper. But Alastair seemed to radiate calm and control. It was one of the reasons, Olly realised, that, despite everything, he wanted to please him. A sense of hopelessness, of resentment even, now joined his annoyance. Why did everything always go wrong?

'Let me put it another way,' Alastair said softly. He was watching Olly carefully. 'What makes you angry? Really angry, I mean.'

'Jasper De Borchy.' It came out with the speed of a bullet, before Olly even had time to think about it. He hung his head, aware of expressing something ridiculously petty and personal. Alastair had probably never even heard of Jasper. This would surely be the end of his hopes for a job.

He did not dare look at Alastair Cragg. Instead, Olly stared at the floor. It was covered in hairy grey carpet tiles; one of the stains was shaped a bit like Australia and Olly was just thinking that he should probably try his chances there next when he heard Alastair inhale deeply through his nostrils. He was evidently about to speak.

'That's interesting,' Alastair said, sounding really quite friendly now. 'Very interesting. And why does *he* make you angry?'

Olly lifted his head, scanning the editor's face to make doubly sure he was not being mocked in some way. 'Well, the Bullinger Club, really. He's one of its leading lights.'

The change in Alastair was striking. Gone was the weary irony. His eyes sparkled behind his spectacles and his countenance glowed with vivid speculation. 'So I'd heard,' he agreed. 'Which brings me neatly to the real reason I asked you for interview.'

Olly felt a mild outrage. On the other hand, Alastair was obviously not interested in his features ideas. Being invited on false pretences was better than not being here at all. He listened as the editor now explained that Olly's educational CV had been what caught his eye. In particular, the college Olly had been to.

It was with a growing sense of inevitability that Olly listened as Alastair explained that his first splash for the *Post* was to be an exposé of the inner workings of the Bullinger Club. 'And you're perfect for the job,' he concluded.

Encouraged, Olly nodded. 'I have done some investigation,' he said eagerly. 'One of the university papers I worked on once did an exposé on the price of crisps at college bars . . .'

Alastair was grinning. 'Spare me the details. The reason you're perfect is that you're cheap, you're young, you're desperate and, most important of all, you have a motive. When I saw you'd been to St Alwine's, it was fifty-fifty.'

'Fifty-fifty?' Olly was mystified, and not in a good way. He was still absorbing the fact that his lack of a job and burning sense of defeat and resentment was what Alastair was most interested in. His status as a loser, in other words.

Alastair was nodding. His glasses flashed in the flickering strip light. 'I knew you'd be one of two things: either a roaring hooray, or someone who hates them and everything they stand for.' He paused. 'And I could tell by the suit that you weren't the former.'

Olly's mouth dropped open. Then he shut it and tried to look gratified. It was, in a way, a compliment.

'And also because time is running out,' Alastair added, talking rapidly now. 'The Bullinger's having its big bash this weekend. "Bash" being the operative word, of course.'

'Of course,' Olly said feelingly.

'The Bullinger Ball: I want you to infiltrate it. Get all the grisly details. Get me the front-page story that'll launch us into the stratosphere.' He leant forward, his smile now a hard and serious line. 'In fact, you have to. We're launching next week and at the moment we've got nothing.'

Olly sat frozen to his chair. A minute ago he had felt an utter failure but now he was being charged with the success of Alastair's entire enterprise. 'Nothing?' he repeated, temporarily dazed at the crushing responsibility that had landed so unexpectedly on his shoulders.

Alastair's shoulders rose and fell. He sighed. 'I was hoping for drugs.'

Olly looked back at him doubtfully. He had heard that newspaper people often operated under the influence of illegal stimulants. But it was unexpected to hear it confirmed, and at their first meeting too.

Alastair gave a sudden roar of unexpectedly infectious laughter. 'I don't mean *me*, you muppet. I meant that I was hoping for a drugs *story*. There's something going on, something big. Dealing in the colleges seems to have stepped up a gear. But all the avenues I've followed up haven't delivered. Not yet, anyway. So it's up to you, OK? Your mission, should you choose to accept it. Goes without saying, of course, that, if you pull it off, you get the job.'

Olly hesitated. But not out of doubt. He was savouring the unprecedented sensation of being at a turning point in his life and being absolutely, unmistakeably, aware of the fact. He smiled at Alastair. 'I accept it.'

Chapter 26

Isabel meant to arrive at Professor Green's session early. She had missed so many supervisions now and was determined to make an effort for this one. But Jasper had dragged her back into bed and, in the end, there had been no time even to get her coat. Even though it was freezing outside. The weather had turned suddenly. From mild, sunny autumn it had become bitter winter.

As she hurried along, her phone buzzed in her bag. She dragged it out, breathless. Jasper? Ringing her so soon? Did he miss her already? Her nerves surged with an answering, golden rush of love.

'Hello, stranger!' Mum exclaimed affectionately.

'Oh . . . hi.' Isabel struggled not to sound disappointed.

'What's the matter?' Mum asked immediately.

'Oh . . . nothing . . . It's all fine . . .'

'You sound a bit distracted. Working hard?'

'Ye-es . . . Um, what's happening up there, Mum? Lochalan behaving itself?' Isabel began to walk along rapidly.

Mum took a deep breath and began. Isabel hardly listened. Lochalan and Mum seemed strangely distant now. It seemed a long time since they had even crossed her mind.

'You still there, love?'

'Mmm.'

'Thought you'd been cut off. You're very quiet.'

Isabel was wondering about telling Mum about Jasper. But

did she trust herself to drop him, now, casually into the conversation? Mum would detect from her voice that this was no run-of-the-mill acquaintance.

'How's your friend?' Mum asked suddenly.

Shock rippled through Isabel. Had she mentioned Jasper without realising? Had Mum guessed? 'My *friend*?'

'That boy,' Mum said easily. 'He sounded lovely. What was his name again?'

'Er . . .'

'Olly, that was it.'

Isabel let out a slow sigh of relief. 'Olly; oh, yes,' she said casually. It felt like a name from a long time ago.

'You haven't talked about him lately. How's he doing with his newspaper interviews?'

Isabel blinked. Olly? She struggled to recall a single thing about him. 'I'm not sure,' she demurred eventually.

'I hope you haven't fallen out with him,' Mum said sternly. 'I thought he sounded lovely. Really kind.'

Isabel rarely, if ever, got cross with Mum, but irritation rose within her now. She, Isabel, would choose her own friends, not have her mother – her adoptive mother, to boot – controlling her choices from afar.

On the other hand, there was something she needed to ask her. Something she had been intending to call about for some days, in fact. Isabel reined in her chagrin. 'Mum,' she said now, breaking into the stream of compliments about Olly, 'is there . . .' she took a deep breath, 'any chance you could send me a bit more money?'

Her mother stopped with a gasp. '*Money?*'

'Money, yes.' Isabel fought the shamed mutter in which this threatened to come out. 'Please. If you could,' she added in as matter-of-fact a tone as she could manage.

'You need more money already?' Her mother's voice mingled amazement with alarm. 'But you worked it all out so carefully, how much you'd need every week . . .' Mum stopped.

'I didn't work it out very well. You know how bad my maths always was,' Isabel forced herself to joke. Something was twisting inside her; she could hear her mother's distress but she had to maintain the façade. Admitting to paying for every date she and Jasper had ever had would horrify Mum. She would never accept him after that.

There was a silence during which Mum was clearly wondering what questions to ask and whether to ask them at all in the face of the uninformative and expectant silence Isabel forced herself to maintain. She was horribly aware of how coldly demanding she must sound and how little Mum deserved it. And how little Mum had to spare, too. But what option was there?

Eventually Mum said, sounding more bewildered and hurt than angry, that she would see what she could do.

'Thank you,' Isabel said, her eyes pricking with gratitude and relief. And guilt. She ended the call quickly after that.

The English group were already assembled outside the dark wooden door of Professor Green's room when Isabel panted up. Just in time, she saw with relief.

She realised her colleagues were all staring at her: Lorien and Paul with concern at her coatless state, Kate with more general annoyance. 'Good of you to turn up,' she said acidly.

Her hostility remained as complete as on the day it was formed, Isabel thought. As Ellie's had. But so what? What did any of it matter now she had Jasper? Isabel raised her cold-reddened chin defensively, reminding herself that she had been living literature recently, rather than studying it. As Jasper was fond of saying, it all boiled down to sex in the end.

'I haven't missed *that* many supervisions,' she retaliated. Not as many as Amber, say. The rumour that her neighbour would not be returning next term had reached even Isabel's distracted ear. She was to be sent down – expelled, in other words.

'Oh, no?' Kate jeered. 'There was the Brontë one, for a start.'

A faint echo of what might have been regret rippled through

Isabel. Yes, she had missed that, Kate was right. And it had been a shame, because she loved the Brontës.

'And Mrs Gaskell, last week.'

Isabel swallowed. She had prepared Mrs Gaskell for *this* session. Somehow she had got confused, or not read the timetable properly. So what were they doing this week? She had no idea. The subject of the next hour's close study with one of the world's leading literary brains was completely unknown to her.

Her heart began to gallop. She did not dare ask the others what it was. Even glancing at the books they held would give the game away. Kate's scorn if she did was all too easy to picture and, anyway, it was far too late.

There was a sliding of handle mechanisms and creaking of wood as Professor Green opened her door. As usual, she wore her grey hair in a bun, an all-concealing purple paisley dress and a lofty, stately manner. She looked at Isabel from beneath beautifully shaped raised eyebrows.

'Ah, Isabel,' she said in her fruity vibrato. 'Good of you to join us. If you'd missed another supervision, I'd have had to send out a Missing-Persons report on you.'

Isabel looked at the orange carpet and reddened. 'I'm sorry, Professor Green.'

The group shuffled in. Isabel realised she had almost forgotten how pleasant Professor Green's room was. The exposed brick walls were covered in framed RSC posters, a scented candle exuded warm lavender and the comfortable chairs and sofas were upholstered in bright, soft fabrics. Isabel felt suddenly glad to be here, eager to be part of this world once again.

'Right,' said Professor Green, smiling warmly round. 'Edith Wharton. Who's going to start us off?' Isabel looked quickly at the carpet. Edith Wharton! Nineteenth-century American women writers! Her mind had gone completely blank.

'Kate!'

As Kate began expounding, Isabel realised with rising panic how absolutely out of her depth she was. Never in the course of her whole life had she arrived at a lesson without preparing. To turn up, now, without having read *The Age Of Innocence* was a stupid mistake, albeit one Isabel endeavoured desperately to conceal as the others talked knowledgably on.

Being forced, through ignorance, to remain silent was a new and horrible experience for one, like her, accustomed to dominating through sheer knowledge and enthusiasm almost every session she had ever been in. That role now went to Kate. The looks of apprehension she had initially darted at Isabel – expecting her to interrupt, it seemed – now deepened to triumph as the tutorial progressed. She was clearly enjoying herself.

Isabel was even unable to answer a simple question about the heroine's background. Professor Green's glance, expectation turning to surprise, lingered on her. An agonising, apparently endless silence elapsed before Lorien provided the answer. Isabel hunched as she sat, turned down her mouth, tried to look ill, hoping that Professor Green would take that as the reason. But she was not surprised when, as the others filed out at the end of the session, the tutor signalled to her to remain behind.

As the door shut behind Paul, Isabel felt a leaden dread in her stomach. She knew that, unlike at the beginning of the term, she was not being detained for positive reasons.

'I'll get straight to the point,' the don said, folding her large hands in her lap and leaning her paisley bust towards Isabel. 'The English Faculty is concerned about you.'

Isabel sat bolt upright, eagerly. 'I'll work harder. I suppose I've been a bit . . . distracted.'

Professor Green nodded and gave a faint smile. 'Isabel, you need to tell me if there are any special circumstances. Any trouble at home?'

Isabel shook her head, perhaps too vehemently because her supervisor's eyes now kindled sympathetically. 'I can imagine,' she added gently, 'that as an only child of a single parent you are under a certain amount of pressure. Not least from yourself. It is possible that may get too much sometimes.'

Isabel was surprised at the depth of her supervisor's perception. She shook her head, however. 'I'm fine, honestly,' she assured the professor.

Gillian Green sat back. 'In that case, are there any other issues affecting you?'

Was Jasper an issue affecting her? That was one way of putting it, certainly. Partly from nerves, Isabel felt the sudden urge to laugh, but fought desperately to keep her face still.

Obviously she did not entirely succeed. 'I can see you think it's none of my business,' Professor Green said dryly. 'But I have to tell you that what is very much my business is the quality of your work. You came to this university with an excellent reputation and we all had very high hopes for you. But on present form, you'll be lucky to scrape a third.'

Isabel stared at her in shock. She felt as if she had been punched in the stomach. Then she hung her head, her heart racing as she stared at her jeans. She was, she noticed vaguely, much thinner than she used to be. But you couldn't be too rich or too thin, wasn't that right? Funny, they were the only kind of quotes she could remember these days. Her concentration seemed completely shot.

'I'll try harder, Professor Green,' she said, noticing, now, that the other woman had stopped speaking.

'You'll need to,' was the acid reply.

Dismissed, Isabel rushed out of the faculty building and into the leafy road. She was ashamed and embarrassed and wanted to run away from the feeling. She must reach Jasper. Once she was in his arms, everything would be all right.

Chapter 27

There was, Richard felt, nowhere to run. Sara and Milo had completely taken over his home. She seemed somehow to be everywhere at once: half-dressed in his bathroom; lounging in low-cut dresses over his sofas; clacking across the Lodge's concrete floors in leather trousers and stilettos; seemingly forever on his (much lower) heels.

'Do I look nice in this?' she endlessly asked him, twirling in some flimsy, figure-hugging scrap that seemed to him indistinguishable from any other of her flimsy, figure-hugging scraps. They were all, he felt, unsuitable for someone her age and the idea of her wearing them in public at the alumni dinner made his toes curl. Yet this was the purpose of the fashion show. She was, Sara claimed, trying to hit on the exact right outfit. While in most respects he dreaded it, Richard also longed for the weekend to come, for the dinner to be over. Then, as he sought to remind her at every opportunity, she would leave.

His desperation for her to do so redoubled after finding her in his bed. She had, she claimed, mistaken his door for hers. As Richard had stood there, pondering this unlikely excuse, she had lain below him, naked and pouting, arms above her head and writhing energetically against his sheets. While insisting, with what voice he could summon, that she return to her room, he had done his best to avert his eyes firmly from her erect, cone-shaped breasts and the strange sparkle about her magenta-dyed and heart-shaped pubic region. But the image had haunted him in his dreams: in a fur coat of a violent rose-colour, he had run through a storage depot of vast pink ballistic missiles, searching for the way out.

So unruffled by the incident did Sara seem afterwards that he wondered whether he really had dreamt the whole thing. This possibility seemed almost more worrying even than if it had been real.

He started to avoid her, to keep away from rooms she was in. He had realised fairly early on that the kitchen was not Sara's favourite place. She seemed unfamiliar – more so even than him – with the various objects it contained; he had to show her how to switch on the electric kettle.

It was in the kitchen that Richard was, hastily, eating a piece of Marmite toast, when Sara unexpectedly entered. He doubled his haste immediately, his jaws crashing so hard on the toast that he could barely hear her speak.

'What?' he asked, having swallowed.

'I need to talk to you,' Sara gasped.

Richard glared from under his brows. He hoped it wasn't about dinner parties again. Much of her conversation was a stream-of-consciousness about her former life in London, which she was labouring under the illusion would interest him. She seemed especially keen to emphasise her abilities as a hostess, her experience of dinner parties for influential people. As if he cared!

'It's about Milo.'

Milo. The very name made Richard frown. Whenever he entered the sitting room it was to find the ghastly child and his violent video games scattered over the floor.

Richard cleared his throat. 'I'm glad you've brought the subject up.'

Sara threw back her hair and beamed hugely. 'He's simply desperate to be a neurotic— I mean, neurologist. He'd love to come with you to the labs again.'

Richard summoned up what little remained of his patience.

Of all the week's enervating events, worst of all, worse even than the bed episode, was Milo's visit to the labs.

It had been as unscheduled and unsanctioned as Sara's own first appearance at his place of work. That seemed to be the Oopvard way. And, contrary to his mother's assurances, Milo was not the least bit interested in neurology. Richard's attempts to explain how he was training his worms to recognise colour and smell met with the usual unsettling blank stare. This, and the fact the boy spent most of the time playing on his iPad, seemed to belie Sara's claims concerning her son's intelligence. 'Top of his class at school and off the scale at Mensa; they'd never seen results like his,' she had invented wildly. Richard could well believe the latter.

He was about to say as much when Sara jerked her cleavage meaningfully in his direction. 'After all,' she trilled, 'you do rather owe me one, after I saved you from Diana's evil clutches!'

He was about to object, but the breasts rose in his face again and she got there first.

'Milo just adored it last time.'

'He had a funny way of showing it,' Richard confined himself to remarking. 'I'll have to think about it,' he added as discouragingly as possible, and escaped to the labs with all speed after that.

He had only just started work when the phone on his desk shrilled.

'Is that you, Master?'

Richard suppressed a groan. The Bursar again. His colleague seemed to have been reduced to a state of near-paralysis by the looming prospect of the alumni dinner and, in particular, the looming prospect of the wealthy guests of honour, the Snodgrasses.

'What's a thread count?' the Bursar asked.

'No idea,' Richard said shortly, one eye on his worms. 'Why?'

'Mrs Snodgrass can't cope with less than nine hundred.'

Richard was sufficiently distracted as to enter the worms'

direction in the colour box into the wrong row of figures. Now all his calculations were confused. He cursed under his breath.

The Bursar, meanwhile, was getting into his complaining stride. 'And Mr Snodgrass only drinks filtered tap water. At room temperature, not a degree above or below.'

By the time Richard had put the phone down he had had enough. These people were mad. He was mad, for staying here. What for, anyway? Nothing had worked out for him here. He was in the wrong place, in England. Why didn't he just go back to America?

Nothing was what it had seemed, from Diana to the job as Master. The college had assured him he would be left alone to work, but his time was continually taken up with absentee students, drugs, alumni dinners. And this winter was shaping up to be an absolute bum; he had not realised how hard it was to cycle on icy roads. You had to progress down other people's grooves and the risk of falling over was ever-present. Richard wasn't a literary man but he could recognise a metaphor when he saw it.

And Christmas was coming, with all that meant. Excited children. Carol services. Other people's happiness. Amy had always loved Christmas; apart from spring, it had been her favourite time of year. He still felt his wife all around him, more than ever just at the moment. What would Christmas be like here, that season of cheerful excess, among the bleak sixties futuristic architecture? Unbearable, frankly. Who would he spend it with? Most probably his worms. Perhaps he'd light them up in green and red for the festive season. He felt a miserable loneliness, a feeling of being hopelessly adrift. He wanted to run away.

Diana was picking Rosie up from a friend's house. Not Shanna-Mae's, obviously. Just as Debs would not speak to Diana, Shanna-Mae had since ignored Rosie.

'She's got a bunk bed,' Rosie was saying eagerly about her

friend. 'Can I have a bunk bed, Mum? Handy for when people come to stay,' she added, without irony, it seemed.

'Mmm,' Diana said, not really listening. She was unable to concentrate on anything at the moment. Her thoughts ricocheted between a murderous loathing of Sara, anguish about Debs and a combination of anguish and loathing when it came to Richard. He was taking Sara to the dinner instead of her! How could he? How had it happened?

It was not a real question, of course. Diana had no doubt, now, why Richard had not been in touch. Sara had poisoned him against her as she had earlier poisoned Debs. And now Sara had moved in to the Master's Lodge and was no doubt sizing Richard up as a replacement for Henrik.

Diana could see it all now, horribly clearly – almost as if she had been Sara herself. She had been the victim of a plot. Sara had money after the divorce, but no importance. Richard was a widower and Master of a prestigious university college. It was all so obvious.

Obviously, too, Diana would now have to go. Christmas approaching or not, there was no question of remaining at Branston after Sara became – as Diana did not doubt she would – the Master's wife. In one fell swoop, over one catastrophic weekend, Sara had destroyed her closest new friendship, her burgeoning romance and her job prospects.

She had tried to salvage the situation with Debs. Only this morning they had walked down their respective garden paths at exactly the same time and Diana, swallowing her fear, had tried to rekindle some spark of friendship. But Debs had stonewalled her completely. She had not betrayed by as much as a glance that she was aware of Diana's presence.

'And she's having a *Strictly Come Dancing* disco birthday party,' Rosie added as Diana turned into the Campion Estate. 'Could I have one of those, Mum?'

Diana closed her eyes and took a deep breath. She must not get annoyed. None of it was Rosie's fault. She was blameless;

indeed, she had made more than the best of her new situation. Whereas she herself . . .

'Of course you can,' she forced herself to say through the hard ball suddenly rolling up her throat.

'Oooh, great! . . . What's the matter, Mum?' Rosie's elation gave way to concern. 'Are you crying?'

Diana shook her head hard. 'No . . .' But it came out as a gulp.

'You *are* crying, Mum! What's the matter?'

Diana pulled in. The car behind, which had been following too close, with over-bright headlights, zoomed past with a rude admonitory parp. It added to her crushing sense of failure.

She had tried to make a go of it, to work hard, remain cheerful, adapt uncomplainingly to her new circumstances. She had imagined she was building something solid. But it had taken only one short visit from Sara Oopvard for everything to collapse. What had been the point of it all?

Light fingers were pressing her hand. 'Mum!'

Diana sniffed, and with the mightiest of efforts pulled herself back from the brink of hysterical sobs. She could not cry in front of Rosie.

'Come on, Mum!' Rosie was urging.

Diana's head, which had been bent, now slowly raised itself back up.

'I'm sorry,' she muttered dully, rummaging for a hanky and feeling that roles had somehow been reversed. Rosie had become the mother, all resolve and encouragement, and she the defeated small daughter.

The impression intensified as Rosie produced a scrunched-up tissue from her school cardigan pocket. 'Here.'

Diana took it, and dabbed fitfully at her eyes. A sense of shame gathered within. What was the matter with her? Not only had she allowed Sara Oopvard to ruin her life, she was showing less spirit than a nine-year-old. Had she, Diana asked herself fiercely, learnt nothing from what had happened to her?

Rosie's voice went on, patient and encouraging as before, but now unmistakeably desperate too. 'You *can't* just give up because of horrible Sara Oopvard. And even more horrible Milo. You *can't* let them win.'

Her daughter was right, Diana realised. She mustn't let Sara defeat her. Not just for her own sake, but for Rosie's.

Like a smouldering log suddenly bursting into flames, a violent rage leapt within her, of an intensity that vaporised the misery she had felt. Flamelike, it scorched up and down her nerves. She clenched her fists; the pain as her nails dug into her palms was almost welcome.

'I won't let them beat us,' she muttered.

'You go girl!' cheered Rosie. 'You go get 'em!'

This unaccustomed phrase – from her daughter, anyway – stopped Diana in her tracks sufficiently to allow doubt to catch up again. Because what could she do about any of it? Wouldn't appearing at the dinner be just a horrible humiliation? Wasn't what was done, done?

Doubt now held a blanket over the flames of fury just felt. Doubt was about to drop this blanket and extinguish them. It was all very well when you were nine, Diana thought. Things were simple. Her daughter had no idea of the million and one reasons why she could not just 'go get 'em', as suggested – Sara or Richard. There was also the mess next door, with Debs and Shanna-Mae.

'I'll try not to let them beat us,' she amended her earlier assertion, shrinking inside at the disappointed look her daughter turned on her.

'Come on, Mum,' Rosie began urging again. 'You go and sort it out. And if you don't,' she added boldly, 'I will.'

'*You* will?' Diana regarded her daughter with a sort of amused hopelessness. 'What could you do?'

Rosie crossed small but capable forearms. 'I've sorted out next door, haven't I?'

'Have you?' Diana gasped.

'Didn't I say? Yeah, I saw Shanna-Mae at school today and we had a good talk in the sixth-form area. I told her that you didn't know about what Dad did and you were upset because Sara stole your boyfriend . . .'

'You said *what*?' burst in Diana. *Boyfriend!*

Rosie carried on regardless. 'And so I said Debs had to go easy on you. Shanna-Mae promised to speak to her mum. She says Debs feels awful, anyway, about all the things she said to you. So it'll be fine, Mum, honestly,' Rosie finished, breathless and cheerful. 'It will, honestly.'

And perhaps it would. For, at the sight of her daughter's brave little face, her resolute little eyes, Diana felt a new strength radiate from her heart and travel with a slow, steady warmth along her veins and nerves.

Chapter 28

Isabel had already started to plan the Christmas holidays. She was eager to move things on and meeting each other's parents was the next step. Would Jasper come and stay with her or would she go to him?

She longed to show him off. The thought of him in Lochalan made her thrill with pride. His exotic blond beauty would have an electric effect on the village. She could imagine the buzz of gossip in the teashop, in the supermarket – how well Isabel Murray had done for herself! What was less easy to imagine was how Mum would view it all.

Her mother now, finally, knew about the existence of Jasper. Isabel had taken a deep breath and dropped him into the conversation as casually as one might – if one took it – drop a sugar lump into tea. She had told Mum how handsome he was, how well dressed, but Mum had seemed unimpressed. 'Fine feathers make fine birds,' she had sniffed.

After that, Isabel had been careful to keep mentions of Jasper to a minimum. If Mum was jealous, the most likely explanation, it would be unwise to fan the flames. Once Mum had met Jasper herself and seen how wonderful he was, everything would be fine.

There was but one shadow on her happiness: the feeling that something, somewhere, was a tiny bit not quite right. Or might even be wrong.

Resist the thought as she might, she could not entirely shake off the impression that Jasper had been evasive these past few days. Her calls and texts had gone unreturned and twice when she had gone to his room he had not been there. She had hurtled happily up his staircase to find the door shut, not ajar as generally it was. She knocked on the brittle oak, the impact painful on her chilly knuckles. No answer. She knocked again and stood there for a few moments, her heart beating fast in a silence that smelled of furniture polish. He was not there, however. She could sense it. Beyond the door, the room was empty.

Both times she had gone back through the slippery streets to Branston. The ringing bells had seemed to taunt her, the ice beneath her feet trying to bring her down. The last time, she had watched as a couple of cyclists wobbled and then slid over, shouting curses as they hit the road surface.

Yes, somehow, for some reason, some of the earlier magic had gone.

Nothing had changed, yet everything had. Alastair, Olly felt, had saved him. In giving him a job, the editor had enabled him to take up once more the cudgels of life. He felt enormously relieved, and newly determined.

He felt he could see things more clearly. Even Isabel. Especially Isabel. It seemed to Olly that his thwarted passion and burning resentment now had the perfect outlet in the story Alastair wanted him to do. And Alastair, it turned out, had more than mere editorial glory in mind when dreaming the stunt up.

He too had an axe to grind. He too had suffered at the hands of the De Borchys. The paper he had previously worked on had been owned by the family and summarily shut down. Many of Alastair's former colleagues were still attempting – with diminishing hope – to get some compensation. To expose the Bullinger, Alastair felt, was to hit back to some extent.

But there was even more than that in it for Olly. Try as he might, he could not extinguish the hope – there was always hope

– of Isabel's passion for Jasper being mere infatuation: a moment of madness that would burn itself out. Perhaps, after her boy-friend's idea of fun had been splashed all over the *Post*, it finally would. And, as Isabel stood in the smoking ruins, he, Olly, would be there.

The *Post* office was all preparation for the great denouement. He would, Olly discovered, be expected to dress up.

'Not as one of the actual club,' he said to Alastair in horror. 'Pink's not my colour really.'

The editor laughed. 'Hardly. Those panto get-ups cost a good five grand a shot. No, you're going to dress up as a waiter. Oldest trick in the book. My friend Charlie runs a staff agency and he's happy to help in return for a credit.'

Olly stared. 'Well, how's that going to work, then? "By our undercover reporter, Oliver Summers, undercover courtesy of Jeeves Staff Agency, supplier of high-class-events personnel to the carriage trade"?'

Alastair snorted. 'Course not. We'll just do an advertorial or something about them, next issue. Come on.' He stood up behind his desk. 'Dress rehearsal. Charlie's sent a couple of penguin suits.' He opened the cupboard behind his chair and pulled out a coat hanger with a long plastic bag attached.

'I get a choice?' Olly noted the plural. He took the suit and pulled off the plastic. An odour of dry cleaning fluid arose from the jacket within. It was too long in the sleeves but otherwise it fitted reasonably well.

'Nah. Anna-Lou's coming with you.'

Olly, pulling off his jeans to try on the trousers, noted the new name. He had not met an Anna-Lou so far. He had been to the office just twice since the interview and the only other staff member he had met was Annabel, Alastair's wife, who doubled up as part-time secretary in the hours the couple's two daughters were at school. There were other employees, designers and sub-editors, but they worked remotely, from home and online. Such was the nature of the modern, family-friendly newspaper, Alastair had explained.

Who's Anna-Lou? Olly was about to ask, when the door of the office opened and a woman came in. A very good-looking woman, Olly noted, scrabbling desperately to cover his boxer shorts. She stood a good six feet in heels, with high cheekbones and blond hair that swished about her waist.

'Hi,' said the blonde vision, striding towards Olly with a hand outstretched. 'I'm Anna-Lou.'

'The staff photographer,' Alastair put in, sounding amused. 'To take the incriminating snaps.' Shaking hands while pulling up his trousers, Olly found, required more dexterity than he had at his command. He nodded at the tall blonde, red-faced and feeling utterly disadvantaged. And not only in one way; Alastair was explaining that Anna-Lou was actually a wildlife photographer but was taking a year's sabbatical on a newspaper to extend her skills. She was, Olly realised, quite a woman.

'So where is it, this ball?' she asked Alastair, swinging her hair. She seemed very relaxed about it all, Olly thought enviously.

Alastair was frowning into his Blackberry. 'That's the only thing I can't quite find out.'

Olly blinked. 'You don't know where the ball is?'

The editor looked up. 'You needn't take that tone,' he objected. 'Bullinger Balls are always secret.'

Olly nodded. Alastair was right, of course. While officially non-existent, the Bullinger Balls were the most notorious of all the notorious society's events. At the balls that hadn't happened during Olly's years at St Alwine's, someone hadn't got so drunk they'd drowned and someone else under the influence hadn't jumped out of a top-floor window; this alongside the usual, run-of-the-mill mayhem that hadn't happened either – surprisingly little of which ever got reported. Until now, of course, Olly thought, examining his putative boss's determined face.

'I've got feelers out,' Alastair said, 'but nothing so far.' He looked hard at Olly. 'Perhaps you could stir up some of your old Wino's contacts and find out.'

'I don't have any contacts at St Alwine's,' Olly said quickly, desperate to dodge this particularly onerous responsibility. 'I didn't form especially close friendships while I was there. Misogyny, racism and rampant snobbery not being my thing, and all that,' he added with an expectant, inclusive smile.

But Alastair was leaning back in his chair, arms folded. 'No contacts?' His lip gave a contemptuous twitch upwards. 'And you want to be a journalist? You'd better get some, then. Or else, make a better job of lying about not having any.'

Olly felt his knees start to tremble. His entire future seemed to hang in the balance. Then he felt a hand on his arm: Anna-Lou's long, white one.

'Don't take any notice of him,' she said. 'His bark is worse than his bite. He wouldn't have taken you on if he didn't think you could do it. We're going to do a great job, don't worry. It's going to be fun.'

'Yes,' Olly said, looking gratefully back at her and shyly at Alastair, who was smiling himself now. He felt a sudden great burst of excitement and determination. 'Yes. I think that it is.'

Later, Olly stood before Hero's door. He had been at the *Post* all day, but as his new job had yet to pay him anything, it seemed impolite to abandon his cleaning duties. The Hoover was in his hand.

A picture of a poodle had joined the gallery stuck on the door's outside, he noticed. Did this mean Hero was joining the human race or moving further away from it?

There was no noise at all coming from behind the door. Perhaps Hero was out. Dog walking, possibly. Particularly after a long day at work, he felt relieved not to have to face her.

Olly pushed open the door and felt a burst of shock to see Hero's long, lean, black-legged form stretched out on the bed. She was breathing gently, evidently asleep. Grasping the Hoover, Olly was preparing to back out of the room when he heard a sudden exclamation. He turned to find himself staring into a pair of heavily ringed, very angry black eyes. 'What the hell do you think you're doing?' Hero demanded. 'Can't you see I'm resting?'

Olly looked stonily back at her. 'Do you ever do anything else?'

She glowered at him from beneath a hanging, purple-tinged black fringe. 'So what?' she said defiantly.

'My business. No one else's.'

Olly had not intended to shout. He was not, as a rule, the shouting sort. But what Hero had just said seemed to light a blue touchpaper within him. He drew himself up. He let fly.

'No one else's?' he roared. 'What about your parents, Hero? They *love* you. Both of them are worried *sick* about you. They'd do *anything* for you. But you won't do anything at all!'

'How dare you say that to me!' Hero shouted back. 'Who the hell do *you* think you are? You're just the lodger.'

Olly had a head of steam up now. While his new job had depleted his energy slightly, it had also given him confidence. 'Yes, I am just the lodger,' he roared. 'And that's exactly why I can say things that your parents are too afraid to say themselves. Your mum and dad are good, caring, talented people, Hero. They deserve better than you. You're selfish beyond belief. You're cruel, arrogant, lazy—'

'And you're just a loser!' Hero broke in, thumping her skull-beringed hands against her black duvet.

'Not so much a loser as you are,' Olly bawled back. 'I've got a job now, actually. I'm not buried alive in my bedroom! I'm out there!'

Hero's gaze was mocking. 'I wish you'd get out of *here*,' she said. While her tone remained coolly insolent, he noticed that her fingers in their skull rings were shaking.

He took another huge lungful of breath and steamrollered on. He felt, for all his fury, oddly in control and absolutely justified. What was being said now should have been said long ago. 'How can you,' he shouted, 'waste your life, your youth, your looks – yes, *looks*, Hero – your intelligence and all your opportunities up here in your bedroom? It's interesting that you spend all that time on that graveyard Gothic look, because, frankly, you may as well be dead.'

He stopped. Perhaps the last sentence was going a bit far. The word 'dead' was still ringing in the air.

Hero looked shocked. She was biting her lips now, he saw, and her eyes looked shiny, but he could not stop what he had started. It would have been easier to stop an avalanche. '*Someone's got to tell you, Hero. Get up, get out and do something with what remains of your life.*'

He picked up the Hoover and wrenched open Hero's door. Leaping back before him on to the landing were two crouched figures who had evidently been watching through the keyhole. There would have been no need to listen through it, obviously.

The figures straightened into Dotty and David. Olly looked back at them in horror, expecting them to launch themselves at him with all the fury that over-protective parents could summon.

For a second, both just stared at him. Then Olly felt something clinging round his neck. Looking down, he saw Dotty's familiar raspberry beret. David, to the side, was clearing his throat repeatedly and knitting his brows.

'Thank you,' Dotty bawled into Olly's chest. He could feel her hot tears through his T-shirt.

'Yes,' David said, socking him with grateful and painful violence on the shoulder. 'And, um, no need to carry on with the housework, OK? We'll manage somehow.'

Chapter 29

Richard had made a decision. He would leave. Quit. Go. He'd wait until the wretched alumni dinner was over and then tender his resignation. He had lasted only one term, but so what? He wasn't College Master material. Nothing had gone well for him since he got here. Best to quit while he was ahead – or, at least, not too far behind.

All the same, he felt guilty. The college had been a port in a storm and he had enjoyed his research work. So he would, Richard decided, do his very best for Branston at the dinner. He would bang the drum, talk the talk, walk the walk, raise the money and, in general, try to leave the place in a better state than when he found it.

And now, this Saturday night, the hour had come. And so must the man. Feeling oddly jittery, Richard walked into the Turd for the pre-alumni-dinner reception.

He reminded himself of the reasons to be cheerful. The academic world would be his oyster once he had left Branston. Better still, Sara did not seem to be joining him for the dinner, as she had threatened.

When, earlier, he had passed briefly through the Master's Lodge to pick up his black tie, his unwelcome house guest had been absent. For a few moments Richard's heart had soared in the hope that she had left altogether. But then he had discovered

Milo conducting virtual germ warfare in one of the bedrooms. And the bathroom was still a bombsite of Sara's emollients and potions. She was still here, all right. But there was always the possibility she had had a better offer for this evening. This town was full of influential people, after all.

Now he had made his mind up to leave the place, Richard was surprised to find he felt almost fond of Branston. The Turd looked surprisingly respectable, almost festive. Someone – Flora, presumably – had strung fairy lights along the bar front and decorated the concrete stairs from the ground floor with tea lights in small glass holders, pressed right against the wall to be out of the way.

Flora appeared in an unusually becoming red dress. The guests started to arrive. A stately trout with a withering expression and a carefully arranged pile of spun-sugar hair was talking to a bishop wearing a bristly grey tweed jacket over his dark shirt and dog collar. Hanging round his neck was a large, thick silver cross, which seemed to Richard to be dangling dangerously near the dish of hummus being passed round.

Remembering his vow to be solicitous, Richard looked about to make sure everyone was talking to someone. An unsmiling couple stood silently near one of the walls. A pink fascinator was plunged in her rug-like dark hair, clashing with a big pair of pink-framed glasses. Her companion held his wineglass in both hands and was looking about with an unimpressed air. Richard was uncertain he could rescue things for them, but recognised he was bound to try. It was his last duty to his college. Taking a deep breath, he stepped towards them.

He was interrupted by the Bursar, who bore down on him, looking anxious. 'The Snodgrasses!' he hissed.

Richard's heart sank. 'Where?' he asked, resignedly.

'Nowhere! That's the point. They're not here!' the Bursar wailed, looking as if he might burst into tears. 'They haven't checked into their hotel or anything!'

Richard's reply was drowned in a series of loud crashes. A

harassed-looking man hurtled into the bar. He had evidently just fallen down the stairs. Two small and very untidy children shot in after him, both cackling with delight and bearing tea lights like Olympic torches.

'Buster! Django! Get back here!' screamed the harassed man. He then drew a hand over his mouth and looked apologetically round. 'Sorry, folks.'

Tenebris Hasp of South London, Richard guessed, remembering the cross-purposes phone call about the bank loan. Matters had obviously not improved since. Tenebris Hasp had gone straight to the bar and was tipping one glass of wine down his throat while his fist clutched another. The children continued to run around, screeching.

Richard stared hard at Flora. She was busy calming down the Bursar; eventually, however, he caught her eye. 'Get – them – out – of – here,' he mouthed silently.

Flora got the picture. She bore down on the gulping Hasp at speed. 'Welcome,' she said smoothly. 'I see you've brought your family with you.' She looked down at the boys, her tone commanding. 'Shall we go to your room?'

'That's amazing,' Hasp spluttered as his sons stared up, evidently stunned. 'I can tell already that they really respect you. I don't think you're going to have any trouble with them.'

Flora paused a few treads up the concrete stairs. 'Let there be no misunderstanding here,' she said in firm tones. 'I am not babysitting your children.'

Tenebris Hasp looked aghast. 'Well, if you're not,' he asked, 'who is? Because it's not me, let me tell you.' His voice rose to a tearful bleat. 'I've had a bloody awful week looking after these two –' he shot a resentful glance at Buster and Django – 'and I've come to this dinner to get completely wrecked and forget how bloody awful my whole bloody life is.'

As Flora hustled him away, Richard felt an unexpected sympathy for Hasp. His own life was pretty bloody awful at the moment too. But at least he could make a new start elsewhere.

On Monday he would make the first move, tell the college, begin looking about.

An angry cry broke into his thoughts. His fears for the bishop's cross and the savoury dips had, it seemed, been justified. The cross had just swung like a censer through the yellow slurry, carrying on its exiting trajectory a considerable amount of garlicky slop which it had deposited smartly over the trout with the spun-sugar hair. The bishop was currently scrubbing her left breast hard with a paper napkin.

Richard felt a sharp finger painfully prodding the soft tissue between his neck and his shoulder.

'Dick!'

He turned in horror. He had never been called Dick in his life.

Standing before him was a skinny woman in a skin-tight white dress exposing a great deal of tanned flesh. Her glittering blond hair was piled loosely up on her head and hung in tendrils around her skull-like face. Her red-lipsticked smile hit him like a hail of bullets. Sara Oopvard. Just when he had thought it was safe.

He could have looked more pleased to see her, Sara thought. But if she had learnt one thing from her banker ex-husband, it was that aggressive and upfront tactics succeeded. She gave a roguish toss of her chignon; making it look as if she had twisted it up in seconds had taken over three hours and entire cans of Elnett and was the main reason she was late. Although Milo's being difficult hadn't helped; in the end she'd had to go to extreme lengths to entertain him. He'd expressed a great interest in seeing Richard's laboratory and she'd dropped him off there on the way. Something warned her not to mention this to Richard, though; not at this point in the evening, anyway.

As she chucked him playfully under the chin, Richard felt his spine freeze.

'You must have really wondered if I was coming or not!' exclaimed Sara, grasping his shoulders and planting on his lips a prolonged and possessive kiss.

* * *

Of course, Isabel told herself, nothing was wrong. Of course Jasper still loved her. He had told her so.

So why did she feel so nervous? Why the sense of impending doom? Jasper was just a bit busy, that was all – with what, he did not say. And tonight he had a dinner to which Isabel was not invited.

He had been charming but evasive about it and she guessed it had something to do with the Bullinger Club. She did not ask directly, however, and indeed had been careful to avoid any reference to his membership since bringing it up so unexpectedly on their first night together. Especially now that he had become so distant all of a sudden; she feared appearing censorious.

Of *course* there was nothing wrong. She tried to look at the situation sensibly. Jasper was entitled to have an evening without her if he wanted to and she didn't in any case want to have dinner with his friends. She had met a few of them in passing, on the staircase, in the quad; they had been boomingly self-confident, not to mention offensive, to a man. They had either ignored her or swept her up and down with amused stares that were clearly not assessing her intellectual abilities.

No, it would be pleasant to have a night in alone. She could relax. Catch up on some of the reading she had been neglecting of late. Think about some of the essays she had missed. Have a long bath. A bath never failed to calm her down.

Isabel drew the curtains of her room before picking up her sponge bag and towel. The evening sky outside struck her as extraordinary: a burnished lemon that looked somehow tremendous – a background for some huge celestial drama. She was being fanciful, she told herself. She was only having a bath and staying in with a book. No drama there.

But here was Kate outside the bathroom door, pacing the corridor, wrapped in a bath towel. It was like the past repeating itself, like the scene at the very beginning of her Branston career.

The thing that was different was that Amber was not there, nor the dog.

Isabel had not seen Coco since the day she disappeared and had, some time ago, convinced herself that the animal had found a good home. And Amber had not been around. She was being sent down, everyone knew that now. Perhaps she had simply left ahead of schedule.

'Someone nicked the bathroom again?' Isabel made an effort to grin. Christmas was coming; surely Kate could manage a bit of good cheer. Besides, being for once without Jasper was a reminder of how her social circle had shrunk since he had come into her life. She should, Isabel knew, make an effort to build bridges with people.

Kate, however, did not smile. 'It's Her Majesty the Lady Amber.'

'Amber!' Isabel was surprised. Still here, then.

Kate was looking at her ironically. 'She told me she'd be out by six. I can't quite imagine why I believed her, given the lies she tells everyone else.' She paused and hoicked up the towel with a muscly arm. 'She's been in since five.'

Isabel looked at her watch. 'Five!' A long bath, even by Amber's standards. 'But it's almost seven.' She felt a faint bolt of alarm.

'No shit, Sherlock,' Kate snapped. She rattled the handle violently. 'Come on!' she shouted. 'Out of there!'

It was now that Isabel realised that the orange corridor carpet beneath her was wet. She glanced at the base of the bathroom door; a growing pool of water was emerging. If she listened closely, through the thick door, the sound of a gushing tap could be heard.

'Bloody typical!' Kate groaned, now noticing it too. 'Not only is she hogging the bathroom, she's having one of those Japanese baths where you just keep the water running—'

'Kate!' yelled Isabel, gripped by a sudden, horrible conviction. 'It's not that. Something's wrong. I just know it is.'

334

'Don't be stupid. She's just hogging the bathroom as usual—'

'No, she's not!' Isabel gasped in terror, throwing her shoulder against the door. 'Come on. Please, Kate. You've got to help me get this door open.'

Kate's red, angry face radiated amazement. 'Smash it in? Are you joking?'

She had never, in fact, felt less like joking. Isabel was throwing herself wildly at the door. 'Kate! Please! Help me!'

The gushing water within seemed to be pumping around her own head. 'Help me! I'm not strong enough on my own. It's life or death, I'm sure it is.'

Kate gave her one last doubtful look before throwing her powerfully muscled rower's shoulder against the solid door. Again and again they slammed themselves at the unyielding wood. Eventually there was a splintering sound, a crack, and the door gave way. Kate staggered forward into the bathroom with a swoosh of water. Water covered the entire floor, like a shallow swimming pool in which soggy towels lay here and there like islands. And in the bath . . .

The air now filled with a loud, continuous sound: Kate screaming, 'Oh my God! Oh my God!' over and over again.

Isabel had frozen with disbelief. She had been expecting something awful, but never this.

The bath was full to the top. Water ran smoothly over the tub's rolled edges. It was the cold tap that was running, the twisted column of water sending a constant series of ripples over what lay below.

What lay below was Amber – slumped, unmoving, her face blue and her eyes closed.

Chapter 30

As she drove through the dark streets towards Branston, Diana asked herself yet again whether she was doing the right thing. Rosie insisted that she was. Debs, unhesitatingly, had backed Rosie up. Shanna-Mae had been most concerned with the effect of her eye shadow palettes, but had paused whilst applying a lick of liquid eyeliner to opine that she thought Diana couldn't do otherwise. 'You can't let that 'orrible old cow win, can you?'

That all was forgiven next door was the most dizzying relief. Diana's stomach had twisted with terror when she had opened the door to find Debs on the doorstep, Rosie and Shanna-Mae standing behind her. Debs' plump face had been inscrutable and Diana would have feared the worst had not Rosie been behind, beaming and with her thumbs up.

Debs had rolled a suspicious look around Diana's bare hallway. 'Gone, 'as she?'

'Yes,' Diana whispered, recognising these three words for the olive branch they were. The next moment, she was clasped against Debs' broad and squashy bosom.

An hour later, in the kitchen, a bottle and a half of rosé to the good, Debs was weeping tears of mirth at Diana's accounts of Sara Upward in London. 'She actually *paid* people to come in and decorate her Christmas tree for her?'

And now, dressed up, made-up, hair straightened and shining, Diana was about to right some more recent wrongs. She was to confront Richard and Sara. The alumni dinner was the perfect opportunity – in Debs' view, anyway. 'He'll be at the labs avoiding 'er, otherwise.'

'Bit public though.'

'Yeah, but you gotta get 'em together, tell 'im in front of 'er.'

And so, in front of whoever happened to be there at the time, Diana would explain to Richard the truth about her divorce. Tell him, too, about Sara's lies. Sara was unlikely to take any of this calmly, of course, and a violent scene was practically guaranteed.

The thought of such a scene – and Richard's accompanying embarrassment – was torture. But Debs was adamant that Sara should face the consequences of her actions. Making her do so was, Diana sensed, the price she must pay for the resumption of neighbourly relations.

While Diana wavered, Debs was impressively unblinkered in her view of the situation. She had an answer for even the most unanswerable aspects. 'What do you mean you can't believe Richard's let Sara move in? He may be a brain genius, but these academics are all the same. Got no bloody common sense. He might know what's inside 'is own 'ead, but he can't see what's in front of 'is own face. She forced her way in,' was her explanation for Sara's residency at the Master's Lodge. 'She got past you, didn't she? And you know what a pig she is. Richard never met her before. Bet the poor sod's rueing the day he set eyes on her now,' Debs finished with a sniff.

Debs even had an answer for Richard's lack of communication. 'Look, Di, he lost his wife not long ago. And then he goes out with you just twice and all this 'appens. He's just run back to the labs, that's all. And who can blame 'im?'

Diana had doubts, even so. Angry though she was with Richard and Sara, she was most annoyed with herself. Had she been candid with Richard about her past in the first place, had she been honest with Debs about the divorce, none of this would have happened. Sara had merely exploited the opportunity Diana had handed her on a plate.

'Oh, for goodness' sake,' Debs exploded, when Diana hesitantly expressed this. 'Stop blaming yourself, will you? That woman tried to ruin your life. Get angry. If you don't, she wins and you'll have to leave town,' her neighbour baldly pointed out. 'And with Rosie settled at school and you in your job, do you really want to do that? Start all over again, somewhere else?'

It was this that finally galvanised Diana. And so she was driving, this Saturday evening, towards Branston College. Her heart was thumping and her nerves were tense, but the loveliness of the scene outside the steamy windows impressed itself upon her nonetheless.

Christmas was coming, in this most Christmassy of towns. In the gathering darkness the college bells made ripples of sound over the riverside meadows. Candles glowed through the stained glass of the chapels. Through the window that was stuck open, Diana could hear the notes of organs winding out into the freezing air. Did she want to leave? No. Not at all.

She was nearing Branston now and her insides were knotting nervously around each other. She was driving past the university neurological department, Richard's centre of operations. She felt a rush of nostalgia for the night he had shown it to her, that night which had started so well but then gone so wrong.

The building, as she glanced at it, seemed mostly dark. The scientists had all gone home, perhaps for the holidays. And Richard, of course, would be at the dinner.

Or was he? It looked as if there was a light on at the end where Richard worked. Perhaps he'd dropped in to see his worms after all, dinner or no dinner. Perhaps he wasn't going to the dinner at all – which would make all her plans redundant, of course. Flooded with sudden hope, she was tempted for a second to turn round and drive back home.

But then what would Debs say? And, of the two of them – her new neighbour and her old – who did she fear facing the most?

Diana pressed her foot gently down on the accelerator and continued towards Branston.

* * *

How Richard wished he had spent the evening with his worms. They had started to do some interesting things of late and, dumb and sluggish though they were, they were more interesting than most of the people at the dinner.

He had, he felt, kept reasonably calm under the onslaught that was Sara Oopvard, and was remaining that way with the aid of a soothing glass of red and the reflection that she would, finally, be on her way back to London tomorrow.

Sara was, in any case, at a safe distance down the table next to the Bursar, who was drinking away his worries about the non-appearing Americans. From time to time she leant forward and tipped Richard an enormous, very off-putting wink.

However he personally might feel about it, the dinner was going well. The Incinerator looked almost reasonable by candlelight and the food, for once, was palatable. He looked down from the top table to the main body of the hall.

Tenebris Hasp was there; presumably he had managed to get Buster and Django to sleep. How, exactly, was something Richard didn't want to think about.

Richard couldn't see it at first, but he could hear it. And see it. People had begun to jump about and exclaim – scream, in some cases. The disturbance rippled down the long table; one after another people leapt up, like a Mexican wave.

'Under the table!' he heard a man's voice shout.

'There! It just grabbed me!' shrieked the woman next to him.

Then came the crash of a chair being thrown back and a deranged-sounding, evidently very drunken, roaring male voice.

'Buster! Django! Whazzahellyoudoinoutabed? Comeoutfrom-unnerzosetables! NOW!'

But Buster and Django, it seemed, had no intention of doing anything of the sort. They had now reached the top table and were about to complete their mission. Those to the right of Richard were on their feet with fury and Richard himself was about to find out why.

Small bodies now squirmed past his knees and he felt a sharp and painful jab in his crotch, accompanied by manic childish giggling. Nor did the mayhem end there. The unfortunate effect of goosing Sara Oopvard was for her head to tip forward into the candle flame. This immediately seized her big and much-sprayed hair, which in turn went up like a rocket.

Screams – the loudest of which was Sara's – now filled the air. Richard looked about in panic, then grabbed the nearest glass of water and emptied it all over Sara Oopvard's head.

Looking back afterwards, Richard could remember only vaguely the resulting disintegration of the entire dining room into noisy chaos. But he could recall with perfect clarity what happened next: the college porter walked rapidly towards him, followed by people in hi-vis jackets. Policemen. Paramedics.

Amber Piggott had been found dead in the bath.

Isabel had run out of Branston as soon as the emergency services arrived. They had crowded into the bathroom, panting and rustling in their hi-vis jackets and reflective strips, saying things like, 'We'll take over now, Madam.'

Isabel had let them. Left them to it. She had done her best, after all; she and Kate had dragged a heavy, slippery Amber out of the bath and, while Isabel had tried the kiss of life, Kate had run down the hall in her towel, screaming about the police and needing to find the porter.

It had been horrible, being left alone with the body. Blow and pump as Isabel might, no response had been forthcoming. Amber had lain there like a stranded mermaid, naked and shining and lifeless, her water-darkened hair streaming out across the floor.

'Drugs,' one of the paramedics had muttered. 'Gotta be.'

Drugs! The word went through Isabel like a bolt of electricity. She felt as if she were waking up from something.

Drugs. Isabel remembered the last time she had seen Amber, unfocused of gaze and stumbling of gait. She had thought she

341

was drunk, an impression Jasper had confirmed. 'Pissed as a fart sometimes,' he had said. 'We all know she likes her champagne.'

Yes, Isabel knew that. But she knew next to nothing about drugs, or the signs someone was taking them. Did Jasper? There had been that joint, Isabel remembered, that night in her room . . .

She pushed these disloyal reflections violently away. How could she even think it? Jasper was Amber's devoted friend. He would be devastated when he found out what had happened. She must tell him before anyone else.

He was at the Bullinger dinner, but where was that? At his college? She turned herself in the direction of St Alwine's – and ran.

As before, Farthingale and Scavenger were sitting in the porter's lodge drinking tea. A small fire roared in the grate. As Isabel burst in, chest heaving, they regarded her with a studied lack of interest.

'In a rush, are we, Miss?' This in Farthingale's trademark sardonic manner.

Isabel forced down her dislike. She needed him to help her.

'I've got to find Jasper De Borchy,' she said, with as much control as she could summon.

Farthingale's ironic eyes gleamed. 'They all say that, Miss.'

Isabel felt murderous, but persevered. 'He's at a Bullinger Club dinner tonight. Where is it? Do you know?'

Farthingale turned heavily to his colleague. 'Bullinger Club dinner tonight, Mr Scavenger?'

'No, Mr Farthingale.' There was amusement in Scavenger's tone.

Isabel fought incipient hysteria. A tragedy had occurred and these vile porters were toying with her. She wanted to scream.

Farthingale blew out his mottled purple cheeks. 'There's the Bullinger Club Ball, of course.'

'Indeed, Mr Farthingale.'

Jasper had never said it was a ball, Isabel thought. He had made it sound like a low-key dinner. But there could hardly be two Bullinger events on the same night. 'Where is it?' she asked, straight to the point.

'The real question, Miss, is not "where", but "whether". Does it exist at all?' Farthingale said.

Metaphysics now, a despairing Isabel thought. She felt like Alice in some twisted college-porter Wonderland. 'I don't understand,' she said eventually.

'Bullinger Balls don't exist . . .' Farthingale looked again at his sidekick.

'Don't exist,' Scavenger repeated, on cue. 'Except that they do,' he added, with a sudden, terrifying grin that exposed a row of yellow tombstone teeth. 'Although nobody knows where. Secret location.' He tapped his large purple nose.

The Bakelite clock above that fierce little roaring fire indicated time was moving on. She was getting nowhere here. Isabel was about to turn on her heel and stomp out when a remark of Jasper's about the porters shot through her mind: 'They do anything you tell them to. If you slip them enough cash, that is.'

She rummaged in her bag. Her purse was empty apart from one last twenty-pound note, sent by Mum only this morning along with a sad little letter imploring her to be careful: 'I never realised university was so expensive.' It wasn't university that was expensive, of course. It was Jasper.

Shoving Mum determinedly to the back of her mind, Isabel took out the money, put it down on the age-polished oak counter in front of Farthingale and Scavenger and raised her chin expectantly.

Farthingale was the first to react. 'Ah,' he said, putting out a meaty paw, taking the note and holding it up to the light. 'Forgive me,' he said, lowering it. 'But we need to check.'

'Some of the young gentlemen have in the past entertained an elastic concept of what constitutes legal tender,' Scavenger added gravely.

The thick minute hand of the wall clock wobbled forward again. She felt her heart wobble in response. 'Where is the party?' Isabel growled.

Farthingale cleared his throat and sent a light, inquiring smile at Scavenger. Scavenger sent it back.

Farthingale spoke: 'Is it not, Mr Scavenger, on this occasion, at Crewell Place, Crewell village?'

Scavenger put his bowler-hatted head on one side, seemingly to consider. 'You may be right, Mr Farthingale – it being Lord Crewell's turn to host.'

Farthingale shook his head indulgently. 'Most amusing young gentleman.' His tone was fond. 'Quite a chip off the old block.'

'Or a block off the old chip. The family made their fortune from frozen foods, Mr Farthingale, don't forget,' Scavenger reminded his colleague.

'You're right there, Mr Scavenger. Hence m'lord's nickname, Chippy Crewell. Nothing to do with a sense of inferiority, of course.'

'The opposite, indeed,' Scavenger appreciatively agreed.

Isabel, with flying heels, left them to it.

The rain had now increased. It drummed on the road surface so hard it bounced back up again, and so Isabel got soaked twice by the same downpour.

'Come on!' she muttered under her breath, glaring into the hissing, steaming night as she willed a taxi to appear. 'Come *on!*'

At the taxi rank, one battered-looking white car was parked in the bay, its driver settled comfortably behind a newspaper. He looked over his fat shoulder with irritation as Isabel threw herself into the back seat and panted, 'Crewell Place.'

The driver tipped up his flabby, stubbly jaw. 'You students, you're always bloody moaning. Places can be crueller, believe me.'

'I mean that's where I want to go,' Isabel said, exasperated. 'It's a house. Somewhere round here.'

'Where?'

'No idea,' Isabel replied, with a spirit that surprised her. 'I'm not the driver.'

The driver grumbled as he punched the details into his GPS and stuck his foot down hard on the accelerator. Isabel's head slammed back against the plastic ribbing of the rear seat. For a second she saw stars.

The taxi was torture. It wasn't just the initial startling velocity and the subsequent halting progress through what seemed an unprecedented number of traffic lights. There was also the oppressively soothing voice of the sat nav, the pounding yet slightly off-dial local radio and the sickening smell of air freshener, made worse by the overpowering heating. The taxi driver, who sat on a sort of mat made of small wooden balls, also kept up a litany of growling complaint. Most things seemed to irk his ire: the students, their bikes, the weather, the city council's road repair programme. Isabel wondered if he would feel better if he didn't have those hard-looking wooden ball things pressing into his back.

Her eyes stayed to the meter, whose green digital figures were increasing with merciless speed. It provoked the alarming recollection of giving twenty pounds to Farthingale and Scavenger. Was that really all she had had?

With deceptively calm movements, so as not to attract the attention of her chauffeur, Isabel reached for her bag and opened her purse. The note section was empty. Frenziedly dragging back the zip on the coin pocket, Isabel found two pounds forty nine pence in change. She grabbed her bag and rummaged wildly in it. Rather as she had suspected, no spare twenty-pound notes had slipped in there and become twisted in the debris.

She looked, panicked, out of the window. They were far out in the countryside now, miles from any cashpoint, in the unlikely event any such machine would oblige her. That Jasper had used up the last of her credit with the bank was the reason she was now forced to ask for cash from Mum. Her best bet was to say nothing until Crewell Place. Then she would face the music, or, more likely, the shouting.

But Isabel was a fundamentally honest person. She deplored deceit, and was ashamed of her recent obfuscation in money matters. Tonight's act of bribery, necessary though it had been, seemed to her to mark a boundary. She must go no further. Her current predicament, in this car, was a sign. She must tread a more honest path from now on and not ask her mother for any more money. Jasper would just have to pay his way.

Having thus straightened out her own conscience, Isabel decided to place her faith in the taxi driver's reaction to her penury. Perhaps, like many growly people, he had a heart of gold beneath. She cleared her throat. 'I'm awfully sorry,' she began. 'But I actually haven't got any money and—'

The violence of the brakes slamming almost knocked the breath out of her. This time she was flung against the furthermost extension of the seatbelt.

'Get out,' said the taxi driver, tipping back his head and glaring at Isabel in the rear-view mirror. 'I know your sort. Get out. Now.'

Isabel was incredulous. 'You don't understand—' she began.

'I understand all right,' he cut in. 'You don't have any money. What else is there to understand? What you doing taking a cab for if you don't have the cash?'

'I didn't realise,' Isabel gibbered. 'It was a mistake.'

This seemed to tip him over the edge for some reason. 'Do me a favour!' he roared. 'They all say that! Get out! Now!'

Isabel got out, hurriedly. He was big and frightening and she obviously had no choice. But, after the heat of his car, the outside air round her legs was a freezing shock. 'You can't leave me here,' she yelped disbelievingly from outside on the damp verge. It was a winter evening and, by now, very dark. Mist was gathering.

'Try me,' he responded, revving his engine and looking each way down the road. Beneath his shaggy brows, his small eyes glittered with grim satisfaction.

'I'm going to be late,' Isabel squeaked. 'Really, really late.' She had no idea how near or far she was from Crewell Place.

'Better start walking then,' the taxi driver replied nastily. He pointed up the road with a thick finger. 'It's that way.'

As there was clearly no point in arguing, Isabel ran off. There was no time to walk and the agitation she felt demanded some arduous physical outlet. She plunged down the road in the rain. From time to time, cars passed, tyres hissing in the wet. Soon her legs were protesting painfully and despite all she had absorbed as a teenager about not accepting lifts with strangers, let alone soliciting them, the idea of sticking out her thumb was growing within.

She would, she promised herself, flag down the next car that passed.

Of course, from that moment on, the road traffic dried up completely.

There was no choice but to pound on. Ghastly pictures and impressions started to form in the drizzly darkness. Amber's face seemed to hang before her, as Isabel had last seen her. Helpless beneath the water, head lolling, mouth open, hair stirring the surface in a hopeless, ironic imitation of life. Isabel had never thought it possible to feel sorry for her, or see her as a victim. But now the waste, the pity of it all, squeezed her heart as much as the running was straining it.

'*Drugs,*' *the paramedic had said.*

Someone had given Amber those drugs. Someone in this town, very possibly. The raging hate she felt for them gave Isabel fresh energy. Just wait until she told Jasper. He would be furious too – more so, if anything.

After what seemed like hours, she saw on her right hand side a pair of ivy-swathed gateposts topped with hideously contorted, sharp-beaked gargoyles. They would have looked bad enough in full sunshine, but looked positively terrifying in the dark, gleaming with rain. To Isabel, however, they were the most welcome of sights. Below them, a verdigris metal plaque announced this to be Crewell Place, and them, by extension, its guardian spirits. She was here.

Chapter 31

'Crewell Place,' exclaimed Alastair.

'Isn't it just?' groaned Olly, turning from his computer screen. Coming in to work on Saturday had been a shock to the system. He had had no choice, however; Alastair had demanded all hands on deck to locate the still-elusive Bullinger party.

So far, despite frequently ingenious effort, they had come up with nothing. It was now, presumably, just a matter of hours before the party began. And while an outwardly relaxed Alastair was clearly not giving up – everything, after all, depended on it for him – Olly had started to detect a certain nervousness, although the editor's tone now was almost boisterous.

'Pull yourself together, man,' Alastair said, the relief in his voice evident. 'Crewell Place is a house. It's where the Bullinger party's being held. I've just found out; mind you, it's bloody cost me.'

'What do you mean?'

Alastair looked at Olly, a hint of incredulity in the eyes behind the glasses. 'They're called contacts. We talked about them before, remember? You'll find them quite useful. If you stay the course,' he added darkly.

Olly's insides shrank in terror. He could not afford to lose this job. He would not. 'What contacts told you about Crewell Place?' he asked.

Alastair gave him a cryptic half-smile. 'A journalist never reveals his sources, remember?'

Olly reddened. His only real talent at the job, it seemed, was saying all the wrong things. Across the room, Anna-Lou caught his eye from behind her screen. She winked and immediately he felt better.

Alastair had not finished; however, he sounded friendlier now. 'But, as you're one of us, I can exclusively reveal that it's the porter's lodge at St Alwine's.'

Olly was amazed. But was it such a surprise, really? Farty and Skinflint, as they were known in college, had been keen extortioners. He had once had to hand over five pounds for shackling his bike to the wrong railing. The correct railing, Skinflint had enlightened him, was the one next to the one he had used, a mere few inches to the right. So Farty and Skinflint had another sideline in selling information.

But that was not the conversation's most significant revelation. 'One of us,' Alastair had said. Olly felt wildly proud, and determined to justify the editor's faith in him. Now they knew the location, he and Anna-Lou could get to work.

He hurried to put on the waiter suit. 'Hardly Fred Astaire,' Alastair remarked, stroking his stubbly chin with one hand. 'More Charlie Chaplin. While you, my dear,' he added, turning to Anna-Lou, 'look like something out of *Cabaret*.'

Anna-Lou, who had disappeared into Alastair's cupboard to change, now emerged looking spectacular indeed. Her tall frame was shown to stunning advantage in the long black trousers, while the monochrome bow tie and white shirt were the perfect background to her fall of golden hair. Alastair was right, Olly felt. She did look as if she were going to high-kick down some illuminated staircase.

'Shouldn't you put your hair up?' Olly queried.

Anna-Lou smiled and held up her hair in both hands. Hanging down the back was a small but definitely professional-looking camera. The shining tresses, replaced, hid it entirely.

Both Alastair and Anna-Lou, Olly saw, perfectly understood the job. They felt confident about it; were even looking forward to it. He, on the other hand, was full of a sudden, sickening, all-consuming fear. 'What makes you think,' he jabbered at Alastair, 'that we'll get past the doormen? Just looking like waiters might not be enough. We might get thrown out. Anna-Lou's very obviously a girl, for one thing.'

Alastair did not reply immediately. He leant his close-cropped head on one hand and looked wearily at Olly. 'You might get thrown out,' he agreed. 'And it might not be enough. There are no guarantees.'

Olly's heart, already thumping, thumped louder. He felt nauseous with nerves.

'But you have to make it work, that's all,' Alastair went on quietly. 'Your own job depends on it. My job depends on it. And you want to get Jasper De Borchy, don't you?'

The trilling nerves feeding Olly's fear now seemed to burst into flames. A violent rage leapt within him, of an intensity that vaporised the apprehension he had felt. 'Yes,' he said, over his thumping heart.

'And I don't think it matters that Anna-Lou looks like a girl,' he heard Alastair say over the thumping. 'They go for that androgynous thing, those Bullinger types.'

An expression of disgust crossed Anna-Lou's face. 'Well, they won't be "going for" me.'

They wouldn't, either, Olly thought. Anna-Lou had fended off tigers and lions; the Bullinger Club would be child's play.

As they prepared to leave, Alastair was frowning into his screen again. 'Story coming through,' he said. 'Some girl collapsed in the bath in one of the colleges. Drugs, it looks like.' He shook his head. 'Again. Why can we never get these creeps?' He rubbed his eyes and reached for the phone. 'Better see what the guys at the station have to say about it.'

Olly and Anna-Lou left quietly. It was evident that their leader's mind was on other things.

'Oh, and by the way,' Alastair shouted from behind them.
'What?' called back Anna-Lou from the chilly stairwell.
'Good luck!'

It was raining outside; nonetheless, they flagged down a cab in minutes. Or, rather, his colleague did. Few taxi drivers, Olly reasoned, would have been able to resist the sight of six feet of gorgeous blonde at the roadside. Hopefully this luck would keep up.

As they rattled along to Crewell Place, Anna-Lou, unruffled as ever, was telling him of her adventures photographing tigers.

'You see,' she said earnestly, 'they don't mean it when they growl at you the first time. But if you don't get out of the way then, you've had it.'

Normally, Olly supposed, he would have fallen in love with Anna-Lou. But it was unlikely to be reciprocated; her heart obviously belonged to faster, stronger, more exotic and exciting males than himself. And his own heart these days felt like a car that wouldn't start, until, that was, he thought of Isabel. Then the lights went on, the heater whirred, everything roared into life.

He wondered where she was and what she was doing now.

Isabel was almost too tired to feel now, but turning the last bend in the Crewell Place driveway, she was conscious of a certain faint relief. Soon, any time now, she would be with Jasper.

Her battered senses took in only that the house seemed a shapeless lump in the darkness. Light was spilling down a wide flight of steps. Staggering up it, Isabel found herself in a lobby. Light from flaming torches licked the faces of bored-looking waiters holding trays of champagne. 'No, thanks,' she muttered, stumbling past.

She plunged into the crowd beyond the lobby. She registered vaguely that a lot of the men wore the same thing: pink coat, yellow waistcoat and yellow bow tie. But so what? She was not here to look at clothes.

'Where's Jasper?' she bawled at the nearest person. 'Jasper De Borchy! Where is he?'

The man she had chosen to interrogate was startlingly tall and thin. He had wispy, strawlike hair and a strangely squashed-looking face. As, now, he opened his mouth, it was to display teeth that bent inwards.

'I say,' he said, swaying like a reed in the wind. 'You strike me as very good breeding stock.'

He was, Isabel saw, so drunk that only the fact he was in a crowd and being supported on each side by the people next to him prevented him falling. Her theory was proved as his neighbours now moved away and, after swaying back and forth on heels and toes, he headed face-first towards the parquet floor with the force of a felled redwood. 'Timber!' shouted someone behind Isabel. 'Chippy's down!'

As Chippy's face made contact with the ground, Isabel understood why he looked the way he did. She also realised, from the name, that the prone form at her feet was the amusing young gentleman of whom the St Alwine's porters had spoken so highly and whose family dominated the frozen food market.

She pushed on. The urge to get out was growing irresistible. She had not found Jasper and her object in doing so seemed less clear now . . . Perhaps he would not thank her for the intelligence about Amber; he might shoot the messenger; perhaps ignorance was bliss. She felt confused and very tired. Pressing insistently upon her thoughts was the question of what someone as charming as Jasper was doing at such an awful event. He had said that his family had always been Bullinger members. He must have to be here for some reason. He must hate it, she was sure.

Dredging up her last reserves of spirit, Isabel fought through the crowd towards the distant wall where she could see the top of a giant doorcase carved in marble the colour of liver pâté. From the centre of a pediment grinned one of the griffins she had seen on the gateposts. The aesthetics of it all, however, concerned Isabel less than the fact that it promised a way out.

She approached to find that a fat teenager leaping about to Status Quo was blocking her escape route. Isabel sidled past but then a great shove from the rear propelled her into the huge mahogany door with a velocity not unlike that with which Chippy Crewell had met the floor. The door gave way and she shot through.

Olly had never seen anywhere so creepy. The drive to Crewell Place was like a Hammer Horror: long and twisting, flanked by contorted, thick-trunked trees. At the end, the house loomed large and forbidding. Castellations jutted up from the roof like teeth. In the dark walls, long slashes of windows threw light into the rain.

As the taxi drove away, Olly fought the urge to run after it. Terror welled up within him again. There was no chance they would get away with it! They were miles from any help; what would the famously savage Bullinger Club do to them if they caught them?

'Come on,' Anna-Lou said, confidently. 'That bastard De Borchy's in there. Let's go get him.'

Olly felt better instantly. They were here to expose De Borchy and his like. And even if they died in the attempt – which hopefully they wouldn't – it was a noble cause. Nonetheless, he ascended the steps in Anna-Lou's wake hoping no one would notice his trembling hands.

No one at the door noticed anything, however. As Anna-Lou sailed through as if it were the most natural thing in the world, the doormen stared, blank-faced, into the middle distance.

A strange place, was Olly's immediate impression. There was something louche and licentious about it. The painted ceiling above them seemed to feature nothing but fat pink bottoms. Beyond was a great room in which two blazing chandeliers hung like vast illuminated breasts. Olly and Anna-Lou pushed on, into it.

It was boiling hot and the crowd was rough and noisy.

Looking about him, Olly was struck by how strange many of them looked. No one looked normal. Some were unnaturally handsome, with smooth faces, full lips and long, blank eyes. Others, less fortunate, had features that were either exaggerated – noses for example – or non-existent (chins seemed few and far between). Hair was greased back and side-parted; spectacles were anachronistic and fogeyish.

The silly Bullinger uniform, all yellow and pink, made everyone look like a pear drop, Olly thought. Or, as Alastair said, a pantomime. The pink matched many of the men's faces exactly, as the yellow bow ties did their teeth. Everyone had what looked like an onion rammed into their buttonhole, some with dirt still adhering to the roots. A joke, Olly guessed, although a smelly one, especially in this heat. He had only been in the room a few minutes and sweat was already beading his forehead.

The women, on the whole far better looking than the men, wore fancy dress too. A maid in fishnet stockings was raucously applying a feather duster to the thinning hair of her accompanying swain. A girl in a red leather bondage outfit, complete with chained cap and studded gloves, was hanging unsmilingly on the arm of a languorous youth in a monocle. A woman in a flapper costume, drawing on a long black cigarette holder, was ignoring the male hands feverishly groping her bugle-beaded breasts. The hands belonged to a porcine type with several shining chins.

The woman with the cigarette holder had her mind on other things. Like a spider snatching its prey, she extended one long-black-gloved arm and grabbed a glass of champagne from a passing tray. She tipped it back in one.

Olly's fear he would be spotted as an interloper was fading. And, as Alastair had predicted, Anna-Lou had passed muster; a lot of the men here were unusually tall. The crowd, anyway, was in no state to notice anything much. The noise was increasing. Everyone was yelling.

'Unbelievable,' Anna-Lou shouted from behind. 'They sound like a jungle.'

'More a farmyard,' Olly returned. His ears were full of people braying like donkeys or whinnying like horses.

Champagne bottles popped like gunfire and intimate items had started flying through the air. A youth before Olly slowly peeled a G-string off his nose before looking carefully at the label. A red lacy garter whirled over Anna-Lou's head. Bras shot past like double-headed comets. A pair of leopardskin-print cups of a particularly generous size described a graceful trajectory over the crowd.

It was the perfect photo opportunity and, right on cue, Olly could see one of Anna-Lou's hands reaching back into her hair. She pulled round the camera and raised it to her eye.

'Hey!' A pink and yellow bison thrust its unlovely countenance into Anna-Lou's face. 'What are you doing?'

Olly's stomach plunged in terror. He felt sweat – more sweat – break out on his forehead. Were they to be unmasked?

But Anna-Lou remained composed. She removed the camera from her eye and blinked at her aggressor, the picture of innocence. 'Is only for my parents,' she said with a heavy Eastern European accent. 'To show my willage I have vorked as vaiter in important English party vith lords and dukes. You smile for me, yes?' She maintained her irresistible beam as she said this and, as an amazed Olly looked on, the burly newcomer melted and gurned into the lens.

'Wow!' he whispered, after the bison had passed on. 'That was cool.'

'But not as cool as this,' Anna-Lou hissed back. Both of them now turned sideways to avoid a waiter coming towards them with great force behind a trolley. It bore what Olly first thought was a large, angled finger made of ice, but realised as it passed that it was in fact an enormous penis, the area around the member heaped with blackly glistening caviar evidently meant to resemble pubic hair. It was melting in the heat, the trail of water soaking into the parquet showing darkly after its progress. People either side of them started to clap, whoop and roar as it passed;

its appearance was, it seemed, a central part of the ritual.

As Anna-Lou's camera exploded in flashes, the bison in pink and yellow, on the other side of the trolley, gave her the thumbs up.

'What a picture!' she gasped, as the penis trundled off.

'Flash, bang, wallop,' agreed Olly.

The chandeliers were now turned off and strobing spotlights began to sweep the crowd. The music, which had throbbed faintly before, was now turned up enormously. Fists punched the air. As the chorus approached, the music suddenly disappeared. 'And it's Hi, Ho, Silver Linin',' roared the crowd into the void.

The eighties wedding disco from hell, Olly thought.

'Why do people like this always have music like this?' asked Anna-Lou, raising her camera.

As they passed on, something was barring their way. 'There's a man on the floor!' Anna-Lou exclaimed. 'People are jumping all over him.'

Someone, Olly saw, was indeed being crushed to a pulp beneath people obeying the strictures of Van Halen.

As his colleague snapped away again, it was left to Olly to alert the dancers that the prone and crumpled form beneath them was a person. 'Good lord!' said one of them, looking down in astonishment. 'It's Chippy!'

'More like squashy now,' Anna-Lou observed as they moved on.

No longer bothering with the niceties of glasses, people were swigging champagne direct from bottles. Not all of it was hitting their mouths. The music had switched to the Sex Pistols and both men and women were jumping up and down, landing uncertainly on a floor slippery and sticky with wine.

Someone cannoned across the floor and, bowling-pin-like, brought down several others. There was a scream to Olly's side as a hefty woman in stilettos came down on her partner's foot.

The music changed again. 'Wo-oh-oh-oh-oh-oh-oh . . .' began Billy Joel. 'Uptown Girrrullll . . .'

* * *

Isabel struggled to her feet, blinking round in the gloom. The hall seemed to be at the end of the building and no doors led out of it at ground level. A flight of shallow, enormously wide stone stairs led up between fat stone balustrades. Isabel unhesitatingly followed them.

At the top of the stairs a wide landing stretched into shadows punctuated by deep-set doors. They looked like they might lead into bedrooms. Might Jasper be in one of them? Making a stand of some sort? Refusing to take part? Hiding from the horrors downstairs?

It was an encouraging thought; he would be pleased to see her. She pushed the first door open.

The room exposed was huge, shadowy and dominated by a four-poster bed whose enormously tall canopy was draped with dark curtains and topped with black plumes. Dim lamps against the walls near the door illuminated a gloomy painted scene, which seemed to cover the whole room. In it, muscled men on horseback were making off with screaming, naked females. The thought flew through Isabel's mind that, with such early influences, it was unsurprising that men like Chippy nursed the attitudes they did towards women.

Over the nervous rushing in her ears she could hear nothing but a pounding silence. But now she could hear voices. Coming, it seemed, from behind the curtains of the bed. On the broad, dark-oak floorboards beside it lay a scrunched-up pink jacket, a hastily cast-off blue waistcoat. And a pair of high-heeled shoes.

Isabel shot across the polished floor. In a flash, she was at the bedside and wrenching back the drapes. The padded red interior was lit by a lamp mounted above the pillows. A dark-haired woman and a blond man lay on the counterpane.

Jasper was sprawled on his front over the red bedspread. His head was bent over a small mirror on which rows of white powder were arranged in neat lines. Connecting his elegant nose to the mirror was a small silver straw.

Isabel swayed and clutched at the velvet curtains.

Jasper's companion now looked up. 'Hello!' she said cheerily to Isabel. 'Want to join in?'

Jasper now lifted his familiar, curly, golden head and stared back at her. It was, she decided afterwards, the absolute lack of shame on his face that angered her more than anything.

She reached for the nearest object, one of the high-heeled shoes on the floor. But in her fury she misfired; it whizzed past its intended target and through the curtains on the bed's other side. A few second later, there was an explosion of breaking glass.

'Hurray!' said the dark-haired girl. 'I was wondering when the window-smashing was going to start.'

'Brown Sugar' had started up now to ecstatic shrieks from the crowd. Olly had seen enough; certainly he had heard enough. He had got the idea. He did not need to see the entire Bullinger Club in their ridiculous uniforms pretending to be Mick Jagger.

'What now?' asked Anna-Lou. She had, he knew, got lots of photos of silly people doing silly things. But there was nothing exactly incriminating. And nothing at all of Jasper De Borchy, who had been conspicuous by his absence.

'It's all more of the same, really,' Anna-Lou observed as they reached the wall and looked back at a sea of twisting wrists and shaking heads.

They stood watching, spirits sinking. Must they, Olly thought, return to Alastair with nothing better to show for their efforts than a frozen willy? But even the indomitable Anna-Lou was flagging now, he saw. She looked pale and exhausted and all the amused confidence had gone from her gaze.

The drunken crowd were now shouting along to Meatloaf. It was a sight to depress even the most resolute, which he and Anna-Lou no longer were. The momentum was going, Olly knew. Their drive, their purpose, was evaporating. He had to get it back, fire Anna-Lou up again. Find her something good to photograph. 'We haven't tried upstairs yet,' he pointed out. 'They might be bonking on the coats.'

'Or just being sick,' Anna-Lou groaned as someone nearby vomited copiously on the parquet. With a jaded air, she pulled out her camera to record the event.

She followed him, anyway, as he sidled along the wall to the nearest doorway and out into a large stone hall where a flight of wide stone steps led to the upper level. The bottom of the stairs was flanked by stone posts bearing yet more gargoyles, like the monsters at the gate. Olly felt, briefly, almost sorry for whoever lived here with these hideous objects.

'Come on,' he urged Anna-Lou, as he headed up the stairs. Twisting backwards to encourage his colleague, Olly did not see the figure now coming downstairs towards him – rushing, unseeing, right into him.

She was falling, down, into the gloom at the bottom of the stairs. Someone was beneath her, grabbing at her as they rolled over and over, the stair-treads hitting back, knee, elbow.

'What the hell?' yelled Olly. The figure had come out of nowhere. It had knocked him completely off his feet. Thankfully, he was only a few steps up; it could have been fatal otherwise. As they lay tangled together on the cold stone at the bottom of the flight, he could see now who his attacker was.

'Isabel!' Olly gasped.

'Olly!'

'What the hell are you doing . . . ?' He could hardly speak. The pounding pain of his fall was nothing beside the searing agony of seeing Isabel at a Bullinger event.

He could hear her voice. 'I'm sorry!' Isabel was repeating. 'I'm so, so sorry.'

It was, he thought, too little too late. The realisation that she was Jasper De Borchy's, body and soul, drained the remainder of the fight from him. Olly no longer cared about the *Post* story, his job or anything else. He lay back on the cold, hard stone and stared into the darkness; it seemed an appropriate metaphor for the future.

'You've got a camera,' Isabel now gasped at Anna-Lou.

'So?' Anna-Lou returned laconically, as if she too had given up.

'First room on the right,' Isabel croaked. 'Jasper De Borchy's snorting coke.'

Then she turned and rushed out of the hall.

Chapter 32

It was, Richard thought, one nightmare after another. First Sara Upward catching fire. Then the whole dinner dissolving into chaos. But worst of all – far, far worse – was the news about Amber Piggott.

And now the news from the Bursar that a personal catastrophe had prevented the Chuck Snodgrasses making the plane trip. It seemed that their usual seats in first class had been unavailable on the plane. 'I think,' Richard said to his hysterical colleague, 'that we have to keep a sense of proportion about all this, don't you? Someone almost died here tonight.'

The bathroom in question had been sealed off. Police tape stretched over the shattered door. Forensics were in there. They were in Amber's room too. Police tape was stretched across the entrance to the staircase.

But Amber was not dead. The girl who had discovered her had saved her, although it was likely she did not know it. It was after she had – unaccountably – disappeared that the paramedics, continuing her efforts, had extracted the first choking breaths of life.

The Scottish English student, Richard gathered. The one Diana liked so much. 'Isabel's the heroine, not me,' the other girl insisted. 'She's the one who insisted we break the door down.' But where was this heroine of the hour?

It was drugs, the police said. They were still checking which ones. It looked, at this stage, like a mixture of just about everything imaginable. The source was probably the usual one, the one they were unable to trace but whose tentacles seemed to be spreading further daily throughout the city.

Richard was shocked and upset, but ashamed, most of all. How much was he to blame for all this? As Master of the college, was he not in *loco parentis*? Yet, throughout his time here, up until now, he had avoided all but the most essential direct involvement with the students. He had never even spoken to Amber Piggott. Had he reneged on his responsibilities?

Was it his fault, now, that the college was overrun with policemen in hi-vis jackets? Could he have done more to stop life's frightening and unpleasant side invading this protected environment, this ivory – if concrete – tower?

His suspicion that, yes, he could have, coloured everything at the moment. The disaster of the dinner, even the presence of Sara, seemed unimportant by comparison. He tried to compensate for his perceived neglect by being as helpful as possible to the various people now crowding his office. But inside he had a horrible sense of shut stable doors after horses had bolted. Making everything even worse was his growing and unstoppable wish that Diana was here to help him, with her sweet face and wide, concerned eyes. Instead of Sara Oopvard, stumbling and shrieking about with smoking hair.

Sara, in her own mind, at least, was ably commanding the situation, ordering the emergency services left, right and centre. Inside, she was furious. She had been getting on so well at the dinner, charming all the influential donors on Richard's behalf. But then all hell had broken loose. In quick succession, someone had grabbed her crotch, her hair had been engulfed in flames and cold water had been thrown all over her head.

What was worse, her sore and half-naked scalp remained on display. No late-night salon seemed to exist in the godforsaken provinces. She had tried all the directories without success. The smoking ruins of her hair were plastered to the streaky ruins of her make-up. What must people think?

Old habits died hard all the same and she was determined to turn even this situation to her advantage. As future wife of the Master of the college, she would seize this cast-iron opportunity to show her mettle in an emergency.

'I don't know what everyone's making such a fuss about,' she opined loudly to no one in particular. 'People get gunned down in West London all the time.'

The telephone on Richard's desk rang and Sara swept it commandingly up. 'Yes?'

It was the security guard at Richard's laboratory.

'You can speak to me,' Sara loftily informed him. Had any of the preoccupied bodies filling Richard's office had a second to spare, they might now have noticed Sara's soot-smudged face change as emotion fought with Botox to produce an expression of subdued but still obvious horror.

'His *worms*?' Sara shot a terrified glance at Richard deep in conversation with the detective. 'Er, I'll pass it on,' she stammered. 'He's a bit tied up just now. Some hamsters as well, you say?'

'Your son said he'd left something there when he came before with you, that's why I let him in,' the guard stated. 'Seemed harmless enough.'

'Milo *is* harmless,' Sara insisted.

'Apart from attacking all these creatures with a razor blade, Madam. He's vandalised all the experiments, as well. Slices of brain all over the lab, there are, Madam.'

At Sara's appalled gasp, Richard glanced over to her in concern. Immediately, Sara forced her features into a reassuring smile. 'Thanks so much for letting me know,' she trilled loudly into the handset, before replacing the receiver and clacking out of the office on her high heels.

Diana was expecting drama at Branston this evening. She was actually expecting to be the cause of it. So to arrive in the staff car park and find it full of emergency vehicles was a shock.

She had passed an ambulance, sirens screaming, a few minutes down the road. Some accident, it seemed.

Fear that Richard was involved froze her heart. Despite the wall he had thrown up, despite the misapprehensions he no doubt harboured about her, despite herself even, the seed of something like love for him had rooted and begun to grow. What on earth was she to do about it? She could almost see the forthcoming confrontation: Sara and Richard together, laughing at her.

Diana parked and got out. She leant for a moment against her battered car, taking deep breaths, gathering strength.

A movement caught her eye. In the glow of the sulphurous car-park security light a figure could be seen: a slightly built woman in high heels and a flimsy dress, a mobile clamped to her ear.

Diana leant forward, astonished. Was she imagining it? But no, if she listened, she could hear the woman talking. Shouting, actually. It was, it really was – Sara Oopvard. But what had happened to her hair?

Sara was bristling with fury as well as shivering with the cold. Milo was not answering his phone. She shoved her mobile into her clutch and folded her arms crossly. What now?

Despair swept over her. She was frozen and largely bald and her shoes were crippling.

And – what was this? Someone was coming. The person she least wanted to see, too. Her great rival, Diana, was crossing the car park towards her.

Distracted as she was, Sara could recognise a change. Diana's expression was not the conciliatory one of old, the one that could be lied to or shouted down. It was clear that something apocalyptic had happened. Something from which there was no coming back. No one had yet spoken, but Sara could tell that this scenario was terminal.

With an almost romantic longing, now, she recalled the

comforts of home. Perhaps, after all, she could survive life without a famous academic for a husband. If she could survive so many nights in social housing, in a non-super-king-sized double bed in a bedroom without an en suite, then she could survive anything. She had learnt that much about herself.

Sara looked at Diana, who was trying to summon the words to start. She raised her hand. 'Don't,' she said. 'Save your breath. We're going, Milo and I. We're leaving. You'll never see us again. Just let me go and pack our things.'

Diana stood in the security light and watched Sara totter off towards the Lodge. She closed her eyes and let the great sense of calm flood through her. Then, slowly, she walked towards the college.

The foyer of Branston was full of people, students mostly, all in a state of high excitement. Diana did not stop to gather the details. She pressed on into the corridors that led to Richard's office. Policemen were milling about outside. She pushed through, hardly aware of them. There he was, leaning over his desk, looking grey, exhausted and utterly defeated.

Then he looked up and saw her and the joy that shot across his face went straight to her heart. He was over beside her in seconds. 'I'm so pleased you're here,' he whispered. His strong hand closed over hers, holding it tight. His breath was warm in her ear. 'Stay with me, won't you? For ever? I need you, Diana. You've no idea how much.'

Isabel was running up the grass verge of the road, in the darkness, under the trees. They dripped on her with a concentrated remorselessness. It felt horribly personal, as if the very heavens were victimising her.

She had been wrong. Pathetically, stupidly, despicably, inexcusably wrong. Jasper had never loved her. He had lied. He had taken her money. He had ruined her life. But much worse than that, he had killed Amber. Isabel had no doubt now that he had supplied whatever she had taken.

The thin soles of her shoes pounded down on the glistening black tarmac. She had made all the wrong choices. Olly, for example. The sight of him here, tonight, had made her want to throw herself in his arms. Dear, sensible, warm, loving, funny, caring, clever Olly. But he had been there with that other woman, the one with the camera. Isabel had missed the boat.

And then there was her work. Professor Green: 'You'll be lucky to scrape a third.'

Despair overwhelmed her. She did not deserve to live. The urge to lie down in the road and be crushed by the next passing car was violent and powerful. But what would dying achieve? One dead person was enough.

She was in trouble – lots of it. For running away from Branston and leaving Amber's body. For rushing off to St Alwine's, bribing the porters and then hailing a cab she could not afford to take her to the debauched party of a notorious student society. Would she have to go to jail now?

She could no longer think straight, and she could run straight still less. She was heading for Branston but wanted more than anything to run to her mother, the one person who always had, who always could, make everything all right again. But she had been avoiding Mum's calls.

Isabel was limping and lurching now, sick with pain and self-disgust. Mum had been so proud of her, so loving and supportive. She had been repaid by constant demands for money and the idea that an adoptive mother was inferior compared to a family who could trace themselves back a thousand years.

Isabel was sobbing now. Despicable ingrate as she was, how could Mum want her after this? Let alone love her? She wasn't even her child in the first place. When she found out, Mum would regret the day she ever saw her. Perhaps she should just run away . . .

As, much later, an exhausted Isabel reeled up to Branston's entrance, the red digits of the clock blurred and wiggled across her sight. She felt about to die as she stumbled into a foyer so bright she could almost hear it.

Someone within leapt to their feet, but as they rose, Isabel fell. The floor had come up to meet her and Isabel's fingers were splayed on the carpet. It was warm and dry and she wanted to melt into the red behind her eyes.

'Isabel!'

Isabel opened her eyes. She rolled over and stared up. Within a halo of blazing strip lights, a face was looking down at her.

Isabel gasped. And yet there was, in this face, none of the censure she feared or felt she deserved. All Isabel could read there was concern.

'Mum?'

The face nodded. Was it a dream? Isabel asked herself. But no, her fingers were pressed into the gritty pile of the carpet. It was real, if unbelievable.

'What are you . . . doing here?'

Her mother was kneeling beside her now, hugging her hard. 'You weren't answering my calls. And, when you did, you sounded, well, not like you. I had a feeling.'

Isabel's heart squeezed with guilt. A *feeling*. A maternal feeling. A sixth sense that could only be love. She struggled to sit up, but fell back again.

'I just knew something wasn't right,' her mother went on in her soft Scottish voice. 'I got here earlier this evening. Got to Branston in the end, you see!'

It was a brave attempt at a joke, but her mouth quivered with the effort to smile and there was no laughter in her eyes. She surveyed the wreck of her daughter with an expression of wild distraction. 'Look at you!' She shook her head. 'Isabel! You're so *thin . . .*'

The love and fear in her voice sent new strength into Isabel. She rose up, clung and sobbed into the blessedly familiar shoulder. 'Oh, Mum. I'm so glad you're here.'

The arms round her tightened. Isabel closed her eyes and felt her mother's face against her head, her mother's voice crooning comfortingly into her hair: 'Don't worry. Everything's all right.'

'No, it isn't!' sobbed Isabel. 'And it won't be ever again.' Mum didn't know the half of it.

'Rubbish,' her mother replied robustly. 'You're a heroine, you know. You saved someone's life.' She paused, and Isabel felt the body holding hers straining with the effort of holding back volcanic emotion. 'I'm so proud of you,' came her mother's ragged whisper. 'So proud that you're my daughter.'

Chapter 33

The scales had fallen from her eyes in a manner more dramatic than even Olly could have hoped for. And he had further hopes of Isabel, even though things were at an early and delicate stage between them. Partly still in shock at the ease with which De Borchy had deceived her, Isabel was understandably cautious about starting another relationship. And, when she wasn't being cautious, she was locked in the library trying to make up lost academic ground.

Olly was giving her time. He could afford to. He was busy himself, happily occupied now the *Post* was going full throttle. *Press Baron's Son In Drugs Shame.* What a great first-day front-page it had been. That Jasper De Borchy had been the missing link in the university drugs ring had been a discovery beyond Alastair's wildest dreams.

And then there were Olly's landlords. The Stringer household was on the up. Hero had not only started going to school again but had taken a weekend job at the dogs' home where Coco the ever-escaping poodle was supposed to be incarcerated. She could be seen about town on Saturdays, taking Coco for walks. Scrubbed of make-up, hair shining, she was unrecognisable from her former incarnation. And she seemed to bear him no grudge about his outburst – on the contrary, she seemed almost grateful.

Dotty's clients were building slowly up again – although thankfully the Lintles had not returned. David's career too was gradually righting itself. Hero had also, by way of apology, revamped her father's online presence; it now looked better than any rival lecturer's.

Olly supposed it was good news that Amber Piggott was making progress in hospital. And Isabel was definitely thrilled about the relationship between the Master of Branston and her friend, Diana, the college gardener. She had, apparently, moved into the Lodge and it looked like a florist's inside, these days, according to David, who, with Dotty, had been invited to the dinners the Master kept giving for his students and staff. Also according to David, Richard Black had a permanent smile on his face.

Chapter 34

Press Baron's Son In Drugs Shame. Diana put the newspaper with its enormous – really, *really* enormous – headline back on Richard's desk. Dramatic times, she thought. The paper dated from some months ago – the week before last Christmas, in fact – but it brought it all back.

Feeling a wave of sudden nausea – she was sicker this time round than when pregnant with Rosie – she sat down. Beneath the *Post* on the desk were many other papers containing stories relating to Branston. They were awaiting insertion in the cuttings book, the maintenance of which was the responsibility of Flora. But she and the Bursar were still on honeymoon.

Diana moved a few papers. Exposed were the bills for the post-alumni dinner clean-up operation in college. It had taken weeks for the wreckage to be entirely removed from the Incinerator, and college claret had proved impossible to remove from concrete floors. Elsewhere, a black smoky patch recalled the fact that there was a corner of Branston College that would forever be Sara Oopvard.

Sara's departure was only one, Diana thought, of the many unexpected ways the alumni dinner had been a blessing – to the college as well as herself. Among the students it had attained a notorious, even legendary status and Diana sensed the hope bright among them that something even worse would happen next time.

As a result, Flora – when she came back – had an enormous number of volunteers to help work through the updated alumni list. Those potential donors to whom news about the dinner had got out seemed to be newly interested in their alma mater as a result. Money was flowing in.

Some of this had been invested in a new website. There were sections on the college staff – as Head Gardener and soon-to-be wife of the Master, Diana had been put at the top, just underneath Richard himself. The designer had put in a special section on the *Gesamtkunstwerk* and there was another – admittedly small – on celebrity alumnae: 'Famous Picklers'. As a result, applications were firmly on the up, including one from David Stringer's own daughter who was, according to Richard, especially promising and wanted to be a lawyer.

Diana stood and walked to the window. Glossy grass rippled in the breeze. Little green buds were appearing on all the trees. There was laburnum along the lawns and lilacs in white and purple – lilac and laburnum that she had freed from ivies, from rubble, from shadow.

There was so much to look forward to. Gradually, over the next few weeks, the sun would get hotter and the leaves grow bigger. The days would start to smell warm, filled with perfume and butterflies. Her delphiniums would explode in slow motion, that blue row of rockets she had looked forward to seeing for so long. And she had other plans for the garden too, but those might have to wait for a while. She pressed her belly and smiled.

The only cloud in her happy blue sky had been leaving the Campion Estate to move into the Master's Lodge. But then a job as Sally's deputy in the housekeeping department had come up and Debs had not needed Diana's urging to apply – successfully, as it turned out.

So there was no need to lose touch with her old neighbours; besides, Shanna-Mae and Rosie were joined at the hip and both wildly looking forward to the baby, who Shanna-Mae hoped was a girl and Rosie hoped was a boy. Both had eagerly volunteered for babysitting. And both would be bridesmaids at the wedding, registry office though it was. Neither she nor Richard wanted a fuss. Nor a wedding in the egg-shaped chapel, however newly committed to Branston Richard now was.

Who could have imagined it would all turn out so well? She opened the window, breathing in the fresh air. It was the most beautiful spring she could remember; certainly the loveliest there must ever have been at Branston. The bulbs she had planted the previous autumn had transformed what had been scarred, scabbed and unloved grass into a dancing fairyland of pale yellow and soft blue flowers: narcissi, bluebells, primroses and daffodils. A path wound through it.

Diana closed her eyes. Voices floated over to her and she opened them again to see Isabel walking along the path between the primroses with Olly. He had his arm round her and they were laughing.